BETH OVERMYER

THE GOBLETS IMMORTAL

This is a **FLAME TREE PRESS** book

FLAME TREE PRESS
6 Melbray Mews, London, SW6 3NS, UK
flametreepress.com

Distribution and warehouse:
Baker & Taylor Publisher Services (BTPS)
30 Amberwood Parkway, Ashland, OH 44805
btpubservices.com

Publisher's Note: This is a work of fiction. Names, characters, places, and
incidents are a product of the author's imagination. Locales and public names
are sometimes used for atmospheric purposes. Any resemblance to actual
people, living or dead, or to businesses, companies, events, institutions, or
locales is completely coincidental.

Thanks to the Flame Tree Press team, including:
Taylor Bentley, Frances Bodiam, Federica Ciaravella, Don D'Auria,
Chris Herbert, Josie Karani, Molly Rosevear, Will Rough, Mike Spender,
Cat Taylor, Maria Tissot, Nick Wells, Gillian Whitaker.

The cover is created by Flame Tree Studio with
thanks to Nik Keevil and Shutterstock.com.
The font families used are Avenir and Bembo.

Flame Tree Press is an imprint of Flame Tree Publishing Ltd
flametreepublishing.com

A copy of the CIP data for this book is available from the British Library
and the Library of Congress.

HB ISBN: 978-1-78758-362-7
PB ISBN: 978-1-78758-360-3
ebook ISBN: 978-1-78758-363-4

Printed in the UK at Clays, Suffolk

BETH OVERMYER

THE GOBLETS IMMORTAL

FLAME TREE PRESS
London & New York

Know what is to be; everything, you see:
Drink from the Goblet of Seeing.
Lighter than air, float without care:
Drink from the Goblet of Drifting.
Strength and survival, no beast is your rival:
Drink from the Goblet of Enduring.
Strategic and cunning, to war shall be running:
Drink from the Goblet of Warring.
Take what you can, banish at hand:
Drink from the Goblet of Summoning.
Luck is your friend, all others must bend:
Drink from the Goblet of Questing.
Immortality to he who drinks from one and the rest—
And a curse for the soul who was born as a Blest.

CHAPTER ONE

Aidan cut his hand and watched his blood pool in the inkwell. When the flow came to a standstill, he cursed and squeezed until the crimson flowed again. "You've the pen?" he asked Tristram, the only person who would buy land from a wanted man.

Tristram passed the iron quill. "You won't regret this, Aidan."

"I never have regrets." He pressed his lips into a hard, thin line and paused before dipping the nib into the blood.

Tristram laughed, a nervous sound. Aidan could imagine him raking his lily-white hands through his corn-blond hair. It took all of Aidan's strength not to tear at his own dark locks. Below his breath, he swore.

For the last ten years, he'd lived in peace. That was before the money he possessed had run out, and he was forced to return once again to Breckstone. If Lord Dewhurst got wind that he was still alive....

After a moment, the scratching ceased, and the deed was done. "There." Aidan set down the pen and stanched the flow from his hand. "It's over." When his friend said nothing, Aidan looked up. "Am I keeping you from some pressing engagement?"

Tristram stowed his timepiece in his waistcoat. "Not at all. We just need to be mindful of the time, that's all. Jina's due home in half an hour."

Aidan's brows drew together. He looked around the parlor. The Prewitts had painted again, and the pianoforte occupied a different position in the room. Other than that, the place had not changed since he and Tristram had snuck in there as boys for sugar cubes.

The aroma of baking bread wafted in from the kitchen at that moment. Aidan's stomach rumbled and then clenched. He swallowed a mouthful of bile and nearly crushed the signed paper in his fist.

Tristram cleared his throat. "That should be dry now."

Aidan nodded and extended the deed over to his friend. But before the other's fingers could close on it, Aidan withdrew and said, "Money first."

Tristram snorted. "You trust me so little?"

Clank went the pen into the well. Aidan looked up. "In my position, you can afford to trust no one."

"And yet here you are, in my parlor, no exits but the window and the door." Tristram laughed. "Don't think I didn't notice you making escape plans. Just in case, of course."

Aidan managed to crack a slight smile as his friend opened his billfold. "Of course." The deed and money exchanged hands, and they shook on the deal.

"You won't regret this." It needed repeating, but it did no good.

It was signed in his blood. No amount of regret could wash that magic away. Aidan sucked on his hand, which still oozed, and reached for the inkwell. "You keep a lot of iron in here," he noted, Dismissing his lifeblood from the well and getting to his feet.

Tristram laughed. "I'll never get over how you do that." He waved his hand with a flourish. "Just simply willing objects away. Wish I was so able."

"No, you don't." He clapped his friend on the shoulder. "Thank you, Tristram. This means a lot to me."

Tristram made to cut him off. "Going so soon? How about taking tea with me?"

And risk having a servant spying him there? "No, thank you. I'll just be going out the back way and—" He moved to the front window, having felt a human Pull. Sure enough, there was a woman coming up the walk. A middle-aged, wire-thin woman with a yellowing lace shawl draped around her shoulders. Aidan moved into the shadows. "What the devil is this?"

Tristram was beside him, pulling back the curtains. "I don't— Oh, that Roma woman. She's been pestering my wife and me these last ten days at least."

"For what?" Aidan Dismissed the money and donned his hole-riddled riding cloak. His heart pumped hot blood hard through his veins, which prickled as they always did when he scented danger. But what could be wrong? Aidan pushed the feelings aside and repeated himself. "What does she want?"

"To tell us our fortunes, of course." Tristram hesitated, still peering out the window. "Blast. She's going to the back. You'll have to wait here 'til I've gotten rid of her, I'm afraid."

Aidan grimaced. "I shall leave through the kitchen."

Tristram was already moving to the hall. "No good. I ordered all of the servants to stay in there 'til they're told otherwise."

"Then I'll just have to leave through the back and risk the Roma." Aidan picked up his riding bag and Dismissed it. He'd left his horse, Triumph, out in the back wood, tied off to a tree. *Please don't wander off.*

Tristram was on his heels as he moved to the back door. "Are you sure that's a good idea? What if she's a spy?" He grabbed Aidan by the arm and stayed him. "It's not worth the risk. For any of us."

That made Aidan hesitate. If he was caught on the property, it wasn't his life and freedom alone at stake. He turned and looked into his friend's eyes.

"Please."

A vein throbbed in Aidan's forehead. So many ghosts in this town, in this house even. A starving child at an iron gate. Two soft hands bearing food. There was laughter, good times, even. *Fool. You are a sentimental fool.* Aidan's spine stiffened but he moved back into the parlor. "Very well."

"You're a good man, Aidan." Tristram turned to go, saying over his shoulder, "Have a seat. And take some refreshment. You haven't touched your brandy."

Aidan took a seat, but once he heard his friend's footsteps falling away, he sprang to his feet as one burned. "Too much iron. If I were trapped here...." For whatever reason, he could not Summon or Dismiss iron. Perhaps because he could not feel it, like he felt the wooden side table tugging at his core, or the woolen rug, the glass lamp, the glass and silver chandelier. All these things were alive to him, just waiting for a nudge or a tug.

By turn, Aidan's gaze took in the iron fire poker, the iron letter openers, the iron fire grate. Where had his friend come across so much of the metal...and why? To comfort himself, he sent a pillow sailing across the room with a thought, and then allowed it to wink out of existence. He exhaled sharply and Summoned the cushion back into being.

Footsteps pounded down the hall, two sets, two human Pulls. Aidan's nerves tingled, and he fidgeted in a moment of inaction before searching for a weapon. If it weren't so heavy, perhaps he could use the poker as a sword. He'd wielded iron before with his bare hands. It never felt right. There was no bringing himself to adjust to it in time now.

The doorknob turned, and in walked the woman with the shawl. She studied the pianoforte for a moment, and when she turned, her expression was as empty as Aidan's stomach. When she spoke, her voice was as deep as a man's. "Nine days I've come, and at last you arrive, Lord Ingledark."

Aidan's fists clenched but he otherwise kept his reactions in check. "Who's asking?"

Her lips drew up into a thin smile. "I'm not asking. I know who you are and what you're doing here." At once her eyes flickered in suggestion at the writing desk where now lay the deed, signed in his own red blood.

Aidan cursed himself for leaving his copper dagger out of Calling distance. It was too far away now to safely bring it sailing into his waiting hand. He should have Dismissed it into Nothingness before he left his horse so that he could Summon it from seemingly nowhere now.

The fortune-teller laughed and raised her hands in truce. "Do not be alarmed. I know because I am the seer."

"Relax, I'm sure now that she's harmless," Tristram said.

Aidan did not relax. "So, you're a seer," he said, closing the curtains. There were servants out there; he felt their Pulls on him. Too heavy to Call, but still Pulls, anchors, slowing him down.

"Hmm. You're worried, Aidan Ingledark."

"Am I, now?" Gathering his wits, he made for the door, which Tristram barred. "I'm sorry, Tris. I must leave at once."

Tristram opened his mouth as if to object, but closed it. "I understand. Farewell, friend." Ashen now, he pushed past Aidan, took a seat, and finished the full glass of brandy.

With a frown, Aidan again made to leave, but the seer stopped him with her words.

"I know where you sent them and how you might get them back."

Aidan stood in the doorway, his fingers tingling. *Run. Run. Run.* He answered, "I have no idea what you're talking about."

"Don't you, now?" The cursed woman smiled with her teeth this time, exposing a large gap between her left incisor and the tooth next to it. "You don't smoke, do you, milord?"

Aidan's legs had turned to lead. "You would be the one to know, wouldn't you?"

Another laugh. "So you believe me when I say I know what happened to Lord and Lady Clement Ingledark and their wee boy. Samuel, wasn't it?"

As if compelled, Aidan found himself nodding. His limbs had gone numb, and he cursed his need to know. Yet every beat of his heart thumped, *my fault, my fault, my fault.*

"There is but one who can help you," the seer was saying. "And if you are to seek her, you'd better start out immediately." Here the woman gave Tristram a pointed glance before looking back at Aidan. "Walk with me, milord?"

Tristram intervened. "Lord Ingledark cannot draw attention to himself. You would draw that attention, woman. I'm so sorry, Aidan, I thought she might amuse you. It would seem she's now going to be trouble." He put his hand up to grab the seer by the elbow, but Aidan motioned for him to stop.

"What must I do and whom must I seek?"

The Roma woman licked her lips and her hands fluttered around. "I saw – so much pain. Lord Ingledark, should you succeed you must seek out Meraude and unite the Immortal."

His fists unclenched, and the blood came rushing painfully back. "I'm sorry…unite the what?"

She nodded. "You heard me. The first one lies in your path. The others shall prove most difficult to come by." The woman shuddered. "But for more information, it'll cost you."

"Cost me what?"

She was silent, as if considering. "Your blood."

"How much?"

The shawl around her fluttered to the ground, pooling at her feet. "All of it."

And that is when Aidan realized the human Pulls on his being had tripled since he'd arrived. "Tris, the house is surrounded. I am so sorry."

Tristram was shaking. "God help us."

"Why do you have so much blasted iron? I need lead. Have you any lead or copper?"

The man shook his head. He did nothing. He sat there as one in shock, staring at the amber bottle of whiskey. "I'm the one who is sorry."

Aidan tore from the room, Calling objects to his side as he ran, only to Release them as he realized their uselessness. "I've been a fool." He made it to the back door, Calling a paring knife from the kitchen, the only object of use he could feel. It jammed into the wall before it even got to his hand.

"Aidan Ingledark," boomed a deep voice from the front of the house. Footsteps crashed overhead. How had he not felt the hidden soldiers' Pulls? "More iron," he snarled. Had Tristram padded rooms with panels of the metal in anticipation of this visit?

"Wound him if you have to, but I'd rather take him whole," said a voice belonging to Lord Dewhurst.

Aidan ducked into the kitchen, sending the scullery maid scuttling up the servants' staircase. He raced out the kitchen door.

Three arrows whizzed past his face and embedded into the wooden frame. He felt the archers' Pulls. Five of them in the brush, two in the haymow in the barn. Those had been warning shots; Lord Dewhurst's bowmen were renowned for their accuracy.

The arrow tips, of course, were iron. But the bows were mere wood. Those he could deal with.

Aidan closed his eyes, feeling for the bows and, one by one, Dismissed them from their respective archers. It was on the fourth bow that another arrow flew. Aidan felt its approach, and hastily Dismissed the shaft. Unbalanced, the arrow tip missed its mark yet still came within dangerous proximity to Aidan's person.

He grimaced as he ran across the yard. *Get to Triumph and you'll be free. Get to Triumph*, Aidan told himself.

But the archers were not through with him, and the men in the house and around the house were closing in. The bowmen in the loft threw wood at Aidan, but he Pushed each log, block, and board back at them, not pausing to see if his aim was true.

The men in the brush charged with their iron pokers. Aidan sensed the Pull of the new bows being drawn behind his back.

He didn't stand a chance running backward, forward, left or right. There was only one option open, the trick up his sleeve. Aidan stopped and closed his eyes. He hadn't done this since he was a boy, hadn't needed or, rather, wanted to. Not even Tristram knew of this part of his blasted abilities.

Aidan let the tension leak out of his body as if Dismissing it. His knees became weak. He relaxed, Releasing every object and every person's Pull on him.

He was now surrounded, and he could still feel at least two persons whom he'd yet to Release himself from.

"What is he doing? Seize him."

They were too late. Aidan let go of his Existence, and Dismissed himself into Nothingness.

★   ★   ★

The oddest thing about Nothingness, Aidan always found, is that you still know. You can't feel, which makes re-gripping Existence difficult, never mind breathing properly. And no matter how long you think you've vanished for, it will always have been an hour.

As Aidan struggled to reappear, he could only hope that the yard would be clear of soldiers. If they had remained where they stood…well, he would have given up his great secret for nothing.

Aidan imagined tightening his muscles, feeling the Pull of Existence and everything in it. He allowed anxiety to roil through his being, guilt to take over his thoughts until he experienced the sensation of being yanked between two great forces. Existence and Nothingness were warring over him. He grabbed on to thoughts of his family. "My fault," he repeated over and over again in his mind. "I shall make this right. I shall. I shall."

The image of a young boy filled his thoughts. In his mind, the raven-haired lad was screaming for help. Aidan could not help in Nothingness. He could not help the woman and the man he called his parents, either. So he beat himself with the thoughts over and over, allowing himself to feel the pull of his responsibility until, at last, he was thrown back to the yard with a none-too-gentle thud.

The world was so bright at first, Aidan could not see, nor could he move. He lay there, catching his breath.

All was silent, save for the upset clucking of chickens and the indignant crow of a rooster. Aidan tried his eyes again. The world came into focus, and he was relieved to see that he was alone.

Strength returned to him at that moment, so he stumbled to his feet and ran into the wood, praying that Triumph hadn't been discovered.

He ran one mile, then another. There were no signs of disturbance up ahead. But where was his blasted horse?

Aidan looked around him, caught his breath, and whistled. Triumph nickered nearby. "Well, come on, then." He turned, and there was his black stallion, grazing on what grass he could find. "Any day now would be wonderful."

Triumph snorted and tossed his head but made no move toward his master.

"Stubborn beast," Aidan muttered, coming to Triumph and seizing the reins. He mounted and kicked the horse's flanks. Triumph started forward at a gentle walk. "We've been betrayed. Tris betrayed us."

The horse seemed to understand the urgency in his master's voice, and broke into a canter, putting Tristram's estate behind them.

A setback, indeed, Aidan thought as he leaned forward. His only ally had turned on him. "At least he gave me the money first. Yah! Fly, you devil, fly!"

CHAPTER TWO

How much the betrayal would cost him, Aidan couldn't say. It would all depend on how much Tristram knew and how much of it he had told. On the one hand, Tristram was a fool. He probably thought his old friend had simply vanished and relocated anywhere he pleased. However, Lord Dewhurst's advisors were not so foolish; they would tell their lord to continue scouring the area for signs, to listen to whispers and rumors of strangers in the vicinity.

Aidan rode on for hours, staying off the main ways as much as possible. But the woods were overgrown in many places, and not much of his old secret path remained. Twice he had to pass well-to-do persons on the road, stopping to make the polite tip of the hat that manners would require. If he did not, suspicions might be raised. Still, he kept his head down like a common man would, and prayed they did not question him. They did not.

It was when the sun was near the end of its descent that Aidan re-entered the woods by a stream. His steed let out a great huff before dipping a grateful muzzle into the water.

Aidan stroked the beast's side, and then tied off the reins, as much good as that would do. That his horse had figured out how to free himself was worrisome. Not that he feared Triumph running off…very far. He was a loyal beast. He would return. But this could prove fatal for them both if he wasn't properly managed.

With a sigh, Aidan pulled his copper dagger from his saddlebag and sliced open a vine from an overhanging branch. He drank several mouthfuls of its juice, draining the plant entirely. He had several water bladders stored in Nothingness – two full, five empty – and he'd been planning on filling them from Tris's well once the deal had been closed. Aidan shook his head. It would do no good now to dwell on it.

Aidan went upstream and splashed his face to cool himself. The water felt so good, though, that he threw caution aside. Without a glance about, he stripped down, cast his garments onto the bank, and waded into the shallow water. With a sigh he sunk under, cleansing himself of a week's worth of grime.

The wood was silent when he emerged, save for the night calls of wild birds and the rushing of water. It would be dark soon. He'd best get started on a shelter. No fire tonight; he couldn't risk it.

After climbing back into his trousers, he went in search of a hollow or some nature-made way of covering himself from the elements. Thunder rumbled in the distance. He knew he should have first made his shelter and then enjoyed the water. Still, he couldn't blame himself for his absent-mindedness. The seer's words still troubled him.

How had she known of his parents? Of Samuel? "My fault." The words came out unbidden, a dark habit of his mouth. It was true, though. Still, Aidan couldn't afford to dwell on that just now.

He shook off his darker thoughts and manually gathered sticks and branches, which he would prop up against the wind and rain that he knew were coming. He could Call objects to himself, saving physical energy for tomorrow. But his mind was exhausted and needed the break, and he wanted to keep up muscle tone, just in case brawn was ever needed.

After the better part of an hour, he had managed to make a decent shelter for himself and was about to start one for his horse. That's when he felt two dozen human Pulls. Twenty-plus people – men or women – approached. They were a mile off yet, but they might very well pass him by. Aidan ran for his horse and swore. Triumph had freed himself and was nowhere to be found. A whistle would surely give his position away, so Aidan had no choice but to hide and pray his horse went undiscovered.

But he had left his shirt on the banks! Aidan Called it, panting hard as it flew into his hand. Now for the saddlebag.... That took more concentration because he wasn't certain where his blasted horse had gotten to. He sat there, feeling for the Pull of the saddle, and had just laid his mind on it, when horse hooves clashed and clattered on his path.

Again he closed his eyes, feeling for the saddlebag. *Got you*, he thought as he Dismissed and then accidentally Summoned it. It landed with a thud next to him. It might as well have been a war cry, how loudly it landed.

The horses' approach stopped. The men's voices quieted.

Aidan felt them spreading out, surrounding him. He could Dismiss himself again…if he weren't so exhausted. No, he would have to hide and wait this one out.

"There's bandits in these here woods," rasped an old man's voice. "Oughtn't we comb through the brush?"

That statement was followed by laughter. "Uncle, you a'feared?"

Someone spat. "Nah. Just careful, 'tis all. Say, what is this?"

Aidan froze. There was a familiar whinny, which was taken up by several other horses. Triumph. Trust the beast to reappear at the least convenient moment.

"His rider can't have gone far."

"Aye. Perhaps he's wounded."

"Nah, he looks all right," said the old man's voice.

"I meant the rider. We'd best spread out an' look." Their footsteps came nearer to Aidan's shelter.

Aidan caught a glimpse of red and orange fabric through the gaps in the branches. Could these men belong to Lord Dewhurst?

"Can't be far," said a new voice, an old woman's. "There be footprints all over the bank."

Aidan cursed himself and his carelessness.

"Well, where do they lead, woman?"

Something was whispered and more footsteps drew nearer. Aidan felt the Pull of eight people, and….

"You'd better show yourself, sir."

He thought of the copper knife stowed in his saddlebag. He had fought off more than five men in the past, but never when this weak from exhaustion. There was only one option left him: let things play out.

With a yawn, Aidan crawled out of his shelter, rose to his full height, and stretched. "May I help you?"

The ragged men before him were no soldiers. Bandits, perhaps. Hired spies, maybe. But Aidan doubted it.

The woman with them laughed. "Well, see, Jeb? One man and an unarmed one at that."

A fat old man grunted. "It could've been worse, woman."

"What is your business in this wood, sir?" said a man with a neat brown beard, his thinning hair pulled back in a tail.

"What is anyone's business here?" Aidan asked him, assuming he was the one in charge.

They studied each other in tense silence, the others frozen, waiting for their leader's verdict. "There was a spot of bother over at Prewitt manor. Apparently there was sightings of a wanted man on the estate."

With effort, Aidan kept his expression neutral. "I'm sorry to hear it. I pray the family is safe."

The head man scratched at his beard. "You know the master there, then?"

Aidan shook his head. "No, but I have had dealings with some of the staff. Good people, Mr. and Mrs. Collins."

"They say Lord Dewhurst had a screaming fit, had to be carted off to a doctor."

He blinked with false surprise. "Lord Dewhurst?"

"You never heard of Lord Dewhurst?"

"Yes, of course I have. What was wrong with him?"

"Well, he was after the wanted man."

Aidan nodded. "I see."

The others laughed, and the old man said, "No, you don't. That wanted man supposedly vanished. Right into thin air." He waved his hands around vaguely, his eyes wide with wonder. "Scared the livin' daylights out of his lordship, serves the old rascal right."

"And you've just come from there, from Prewitt manor?" Aidan felt for the Pulls of the men's swords. All were copper or lead. He took in their wagon and suppressed a grimace. Romas. He could only hope that the so-called seer wasn't among their number.

"You haven't figured it out, then?" said the man in charge. "We're no friend of his lordship." He spat, and the others followed suit, even the woman. "So, what brings you into these godforsaken woods?"

Aidan frowned and let out a soft chuckle. "Godforsaken, you say?"

"We do say, sir, we do," said the older gent. "There be bandits hereabouts. S'not right to be romping about on one's own. Ain't safe."

The men grunted in agreement. The woman spat again before saying, "What isn't to say he ain't a bandit?"

Aidan folded his arms. "What's to say you aren't?"

That caused the men to laugh and relax. "He's got a point there, Trudy," said the man in charge. "I'm Isaac. Isaac Pensworth, at your service." Isaac extended his hand, and he and Aidan gripped forearms.

"Aidan Powell at yours." Powell was his mother's maiden name, and by the look on the other man's face, he knew that it wasn't Aidan's own.

Isaac cleared his throat and let his hand drop. "Well then, you can stop hiding in that brush there. We've an extra tent that might accommodate you during the storm...for a price, of course." His eyes wandered to Aidan's saddlebag, which sat just behind him. "Might want to keep a good grip on that, sir. The family has sticky fingers, each and every last one of us."

The Romas were spreading out, assembling camp as the wind picked up. Thunder rumbled a few miles off after lightning streaked across the darkening sky.

"I only have eight pence to my name, sir." He brushed a spider's web from his bare shoulder, ignoring the scurrying of eight legs down his back.

"Please, it's just Isaac – and five will do, *milord*."

Aidan met his stare, all the while his heart thudding hard in his chest. *They can't know who I am...can they?* he wondered. Surely they knew he was the criminal just escaped from Prewitt manor. But what else did they suspect?

Isaac laughed and motioned for Aidan to follow him. "Come, fetch your things, milord. Keep 'em close. Eight pence is enough to buy labor as well."

"I can pull my own weight, but I thank you, Isaac."

"I'm sure he can," the woman named Trudy said, her eyes traveling over Aidan's bare torso. "Not a very gentlemanly gentleman, is he, now?"

"My apologies, ma'am." He retrieved his shirt and quickly dressed, ignoring the woman's laughter.

★　★　★

When no one was looking, Aidan Dismissed his belongings, planning on Summoning what he needed later whilst the company of Romas slept. He'd known Romas before, and they were as Isaac said: sticky fingers, quite a few of them.

With everyone working, the tents were pitched in no time, and the horses were taken undercover as well. "Will these withstand the wind?" Aidan said above the roar.

Isaac looked heavenward and tested one of the ropes. "Aye, they'll weather all right." Lightning crackled against the gray clouds, and what had been a light sprinkling of droplets now became a heavy downpour. "Join us in the main tent when you're able. Supper should be ready shortly."

For a moment, he hesitated. The offer was as tempting as it was repulsive, though he would not admit either to the man. Aidan needed to be alone, to puzzle through the day's events and then catch a few winks of sleep before he snuck out of camp. On the other hand, the last conversation he'd had before the one with Tristram had been two and a half weeks prior. After pausing too long, Aidan finally came out with, "I would not dream of troubling you."

"For eight pence and a turn at keeping watch? That'll put some food in your stomach." He gave Aidan a sympathetic smile and ducked out of the tent.

His shoulders dropped and he shook his head. There would be a price, Aidan knew. There was always a price. Still, he hadn't eaten since the previous day. Whatever the Romas demanded, he could probably afford. He *hoped* he could afford.

He Summoned his saddlebag, pulled out eight pence, stuck them in his money purse, then Dismissed the saddlebag again. He tucked in his shirt, smoothed back his hair, and joined the Romas in the main tent.

There was no making a fire that night, what with the rain falling and the winds gusting. The group of vagabonds dined on tinned meats and dried fruit, which they shared freely with their guest. "Some wine, milord?"

"Lord?" the old man laughed. "I doubt it."

"Now, Uncle," said Trudy, filling a tankard and passing it to Aidan, "Isaac's just usin' his manners, ain't he?" She shot Isaac a look.

"Oh, aye," said Isaac after dragging a long draft from his stein.

"So, where're ye from, Mr. Aidan Powell?" said a young woman he had mistaken for a boy earlier.

Aidan swallowed a small mouthful of the cherry wine and shook his head. "Just Aidan, if you please." He set the glass aside, though kept his hand over the opening, should he care to take another sip.

The young woman leered at him for a moment, then her eyes fell down to her plate. "Is you from these parts?"

"Now, Pol, keep yourn mouth shut. Our guest don' have to answer no questions." Trudy winked at Aidan, then nodded at Isaac.

"Don't he?" asked another man. "We could be takin' a murderer into our company."

Pol hissed, Trudy tutted, and Isaac wouldn't meet anyone's eye.

Silence fell over them like a blanket. *Am I a murderer?* Aidan wondered for the millionth time. *I surely hope not.* Aloud he said, "No, he is right to be wary. Any man should be wary of a stranger."

"But you ever kill a person?" asked the gruff old man.

Aidan took another sip of the wine, feeling all the eyes on him. He wiped his mouth clean with the back of his hand and set down his glass, this time for good. "Not that I'm aware of."

That eased the tension a little. A few even laughed.

"As it is," said Aidan, "you'll be rid of me tomorrow."

"Don't be too sure of that," said Isaac. "You're low on supplies, and this storm could go on for days. No, you'd better plan on spending more than tonight in our company."

And plan on spending more than eight pence. Rather than making a fuss, Aidan simply nodded.

The old man belched and stretched. "Who be on for the first watch?"

All looked to Isaac, who gave a dramatic sigh. "Very well. We'll draw for it." He reached into his inner vest and pulled out a handful of twigs. "The short straw gets the pick of the watches." Isaac rose and went to each man, having them pick one of the twigs from his fist. "The longest gets the second pick."

"Any paying a man to take my watch?" asked one of the men.

"That isn't fair, an' you know it," Trudy spat. "You're the keeper of everyone's wages, you indecent—"

"Now, Trudy." Isaac held up a callused hand. "No need to get after the old man for trying."

Aidan took his twig from Isaac and fisted it. His whole body seemed to relax into the cushion he sat on. No, he would not be awake for long. He would allow himself to sleep lightly, and Dismiss all of his belongings. Then, he hoped, he would be left alone.

As it turned out, Aidan had drawn the middle straw and was at the mercy of the rest of the men. His watch was set for the very middle of the night, the slot nobody wanted.

"Sorry about that," said the man named Algie, an owlish youth with a beaklike nose and large tawny eyes that were set too close together. "Rules are rules."

"Speaking of rules," said Isaac, "I think it's fair to set a few of them, regarding our guest." He cleared his throat and looked each man and woman in the eye. "There will be no disturbing, robbing, or murdering of our guest while he sleeps. Ain't polite."

The men grunted in agreement. "Aye, sir."

Aidan nodded his appreciation, his jaw tensing. "That is quite good of you."

Isaac shrugged. "We're a decent lot." He looked at Algie, a warning. "For the most part. As for our guest – there will be no disturbing, robbing, murdering of us in our sleep, for we're a close-knit group, and there will be retaliation."

Aidan quirked a half-smile. "Understood."

"A deal, then?" Isaac spat in his hand, which he extended to Aidan. Aidan spat into his own, and they shook on it.

★   ★   ★

Back in his tent, Aidan began to feel the effects of the alcohol. He hadn't consumed much, only half a glass. But perhaps that had been unwise.

He dropped where he stood, the candle in his hand hissing, fizzing, and then extinguishing on the damp earth next to him. The world was topsy-turvy, and he scarce could think straight as he crawled away from the entrance of his tent, the wind whipping at the flaps.

The Romas had given him a blanket, but Aidan couldn't muster the strength to find it. "How am I to keep watch in this condition?" he wondered, his whole body shaking with cold. "I haven't been this drunk since I was five and twenty." Seven years. He hadn't even touched a drink since then. Alcohol did strange things to men, he'd observed, made them put their guard down.

"You think he's out?" said a voice in the entryway, one that sounded like Trudy's.

"Do it matter?" answered another, the girl's. "He ain't armed."

"But he's strong, no doubt."

"Aye, and handsome," the girl giggled, fingers feathering Aidan's hair.

"*Shh.* Keep your voice low. Isaac already suspects us."

Aidan tried moving, but it was as if his whole body had been weighted down with iron. *I've been drugged*, he thought, cursing his own stupidity.

"Where do you think he hid his money?" the girl asked with a sigh. She stopped stroking his hair, and her Pull told him she had begun prowling around the tent. "Can't we light a candle?"

"Nay, fool girl. We'll draw the others to us." Trudy cursed. "Is he lying on it?"

"Only one way to find out." They rolled Aidan over onto his back, and he flailed like a dropped ragdoll. "Nothing. You don't think he buried it?"

"If he did, it'll be buried nearby. Do you think he can hear us?"

"Nah. He should be dead, the dose I gave him. Can't imagine how he managed to survive, less he be Blest."

"How could you, Trudy?"

Someone snorted. "What? Poison him? I don't see why not. He ain't done nothing for us."

"True, but I might have liked him." The girl sniffed. "But do you really think he might be Blest?"

"Must be."

Aidan could do nothing but listen to the two chat and prowl around the tent, searching for his money. At his watch, if he lived to see it, he would take his horse and ride as far from these cursed Romas as he could.

"Did you hear that?" asked the girl. "Is he getting up?"

"Nah. You're too easily spooked."

Someone's skirt brushed Aidan's side. "Well, this was fruitless."

"Aye."

"What should we tell Algie?"

"That he can do his own dirty work next time, that's what. C'mon, girl. We'll be missed." And with that, the two left.

The storm raged on, and the tent leaked. Horses whinnied their displeasure nearby. Aidan wondered if his horse and saddle would still be there in the morning, or if the Romas would merely abscond with everything, including the tent over his head. The woman, Trudy, had meant to kill him. What was to stop the others from leaving him there paralyzed, fit to die?

He could try Dismissing the drug from his system. He felt it coursing through his blood. But it was a tricky business, Dismissing foreign objects from one's body. With his luck and current level of alertness, he might end up Dismissing a vital organ or a vein. No, he would have to simply wait and hope that whatever they'd slipped him wore off.

There was some shouting outside, and the tent flaps ripped open. "Well, you'd just best get the bleedin' antidote," said Isaac. "Or I'll skin the both of ya."

"We meant no harm," said Trudy, her voice quavering.

"We're sorry. Truly we are, Isaac," said the girl.

Isaac swore. "And how much did you give him?"

Someone sniffled. "Not more than ten drops."

"Ten drops?" Isaac roared. "He's probably dead."

At last Aidan managed a groan. He might as well be dead, for all the good his limbs were doing him.

"Antidote, now!"

"Yes, sir," said Trudy.

"Can you hear me, milord? Girl, fetch us some water. He ought to be dead, the poor lucky fool." There was some scuttling around, and a wave of ice-cold water hit Aidan in the face.

"If you can hear me, don't try to move. We're going to fix you up. You'll be well again soon."

"I've got it, sir," said Trudy.

There was silence followed by a whine, and then something vile was poured down Aidan's throat. He was about to spit it out, but a hand was clamped over his mouth and his jaw was held shut until he had swallowed every last drop.

"Sorry about this. It'll burn like the dickens."

An inferno swept into Aidan's chest, beat in his heart, and rushed through his veins. And yet, through all this, he could not make a sound, though his mouth was open and he was most definitely screaming. But with the fire came the assurance that feeling and life were re-entering his limbs, that he was no longer paralyzed.

"If the poison didn't kill him, this surely will," the girl whimpered. "Do something, Isaac. He's as white as a ghost."

"Nah, the worst is over. You'd best go back to your tent and pray I don't horsewhip the both of you at dawn."

Aidan gasped as the rest of the antidote coursed through him. He moved his fingers, wiggled his toes, turned a hand over and tried to lift it to his sweaty brow.

Isaac grabbed his arm and held it down. "You'd best not, milord. You'll be weak as anything for the rest of the night at least. Here, let me fetch something for you to drink."

Despite the warning, Aidan sat up. The whole world came back into sharp focus as weakness overtook him and he was forced to flop onto his back. *That's what you get, Aidan*, he thought. *That's what you get for even half-trusting someone.* He watched his breath puff out in great clouds in the darkness. His whole body ached and felt feverish. He wanted to leave. He *needed* to leave. But he knew he was in no condition to ride, and the roads would be in no condition for him to make an escape either.

Isaac returned presently and lifted an iron goblet to Aidan's lips. "Please drink, sir. You've probably sweated the rest of the poison out. You'll be quite weak and thirsty, I'd imagine."

Aidan was not in the position to resist. The water that poured down his throat was cold and fresh, and his mind cleared at once. He said, "I know you did not mean for this to happen, Isaac. Stop blaming yourself."

"I'm glad you understand, milord." He was quiet for a moment, the only sound the rain beating against the canvas. "You don't remember me, do you? Nah, you can't have done. You was but a boy."

Aidan clenched his jaw for a moment before responding. "You do know me, then?"

Isaac laughed without humor. "The poor Ingledark orphan—'scuse me, *presumed* orphan. Never did find your folks, did you?"

Aidan let the silence answer for him. Of course he had never found them. Why else would he be in this position?

"Well, then. You don't remember a beggar named Isaac Taylor, do you?"

He thought for a moment. There had been a man, maybe fifteen years Aidan's senior, that could hardly make a decent wage, so poor were his connections. He'd been put in the stocks twice for thieving, and was suspected of house-breaking, though that last charge couldn't be proven.

"When Lord and Lady Ingledark went missing, taking their youngest and leaving you behind…well, we know your uncle took over your fortune to manage."

"He managed all right," Aidan said, trying and failing to keep the bitterness out of his voice.

"Starved you, he did. Beat you, too, I'd imagine. Is that what led you to—"

"You said you were a beggar, sir," Aidan said, cutting the man off. "I remember no beggar, just a man fallen on hard times."

Isaac clapped him on the shoulder. "You always were a good lad. Gave me your last crust of bread before…well, before that bad business with Dewhurst." He spat. "So, what made you return to Breckstone?"

"Just a visit with an old friend," Aidan said. As kindly as he remembered Isaac, Aidan was not going to mention the sale of his estate and the money it provided him just then. The man would find out soon enough.

"Pol and Trudy will take your and my watches tonight, sir. I'll keep my eye out for ya, in case there's more trouble."

"That won't be necessary."

Isaac snorted. "Proud as an Ingledark, that's for certain. No, I ain't letting anything happen to you in your weakened condition. My fault. It's my fault what happened." The man moved to the mouth of the tent and muttered to himself.

Aidan covered himself with the blanket as best he could, as Isaac repeated, "My fault. All my fault."

Aidan sighed. "And I thought that was *my* mantra."

CHAPTER THREE

"Tethered and tied to the bow of Pridewyn
A maiden cries "Woe!" into the wind
Tossed in the waves that spit in her face
The sea a drunkard at his gin
If only, if only I could take her place
She's freer than I, no ache in her chest
Since thou hast come nigh to me
Ne'er free can we be
The be-cursed children called the Blest."

Aidan awoke with a start. He felt…not himself, but like a great bat hanging upside down from some great height, the blood rushing to his head. When he finally opened his eyes, the sun was up and he was lying in the dirt. "Oh." He looked around for the source of the strange music, but was not enlightened and was now all the crosser for it. Aidan blinked. "Who was singing?"

"Ah, the dead man rises…and hallucinates," said Isaac with a laugh as he stooped into the enclosure. "No worse for the wear, I trust?"

With a grunt, Aidan sat up and tested his arms by shaking the stiffness out. The dream – for it must have been a dream – was now receding into the dark corners of his mind. "All seems to be in working order." *No thanks to your people.*

"You're a good man, milord. A good man." Isaac pulled a bag off his back and tossed it onto the ground near Aidan. "Here."

Aidan eyed it, feeling for the contents. He sensed no real Pull, but it was definitely full of something heavy. *Iron.* "What is this?"

"An apology." A moment passed, and Aidan did not move. Could this be yet another trap? Isaac seemed to have read his thoughts, as he said, "Go on, open it up. It ain't gonna bite you."

With trepidation, Aidan reached inside the large moldy pouch and produced an iron goblet. "Thank you...."

"But you've no use for it?" Isaac chuckled. "You don't understand. That is a magic goblet."

Aidan eyed him askance. "What?"

"Aye. I—I don't rightly know how to say this but I pinched it from your uncle."

Aidan smirked, and turned the vessel around in his fingers, eyeing the design to see if it was familiar. "I doubt he missed it. We had numerous.... What?"

It was Isaac who was now laughing. "You still don't understand. This was his to guard. I took it after – well, after your folks disappeared. I figured it would be safer in my care than his."

The pulse in Aidan's eye began to tic, and he shuddered involuntarily. "Why?" Perhaps if he had not been poisoned by this man's 'family', he wouldn't feel so cross. As it was, a headache was forming. "You said it was magic?"

"Just a hunch."

Aidan quirked a smile. He tried to ignore the repulsion he felt to the metal and the urge to fling it aside; what would Isaac think of him? What would he suspect? "Magic," he repeated. "So, are you going to tell me that you're my fairy godfather or some other nonsense?"

The man grinned at that. "Nah. Me? I've not got a drop of magic in my blood. I am not Blest." Ah, there it was. Before Aidan could open his mouth to protest, Isaac broke in. "You survived that poisoning when no man thrice your size should have." His breath reeked of breakfast – sardines and burnt toast, it would seem – as he leaned in and whispered, "You're Blest, aren't you?"

Aidan set the goblet down and rubbed the remainder of sleep from his eyes. "I've heard that word applied to me before. I don't know what it means."

"Blest," Isaac said again. "You're an invincible, aren't you? Like in the days of old? Legend says...." He looked around before continuing in a lower voice. "Legend says that you can do things that no ordinary man ought to be able to."

As if to answer Isaac's question, Aidan lost control of himself for a moment and Summoned his saddlebag, which thudded between them. He closed his eyes. This was not his day. "Oh."

"Wowee." Isaac whistled. "You *are* one of the Blest."

"You mean there are others?" Aidan asked, knowing he was good and outed. The headache was not abating, and he had to make water rather urgently. He stumbled to his feet, Dismissed his bag again, and made his way away from the camp.

Isaac followed closely on his heels. "I always wondered how you survived. Why Dewhurst is really after you."

Aidan found some brush and relieved himself there. To his surprise, Isaac continued to chatter from behind his back.

Aidan interrupted. "And there are others? Others like me? And what of the goblet? You said it was magical." He made himself decent and followed the man back toward where the others were working.

"Goodness me, how would I know any of this? I only just started believing the rumors." Isaac shook his head. "That goblet always did make me feel strange. It must really be magical. It must."

"And you've kept these notions to yourself?" Aidan continued to look straight ahead. Everyone, he noted with his peripheral vision, was avoiding his gaze.

"The notion that a man can survive being murdered like that?" Again Isaac whistled. "Naturally, word got around camp."

Aidan put out an arm and caught Isaac. "And you'll keep it in camp?" He turned and extended his hand. "You'll give me your word to keep this from traveling far and wide?"

Isaac bit his lower lip and gave a quick look around. "Yes, milord." They both spat in their hands, shook, and returned to Aidan's tent. There in the middle of the floor sat the chalice.

"And you are certain you want to part with the goblet?" Even now as he studied it, he sensed there was some truth to Isaac's words. The vessel repulsed him, that was for certain; but there was something else there. It almost had a Pull as well…but that was impossible. Aidan shook himself out of a daze. "Perhaps someone could melt it down and find use for the metal."

Isaac clucked his tongue once. "No, and don't think we haven't tried. It just won't melt."

Aidan scratched at the beginnings of a beard. Metal that wouldn't melt…something felt off about this whole thing. He Summoned his saddlebag and put the goblet inside. "Is there anything you're not telling me?"

"About the goblet? Or about legend concerning yourself?"

"Both."

Isaac popped outside the tent for a moment, yelled at some of his crew, and then returned. "For the goblet, I have no idea. Probably won't melt because of its magic. But as for yourself.... Legend says that there were men and women among us who could do all sorts of remarkable things. Making objects appear and disappear at will." He nodded at Aidan. "They also had incredible luck, succeeding in everything they tried. Some say that they'd seen these mysterious folk – well, fly."

Aidan could only nod like he understood. His luck had been abominable most of his life, and flying? If only that were possible for him. It would save him a sore seat after riding horseback for hours on end.

Isaac looked at him with a knowing eye. "Maybe these abilities haven't come about yet. But I wonder.... Well, where did these abilities come from? Why some and not others? Luck? Fate?" A moment passed between them in uncomfortable silence. It would seem Isaac was warring with himself over something. A few times he opened and closed his mouth, his weight shifting as he looked heavenward and muttered a blessing. "All right. There's one who might know, and her you'll want to avoid."

With arms crossed over his chest, Aidan turned the Roma's words over in his mind. If he could discover the origins and limits of his abilities, perhaps he could find a way to undo the damage he had done. "Tell me."

Isaac shuddered and muttered something that sounded like, "Curse my hide," before coming out with, "The mage's name is Meraude." He scratched his beard. "She's...well, she's not a good sort. Some say she hunts down magic folk and kills them."

Aidan tried to keep a neutral expression, his heart racing all the while. Isaac, he remembered, had not been the first to mention that name. "How would I go about finding this Meraude?"

Again Isaac hesitated before admitting, "There are four sisters who could tell you. In truth, they're elves, but—"

"Elves?" That caused an uneasy stirring in Aidan's stomach. He'd had dealings with elves in his youth, when he was still naïve and wandered too far into a certain wood. He'd barely escaped two of the 'fair' folk with his life, and he had the scars on his back to show for it. "What are their names?"

But Isaac was shaking his head. "They go by many. But I won't be telling you any of them. No, the sisters would know I told you about them, and above all, you must not say it was I that sent you. They'll accuse me of working for Meraude, see?"

Aidan nodded. "How shall I know these sisters?"

"Deep calls to deep. Most likely, if you want to find them, and they wish to be found, *they'll* find *you*." He nodded at the goblet. "Keep your belongings close to your person, and make no deals with them. But when you do make a deal, make sure you don't break it, or there'll be hell to pay."

"Yes, but what do they look like?"

Isaac sighed. "Well, they use Glamour, don't they? Their faces must change half a dozen times a day. At least, that's how I would work that sort of magic."

Aidan had seen Glamour before, of course. It always looked like a puff of colored smoke to him, a thin screen in front of the real image. Perhaps it had to do with his other abilities that he could see through it.

"Thank you, Isaac. For everything."

The man blushed beneath his beard. "Nah, no trouble. No trouble. And truly, I'm rightly sorry for what went on last night with the women. If there's ever any way I can make up for it...."

"No harm done." Aidan extended his hand, and the men shook.

"If ever you need anything, know that the Bartlett Band of Romas is always at your service."

"I shall hold you to that," Aidan said with a smile, leaving the tent behind.

"Milord?"

"Hmm?"

"I hope you find happiness," Isaac said through a pained smile.

Aidan shrugged and replied, "I neither need nor seek it. But I thank you all the same."

He untethered his steed. The beast turned his head to look at his master, and then went back to grazing on a bag of feed that had been left him. Aidan patted Triumph's side. "Getting fatter, are we?"

The horse whinnied. And that is when Aidan felt a strong Pull.

Pulls of varying degrees of strength were not uncommon to Aidan. He experienced them on a daily basis from everything and everyone. But human Pulls were the strongest. The more people within a mile, the more he felt anchored down.

What he felt now was pure magnetic misery. He'd never experienced anything like it, not by a half-fold. It was as if – but no, the thought was crazy. And yet…and yet it felt like someone was Calling him. But you couldn't Call a person; their strong Pull would hold them where they were as an anchor. *I'm being absurd.*

The feeling abated, and Aidan decided that he had imagined it, until he involuntarily skidded two paces from a standstill position. He frowned. *Who would try to Call me?* Lord Dewhurst? The man didn't have a drop of magic running through his veins.

Aidan's stomach lurched, and he gave whatever was bothering him a tentative Pull, knocking himself onto his bottom. With a grimace, he leapt to his feet, mounted his horse, and walked him out to the main road.

"How about some exercise?" Aidan turned the reins in his hands, and left the company and so-called protection of the Roma camp.

★   ★   ★

Aidan rode through the day and into the early afternoon, guided by no map, no memory, but by the Pull, foolish though it was. And whenever he thought he might doze off in his saddle, that Pull would jerk him awake.

When noon came and went, Aidan was scarcely able to remain in his saddle, so strong and sudden was the tug in his gut. He'd lived in villages of hundreds, but each person's Pull tugged him in a distinctly different direction. The Pull he felt now was urgent and centered in one direction alone. But despite the strength of the Pull, Aidan could only sense five humans in the near distance. Four had a Pull lesser than the average human, but one was making it hard to breathe. *One person with that strong a tug on me?* he scoffed. *I must be delirious.*

Triumph seemed to sense his master's urgency, for he broke into a gallop, whinnying.

Aidan leaned back, pulling on the reins. "Whoa. Easy there." Whether he said this to himself or his horse, he was uncertain.

Blue smoke wafted over the hill up yonder. Aidan continued to calm his beast and resist the urge to run perhaps into a trap. It wasn't easy; the closer he got, the more he wanted to shout in frustration. The Pull was nigh unbearable.

At last he gave in to his temptations and followed the path to the source of his longing. The trees thinned shortly, and there sat an open wagon pulled by four milk-white horses. *Glamour*, he thought with both excitement and dread. A haze hung over all, and the image of how things were was clouded by shadows of how things were wished to be seen.

It was too late to retreat. Whoever was casting the Glamour knew a stranger was near. Why cast it otherwise?

Aidan dismounted and called out a greeting. The one with the strong Pull, he could tell, had run off into the brush beyond the small encampment, but he could feel that four beings remained near at hand. Aidan blinked, trying to separate reality from illusion so he wouldn't trip, and entered into the four's line of sight.

Four old women sat around a fire, though the Glamour showed him quite a different picture. In the illusion, three young noble women stood to greet him, their green frocks whipping in a non-existent breeze. They were beautiful beyond compare, quite a contrast to reality. The sight of them put lead in Aidan's stomach, and when they spoke, the back of his neck prickled uncomfortably. "Who are you and what do you want?" one of the women asked.

Aidan made sure to look at the illusion instead of the person who was really speaking. The fact that he could see through Glamour could be the trick up his sleeve that he needed. He'd hesitated too long.

"Speak up, my good man. We are not seers to know your mind."

Aidan smiled with difficulty. He was no actor, but this surely was a charade of the most dangerous and irksome kind. "Of course. I am called Aidan, and my business concerns—"

"Where did that urchin get off to?" said one of the old ladies, her voice raspy and thick with phlegm. "I be needin' my tea."

"Hush, Treevein," said one of the others.

The three illusions and the four real women stared at him, until, with a pop, the Glamour faded. It took them a moment, but squinting, the leathery-skinned horrors seemed to realize that they were no longer protected from view. "Leech, what did you let it drop for? We had him good and rightly fooled. Look at how shocked the poor man is."

The largest of them, presumably Leech, grunted and shrugged and muttered something about it not being her fault.

"Aye it were," said the smallest of them. She leered at Aidan, who pretended to shake himself out of a daze. "Now we'll have to kill him or hear him out."

"Not a good idea to attempt a murder," said the one they called Treevein. "Not before tea at least, and definitely not before we know whether or not he's got power."

"Of course he ain't got power," said Leech. "Look at the boy. He's got mortal written all over his face."

"Where is the urchin? She could sort this out for us." The oldest woman turned her wrinkly head to address Aidan. "She's been complaining of a headache for the last twenty-four hours, but we all know she was having one of her fits."

"Fiddle-faddle. Slaíne don't have no fits," said Treevein. "Jus' loses control, 'tis all."

As they spoke, Aidan sensed this Slaíne moving about in the wood. The Pull distracted him from the banter, making him an easy target for the four elves – for he was certain that was what they were – if they were to turn on him. He knew this, berated himself for it, and yet could not control his steps that led past the brush.

All four began hissing and spitting at him in protest. "Now where do you think you're going, me good lad? Ain't nothing worth havin' back in the wood. Unless you're in the market for a no good, lazy, dawdling servant," Leech said, then she shouted, "Slaíne, show yourself."

The one with the large wart on her nose chimed in. "Yeah, girl. Pour us some tea. We have a guest."

Aidan felt Slaíne come nearer to the camp, and strained to see what made his heart leap with excitement. Instead of enlightenment, he found himself puzzled.

She was a wisp of a girl, so thin it physically pained Aidan. She wore the clothing of a boy and seemed to have the bearing of one. Her gray eyes locked on Aidan, accusing, before she turned to her mistresses.

This is what's Pulling at me? This mite of a girl? Perhaps there is someone yet in the woods. But as he studied her, explored her Pull on him, he realized there was no one else within a mile, and even if there were, he would not give them a second thought.

The elves must have noticed him staring at their servant, for the fattest one said, "Oi! Girl, show the man your hair."

Aidan resisted the urge to groan. "Really, that's all right."

"You not in the market for a serving wench, then?"

The girl peered at him sideways and stumbled over to the woodpile.

Aidan unwittingly took a step in her direction. "No, I have no use for a servant."

The four elves shared a knowing look. "But you ought to at least have a look. She might change your mind," said the smallest elf. "Girl, leave the woodpile. The gentleman needs some tea."

"That is not necessary," Aidan assured them. It would seem that either the Pull or some Glamour were muddling his thoughts, distracting him from his purpose. "I was – wondering...." And then he forgot.

The girl fetched a tin cup, filled it, and approached Aidan hastily without saying a word.

Relief washed over him as the girl placed the cup in his hands. "Thank you," he said.

She seemed relieved, too. But then she scowled at him all the same and stalked away.

One of the elves piped up again, still trying to drive a sale. "She's a docile little thing, never mind that flaming mane of hers."

The girl was tucking strands of fiery red hair back into her cap, her eyes on him defiant. *Bother me and I'll show you just how docile I am*, she seemed to say.

Aidan raised his eyebrows. *Docile? My horse.* But still he continued to watch her.

She moved about lithely, each step measured, like some wild cats he'd seen skirting around him in the shadows. *I'd put some meat on those bones*, he found himself thinking. *A strong wind might carry her away.*

The girl stumbled again as she continued to tend to the fire. The elves laughed.

"Not normally so clumsy, this one. She likes you, mark my words."

"Why wouldn't she? He's a handsome man. Strong as an ox, I'd wager. He'd be a good master."

Aidan felt a rush of blood run to his face. *This is getting out of hand. Poor girl.*

"Show him your teeth, Slaíne."

The girl shot her mistresses a dirty look, cringing away when the tall one lifted a whip. Her eyes widened for a moment, her jaw clenched tight as the elves all cackled and taunted her.

"Really," said Aidan, "there's no need for this. I am not in the market for a slave."

"They're straight, those chompers of hers."

"White as milk."

"She won't cost you much. We'll give her in exchange for, say, that Goblet of yours. The one you are hiding in your saddlebag.... Don't look so surprised, sir. It's calling us."

It took Aidan a moment to regain his wits and recall where he was and that he should be mindful of his horse, who he was relieved to see grazing with the four white mares. "I am not—"

"And throw in a gold piece, Mr. Aidan. Gotta be fair to ourselves, ladies."

"Aye," they all said, nodding.

"Blast," he said as he attempted to shake the haze from his brain.

The four sisters laughed. "Something the matter with the both of them."

"Aye. 'Tis a sign."

"Aye, an omen."

Slaíne stared into the fire, her face void of emotion. She didn't move, even as one of her owners grabbed the cap off her head and waves of red curls poured down her shoulders. It would seem she had given up.

Aidan hated to leave her with these cruel women, and the thought of trying to escape her Pull filled him with uneasiness. But what use had he for her? He could scarce take care of himself, never mind adding another mouth. And yet he found himself saying, "I'll think about it. But first, I have some questions in need of—"

The she-elves laughed. "Smart man, this one. Knows a deal when he sees it."

He suppressed a sigh. This conversation would be a long, winding one, he could tell. *Small-talk*, he thought with loathing.

"Oi, Sláine, where be them tea cakes?" The fat one smacked her lips and patted her belly.

"So, you said you had a question," said Leech.

He jumped on the opportunity and got right to the matter: "What do you know of the Immortal, and how would I go about uniting them?"

"Not so hasty, not so hasty," said the fourth she-elf, the one with the warty nose. "We've just met, and that is a personal question."

"Aye, very personal."

"What is personal?" he asked, another wave of befuddlement washing over him. Was he going mad? Or were these elves' particular brand of Glamour unusually strong?

"Personal? What's personal, he wants to know," said Treevain. "Why, it's personal just in the fact that it can get your body killed."

"Yes, nothin' more personal than death."

The four cackled.

Aidan thought of the goblet, and for whatever reason, that cleared his head and distracted him from the ridiculous Pull and the Glamour.

"Well, if you aren't willing to part with that information, I shall move on. Good day, ladies." He turned, hoping to hide his intentions.

His hopes were dashed. "Consider your ruse found out," said Reek. "You need us and our precious information."

Aidan turned to face them, his eyebrows raised. But feigning innocence wouldn't work with these power-wielders, as he very well should have known. It would seem that he would have to bargain. "What do you want for it?"

"What do we want, he asks." The third elf snorted and twisted her ugly head to look over her shoulder. "She's gone farther than she ought."

"Mm. Sláine's not rightly in the head, thinking she can push the boundary."

"Foolish."

"Absurd."

The end to Aidan's patience seemed near in sight. He flattered himself to be a moderate-tempered man. But chitchat...all nonsense and fluff and the match to the tinder of his ire.

"It's not working, Reek," Treevain murmured to the one with the warty nose.

"What did you say?"

"I said your Glamour is not working."

Reek snorted. "Nonsense. It's your Glamour that's off."

"Nay," the former insisted.

"It would seem, ladies," said Leech, "that all our Glamour is off. Shall we start again? Together on three? Two...four.... Erm...."

"Enough!" said the tall one, causing the others to stop and wonder at her. She, however, stared at Aidan, suspicion forming in her gaze. "The Goblet."

"What of it?" Aidan demanded, uncertain why he found himself on the defense.

Treevain nodded. "I wondered."

"I thought so," said Reek.

"We've been fools!"

"Shut up," said the tall one. "He can hear every blasted word we're saying. Glamour does nay work on this one – at least, not entirely."

Aidan tensed, preparing to Summon or Call whatever he needed to make an escape. But the four did not attack as he had expected. Instead, they sat there, contemplating something with ugly bewilderment on their faces. They remained like this for some time, staring and twitching.

Finally, after expelling wind, Reek said, "Well, I think that's decided then. We can't kill him."

"Aye," said the other three, dispirited.

"Too few of you left. What better way than to irk the mage?"

"Mage my warts. That scum bucket of rotting eel souls."

"Mage? You mean Meraude?" Aidan asked.

The four glared at Aidan as if he had uttered a very vulgar, ungentlemanly word. "We'll thank you not to mention that pig snout's name in our presence."

"Oh, aye," Reek and Treevain agreed.

"Sorry," Aidan offered.

The four grunted. "It happens. Only, don't let it happen again," said the fat one. "Time to get to the business of the matter."

Aidan narrowed his eyes, his pulse quickening.

"The choice is left to you: the Goblet for the girl or for the – the ah, what was it he wants again?"

The wart-nosed elf huffed and scratched her backside. "He wants to know about the Goblets."

"Reek! He wants to know about the Immortal."

"Isn't that the same—"

"Silence."

Aidan was hit by another strong attempt at Glamour, which almost knocked him backward. The anchor that kept him from falling over was the Pull between him and the girl, who seemed to have turned around and returned to the elves' camp.

The fattest elf swore. "What will it be, man? And how soon can we make the exchange?"

Aidan rubbed his head, which throbbed to the rhythm of his pulse. So, the goblet had something to do with the Immortal? Perhaps they were merely trying to confuse him.

"Don't make a deal with the elves." Isaac's words continued to echo around in his mind. He knew better than to make a deal with any elf, let alone four, no matter how decrepit they appeared.

He thought of the goblet as the four stared at him, waiting for his answer. If they wanted it so much, then perhaps it wasn't the wisest of ideas to let them have it. "Can I have a night to think on it?" He might as well have asked them for each of their right arms as well, judging by their reactions.

"Wants to wait, does he?" Treevain spat. "No doubt so he can run off with the Goblet and the information we've given him."

"You haven't given me a single piece of information," Aidan reminded her.

The sisters exchanged dark looks. The tallest one shook a bony finger at him. "Ah, but haven't we? We're offering you a good deal here, laddie. I'd take it, if'n I was you."

Aidan's head ached, and he did not think he could match wits much longer, what with their cheating and using Glamour. If he had such a gift at his disposal…. Much more useful than willing things away.

"We'll give you three minutes to think about it, and then…." Reek drew a line across her nose. "We'll slice that fine nose of yours off'n your face."

Aidan narrowed his eyes, which he locked on to hers. "Give me tonight, and you will have your answer in the morning. I vow."

"He vows, does he, sisters?"

"What good is a vow?"

"I'll take it," said Treevain. The others looked at her. "He has truth in his eyes."

The others leaned forward, as if to catch a glimpse of what their sister said. "I don't know about truth," said Reek. "I see pain. Lots of pain. And he's hungry."

Aidan did not change expression at that. He knew elves could be extra perceptive when the moon was near its fullest. Just as he was recalling that fact, the Pull between him and the girl fluctuated, slackening as she stalked back into camp.

"He be wanting to know about the Blest as well. But is he cursed? Hmm. What think you, Gully?"

The one named Gully made a face. "Cursed, yet perhaps not cursed. Pain there, yes. Lots of pain." She sniffed the wind. "And regret. Blames himself for something."

"Might be his hand," Reek suggested. "Maybe he regrets letting it get right an' filthy infected."

The other three tutted.

"We'll throw some salve into the deal. Slaíne! Where be that scheming little blight on the face of humanity?"

"Up a tree?"

"Higher 'n that, I'd wager." All four cackled. Reek said, "Go ahead and make your camp. We'll talk later in the evening."

Aidan nodded, and was glad to be dismissed, seeing as his hand was throbbing painfully behind his back. He'd been ignoring the pain for a day now, where he had hastily sliced himself for blood. He walked back to his horse and examined the wound. The skin was a sickly yellow color, filled with green pus. *Infected.* He could skin himself alive for being so reckless.

As if in answer to his problem, he felt someone come nearer. It was *her.* He looked over his right shoulder. The elves were not watching him and did not seem to notice their serving girl approaching Aidan with something small and round tucked in her hands.

"What do you know of curses?" The girl passed him a jar of salve and stared at a fixed point in the horizon over his shoulder.

Aidan blinked, following her example by hiding the jar in his hands. "Excuse me? Curses?"

She blew a strand of red out of her face, which pinched momentarily as if she were in pain. "No matter. They say only *She* deals in curses now."

Bemused, Aidan stared at her. He wasn't quite sure if that question had been meant for him or not, so decided it best not to answer.

"Well, Meraude will pay...no fortress high enough for me."

That compelled him to ask. "You eavesdropped?"

She shrugged. "'Course."

Of course she had. Aidan shook the fuzz out of his head. "And you know Meraude?"

The girl hissed. "Aye. I know of her, all right."

"But where might I find her? And does she really know of the Immortal?"

Her eyes widened and she shook her head. "Not worth it for me to say."

"Then you know."

She sighed. "Ain't up to me to tell you." Her stormy eyes met his for a moment, and then she stalked away, ripping a low growl from Aidan's throat as if she were taking an unwitting and unwilling piece of him with her.

He looked down at the salve, searched its Pulls, and decided that it was quite without poison or irritant. He sniffed once, made a face, and slathered it onto his oozing hand.

To his surprise, the wound began to heal at once, and the pain all but melted away. It wasn't until later, after he had set up a fire and found sustenance for Triumph and himself, that he heard shrieking and a whip crack. Aidan grimaced and decided to return the salve in secret that evening. *Perhaps it wasn't hers to give.*

★   ★   ★

The remainder of the day found Aidan skirting around the elves and the Pull of the girl, who now flinched at the sight of him. He spent his time gathering common herbs, which he stored in his saddlebag, and brushing his steed and checking his shoes. Triumph was glad to lie down for some deep sleep. The poor creature had no idea what hard riding his master had in store that very night.

When the sun was setting, Aidan dined on a generous handful of mushrooms, which he roasted in his Summoned cooking patera with wild chives, beaver fat, and a few potatoes that he'd filched from Tristram's overstocked kitchen when he'd first set foot inside his friend's house. The elves might have guessed his abilities, had they been paying close attention to how much equipment he produced from nowhere. As it was, they seemed content to check on him infrequently. Suspicious, Aidan kept the goblet with him at all times.

After he'd consumed his supper and the contents of his third-to-last water bladder, Aidan watched as, one-by-one, the elves trotted off to bed. The moon retreated behind a bank of silvery-black clouds, leaving the flickering oranges and yellows of the fire to bathe the campers in dingy light. Soon, the elves snored unawares in their wagon under a thick pile of furs, grunting and farting and making all sorts of distasteful noises Aidan thought only men capable of.

He lay down by his fire and drew his cloak over himself. The goblet was near at hand, and he felt confident that he could defend it long enough to get away. Breaking his deal to talk in the morning, though, was not a feat he relished. He could not in good conscience give the elves what they wanted. *But I need their information*, he thought as a yawn ripped itself from his mouth.

As if in answer to Aidan's silent frustration, the Pull between the elves' serving wench and himself tightened. He squinted, just making out her lithe form prowling around in the shadows. *What keeps you up so late?* he wondered. Careful as not to disturb the elves and alert them to his quickly forming plan, Aidan eased himself to his feet, threw on his cloak, and grabbed the goblet sack.

The girl must have heard his movements, for she froze, the firelight glinting off her eyes in the semi-darkness. She had been humming, he realized, something he had mistaken for insects buzzing in the distance. The air grew tense, crackling with the electricity of an unrealized storm.

Aidan held up his hands, palms and sack revealed. When Slawva – or was it Slaíne? – hissed like a wild cat, a finger flew up to his lips and he shook his head. Then, feeling pathetic, he motioned for her to come closer. He would lure her over, and then…he would have to think on-the-move, for there went the servant farther into the bracken.

After a moment of indecision, he clenched his teeth and set out after her. Aidan moved as stealthily as he was able, but every footfall seemed to find a twig or an angry bullfrog. And the Pull…he wondered if she could feel it, too, and whether or not that would alert her to his exact position in his pursuit.

The Pull grew steadily stronger and stronger. He knew he was feet away. And yet he didn't catch any sight of her. *This is ridiculous*, he thought, shaking his head. How would he keep her quiet long enough to kidnap her? Surely she would shriek bloody murder, drawing the elves' attention to their whereabouts. Once the elves were involved… well, he might as well start running for his life right now.

Something sharp and cold poked him in the back. She didn't say a word. She didn't have to. There was a sword at his back, and judging by the steadiness of her hand, Slaíne had wielded it before. But who would let a slave have a sword, let alone keep them unshackled at night? Arrogance, sheer arrogance on the elves' part.

He made to turn around, but the sword – a thin, silver blade – flew up to his neck, as if to say *Move and you're dead*.

Aidan explored the blade's Pull and, satisfied that there was only one witness, he Dismissed it.

Aidan spun around, and the girl took a step back, eyes wide in the failing light. She opened her mouth as if to scream, but he Summoned the sword into his own hand, blade directed at her neck. "Move."

The girl scowled but did as he said, leading the way back to camp. She seemed to do nothing to mute her footsteps, her feet cracking and breaking twigs, stirring up leaves. But when they got back to camp, the elves were snoring as loud as anything.

"Over there," he whispered, jerking his head toward Triumph, who had risen and now stood dark and watchful.

The girl gave him a shrewd look before tramping over to Aidan's steed, the blade still at her back.

"Pick that up." When she looked back at him, he nodded to the sack, the one he had just let drop.

Aidan made quick work of Dismissing everything else, leaving the fire to be dealt with by the elves. He Dismissed the blade and grabbed the girl. He slapped a hand over her mouth before she could scream, and murmured, "One sound and I'll knock you out cold. Do you understand?" When she didn't move, he took that as a yes. "I'm going to remove my hand now." And he did.

The girl was silent and still.

Well, that was easy enough, he thought. He released her, and nudged her toward his horse.

One of the elves muttered something nonsensical in their sleep, and the others responded with great snorts of their own.

Aidan froze for a moment, before deciding his movements had not disturbed the four, and then mounted Triumph. With a low grunt, he grabbed his prisoner by the waist, pulling her up in front of him.

She didn't resist. It would seem that she was willing to leave her mistresses.

I'm stealing from elves, he thought, shaking his head. *What in this blessed world am I thinking?* There was no choice left to him, though. The elves wanted the goblet, and the girl had the information; he wanted both but wouldn't be given both...so he was taking both.

As if in answer to his thoughts, one of the elves let out a piercing shriek, waking the others. "Bandit! Thief!"

Aidan kicked Triumph into a gallop, leaning forward and into the girl as sparks of green and gold struck at the air around them, near and explosive missiles. The horse picked up speed, but the elves – the elves were somehow keeping pursuit on foot.

He leaned to the left, taking a sharp turn with the reins, nearly throwing him and the girl out of the saddle. Something hot hit him in the shoulder, burning through his clothes and searing his flesh, though the pain disappeared almost instantly. A warning shot...that or they did not want to kill or maim the girl by mistake.

"Give her back! Give her back!" they screamed, murder in their voices.

Aidan didn't dare look behind, but murmured encouragement to his steed. He had hoped to be concealed in the darkness, where he could hide off the side of the road. But with the bolts of magic fire flashing over and around him, the road was as bright as day.

Triumph was already puffing great clouds of steam in the late air.

This pace couldn't be sustained; it would kill the beast. Cursing his luck, Aidan made a last-second decision. The goblet was perhaps important, but not worth his life.

With a grunt, he ripped the goblet out of the girl's hands and tossed it onto the flaming road behind him. Curious, he chanced a glance over his shoulder. Another bolt of green and yellow light was hurled his way, but he managed to dodge it.

The four had stopped their pursuit to have a look at their prize.

Aidan took advantage of their distraction and rode off the road and into the wood, his pace slow, silent, and steady. The moon provided some light to see by, and they rode as far as he dared in the semi-darkness, even as the elves again took up their inhuman shrieking.

"They won't stop lookin' for me," the girl said. "I know too much."

CHAPTER FOUR

Aidan didn't sleep a jot that night, hiding in the brush with Triumph, the girl, and the knowledge that he could be caught and murdered at any moment. At one point, he swore he heard whispering, followed by a quickly hushed cackle. More than once he was tempted to return the girl and save his own skin. But then he thought of his missing family, his responsibility, and the answers this simple girl might hold.

At first he fooled himself, flattered himself that her Pull had nothing to do with his decision. Then, as she fell asleep, he explored the strange tug between them, annoyed more than curious.

He couldn't have anything slowing him down, and what was he thinking bringing her with him? Maybe the elves would have given him the answers that he needed if he had stayed around 'til morning to hear them.

And yet…what was fairer to her? She had given him the salve for his hand, possibly taken a beating for it.

Aidan groaned and Summoned his cloak, which he threw over the girl. "There. We're even." *Almost.*

★   ★   ★

At the dawning, sleep tugging at the corners of his eyes, Aidan took care of some personal business nearby behind a tree and Summoned the meager supply of food he had left. He would have to forage until he could reach Wontworth and replenish his wares.

There were some dried fruits and smoked meats, herbs, beaver fat, and enough water skins to see them through one more day, give or take a few hours, which was worrisome. As for Triumph – he had as much hay and alfalfa as Aidan could possibly hold on to. He Dismissed all but what they needed for the morning, and returned to camp.

The girl was gone.

Aidan cursed himself for being so careless. So distraught was he that he did not think to explore the Pull. But then he strained his hearing and could make out singing in that same strange, lilting voice he had heard whilst at the Roma camp.

> *Tee diddle diddly dee*
> *The sky was clear as can be*
> *The gull called to the sea*
> *And the fish answered to he:*
> *"Wishes is for fishes*
> *A kraken a-washin' the dishes*
> *Go lookin' elsewhere for your fishes*
> *For I am not for thee."*

Relief washed over Aidan and escaped his chest in one great gasp. He drained a few mouthfuls from the sheep's bladder and watched as Triumph dined on several fistfuls of hay.

The singing cut off shortly, and the girl wandered back into the camp, scratched up and dirt-smudged. She didn't give Aidan a second look, but set two eggs in his pile of food supplies.

"Where did you get those?"

The girl – Slaíne, Aidan remembered – shook her head and wiped her brow. "Pigeon's nest."

"A pigeon's nest?" Aidan said, gathering supplies for a fire. "That would be a high climb."

Slaíne shrugged. "Not too high for me." And she turned again, as if to disappear into the woods.

Before Aidan could stop himself, he stood upright and said quite firmly, "Where are you going?"

"To find water. Is that all right with you?" she snapped.

"How do I know you're not going to just run off and find your mistresses again?"

Her face pinched. "They ain't my mistresses. 'Sides, coulda run off whilst you were occupied earlier, now couldn't I?" She rolled her eyes and continued to leave.

Irritation replaced relief, and Aidan followed her. "How much have your mistresses told you of the Immortal?"

"They ain't my mistresses," she repeated.

Aidan nodded. "Fair enough." He waited, hoping she would offer something. When she did not, he crossed his arms and stared her straight in the eyes. "What do you know?"

Sláine worried her lower lip, squinting against the sun. "An' I'm supposed to tell you all I know, jus' like that?" A smirk taunted her lips but did not meet her hard eyes.

His biceps tightened. "So you *do* know about the Immortal."

She snorted. "So what if I do? What makes you think I'm just gonna tell you everything I know?" Her gaze held on to his, though she brought up a hand to her eyes to shield herself from the overhead blaze.

Aidan scratched at his chin stubble. "You talked of this Meraude. You seemed to hate her."

"What of it?"

"Well, perhaps I could help you with her."

"Help me with her? What could you possibly do against a mage?" When he opened his mouth to remind her of what he had done to her blade, she interrupted. "Yes, making things disappear an' all that. What good will that do against a mage?"

"More than a scrawny girl could do alone."

She hissed and bared her teeth, reminding Aidan of a feral cat, one that he was trying to pet. "I'm no girl. Two and twenty, and don't you forget."

Aidan raised his hands. "All right. Still...." He followed her farther into the brush and bracken. "You're not going to accomplish anything on your own. We might as well help each other." He bumped into her when she stopped short, eliciting a yelp. "Why don't you tell me everything you know about the Immortal, and I'll help you find and avenge yourself against Meraude."

Sláine cocked her head to the side, her gaze wary. "You want something from her, though."

"So I'll get that, and then we'll see about taking your revenge, hmm?"

She scoffed and was silent for a moment, biting her lower lip. At last she said, "Let me just see how much you can be trusted before I say a thing."

Aidan glowered. He did not like having to wait on others' whims, and he knew this girl was going to drag this out as long as she could. "But if I'm—"

She turned and continued walking.

Without thinking, he reached out, grabbed her shoulder, and spun her around. Aidan was used to dealing with men, and her reaction surprised him.

Sláine, for all her bravado, cringed away like he was about to strike. Hate filled her eyes and she stalked around him, back toward their camp, stretching the Pull between them.

Confused and ashamed, Aidan looked down at his hand, which was wet with blood. He frowned until he recalled the whip crack he had heard the previous evening. "Idiot," he groaned, taking a step back. "I am such an idiot." Not only was he no closer to getting the answers he sought, he now had to tiptoe, something he was not good at. He was tempted to follow her and apologize, but she started singing again, and he knew that she could wait.

Satisfied that the girl was still close by but not within earshot, Aidan sat beneath a tree, crossed his legs, and attempted something he hadn't done in ages.

At first he closed his eyes and explored the Pulls around him. He was struck again by the strength of Sláine's Pull, but he felt around it. Something small skittered down below the ground. Its Pull was easy enough to let go. He reached out farther, feeling snakes in all their thin, wriggling insubstantiality. Then there were fair-sized rodents, or so Aidan assumed; he couldn't actually differentiate between most mammal species. Then he found Triumph's Pull, a few deer, and maybe even a coyote.

"All right," he breathed and braced himself. The girl's Pull wasn't easy now to navigate around, but he was not looking to Call anything. He was looking to Summon.

He held back his cache of supplies in Nothingness, things he did not want to Summon at the moment, and attempted to find his family. If he could Dismiss himself, surely he could Dismiss and Summon others. His family might be in Nothingness this very moment, and all he needed to do was bring them back. But he'd tried this many times, and no matter how hard he stretched and strained, all he produced was sweat.

This time proved to be no different. Aidan sat and focused as hard as he could, trying to draw his mother, father, and Sam out of the abyss.

"Useless," he shouted after an hour, spittle flying from his mouth. His eyes opened as neighboring birds took flight. Disgusted with himself, Aidan hung his head and tried to bring his emotions back under control. He drew in deep breaths and let them out slowly.

His heart continued to race, and it felt as though he had run a mile through waist-deep mud. But he stumbled to his feet and made his way back to camp, where he could smell a fire and the beginnings of something cooking. He sniffed outside of the small clearing, and wondered at what he smelled and saw. Meat? Where had she found meat? And why hadn't she run away? Not that he wanted her to, but this whole situation was as odd as it was vexing.

He spied her then, emerging from the woods across the way. Her hands were bright red, as if coated in blood. "Are you hurt?" he called out.

Even from this distance, he could see the glower on her face. "'Course not."

Aidan remembered the blood on his own hand, and then he wasn't so sure he believed her. Twigs snapped under his mucky boots as he tramped toward her, upsetting the peaceful crackling of the fire. He stopped at the makeshift spit and stared. There were two birds roasting – pigeons, he'd bet his money on. "How the blazes did you manage all this?" he asked.

Sláine froze where she stood, her eyes narrowed.

Aidan stopped and raised his hands. "I'm sorry."

She shrugged. "I snuck up on them."

His eyebrows shot up of their own accord. "You snuck up on them?"

"I didn't steal them, if that's what you're accusin'."

Aidan had to laugh at this. "Pigeons are wild birds and don't fall under poaching laws."

The girl didn't seem to know what to say to that statement, and went back to turning the spit again. "I ate the eggs."

Aidan suppressed a grin. "I see."

"I'm sorry," she snarled.

The grin broke through. "No need to apologize. You did all the work."

The girl seemed to be deciding if he was making fun of her or not.

Stooped over the small blaze, she returned her attention to the task at hand.

"Eggs are hard to Dismiss and save for later, anyway. All that brittle shell." That drew no comment from her, so he tried a different approach to getting her to talk. "And you managed to catch, pluck, and gut them within half an hour's time?"

If he didn't know better, he'd wager a smile was fighting its way onto her face. She grimaced. "Took two hours or so, but I've got fast fingers."

Aidan rubbed the backs of his hands over his eyes. "Two hours? Was I really gone that long?" He'd said it more to himself than to her. "One loses track of time when one's punishing oneself."

★   ★   ★

The birds cooked through, Aidan removed them from the spit and placed the carcasses on slabs of bark he pried from a nearby tree. After dining on nothing but cold food and under-cooked tubers for a month, this was a treat. He ate slowly, savoring.

Slaíne, on the other hand, ate as though her next meal weren't guaranteed. Grease dribbled down her chin, and she didn't mop herself up until every morsel had been chewed off the bones.

Aidan wondered if he should offer her some of his, but decided it might hurt the strange girl's feelings. He handed her a water bladder and said, "Thank you. I didn't expect...."

She was already waving the words away and drinking. When she came up for air, she said, "There enough water for me to drink a few more?"

"A few more...?"

"Mouthfuls."

Aidan felt the bladder. She had already drained more than he could afford. "No. Sorry."

With apparent reluctance, she passed the bladder back. "Vines."

"Hmm?"

She looked around the woods, and his gaze followed hers. "Blast. Naught but poisonous things." Of all things, she reached to the ground, dusted off a few pebbles, and stuffed them in her mouth. When she caught him staring, she frowned and went about cleaning up after the meal.

"Do you think your m—the elves are following us?"

Slaíne shrugged and swept ashes onto the fire with a thick stick.

Aidan wandered off to feed and water Triumph while the girl worked, keeping mindful of her Pull and the other Pulls surrounding him. There were no other humans nearby, nor did he sense the elves. They might be safe. Still, best not to leave anything to chance.

Once he'd finished with his horse, he returned to the camp, where the girl had piled all his belongings.

Slaíne watched him, silent expectation written on her face.

Amused, Aidan made a show of waving his hand and Dismissed everything.

The girl nodded once to herself, as if a burning question had been answered, and wiped her hands down her skirts. "Right. Where're you off to now?"

His eyes narrowed. "*We* are headed for a town."

She snorted. "Right. And what town might that be?"

He frowned. "That is my concern." If the elves found her before they found him, he would still have a chance of escaping. It wouldn't do to give away his plans to her...especially since he didn't know where her loyalties lay.

With a scowl, Slaíne put her bony hands on her bony hips. Her look said it all: "So *that's* how it is."

That rankled. "See here, I haven't time to explain myself. If we're to make it to W—the *village*, I mean...."

She smirked at him.

Exasperated, he jabbed his finger in her direction. "If we're to make it to the village before nightfall, I need your utmost cooperation. Is that understood?"

Eyes ablaze, the girl snapped him a smart salute—"Aye, sir."—causing her loose shirt to dip down over her shoulder.

Aidan froze. "What is that?" He was looking at a bloody gash the size and shape of a whip lash. Recalling the dried blood on his hand, he again berated himself. He needed to take care of this, before it could get much worse. Left untended, it could be deadly. "Come here."

It was her turn to freeze. "Nah, sir."

He pointed at the wound, which she was covering up as best she could. "That's going to become infected."

To his frustration, the girl merely shrugged and muttered something that sounded like 'ruddy meddler'.

"Let me have a look." Aidan made a move for her, but she skirted out of his reach. "Slaíne, please, I'm only trying to help you."

"I can manage m'self."

He decided to change tactics. With a sigh, he threw up his hands and moved toward his horse. "I'm sure you can. Now, can we ride?"

Slaíne gave him a suspicious look, hesitated, and finally approached Triumph, who was huffing impatiently. She was ready to mount the steed, when Aidan grabbed her around the waist and pinned her against the horse's side. "Gerroff!"

Aidan Summoned a clean rag and dabbed at the green pus oozing around the edges of the wound. He tried to ignore her Pull as he held, examined, and cleaned her up. It wasn't easy, and she thrashed against him with surprising strength for someone so slight. "I should not have returned the salve. You didn't manage to slip it out of camp, I assume?"

She swore at him. "'Course I didn't. Get off!" She pushed off Triumph, who snorted and took a few steps ahead, which left Slaíne to fall on her side.

Suppressing a laugh, Aidan held out his hand to help her up. "Come now," he said as she ignored him, "I'm just trying to help."

The glare on her face told Aidan she didn't believe him. Slaíne gathered the opening of her blouse tightly about her neck and stumbled to her feet.

He gestured to the horse, his hands outstretched and his eyebrows raised. "Need help mou—"

The girl leapt astride Triumph with grace that didn't fit her manners, and took the reins in her hands. "Anytime you're ready, *sir.*"

The smirk faded from his face as good humor left him. One foot in a stirrup, he raised himself up into the saddle. Next to her, he mounted like a clumsy oaf, and that hurt his pride. "Hold on tight." When the girl failed to grab him round the waist, he almost said something, but contented himself with wildly slapping the reins, and they flew off into the distance.

★　　★　　★

They rode off and on again into the evening, when the sun melted into the hill-capped horizon, and the waxing moon crested the burgeoning trees. Glowworms flittered like many lanterns in the gloom, and bats scurried about in the sky. Slaíne seemed to have fallen asleep. She was still. Too still. It was almost as though she was trying to lull Aidan into a false sense of security.

For her sake or his own, he kept quiet, pretending not to know what she was up to. *Let her scheme.* He waited and rode, expecting her to attempt an escape at any moment. She didn't. Nor had the elves pursued them. Odd, that.

The great galleon in the sky continued to climb, and soon all was plunged into its dusky light. They could travel no farther that day, for the town was still nigh fifteen miles off. Triumph was growing weary and cantankerous – so was the horse's master. "Girl, wake up," he said, steering his steed off the road. "We need to make camp."

To his surprise, she did not move but let out a great almighty snort and lolloped even further forward in the saddle, forcing Aidan to catch her before she could plummet to the ground.

He pinched her, eliciting a few choice words he thought unnecessary, and hoisted himself to the ground. "We're making camp. On your feet."

Slaíne shivered and tucked her arms tightly about her torso. "Yessir."

Aidan rolled his eyes. "Come on, we haven't all day."

"No, but we've all night, haven't we?" Then, without waiting for Aidan to help her, Slaíne jumped from Triumph's back, giving the beast a start.

Aidan waited for the sound of her feet hitting the ground. There was only silence. *Odd one, she.*

"See about collecting some tinder for a fire," he said snappishly before he could stop himself. The way the girl glared at him was unnerving. For a moment, he thought she was going to tell him where he could shove his fire. But she turned and tread off into the woods, making nary a sound.

Satisfying himself that his one connection to information couldn't run off without her Pull informing him, Aidan licked his right pointing finger and held it aloft. The air was still, and there were no clouds in sight. They should have a cold, clear night. Perhaps it was folly, lighting a fire that could easily draw the elves to them. Though, something told

Aidan that if the four sisters had wanted to follow them, they would have caught up already.

He dragged some branches that were tolerably dry into a row, and went about Dismissing small sections away, thus separating the wood into logs. Once the logs had been consumed by the fire, he could Summon what he had Dismissed and use them in another blaze. He arranged them as he had done many times before, making a tepee which would shelter the tinder in the middle. He removed his flint and the stick of magnesium from the pouch he kept in Nothingness.

Soon there would be no light to be guided by as he struck the flint with his tools. He might slice right through a finger or worse. He needed that tinder. He needed it now.

Anxious, Aidan checked the Pulls around him and noted that the girl was less than five yards off. "Bring what you've gathered," he said, trying to keep any ire out of his voice. Why was he so angry with her? There was no putting his finger on it. Maybe it had something to do with her attitude. That was most likely. He had saved her from those elves, and how did she repay him? By taking her blasted time gathering the essential starting ingredients for a fire.

Well, she might be having difficulties finding anything in the shadows, said the voice of fairness in the back of his mind.

He ignored it. "Girl, where are you?"

Her approach was much noisier than her departure – *Crunch! Crash! Thud! Thunk!* – followed by swearing, muffled by the back of her hand, which swiped at her mouth. When she stepped into the waning light, it was obvious what had taken her so long. She had enough dry grass to make several fires.

Aidan bit down on the corners of his mouth. Had she never made a fire before?

As if reading his expression, she snorted and handed him a fistful. "Some's for your steed, of course."

Oh. He hadn't thought of Triumph. "Thank you."

Soon, he had a large blaze crackling before him, and the warmth soaked into his bones, driving all ill humor out of his body. He Summoned his rations and divided them between the girl and himself. It was a gamble, finishing the meager amount off, but he was optimistic that they would reach Wontworth before noon the next day.

With a yawn, he shot a glance over at his traveling companion, who was hunched over and staring mutely into the blaze. "You should get some rest."

She didn't answer at first. The firelight danced in her glassy eyes, and she moved nary a muscle. It was almost as if she had fallen into a trance. She was too still.

"Slaíne? Are you all right?"

"I'll keep first watch."

"You don't have to."

"There's a storm coming." Lightning crackled in the west, and the sky darkened.

Aidan felt the wind. "It should pass us."

"That's not what I meant."

He opened his mouth to ask her what she *did* mean, but she turned her back to the fire and himself, ending the conversation. Well, if she wanted to keep guard, that was up to her. Not that he trusted Slaíne, but he was fairly certain he could rest. Her Pull would alert him if she moved too far…he hoped. There was little choice left to him.

Aidan yawned, stretched, and lay down on his side. He was sore from riding and exhausted from the week's trials. Before long, his eyelids flickered closed, the yellow flames dancing on the other side as sleep overtook him.

★   ★   ★

He was standing in a great room. If he didn't know that his country had no true royalty, he would say he was standing in a palace hall.

The structure was made of gleaming white stones, bricked together so seamlessly that the octagonal room's walls might've been carved from a single rock. But that couldn't be. There were no windows, no door, but the ceiling was open to the elements, and silver moonlight poured in.

A crystal-blue carpet runner spilled out before him, twisting and winding its way from where Aidan stood in the middle of the room to an unoccupied glass throne against the wall on his left. He turned toward it and took a tentative step forward, but ran into some invisible barrier. Not one to quit, Aidan rose and tried again with the same results. Without being told, he knew he had to reach that throne before someone else did. Someone wicked. But short of cursing, there was nothing he could do. "What is this place?"

"You are dreaming, Aidan Ingledark." It was a woman who spoke, her voice a deep, rich roar.

Aidan made to turn around, but found himself paralyzed from the waist down. Panic seized hold of him and he pounded with his fists on the invisible wall, making no sound. Sore, he paused. "What is this magic?"

A woman – no, an *angel* stepped out of the throne's shadow and approached him. Her hair was blacker than the deepest night, her face as pale as snow, and the silver circlet atop her waves suggested that she was in fact a queen. But the land had no queen. This made no sense.

"You are wondering why I summoned you here."

He shivered, trying and failing to meet her gaze. He settled instead for staring at a spot just over her left shoulder. "Summoned? What do you mean?"

She laughed, a lovely sound that made Aidan think of children playing in summertime. "No, Aidan Ingledark, not the sort of Summoning you are thinking of." Her smile widened as she glided toward him without making a sound.

"What am I doing here? Who are you?"

The woman tut-tutted him. "They told me you were a suspicious one. I see that they did not express the half of it." With a sigh, she reached out as if to touch Aidan's face, but her hand swept right through him. "I told you. You are not here. You are dreaming. That is how I brought your Inner Man to this place." Her smile went lopsided when he opened his mouth to protest. "You'll be gone as soon as you wake. There is no keeping the living in this room."

Aidan swallowed. "So, am I dead? And you are...?"

"We're both very much alive. Aidan Ingledark, I need your help uniting the Immortal." Her eyes became two pools of fire at the word, and Aidan grew afraid, though he knew not why. It passed soon enough, along with the memory of the sensation.

The Immortal. There was that word again. But what did it mean? "The Immortal? Who?"

She shook her head. "Not who. *What.*"

He considered this for a moment. "I've heard of you."

"I assumed no less."

"You are Meraude, then. They say...." He hesitated. The reports he had on her were conflicting. The girl, Sláine, apparently wanted the mage dead. The elves and the Romas had warned him that she wanted all magical beings dead. Yet the seer at Prewitt Manor had said Meraude would be able to help him. That she was the only one who could help him.

The mage gave him a knowing look. "I am neither good nor bad, Lord Ingledark."

"What do you want with the Immortal?"

Her eyes twinkled in the moonlight and she whispered, "That is my own concern, milord. I need the Goblets Immortal, and you are the one who can get them for me."

He stalled. "The Goblets?"

She nodded. "You know of what I speak. You are Blest."

"Blest?"

How could a smile be benign and so piercingly cold at the same time? "I warn you, do not play the fool with me. Lady Meraude knows." The room trembled at the sound of her name. So did Aidan, for that matter. "You met with one of my servants. It has been said you are on the road leading toward the Warring Goblet. Have you found it?"

He'd run into her servant? When? Who? The truth slipped out of Aidan's mouth without his meaning it to. "I came across a Goblet."

Her grin widened. "And did you Claim it?"

"Claim it? No. The elves took it."

Lady Meraude scowled and put a pale white finger to her brown lips. "Interesting. No matter. No matter. It shall be recovered soon enough. I thank you for your honesty, Lord Ingledark."

What could Aidan do but nod his acknowledgement? His voice seemed to have temporarily left him...along with his wits.

When she looked at him again, the smile had returned. "You will need to be careful in Wontworth. There is talk of murders and robberies there. And don't look so surprised. It was the general direction you were headed, was it not?"

Aidan nodded mutely.

"I think I like you, Lord Ingledark." She circled, appraising him. "Hmm. Yes, I think I owe you a favor for your services."

Aidan's voice returned to him. "What services? I'm afraid I haven't agreed to anything, and even if I had, I have no idea where this Warring Goblet is."

"You needn't worry about that one. My servant will collect it. No, what you need to concern yourself with is the Questing Goblet."

"My lady?"

"It should be buried in old Cedric's grave. Unfortunately, I cannot be allowed the honor of retrieving it." He was about to protest, but she cut him off with a wave of her hand. "For your services, I have certain gifts within my means to deliver unto you your heart's desire."

What did she know of his heart's desire? This was some nonsense dream. It was time to wake up.

"When you wake, do not speak of this to anyone. Trust no one, Lord Ingledark. The Questing Goblet is your job alone. Retrieve it and I will bring them back."

Aidan scoffed. "You mean my family, I assume. You'll bring my family back? Even *I* cannot do that."

She practically beamed at that. "Because you know not where they are."

"But—"

"Disregard me and my request, and I will make certain of your death. Please me, and you will be reunited with those you have lost. Go now. I grow weary."

"Wait, I don't understand...." Aidan looked down on his shoulder, where a dove had alighted. Its weight was comforting, even though it dug its clawed feet into his flesh. That is when he opened his eyes, leaving Meraude and the throne room behind.

CHAPTER FIVE

"Sir, wake up. Sir?"

Aidan blinked his eyes rapidly, the dream still burned into his vision. Such light, such beauty. Gone. All of it, except for the pressure on his shoulder. He looked up, and it was no dove perched on him, but a freckle-riddled hand.

"Sir, you need to wake up."

He recognized the voice but couldn't place it. "Meraude?"

"Does I have to do everything myself?" the girl's voice asked.

Aidan opened his eyes in time to have his face slapped good and hard. "Take care!" he said, flailing and stumbling to his feet. His eyes locked on Slaíne's fearful ones, and he let out a great huff of air. "I'm sorry. Slaíne, I'm not going to hurt you. You – you startled me, that's all." Something was wrong. His gaze wandered about in the darkness. Darkness? "Why did you wake me?"

"Your horse ran off."

He went to grab her by the shoulders to steady himself, but decided against it. "When?"

"Moments ago. I tried wakin' you before. He – he whinnied and cantered off." She lowered her gaze. "I'm sorry, sir."

Aidan swore. Closing his eyes, he felt for Triumph's Pull. To his annoyance, he felt only Slaíne's, and for whatever reason, it had grown stronger overnight. "Could you maybe try standing over there for a minute?"

Brow furrowed, the girl took a step around the dying embers and stood on the other side. She looked at him, expectant and confused. "That better, sir?"

No, it wasn't. Not at all. Aidan shook his head and rubbed his temples. "Walk away."

"Where?"

"Into the woods a ways. I'll let you know when to stop." Perhaps putting her at a distance would give him a better sense of the other Pulls around him.

But the girl wasn't moving and didn't seem ready to. If anything, she seemed terrified. "How far?"

They didn't have time for this. Triumph had never wandered far, but there was a first time for everything. "Stay put." Aidan turned and ran off into the woods.

"Don't, sir!" she screeched.

The sound froze him to the core. It was the sound wild animals made when in pain. He turned around to face her, and found that she was moving toward him. "What are you doing? What's wrong?"

"The curse, sir."

"Curse?"

She sighed, exasperated. "The curse. The one that was put on me."

Aidan did not believe in curses. Bad luck, for certain, but cursing was for wizards, and there was no such thing as they anymore. "I need you to stay where you are. That is an order." He gave her a small smile of reassurance. "I won't go far. You'll be perfectly safe."

Her face paled further in the moonlight, but she mashed her lips together and nodded once. "All right."

Without another interruption, Aidan took off into the semi-darkness, feeling for Pulls. He felt trees, grass, all minor life forms that hardly tugged at him at all. What was wrong with him? It was as if his ability had left, or.... *Iron. There must be an iron mine nearby or something.* Well, he wasn't about to go searching for one in the dark. It was too dangerous. In trouble or not, Triumph would have to wait 'til morning, as much as Aidan hated the thought. He turned around and made his way back to camp.

He'd gone farther than he'd thought, and the way became difficult as the moon disappeared behind a bank of clouds. Plunged into darkness, Aidan walked as a blind man, hands outstretched before him to keep branches and bracken out of his face. "There's no finding him tonight," he said as he re-entered the camp. "It's too dangerous." Aidan paused.

There, where she'd been standing minutes before, the girl was sprawled out on the ground, her chest rising and falling rapidly.

"Looks like I'll be keeping watch now." And judging by the moon's position in the sky, that would be another hour or two. Day would break soon enough. She could sleep.

★   ★   ★

Aidan remained vigilant throughout the night. He listened for sounds of his steed's return, but was met only with the silent keening of insects and the occasional hoot and howl of other wildlife.

He thought of his dream, wondering what he ought to do. Meraude had made no subtle allusion to her intents: if he did not provide her with the Goblets Immortal, life was going to get worse for him. But if he helped her.... Could she really bring his family back, as she so claimed?

Find the Questing Goblet, the mage had said before Slaíne woke him. There might have been something else, but the more he tried to grasp at the details, the hazier the memory became. Maybe his mind had conjured images and promises of things he wanted, rather than images of things that were. He'd been thinking and speaking of Meraude earlier, hadn't he? Surely it was the power of suggestion influencing his sleeping mind.

And yet Aidan knew he had a poor imagination. To invent something so particular as the shape of the room, the woman and her fiery eyes, the unclaimed throne…it did not feel right. Something either was changing inside him – which, at the age of two and thirty, was ridiculous – or he really had been transported in his sleep to a different place and had conversed with this elusive witch. He looked at the girl. Perhaps he should share what knowledge he had with her. That, plus some persuasion, might convince her to open up.

Before dawn's breaking, the air grew unbearably cold, and he was forced to build up the fire again, which he'd been feeding handfuls of dry grass since waking. Where had Triumph gone to? Aidan feared he was right about the iron mine. If that blasted horse had fallen into anything, there would be no rescuing him.

Shuddering, he looked over at the girl. *That can't be comfortable*, he thought, seeing her arms and legs turned out at odd angles. He clambered to his feet and, seeing that she was shivering, threw his cloak over her small form.

When the sun overcame the horizon entirely, he tapped Slaíne with his boot. "Girl. Are you awake?" With care, he shook her by the shoulder, but she did not wake at first. "Slaíne, will you not help me find my steed?"

Her eyes blinked open a crack. "How long I been alseep?" Shaking, she sat up, and Aidan's cloak fell to her lap. She looked him full on in the face, and it was startling to observe that a blood vessel had burst, making the white of her left eye crimson.

"Are you all right?" He scarcely could wait for her answer; he needed to find Triumph, the poor beast.

Slaíne started to stand and crumpled to the ground. "I'm fine." Her voice was rather soft. "I'll be up and about presently."

Wasting not another moment, Aidan ran off into the woods surrounding their alcove, feeling for Pulls. When there were none significant to be found, Aidan closed his eyes and felt for the absence of things. His senses slid over the ground, probing and grasping at what could not be grasped. All the while he listened. Birds. Blasted birds twittering in the sky, fouling his mood further. He pushed his explorations deeper and wider. Nothing. No absences, no possibility of an iron mine, no Triumph.

He opened his eyes. He hadn't gone nearly as far as he'd done the night before, but was there a point? Surely the horse—

Aidan started. There, leading toward his camp, were hoof prints in the soil...clustered with another set of strange ones. He followed them back to camp.

"Any sign of—" She stopped herself when their eyes locked.

"Do you know which way he went?" Aidan started off in the opposite direction that he had just explored, and he could feel from her Pull that she was trying to keep pace with him.

"Sir, please wait. I ain't not meself again just yet."

Without looking back, he frowned. "How's that?"

She seemed unwilling to speak at first, and when she did, it came out more of a croak. "The curse, sir."

Aidan held up a hand for her to stop. "You may return to camp." The smell had just met his nostrils; no woman should be forced to witness what was downwind of their fire. "Please return at once." It was all he could do to keep his voice from breaking on the words. He hoped he was wrong. If he were a religious man, he'd be praying that he was wrong. "Go back."

Slaíne ignored that and continued her approach.

Handkerchief drawn, he looked back over his shoulder and handed her the cloth. "You're going to need this, then." He Summoned the sword he had taken from her and, parting a cluster of branches, stepped toward the source of the stench.

What he saw had not been the sore sight he'd expected, though it was indeed a disgusting mess. The mangled corpse of a sun-rotting goblin littered their path. Limbs here, heart there, it was a gruesome sight. But there was no sign of Triumph, other than hoof prints that grew fainter and finally disappeared into nowhere.

"Sir."

Aidan turned to face Slaíne. "What is it?"

"There was a struggle here, if you don't mind me sayin'." She pointed at the ground a stone's throw from where she stood. "The goblin's body was dragged." She took a few steps into a heavily wooded area, and emerged hauling a saddle.

Aidan groaned. "Anything else over there?" He felt for Pulls. There was nothing. But how could he not feel the goblin's? They must have none.

Slaíne frowned at him as she handed over the saddle. "There's no blood on the girth or any part of the saddle really." Slaíne bit her lower lip.

"Go on."

"Looks like they took your steed alive, sir. Goblins, they're good at hypnotizin' creatures. I've seen it done before." She shuddered, and Aidan began to wonder at her. Who went around watching goblins?

She seemed to have read his thoughts. "Elves are cousins to goblins. I'm lucky the four didn't let them eat me."

Aidan sighed. "And I'll be lucky if they don't eat my horse." He Dismissed the saddle and the sword. "Well, it looks like we'll be on foot now. And we'd best hurry. If there are goblins in these parts, I don't want to meet them in the dark."

With a curt nod, Slaíne handed him back his handkerchief. She hadn't even flinched at the smell, which made Aidan's stomach turn. "We won't make it far on foot."

"I'll be picking up another steed in Wontworth."

She smirked at him. "So that *is* where we're headed."

Aidan opened his mouth to deny it, but he hadn't the heart or energy. His horse was gone, and they had a rough journey ahead of them.

★   ★   ★

Their going was slow. The girl still claimed some nonsense of a curse was to blame, but wouldn't go into details. Aidan wondered if she'd had a worse beating from the elves than he'd first thought, but he said nothing. The common mood between them was cordial enough, and he did not wish to bring it crashing down around their ears if he could help it.

They'd finished their food rations the previous night. That was a worry. Some berries were in season, but none were edible. After a rough hike through six miles of bracken, their mutual amiability had dissolved into a cross silence. They needed to exert themselves, to pick up their speed if they were to reach the town before nightfall. But she was struggling to keep pace with him. She fell twice, injuring nothing. And as the sun had reached its highest, the sweat-drenched travelers decided to rest and refresh themselves with a few sips of water.

But the water did not refresh. If anything, it made Aidan want more, and he knew the girl felt the same way, though she said nothing of it. He feared this had been a poor trade for her. She'd gone from living in peace with four evil elves to living in thirst with…. He couldn't think. There would be no going further until they'd had a decent rest.

Stomach snarling like some ferocious beast, Aidan leaned against the trunk of a large oak. A dreadful thought came to him: in their haste to depart that morning, and in the confusion of losing Triumph, he'd got them turned around. They were headed too far southwest. Their course would need to be corrected, costing them an additional ten miles. No wonder they hadn't seen any signs of civilization. "I am an utter fool."

Slaíne, who was resting a few feet off on a patch of crabgrass, lifted her head. "Sir?"

Aidan opened his mouth but hesitated. It wouldn't do to worry her. "I should have gone after Triumph as soon as he went missing."

He half-expected her to give some encouragement that he'd done the right thing, but it would seem that the girl had fallen asleep.

Though the sun continued to beat down on them, the air held a chill, and the clothes that clung to his body with sweat now made him shiver. He Summoned his cloak and covered up. With nothing else to do but rest, Aidan reached out and felt for Pulls. There was no one within his reach…at least, as far as he could tell. It wasn't getting any easier to ignore the girl's Pull, and he was starting to wonder why. He reached out tentatively and closed his eyes. Concentrating with all his might, he opened his eyes, latched onto her Pull and tugged against it.

Screeching in surprise or pain, Slaíne shot toward Aidan like an arrow, landing at his feet. Well, that was new.

She glared up at him. "What'd you go and do that for?"

Aidan fought a grin. He hadn't quite meant to do it, didn't think it would work, but for the first time since his abilities had developed, he'd managed to Call another living being. This could be the answer he needed to whether or not he'd ever see his family again. "You're all right, then?"

"What ruddy sort of question is that? 'Course I'm all right." Grumbling still, she stumbled to her feet and returned to her place of rest. There, she flopped back down, and at once began to snore again.

Aidan looked at her amazed for a while. Was this an everyday occurrence to her? She must not know how his abilities worked, but why should she? *But she knows of the Goblets*, he reasoned. *She must know something of my condition.* He was about to wake her again, but thought better of it. It was obvious she did not care for him one jot, not as a friend nor as an ally. Why would she trade information? Would it be wise for him to say anything? There was only one way to find out, and he was no coward. He began. "Girl, wake up."

She let out an almighty, earth-shaking snort and rolled over onto her side to face him. Her face was dirt-smudged and cross, and she looked positively ready to lose her temper. "What?"

Only a mite taken aback, Aidan started in. "I didn't know I could do that." The bait having been set, he waited for her to grasp it. But the minutes wore on, and she said nothing.

Her eyes were slits, and it would seem that he was in danger of losing her to sleep again. It was time to try a different tack.

"Please, Slaíne, if you know anything about my condition, I would be most grateful if you told me."

The girl laughed, but, upon looking into his eyes, she stopped. Her expression became thoughtful. At last, she spoke. "If I were to tell you…." She sat up and propped her head on one hand. "How are you at keeping secrets that can get a body tortured and killed?"

Aidan stared deep into her eyes, as if he could Call the secrets from their depths. "I won't speak a word of what you tell me to anyone."

"Not to your family?"

"I have none," he said.

She raised her eyebrows and rose to a sitting position. "Oh. Me neither." She scratched the back of her neck, a nervous gesture. "Friends?"

Aidan didn't blink. "I have no need for them."

If he hadn't known better, he would say there was approval in her eyes. Whatever the case, she nodded and looked off into the distance. "All right. I will tell you some of what I know, Mr. Aidan. But I want somethin' in exchange."

He braced himself. "Name it."

She smirked. "I want my sword back."

"For what end?"

"That's none of your business."

Aidan glowered. "If you mean to kill me with it, then it really is my business."

Slaíne smiled with her teeth this time, threw her head back and laughed. It was a spritely sound, one that he was sure he'd never heard the likes of before. It made the hairs on his arms stand on end, and goose-skin break out all over. Too soon, her laughter ended, and her expression grew very serious. "No, I can't kill you. You're quite safe."

"Can't kill me? Or won't?" he asked before he could stop himself.

Her face fell. "You're safe from me. Shouldn't that be enough?"

Wondering how he had offended her, he tried smoothing it over before she refused to share her information. "I'm sorry. I shall speak of it no more."

Her smile returned, and he wondered at her. "You don't even know what you're sorry for." She held up her hands. "All right. Give me a moment to collect m'thoughts."

Aidan tried to appear impassive, but he could feel the tension of anticipation tightening his muscles and setting his jaw. His heart beat so hard it hurt. His hands grew moist, and it took enormous strength of will to remain still, afraid that the slightest movement might make the girl change her mind.

There were several more moments of silence between them 'til at last she spoke. "I don't rightly know much about the Blest...your kind," she amended with a nod toward Aidan. "The Four rarely spoke of such things in front of me."

Aidan gave her a moment before prodding. "Whatever you do know could be of great help to me." They sat in silence for a moment, until he swallowed hard and said, "Please. Please tell me everything you know."

Slaíne looked up at the sun, her face bathed in its glow. "As far as I can understand, there are maybe three or four Goblets. Together, they're called the Immortal." She paused and wetted her lips with the tip of her tongue. "There's the Summoning Goblet, which I'll return to in a moment. There's also something like a War Goblet – or was it Warring?" She bit her lower lip and squinted. "Can't recall. But each Goblet comes with a gift."

"A gift?"

Slaíne nodded. "Yes. Whoever drinks of the Warring Goblet is given the warrior's mind. He's nearly unbeatable in battle. The Summoner – that's you – can make objects disappear, reappear, and can draw or repel them…what you've been calling Summoning and Calling."

Aidan nodded. "How much do you know of the Summoning Goblet?"

"Next to nothing, only what I know about the others: the drinker has the ability for only so long. Until, well, they make water or what have you." She snorted. "Doesn't explain you, though. You don't happen to have a giant iron goblet on your person, do you?"

"I did," Aidan said slowly. "Until I threw it to the elves. What was I thinking?"

"Oh, probably about not getting yourself killed." She smirked at him when he looked up, and then returned her own gaze to the sky. "Might still happen, the dying part. If the Four knew of me telling you this…." She shuddered.

He wanted to press her for more answers, but sensed that if he did so, she'd stop talking altogether. So he removed his intense gaze from her face and stared down at his filthy hands. The cut had healed almost miraculously. His hand felt almost new.

Aidan flexed his fingers, and a clump of weeds tore themselves, roots attached, from the ground and shot into his hand. He hadn't meant to Call them. Their Pulls were so weak, they'd just responded to his feelings, perhaps. He knew without looking that the girl had risen to her feet and took a step to her left.

"That's pretty much all I know. Sorry if it weren't very useful."

Aidan still didn't look up, but twined the blades of grass around his fingers. "What of Cedric's grave?" He looked up, and was not surprised to find her startled. "You do know about old Cedric, then?"

"'Old Cedric', he calls him," she scoffed. "Cedric the Elder's just a legend. Myth."

"No, he's real."

Slaíne narrowed her eyes. "You mean to tell me that you believe the Goblets Immortal were made from wizard blood? Nonsense."

Hoping to lead her to reveal more information, he shrugged. "So, what if I do?"

"Because, Mr. Aidan, it's a very dangerous business, believin' in wizards. An' if you're thinking of lookin' for him...." She tossed her head, and her cap went flying away in a breeze. She didn't seem to notice as her red curls cascaded down her shoulders. "If them legends be true, you're already good as dead."

Aidan held up a finger. "But what if Cedric the Elder is already dead? What if he has something buried with him?"

That brought Slaíne up short. She closed and opened her mouth a few times, and then took to pacing. "You want to go after a wizard's tomb?"

"I might." He tried to sound nonchalant, but the girl saw right through it.

"A wizard's grave would be cursed, of course. You'd better have an awful good reason to want to go diggin' there."

That brought Aidan's temper to the surface, but he let it cool before he spoke again. "Believe me. I do. And I don't believe in curses. That's child's talk."

For all that his words did, he might as well have slapped her. Slaíne recoiled.

Aidan laughed. "You really do believe in them?"

It was her turn to grow angry, it would seem. "How could I not?"

He leaned back, and his manner became playful. "Is this about your supposed curse?"

She took a step back as he rose to his feet. "I don't wish to speak of it."

"Come now. Tell me about it."

She gave him a dark look and said, "How about I show you instead?" And she took off at a run.

Confused, Aidan hesitated before running off after her. "Slaíne! Wait. Please come back. I didn't mean—" He swore as he caught sight of her, just fifteen yards ahead in a circle of maples. "Come back, we don't know if these parts are…safe."

She took a purposeful step back. And another.

The Pull between them warned him before it happened.

Slaíne's body convulsed, and she was thrown up into the sky as if by an invisible hand, and tossed around like a reed in the wind, all before hitting the ground with a dramatic thud and a flash of red light.

The shaking and twitching continued until Aidan came to his senses and ran to her. "What the devil…?" He threw himself down next to her, though was hesitant to touch her.

"Told ya." Her voice was a thin rasp, and her features were gray. A small spasm overtook her once more, before her eyes closed and she lay still, her chest barely rising before it fell.

"Slaíne?" He shook her, and was startled to find that her flesh was cold to the touch. He took her pulse. It was faint at first, but the longer his fingers lingered, the steadier and stronger it became.

Aidan Summoned his cloak and covered her as violent shivers racked her body. "Slaíne," he said more sharply, shaking her.

The girl stirred slightly but did not wake.

So much for reaching Wontworth that day.

CHAPTER SIX

Noon became afternoon, and afternoon ran into evening, and still Sláine did not wake. What had she been thinking? It was apparent that she'd known what would happen to her if she wandered off. And yet....

Aidan knew that he was more than partially to blame. He had, after all, scoffed at the mention of a curse, thus provoking her to take action in order to prove her honesty. To think of the night previous also gave him pain. He had left the girl at the camp, ordering her to stay where she was, oblivious to the fact that it would affect her so. For now, though the exact particulars of the curse were unclear, it was apparent that there was a boundary for her, and that that boundary was attached to a person. Perhaps she could only wander so far from another living being before the curse attacked.

Two fits in two days? The notion pushed all thoughts of the Goblets from his mind and surpassed every worry, even his family, though he was not generous enough to admit it to himself.

The longer she remained comatose, the more unbearable his guilt became. In truth, her color was better, and she'd started to snore softly. Though he could not absolve himself, sitting under the weight of his faults proved misery to the point of pain. It was pointless, as it was done and could not be undone.

Before eventide gave way to night, and the wood was plunged into semi-darkness, Aidan came to his senses and took action. He built a fire. He cut a few vines that seemed safe and drained their fluids into a bone-dry bladder.

The air was chill for late spring, and he sorely wished he'd a second cloak, but didn't think of removing the one he had from his traveling companion. Instead, he built up the blaze to quite a height and reveled in the heat it gave off.

Night fell, overtook, and enveloped them in a cloak of darkness. The sky was overcast, hiding the waning moon, so that the only relief from the inky night was the ravenous blaze, which seemed on the verge of burning out every five minutes, no matter how much fuel he provided.

Aidan Called all manner of dry twigs and branches within the range of his reach. He was separating a larger branch into four separate parts when the girl sat up with a groan. "How are you feeling?" he asked without looking from his work. The sense of guilt again became overwhelming.

"Feels like I've been bludgeoned to death with a burning skillet." Of all things, she laughed. A weak, insincere one, but a laugh nonetheless.

"But you're not dead." He winced at having pointed out the obvious.

This time her laugh had more warmth to it. "Not yet, anyhow." She was on her feet now, he knew, but still didn't even glance at him. The crunching of leaves and the slack in her Pull announced her approach. "Anythin' need doin'?"

Now that it was apparent she was alive, well, and in tolerable condition, Aidan's temper flared. "What were you thinking?"

"No need to shout." She was shouting, too.

"Maybe there is." He turned to her and pointed at the sky. "Not only did you almost get yourself killed—"

"Did not."

Aidan ignored that. "Your fit cost us the remainder of daylight. I should've left you with your rightful masters." He caught her hand mid-strike and did not let go. He'd gone too far and he knew it as regret deepened and he wondered at himself. Why did she bring out such anger in him?

When she spoke, it was through her clenched teeth. "Let. Go."

"Slaíne, please forgive me. I behaved poorly." His grip on her tightened by a degree and, without a thought, he pulled her in closer. "Come, shake hands with me and let's be friends."

Her hand and arm had gone limp. "We can nay be friends."

"But—"

"You shoulda done."

"Should have done what?"

Her look lacked reproach but held plenty of anger. "Left me with the elves. Give me my hand back, sir. I've still need of it." Slaíne's voice was as slack as her arm, but her Pull tightened, contracted, made it strangely unbearable being at such a distance, though a matter of a few inches. Still, he relinquished his grasp and watched her arm fall back to her side.

"Where are you going?"

Slaíne had turned her back to him and was trudging out of the reach of the flames. The look she threw back over her shoulder was grim. "To make water, if that's all right with you."

Aidan grimaced, the girl scoffed, and they both went about their own separate business.

The fire was still ravenous. Nothing, it would seem, could keep it from flickering to the brink of death. Aidan could not use green wood; the fire would smoke. Instead, he Called anything dry that he could sense, driving himself near to the point of mental exhaustion. He'd been at it nigh half an hour when he heard her footsteps returning to camp.

"There you are. I wondered where you'd—" He turned at this point, and a pale fist pummeled him in the side of the head. Stars swam before Aidan's eyes as he tumbled to the ground, marveling at the girl's strength and wrath. He looked up.

Where he'd assumed Slaíne was standing, there stood a stooped figure cloaked in black, its sickly white skin blinding in the fire's light. The fire! Whatever this creature was, he began putting out the blaze, screeching as sparks flew.

Aidan stumbled to his feet, Summoning the girl's blade to his hand. He could not feel the man's Pull, so when the light went out, he swung blindly. He connected with something solid, the silver blade hissing as his opponent collapsed.

The creature gurgled, sputtered, and was silent as the blade began to glow green. From the blade's light, he could see many sets of red eyes peering at him in the darkness beyond. Still he felt no Pulls.

They screeched at such a high pitch!

Aidan's hairs stood on end and he was overwhelmed with dread. "Slaíne," he said as calmly as possible, hoping she could hear him from around the brush. "*Run.*" It would seem a useless exercise at this point, for their alcove was quite surrounded by the red eyes, whose owners' growls and cries pierced the night.

Aidan spun in useless circles, swiping at the sounds as they crowded in. The creatures' fetid breath wafted in on a chill breeze, turning his stomach as he swung out in a wide arc. He caught one of them with the silver sword. The blade again hissed and glowed a brighter green, by which he could now see that these creatures of the night were toying with him, willing to sacrifice the few for sport.

They were there to watch him die. And then? He shuddered at the thought.

"Give us." The voice was a snarl. It reminded Aidan of something primitive, old…feral.

As he swung out again with the blade, there was a shrill cry from the brush, followed by a large flash of light. Perhaps Slaíne had happened across something to fight with, though that was too good to hope for.

Feel for Pulls, you idiot!

So used to feeling them, so desperate now when he could feel nothing but his own imminent demise. Darkness dragged him down to his knees, knocked the sword from his hand, grasped him by the throat and squeezed.

"Where is it?" the night roared.

All grew terribly cold. *I failed them*, was all he could think of his family. *My fault.*

The grip on his windpipe tightened. "Don't touch it too long," rasped a second voice. "It's got power."

It would seem that his body was acting of its own accord. Ignoring his inability to breathe, Aidan reached out and felt for the Pull of his sword. Nothing. But he tried again, and this time there was an odd prickling sensation in the back of his neck. These creatures, these so-called goblins, were not the night nor were they the wind. They were Nothing, and to Nothingness he sent the one clutching him.

Choking and sputtering, Aidan collapsed further still, his skin giving off an eerie green glow.

The goblins had backed away farther, their red eyes averting into the darkness. As one they cried out as wounded things, and were swallowed into the landscape beyond.

Aidan continued to glow, and would have wondered at himself if he had not thought of his poor traveling companion. "Slaíne?" he croaked. He cleared his throat and tried again, though it caused him pain. "Are you all right?"

Her Pull, which had disappeared during the attack, snapped back to life, nearly jerking him to his feet. Relief washed over him.

"They're gone."

Silence. He felt for her Pull again. It was high. Very high. Had she managed to climb a tree before the goblins attacked? Aidan stumbled to his feet and followed the unbearable tug. The farther his steps took him, the brighter his own glow became, until stopping, he could bear the brightness no more. Aidan looked up and there he saw an odd sight. Apparently unconscious, the girl floated in the air above him, glowing a faint blue.

He opened his mouth to shout her name, but a cold iron blade slipped beneath his chin.

"Drop your sword," said the woman he could barely make out in the light of the glow.

Aidan complied. "Who—"

"Another word from you," said a male voice from near his left, "and we shall slit your throat. Attempt anything, and we shall let your lady fair fall."

There was no other option left him. Aidan remained silent and clenched his teeth, furious at himself for being careless that evening. Hot rage pumped hard through his veins. He wanted to help the girl, to free himself, but he was beyond helpless.

"Sleep," said the woman's voice. She snapped her fingers, and the world grew dark. Aidan knew no more.

*　　*　　*

In that dark sleep, Aidan dreamt. He was back in the white stone room, staring at the empty throne, helpless to reach it, as he was frozen in place.

Someone tutted. It was Meraude again, dressed in dark violet. She glided around him, her eyes full of amusement that grated on him. "I take it you haven't discovered Cedric's hallowed grounds?"

Aidan blinked. "What makes you think I'm going to fetch your Goblet?"

She laughed lightly. "You need it as much as I do, Lord Ingledark. Tell me, where are you now?"

"What? You don't know?" He knew he was sleeping. He'd much

rather wake and see what was happening to himself and the girl. Last he'd seen, she was still hovering in the air like a fragile ornament waiting to be dropped.

The woman was speaking again, and Aidan forced himself to attend to what she was saying. "If you wish to see your family again, I and I alone can help you. And in order to help you, I need your location. Where are you?"

Aidan sighed and shrugged. "I was attacked."

Her face fell. "Who attacked?"

"Goblins."

She frowned. "And you survived?"

"Yes." He was growing weary and wished to sit down. "Is it all right if I wake up now? I fear I'm not out of danger yet."

"What do you mean?"

"What I mean is that something must have frightened the goblins off, and now I am with them."

"A prisoner?"

Aidan nodded. "Most assuredly."

Meraude took to pacing, her fair brow wrinkling with either worry or distaste. "This complicates things, to be sure. Can you use your abilities against them?"

He scowled. "You think I didn't try that?"

She held up a hand to waylay his words. "All right. You must find out what they are and what their weakness is. Goblins cannot abide light…. Hmm. Whatever scared them off must be— Ah, most assuredly, you are dealing with nymphs."

Aidan rubbed his temples. "And how do I fight them?"

Meraude sighed. "If you cannot use your abilities, then I'm afraid you're going to have to stay where you are until I free you."

That didn't sound like a good idea. "Couldn't you get inside one of their dreams?"

She raised her eyebrows at this. "Pardon? I don't follow."

"You could appear to them and tell them to let us go…."

"*Us?*"

It was Aidan's turn to be confused. Surely he'd mentioned his traveling companion before. "I met up with someone." He did not like the look she was giving him; it was displeased and bordering on scandalized, so he added, "We'll be parting ways soon," even though he knew there was no possibility of that.

That brought the smile back to Meraude's face. "All right. Let me answer your question: I cannot appear to just anyone."

"But how, then—"

She held up a hand. "And nymphs don't dream. Even if they were to dream, what weight would my words hold with them?"

Aidan shrugged. Isaac the Roma's words were still in the back of his mind. Was it true that Meraude slaughtered magical things? Was he a fool allowing this dream conversation go on? Not that he had much choice. Maybe he should be more careful what information he let slip his lips.

The woman's dark eyes were appraising. "Lord Ingledark, let me be clear. I am trying to help you."

"I know."

"Then you'll have to trust me and stay put with these woodland creatures, all right? No heroics, no escape attempts. Just stay put. Understand?"

Well, that was insulting to his intelligence. Aidan had no intention of staying put and waiting for some possibly evil mage to free them. Nonetheless, he feigned a thoughtful look and finally nodded. "As you wish."

That seemed to satisfy Meraude, for she didn't press the matter. "I suggest that if you have anything to say to me, you say it now."

Aidan shook his head. "I can think of nothing else to say."

Meraude smirked. "How about your location?"

"I don't know where we are. The nymphs—"

"Where were you when the goblins attacked?"

That made Aidan's stomach drop. How best to lie? "If I recall correctly, we were still somewhere on the road to Wontworth." There, the truth but not the truth. They'd been turned around and had wandered in the wrong direction for several miles.

Aidan began to shake and his face stung.

"It would seem someone's trying to rouse you. I suggest you be roused."

The scene dissolved and Aidan was nearly blinded as he returned to reality from his dreaming state. "Ugh." His eyes closed again and he listened. There was lively chatter in the near distance, many fair voices singing and making merry. He heard the crackling of a fire, felt its warmth, and shifted slightly.

Something slapped him in the face again. "Sir!"

Aidan never thought he'd be so relieved to hear a woman's voice in his life. He opened his eyes just as her foot connected with his forehead.

"Ouch!"

"Shh! Sorry…sorry."

Stars swam before his eyes as he tried to focus on her. "Where are we? Wh— Ow. What happened?"

"Some ruddy awful beasts have got us."

He squinted and looked away from Slaíne. They were in a small cave dug out beneath a nest of tree roots. She was chained to an iron pillar. He was free. And the so-called 'awful beasts' that had captured them were beautiful creatures of multicolored light. Had she not been in chains and he with a sore head, he might have had a merry laugh at her odd view of things.

"Are you hurt?"

"Nah," she said as he returned his attention to her. "Can you do anything about these?" Slaíne tugged at the iron chains, which clanked miserably.

Aidan shook his head. "No. I've no abilities with that metal."

"Figured that would be the case. But have you any luck with picking locks?"

Aidan crawled over to her, his head scraping the roof of their enclosure. He studied the chains. He whistled.

"What?"

"You've got some fine bruises."

She snorted. "Can you pick the lock?"

Aidan heaved a great sigh. "Maybe if I had something to pick with that won't break off inside the mechanism." Something was bothering him. He felt for Pulls, and knew at once what the source of his irritation was. Slaíne's Pull was as strong as ever; he'd felt that even in his queer dream. But as for the numerous nymphs surrounding them and their supplies? Nothing. He could not feel their wagons, their tables heavily laden with food and drink, their beds, their blankets. It was almost as if they were figments of a dream. "Blast."

"What's wrong?"

"I can't feel anything of theirs."

Slaíne raised her eyebrows and then frowned. "Explain."

Aidan launched into a short explanation about how his ability worked, how he could feel objects' Pulls, how he couldn't really feel iron, and how everything in the nymph's camp was insubstantial, except maybe the wood that kept their fires going. "It's almost like nothing here is real."

"Oh, it's real." Slaíne gave her bonds a tug to illustrate the point. With a grunt she stopped. Her wrists were now bleeding, indicating she'd been working on getting free for a while. "Do you have any weapons on you?"

Aidan felt for his cache in Nothingness, but to his surprise and horror, everything was gone. It wasn't that he enjoyed his abilities. They were useful and served a purpose when they had to. But he'd become reliant on them. Too reliant. And with nothing in Nothingness, his hopes of escaping these fiends looked slim. "My weapons are missing."

Slaíne bit her lower lip. "Well, at least they left us alive, yeah?"

That might be good enough for her, but Aidan was not used to being bound to something or someone. Freedom was another thing he'd taken for granted, it would seem. Again he looked at her wrists and frowned. "Why are you chained up, and I'm free to move about?"

"Dunno," she said a little too quickly, without quite meeting his gaze.

The music outside their enclosure took a wilder turn, and shrieks of laughter filled the air, causing Aidan's hairs to stand on end. He narrowed his eyes at Slaíne. That is when he noticed the caked blood on her fingernails. He smirked. "I assume the blood I'm seeing isn't all yours?"

Nonchalant, she shrugged. "Might've done."

"So, they can be wounded."

Slaíne laughed without humor. "'Course they can. All livin' things can. But these creatures heal real fast."

Aidan swore. If he had nothing to Summon and nothing to Call, and if he couldn't do much damage to their captors, what was left to be done? He could make a break for it himself, but that would mean leaving the girl behind, which was not a gentlemanly thing to do, so he at once dismissed the idea.

"We need to find out what they are."

"Hmm?"

"I said we need to find out what they are. Every being has a weakness." She paused to sniff. "We gotta find theirs and take advantage."

Aidan raised his eyebrows at her. "What do you know of nymphs?"

If Slaíne wondered how he knew what they were, she didn't let on. "Well, they like light, I s'pose."

Aidan nodded. "It would seem they were made of light, from what I've seen of them." He scratched his chin. "We aren't being guarded very closely."

"Arrogance, ya think?"

He shrugged. "Possibly."

The music slowed to an eerie waltz, and the talking all but ceased. Perhaps it was foolish, the thoughts Aidan was thinking; perhaps his impulse was wrong. Whatever the case, he knew he had to explore the camp and see what they had been snatched up into. "I'll return shortly." He crawled toward the mouth of their enclosure, only to receive a kick in the trousers. "What?"

There was a pause. "Be – be careful."

Aidan smiled to himself and went on his way, leaving the comfort of her Pull behind. It tugged at him frantically as he left her, but he ignored it as best he could and went to listen and observe.

The few beings he saw were translucent when he looked at them full-on, but appeared to be of no substance when he squinted or looked at them from the corner of his eye. To his relief and frustration, they ignored him. He must not appear to be a threat.

As he walked, Aidan continued to feel for Pulls, and continued to feel very little. He tried Calling a jug of water to himself, and nothing happened. The farther he walked around tables and beds and blankets, the more he understood about their captors. They were creatures of comfort. They must want for nothing. And, as far as he could see, they carried no weapons, meaning they were arrogant, ignorant, or relied on magic or some other skill to defend themselves. As far as how many of them there were: now, that was a perplexing problem. Though he'd seen around a dozen of the translucent beings, he heard many more, and the closer he traveled to the bonfires, the more he could see. There had to be at least one hundred of them dancing around and through the flames, which seemed to give them more substance. Aidan wondered what this could mean, but stored that problem away for later. He turned and went in the opposite direction. There were more bonfires and more dancing nymphs. It was then that he realized that he and Slaíne were ringed in.

With a muttered oath, he took to pacing, stopping only when he realized he might draw unwanted attention to himself. Perhaps he would not have been so irritable if he were not so thirsty. As it was, his throat was raw and dry, as if he'd been eating ash, and he could produce no saliva to swallow. And as soon as he realized the extent of his thirst, the more intense it became. Without a second thought, he approached one of the food-laden tables and snatched up a jug. It was an odd sensation, feeling it in his hand without feeling its Pull in his gut. It didn't matter. He put his mouth to the vessel and drank deeply of the coldest, sweetest water he'd ever tasted.

"Mm," he said, setting the empty jug aside. Shame hit him that he hadn't saved any for Slaíne. Flushed, he found another pitcher and brought it back to where she was waiting.

"What'd you find out?" she asked as he ducked back into the enclosure. Before he could answer, she frowned at him. "What've you got?"

He grinned. The water which had gone down cold was spreading warmth throughout his limbs, making him happier than he had been in ages. "Here, drink some." He went to put it to her lips, but she jerked her head away.

"What're you thinkin'?" she said. "Could be poison."

That made Aidan laugh. "Slaíne, it's fine. You're over-scrupulous, I am sure. Have just a taste." He tried again, and this time managed to get it to her mouth.

The girl mashed her lips closed, causing the liquid to pour down her front, and she didn't seem to breathe again until he pulled the jug away. "You look – red."

"Do I?" He did feel rather warm, but it was nothing to grow alarmed about. Aidan undid his collar, letting his shirt gape open. Still he felt as though on fire. Well, that would not do. Flushed and lightheaded, Aidan pulled the entire garment over his head and cast it aside. Slaíne cleared her throat, and he looked at her sideways. "Is something wrong?"

She rolled her eyes and looked away.

Aidan laughed. True, on any normal day, he would hold to decorum. He was, after all, a gentleman, and Slaíne, like anyone, deserved respect. But today…something had changed. What was it?

"Did ya find anything out?"

Slaíne's voice sent a burning jolt through Aidan's body, and he jerked to attention. "Say that again," he said without looking at her. His whole being thrummed, aware of her, her Pull, where she was situated. If he wanted, he could reach out his hand and….

"I said, did ya find anything?"

Something inside of Aidan snapped. Or broke loose. He let the pieces go with a sigh, and embraced his feelings with a feral pleasure. Aidan turned to her. "What do you believe of fate?"

"Fate?"

He moved in closer. "Destiny."

For a moment, Slaíne seemed ready to laugh. But something in his declaration must have alerted her to the fact that he was serious. Her brow furrowed. "Are you drunk or somethin'?"

It was his turn to laugh and he did. Aidan went from giddy and lightheaded to profoundly absorbed with the sight of her lips in the span of three seconds' time. He stared at those two rosy gems, the desire to do something roiling through his being. What was he feeling? There must be a name for it. And yet, as he took her face in his hands, he could not name it, nor did he care.

"What're you doing?" Her voice was thin; Aidan held on to the sound in his mind as he brought his lips to hers. They were soft, supple, warm. He moaned into her open mouth.

She bit him.

He grinned against her touch, even as she drew blood. Aidan deepened the kiss, his hands tangling in her hair, stroking her face, wishing and willing her to kiss him back. She did not.

His heart took off at a mad pace, and the hands which had held her face dared to wander further. Aidan wondered at himself as he took her by the waist and took to kissing her throat. This was unexpected. Pleasant beyond words, but unexpected.

"What're you doing?" she repeated, her words icy needles that almost brought Aidan back to his senses. Almost. When he didn't pause nor come up for air, she spat at him. "Get off!"

Somewhere, the music hit a sour note and voices were raised in higher laughter. But Aidan didn't care about them. Wounded, he peered up at her. What had he done wrong?

"Get off," she repeated.

Perhaps he was a fool, but Aidan felt no desire to move just then, even as he began to wonder if he had lost his senses. Something about this whole thing just felt right. Slaíne, on the other hand, did not seem to share that sentiment.

"You'll ruin it."

"No," he protested, guilt clenching his gut. "Please don't say that."

She was crying now, great big tears running down her pale face. "I don' know what's gotten into you, sir." She jerked away as he leaned in again, hoping to appease her. "Oh, you'll ruin it all. Don't. Get off. Get away from me." With each word, her voice rose in pitch until she was nearly screaming like a mad woman.

Sad that he had offended her apparently, Aidan pulled away, lowered his gaze, and moved off to the other side of the enclosure. And just like that, he was hit with a wave of vertigo, and crawled out into the open, vomiting.

CHAPTER SEVEN

Four hours onward – though it could've been more – Aidan lay outside the enclosure, fit to do nothing but doze, as whatever he had drunk still tormented his body. His head ached. His stomach roiled. Every nerve in his body seemed to fire and misfire. Every muscle convulsed now and then, making voluntary movement impractical, if not impossible.

And for that time, Slaíne said nothing. Not that Aidan blamed her. What had he been thinking, making such advances? It was the water he'd drunk. It had to be. That couldn't have been him kissing the girl of his own volition…could it? On and off he warred with his needs and wants, half-wanting to repeat his actions, half-wanting to repent. He would have to apologize when he felt himself again, that was a given. But was he really sorry?

Aidan turned the sentiment over in his mind, and the findings startled him. He'd enjoyed the experience. In fact, he still enjoyed the memory, except for inflicting obvious pain. "I'm an idiot," he groaned audibly, uncaring as to whether she'd heard him or not. This was all pure nonsense. A distraction. It mattered not, and he would do well to push these foolish urges aside.

By the time the sun should have been setting, the land surrounding them remained as bright as day. Aidan felt more himself with each passing hour, but he was still weak in more ways than one.

At last he was able to pull himself to his knees with a shiver. Aidan dragged himself back to the enclosure, unsurprised to find Slaíne asleep and snoring. His grimace turned into a grin, and he fought himself as he put his shirt back on, not bothering with his collar. Their captors had made no contact with them, which was a suspicious sign. Something told Aidan they were being watched and perhaps listened to; for what purpose, he could only guess. Fine. If they wished to watch, Aidan would watch as well. He would return to their midst and see what intelligence he might be able to gather – but this time, he would avoid their food and drink. He grimaced at the mere thought.

Slaíne stirred.

Aidan froze. This was going to be awkward, whenever it happened, so he might as well get it over with. "Slaíne?"

Her spine went rigid, and her steely eyes locked on to his. "Get it out of your system?"

He paused. What could she mean by that? Did she think that he had acted of his own free will?

She rolled her eyes. "I meant the water."

"I'm sorry. I treated you poorly." He wondered at his own voice, so mechanical at the confession of such an offense. One might think him insincere or insensible to the pain he had caused. Aidan opened his mouth to offer a more heartfelt apology, but Slaíne laughed. He looked at her, bemused.

"Don't you look at me like that. Drinkin' strange water, my lands. How much you drink?"

Aidan flushed. "Enough."

The girl snorted. "Did you find a way out of here?"

If only he had such glad tidings to bring her. As it was, they were perhaps worse off than when they had first started. "We are ringed in."

Slaíne nodded. "And their weakness? Any insights?"

Aidan shook his head. "You said that they heal quickly."

"Right."

"I'm afraid we'll have to stay here awhile longer and observe them."

If the look on the girl's face was anything to go by, Slaíne hated the plan as much as he did. Still, what else could they do?

"You think we can reason with 'em?"

Aidan thought. "We can try."

"Perhaps there's been a misunderstandin'." It was obvious from the way she said it that she didn't believe the words coming out of her own mouth. She said as much in her next breath. "Coming on us like that in the middle of the night. They must've been following us."

"Or were drawn to us by the great racket the goblins were making."

Slaíne cocked her head to the side, and her brow puckered. "Goblins? What goblins?"

Amazed, Aidan told her what had transpired, not pausing to answer the questions he could see forming on her lips.

She listened, the pucker only deepening. "I don't remember no goblins, sir."

"What do you remember?"

Her eyes squinted and her gaze became distant. "The light creatures – nymphs, as you call 'em – pounced on me. They kept saying 'Give us.' I thought them rightly mad, and told them so. That's all I remember. Well, that is, not before...." She hesitated, and looked at Aidan sideways, her face draining of color.

"Before what?"

She shook her head, as though she thought she'd already said too much. Why, Aidan couldn't imagine.

This wouldn't do. "Slaíne, if there's anything that might give us an edge against the creatures, please tell me."

She opened her mouth and closed it again.

Aidan pulled at his shirt, which clung to him with sweat. Upon seeing the girl regarding the motion with abject horror, he ceased. She must be remembering that which he would rather she forgot. After clearing his throat, Aidan pressed the matter further. "Consider carefully. We don't know what they intend for us. You don't know—"

She clenched her teeth. "What they want? 'Course I know what they want. 'Tis plain as day. 'Tis plain as the fact that you are hiding something yourself." The pointed look she gave him sent chills down his spine.

Just the same, Aidan waved away her accusations. Hiding something? What was he hiding? Other than the fact that he'd been communicating with the woman Slaíne so obviously wanted to murder with that silver sword. "Please don't change the subject."

Slaíne growled at him as he inched in closer. "You can stay over there."

"Not if I don't want to be overheard."

The look she gave him could've taken the courage of lesser men. There was something about Slaíne...yes, something powerful – especially when her anger was aroused. It went beyond her Pull, whose strength still remained a mystery; what was it? Aidan could not place a finger on it. They both had their secrets. She was talking again. He'd best clear his mind and attend to her words.

"You want to know what they want."

Shoulder to shoulder, he nodded and leaned in for the answer. "What?"

"It ain't no secret. They're traders."

"Traders?"

Her face had grown dark and hardened, though her eyes flitted about in panic. "Slave traders."

Aidan thought on it for a moment. "But why would they be saying 'Give us.' They must think we have something of value."

Slaíne's shoulders heaved. "Could mean anything. Could mean—"

"The goblins."

"I told you, I don't remember the goblins. Must've been knocked out before then."

Aidan shook his head. "No, I mean the goblins kept demanding that I give them something, too. Perhaps they think we still have the Warring Goblet."

That had been the wrong thing to say. Slaíne's spine went rigid and her steely gaze locked on to him. "What makes you think you had the Warring Goblet?"

Meraude had told him, that's why he knew. He'd been a fool. Was there any excuse to make? Lucky guess? "I thought you said it was the Warring Goblet," he lied, hating himself very much for such base behavior toward her.

His words did not satisfy. She huffed. "You know I told you no such thing. I knew no such thing. What aren't you tellin' me, Ai— Mr. Aidan?"

Was there harm in telling her? *Well*, he thought, *she might try to murder Meraude before I can hold Meraude to her promise of bringing my family back.* On the other hand, there was no proof that the mage could or would do that. Whom could he trust?

Slaíne scented in on the truth. "You've been talking to someone, haven't you?"

"Hmm? When?"

"When you're sleepin'."

It was his turn to stiffen. "What? What are you talking about?"

She scoffed. "Don' play wi' me. You've been muttering strange things in your sleep. Someone's using something to...." Her eyes widened and then narrowed. "You've been in the Seeing Pool."

Was that what brought him to that strange realm in his dreams? He needed to know more. "Slaíne, I have been having strange dreams."

Slaíne waited as one braced for the worst news they could expect to hear. When he didn't continue she turned away from him and whispered. "Did she send for you? Please don't play with me. Tell me the truth."

The truth was fragile on his lips. How to let it break? It mattered not; the look on her face told him that it had already been broken: Slaíne knew that he had been communicating with someone, and that that someone was Meraude, her most hated enemy. Aidan opened his mouth, scrambling for something to excuse himself and put her at ease.

With an exasperated sigh, the girl threw her head back and shouted. It was a quick burst of sound and, quite like her laughter, it raised the hairs on his arms. "Sir, you don't know what you're messin' with." She swore under her breath and closed her eyes, as one would whilst dealing with a rowdy child.

"Slaíne, I know she kills all magical beings. But— No, please listen. What if we could outsmart her? Snare her in the very traps she's setting for us. Think about it." Why did he have to explain himself to her? He almost said as much, but remembered that afternoon where she'd deliberately provoked the wrath of her own curse and bore the consequences. He bit his tongue.

When she spoke again, Slaíne's voice was ragged and her eyes were the eyes of a woman who had seen too much in her short lifespan. "Perhaps it's time to tell you about the curse."

"You don't have to."

She laughed without humor. "Oh, but I think I have to. And not jus' that, we need ter lay out all our information." Slaíne squinted at him. "First, tell me what she offered you."

It was too personal. It was indecent of her to ask. He sat there, warring with his temper and impatience.

Slaíne's patience broke first. "Fine. I'll start." When she began, her gaze flickered off into the distance, and her whole body tensed. "I was not six years of age." Her voice was a millstone, weighting Aidan down as he listened. "The curse, as you may have guessed, is tied to a person."

Aidan nodded. "I gathered as much."

"Whoever takes on the role of master or mistress is the one to which I'm tied. Can only go so far a distance from the person before it takes me. There's only one way out, 'ccording to hearsay, but I won't be puttin' much stake in them rumors."

Aidan frowned. If she wanted to remove the curse, why had she not tried every available route? She was still hiding things.

"Anyway," she continued, scowling at him, "as you'll have guessed, Meraude was a family friend."

"And she did this to you?" he asked, his voice low.

She gave him a quick nod, then shook her head. "She killed my parents. Couldn't do curses back then, I believe. Not powerful enough. Not yet, anyway."

"But she didn't kill you either."

"No, didn't have the chance."

Fighting confusion, Aidan rubbed his brow. "So she didn't put the curse on you?"

"Good as done," she snapped. "Six years old, running on me own. Elves found me 'fore she. They had me cursed, yes, but I'd naught've run afoul of 'em if I'd not been forced to flee myself, see?" The longer she talked, the faster she talked, and the more pronounced her accent became.

Aidan needed to calm her down so he could understand her clearly. "I'm sorry, but please take a moment to collect yourself."

She shook her head. "Nay, if I don' tell you now, I might never have a chance. Mr. Aidan, she murdered me parents. But I was her true target." Despite what she'd said, Slaíne paused and drew in a few deep breaths before continuing. "You wanted to know why the nymphs think me more a threat than you?"

He nodded, his brow furrowing. "I thought it was because you attacked."

"An' you know how I attacked?"

Aidan swallowed. "I assume by lunging—"

She opened her mouth, and he presumed she was going to tell him what she had done, but they were quite rudely interrupted by a loud bang and a blast of light. It would seem the camp was under attack.

CHAPTER EIGHT

Aidan moved without thinking as the ground shook. He felt for the iron chains and tried Dismissing any part of them that wasn't made of the metal, and when that did not work and shouts were taken up in the distance, he explored the Pull of the lock itself. He felt into every corner, every crevice, and smiled when he discovered a lighter, softer metal inside the mechanism. Aidan Dismissed that, and the lock sprung open. "Hurry," he urged, freeing Slaíne from the manacles.

Slaíne crawled out after him as crying filled the air. The landscape grew dimmer for that brief moment when they stepped out into the middle of the clearing. But moments later, the light came flooding back, nearly blinding both of them.

"It serves him right," shouted one of the sprites, her voice an eerie pitch. "He was careless."

The two prisoners exchanged looks. They were surrounded, so there was nowhere to run. Nowhere they could hide where they could not be found. They would have to fight their way out.

As if sensing more trouble, the creatures turned and faced Aidan's way, their eyes flaming in their pale sockets. As one they yelled out a war cry and charged.

"Whatever you did before, care to try again?" Aidan shouted. "Slaíne?" He looked over at the girl to find her shaking her head.

"No good. Can't carry you, now can I?"

Carry him? What did she mean by that? Well, whatever it meant, it was too late now. Their 'hosts' had them ringed in rightly, their iron weapons drawn.

A woman wreathed in blue light pushed through the crush, and the others took a few stooped steps backward. They were bowing to the lady, who wore a circlet of blue ivy on her head. "The mighty slayer of goblins." She turned her gaze from Aidan and sneered at Slaíne. "And his pet."

As if to accentuate the nymph's point, Slaíne actually growled.

"Who are you?" Aidan asked after giving Slaíne a warning glare.

The leader, for that is what Aidan assumed she must be, smirked at him and the girl, the light in her eyes flashing. But she did not answer his question. "Now that you've had some time to gather your wits, tell me, where is it?"

Aidan frowned and glanced at Slaíne, who narrowed her eyes at him. "Where is what?"

Before Aidan could step away, the queen reached out and struck him across the face with the back of her hand, causing him to stagger. "Where have you hidden it?"

He righted himself and ignored the blood gushing out of his nostrils. Aidan felt for a Pull, any Pull. As he had expected, there was none. None from her, her people, or their possessions, that is. The only tangible things were himself, Slaíne, and the firewood. There might be an answer in that, but he would hold that trick up his sleeve as long as he could.

"Mortal, I grow weary of your arrogance. Tell me—"

Aidan spat at her feet.

She struck him again, this time with enough force to knock him off his feet entirely and send him flying a few yards back. He landed with a great thump at Slaíne's feet.

Slaíne reacted like a lightning bolt, jumping at the nymph with a powerful strike from a height. She missed, because the queen was faster and stepped aside. Slaíne recovered with a graceful roll and landed in a crouch.

Aidan didn't have time to wonder at his traveling partner's fighting skills. "Tell us what you want, and perhaps we can come to some arrangement...."

One of the nymphs reached out with an iron rod, meaning to beat Slaíne on the back with it. But before the creature could, or Aidan could warn her for that matter, the girl rolled to the right, then to the left, agilely dodging her attacker's strikes. Her luck couldn't last, Aidan knew, so he intervened. "No, your quarrel is not with her. You want something, yes? Then talk to us. We can behave like rational creatures, or continue to—"

The queen raised a hand, and the attacks on Slaíne stopped.

Panting, Slaíne leapt to her feet and ran out of the creatures' reach, behind Aidan's back. He wondered at her sudden cowardice, until he felt her back pressed against his. Aidan fought a smile; she meant to guard his back.

"We seek what the goblins sought, knowledge."

Aidan took a moment to swipe at his nose. "Knowledge of...?"

The queen's eyes flashed. "You know of what I speak, Aidan Ingledark the Blest. And you can tell your pet that if I wanted to kill both of you, I would've done it ages ago, despite her...blood."

He tilted his head to the side, and his eyes darted about. "Her blood?"

"Tainted."

"With?"

The queen tried to look casual, but Aidan could see that Slaíne had her rattled. With a sniff, the nymph pretended to dust something off of the blue-white collar of her gown. "What? She hasn't told you?"

Behind his back, Slaíne's spine grew rigid. "It don't matter."

The queen leaned in, a cruel smile forming on her lips. "Wizard's blood."

Aidan's brows knit together, but he allowed the expression to clear from his face. His thoughts began to race. Wizard's blood? Was it true? If Slaíne was descended from a wizard, then why hadn't she displayed any signs of magic? This made no sense. "She doesn't even believe in them. What makes you think—"

"You've distracted me long enough, milord. Tell me, what have you done with the Summoning Goblet?"

"He don't have it."

"Don't be foolish, witch." She raised her hand again, only to lower it when Aidan didn't flinch. The light in her eyes waned and she sighed. "Tell me, then, Lord Ingledark, where is the Warring Goblet?"

This was getting them nowhere. He couldn't tell her what he didn't know. And he didn't know what the Goblets together were capable of, but if she were to get her hands on them all, let alone one.... Now Aidan did shudder. "As my traveling companion has already told you, we do not have it."

Again she struck out, though not as hard as the last time. "Where is it?" She struck again. And again. And again, knocking Aidan off his feet.

Stars swam before his eyes. He tasted blood. Aidan pushed himself up again and again, only to be at once kicked back down.

"Oh, for pity's sake!" Slaíne said, coming between the two.

For whatever reason, the nymph hesitated before striking Slaíne, who struck back.

"Slaíne, get out of the way," Aidan growled. When she did not, he grabbed hold of her Pull and sent her sailing farther than he'd meant to Push her.

Though inactive to this point, the nymphs surrounding him, grabbed Slaíne and subdued her. She looked murder at him.

Aidan shook his head. He would apologize later…if they weren't both slaughtered first. "What makes you think we have the Goblet?"

"It belongs to your family. You are Blest. Where else would the Goblet be?"

Aidan laughed without humor as he tried pulling himself to his feet. However, he was exhausted and sore and still recovering from vomiting the contents of his stomach, so he contented himself with sitting. "Only recently did I discover anything about the Goblets. I have been a nomad for the majority of my life, thanks to my uncle. If you want answers about what happened to the Goblet that allegedly belonged to my family, I would suggest you start asking different people, for I am the last who would know."

The nymph queen regarded him for a moment, and nodded. "It would seem that we have been wasting our time. Take him away…but leave the girl. We must have a talk."

Aidan wasn't having any of that. He would not leave Slaíne alone with them, not after the way their queen had kicked and struck him. "You can't have anything to ask of her. She knows nothing more than I know, and certainly less than even you do." That earned him another kick in the shins. Pain shot up his legs, and he held a grimace in check.

The nymph shook her head, and her guards advanced and seized him by the arms. They were strong, too strong to resist as they hoisted him to his feet.

Aidan reached out, feeling for their Pulls. Still nothing but Slaíne and the firewood.

"Take him away." She sounded bored, but the tone belied another: frustration.

Aidan dug in his heels. "Why do you need the Goblets? Hold on a moment."

The queen signaled to her inferiors that they were to stop. "Do you wish to tell me now?"

"Perhaps we have similar goals," he offered. It might be true. He doubted it, but perhaps he could manipulate her into giving him more information. At the very least, he would buy Slaíne some more time if she had any ideas percolating.

The nymph queen's gaze swept over him, piercing like ice daggers. "The Goblets," she said, her tone stern, each syllable articulated with care, "do not belong in the hands of mortals. We wish to see them reunited...and destroyed. Is that your goal, Lord Ingledark?"

Aidan shrugged. "After I get what I want, then yes."

"And what do you want? More power?"

He looked to Slaíne, who shook her head. She was right; if they knew he was making deals with Meraude, they were done for. Meraude wanted the Goblets. It didn't mean she would get them, it didn't mean she was trustworthy. But she seemed like his only option to getting what he wanted most. Aidan knew he must choose his words with care. "I want my name cleared, my life back." *And my family back.* "I have no love for the Goblets Immortal."

The nymph considered him for a moment, her look thoughtful. She surprised Aidan by taking a sudden step forward, motioning for the guards to relinquish their grasp on his arms.

Aidan stumbled to his knees, but he did not stand. He fought the urge to flinch away as she reached out for him, taking his chin in her hand.

The creature turned his head this way and that, her eye contact never wavering. At last she spoke. "I see it. I see it in his eyes."

Aidan wondered what she saw. He hoped not too much.

"So much pain. So much loss. He speaks in half-truths, hoping to hide his intentions." She tapped on his cheek, though not roughly. Her eyes narrowed, and then widened. "This man has been corrupted."

The nymphs backed away, and the queen dropped her hand. "She is coming. Kill them. Kill them both."

CHAPTER NINE

Aidan Called Slaíne, who slipped out of her captor's hand, so strong a tug did he give her. They were ringed in, outnumbered. He could Dismiss himself 'til he turned blue in the face, but something told him the nymphs knew of this trick and were waiting for him to do it. An hour would be wasted, and when he emerged, Slaíne would most likely be dead.

The nymphs had their iron staves pointed toward them. They only needed their leader out of the way, and then they were clear to impale the two prisoners.

Aidan leapt at the queen and locked his arms around her neck.

She responded by shaking him like a dog getting rid of fleas. It took all of his strength to hold on. "Never mind him," she choked. "The girl. Kill the girl first."

"Sir!" Slaíne shouted. "Push me."

"Push you?" What was she doing, distracting him from their one hope?

"Oh, for pity's sake."

The queen shook Aidan free, and he fell onto his back with a great *oomph*. It was in this moment, staring down a stave, that he Pushed Slaíne away from himself, and watched in amazement as the girl sailed over their heads and soared past the circle with great speed.

"The wood!" she shouted. "Aidan, Dismiss the wood!"

Aidan grabbed the end of the stave with his bare hands, fighting the nymph queen's strength with gritted teeth. What good would Dismissing the wood do? The fires would burn out, and…. That was it! Clever girl. Aidan reached out as the nymphs ran screaming toward Slaíne. He Dismissed each log, listening to the anguished cried of the nymphs as they dissolved into mounds of ice and sand.

The she-nymph was not finished yet. Before she could be drawn to her death, she brought the pointed stave down with full force into Aidan's shoulder.

He screamed as pain he'd never felt before coursed through his veins. It burned with three times the strength of the remedy he'd been forced to drink after the Romas had poisoned him. And he saw things. Strange things.

"Don't let her—" Whatever the queen was going to say evaporated in her throat. She broke apart, piece by piece, and ash rained down from the now-dark sky. The only light provided them was the stars and a waning moon.

Aidan lay there panting as his shoulder went cold, his flesh throbbing in time with his crazed heartbeat. He gasped for air. *He was drowning in the ocean. He was being born on the shores inside a strange cave, lit from the light of no sun he'd ever seen before. Light overwhelmed him, and he saw: four Goblets, all an array of colors, all glittering like the eyes of a cat in the semi-darkness. He reached out his hand to grab one, but his arm was weak. His arm was tiny, the size of an infant's. Aidan cried, and the sound that came out of his mouth was so small, so frail.*

"When will it manifest itself?" a slow, deep male voice asked a woman in the shadows.

Aidan silenced his cries; he wanted to hear, though the pain was beyond bearable.

"It is not easy to say," said a familiar voice, though Aidan could not place it. It was a safe voice, if not a happy voice. "We should know before his third year. Any later than that, he'll need a Jolt."

Aidan felt his body go limp and the light flickered in and out. Another face looked down at him, a strange, ugly face that he'd seen before in nightmares. He wept and wept, and the sound rankled the man. That much was obvious. He held Aidan out at arm's length.

The woman spoke. "Brother, I say we take the vessel and escape. With its power...."

Footsteps thundered in the near distance. The man with the beaky nose hushed her. "Shh. We'll discuss this later with your husband." He said the word 'husband' with disdain.

"Aidan?"

Aidan yelled out, struggling against the invisible hands that were shaking him. The world grew dark. Stars. So many stars. He rubbed his eyes of them...or, rather, meant to, but the stabbing pain in his shoulder jolted him back to reality. The echo of many screams chased him back to the present moment.

A woman spoke. "Mr. Aidan, you're hurt. Can you hear me?"

Aidan blinked. He was back in the forest, lying on the ground, staring up at the girl's wintry face. "Where – where was that man?"

Sláine held him down. "Sir, you're in shock. You've been stabbed in the shoulder, and – don't make no sense, sir, but you ain't lost no blood." Her fingers gently pressed into the bruise, drawing a low growl from Aidan's lips. The pressure didn't hurt, but the whole ordeal had been disorienting enough to make the line between friend and foe blur. "Sorry, did nay mean to hurt you." She pulled her hand away, and Aidan relaxed. "Can you get up? I daren't light another fire, lest they come back." She paused. "I don't nay think they can, though."

"They're dead," Aidan said. He was certain of it. "Their life forces were tied to the fires." He shivered and pulled himself up to a sitting position with his good arm, and the other he crossed over his chest.

After a moment, she sat down next to him, shaking as well. Her red hair could pass for fire in the moonlight, and eyes for two embers. "Stop doing that," she said, surprising him.

"What?"

She frowned at him, opened her mouth, and closed it again. "It's nothin'."

"I'm going to look around, see if they kept any of my supplies nearby." Aidan's teeth chattered, and he Summoned the firewood he had Dismissed. Of course the logs were cold to the touch. "Well, that's good to know." With some trouble, he managed to raise himself to his feet. For whatever reason, Sláine did not offer to help him, and for that he was grateful. He'd been unmanned enough that evening. "So," he said, hoping to sound casual. "That was some leap."

Even in the moonlight, he saw the blush creep up to her scalp. "Nice work."

He considered her for a moment. Was this an issue he really wanted to press right now? That leap had been supernatural, even for someone aided with a Push; she was hiding something, that was for certain. At last he turned. "Right."

Aidan used his eyes and his ability to search for his supplies. There were Pulls out there tugging at his core, but nothing that felt familiar. Nothing that belonged to him. Nothing that he could use. The food, the drinks, the tables, and the bedding that belonged to the nymphs had disappeared with the strange creatures, just as Aidan had suspected.

He sensed her coming, but it still made him jump when she spoke.

"The nymphs are really dead?"

"Yes." He continued walking.

She followed, making nary a sound. Odd. How did she manage that? Every step he took crackled, twigs breaking beneath his boots. Slaíne continued. "They as good as well gave themselves away, with all the fires, that is. It was easy enough to sort out."

"You don't have to explain how you knew, Slaíne."

There was a short silence followed by a terse, "I did nay know. I guessed."

Aidan frowned. How could someone so fascinating have such ill timing? Perhaps that was her secret: sheer thick-headedness. He needed peace. Silence. He needed time to adjust to the pain and to clear his befuddled mind. "Slaíne, I believe you."

There was another awkward pause. Slaíne broke it, and it shattered into a million pieces. "Ai – Sir, I lied. About the Goblets."

Aidan froze. This was not what he wanted to hear. He turned to Slaíne. "What did you say?"

Slaíne sighed. "Sir, I said I lied."

"How did you lie?" He approached her in five quick strides. "Answer me!"

She stared up at him, fire rising in her eyes and heat filling her cheeks. "The lot of them, together…. You can't unite them, sir. It would make the drinker an abomination."

Aidan ground his teeth. "Is that all?"

"Is that all, he asks. Blimey, sir, but you can't."

"I have no choice."

Slaíne prodded him in the chest, drawing a low growl from Aidan's mouth. "No choice? You unite those Goblets, Aidan, and you as good as hand that witch immortality." She paused for effect. "You hand her those Goblets, and we're both dead."

"What have you got to do with the Goblets Immortal, Slaíne?" He pushed her pointing finger away. "What are they to you?"

Her eyes darkened. When she spoke, her voice was quiet, dangerous. "I think you know, sir."

He shrugged. Let her keep her secrets; he had his own affairs to deal with, and adding hers to the mix would only muddy the waters. Aidan did not need any more distractions from his main purpose. With a sigh, Aidan shook his head and walked away. "What would you have me do? Ignore the Goblets? I have a chance to make things right, and I'm going to take it."

"To make things right?" She tramped after him, her tiny feet now making enough racket to attract a whole horde of goblins and whatever else might be lurking out in the woods. "What exactly have you done?"

"Sunrise isn't too far off. We should rest."

Slaíne groaned. "If you want me to help you, you're going to have to tell me things."

He almost told her that he didn't want her help, but his lips could not form the words. "Give me time. Slaíne, please. I know I'm a hard man to deal with, but some things...." He waved his hand about vaguely, a gesture he knew she probably missed in the darkness.

Slaíne sighed, and Aidan felt her retreating. "Not everyone's going to betray you, you know." It was said barely above a whisper and with an emotion Aidan couldn't bring himself to decipher. "I'll keep first watch."

Aidan shivered. The night air was cold, and the closer they drew to the dawning, the colder he knew it would get. "No, we'll both rest. But there is a caveat."

Silence.

"Slaíne?" He turned, just making out her tense silhouette in the afterglow of the setting moon.

"I have a feeling I'm not going to like this."

Aidan sighed and rubbed his scratchy chin. "The dew should fall soon." He puffed out his cheeks and took Slaíne by surprise by snatching her hand with his good one and pulling her closer. "You take my meaning?"

The girl frowned, but didn't flinch away as he lowered himself down next to her. She was as warm as a peach tart he'd stolen from the cooling rack as a boy.

His body shivered as he snaked his arms around her and pulled her intimately close. With her hot breath on his wounded shoulder, almost all the pain leaked out of him, and he fell asleep, aware how improper and bizarre his current position was.

★　　★　　★

He was back in the throne room, standing in the middle of the Seeing Pool, if Slaíne had been right. But there was no Meraude this time. In fact, there seemed to be no one within sight.

"Hello?" Aidan called out, but his voice made no sound. Something was different. He turned and was prepared to rouse himself, when he spied movement from behind the throne. A flash of blue light filled the room, and a small voice screamed.

"Larkin, you know better than to hide back there," said a familiar cold voice.

Aidan jumped as the mage herself stepped clean through him. "Blast." He frowned. Something was different about her than what he'd seen before, but Aidan couldn't place his finger on it.

"Away from the throne. It's not yours, nor will it ever be."

A scowling girl with dirty blonde hair crept out from behind the great chair. "Sorry, milady," she said. "But why bring me here if I'm not to have the throne?"

Meraude's brow puckered. "The throne was built for someone else. Someone powerful. Not naughty girls who won't do their mistress's bidding." The words were tart and round, and they gave the speaker obvious pleasure when the little girl cringed and hugged herself.

If Aidan hadn't made up his mind about Meraude, it was made now: the woman was a bully. He took a step forward without thinking, and was able to leave the Seeing Pool altogether.

The girl spoke. "Is the throne for you, then?"

The woman ran a hand through her long hair. "Yes, of course it is."

"Then why don't you sit on it?" With a wicked smile, the little girl looked up at her. Aidan knew that smile; there was a gap in those teeth, right between two of them.

"Where have I seen you before?" he asked, circling closer, but avoiding stepping through Meraude by accident.

The mage struck the girl's grin away with the back of her bejeweled hand.

When she pulled away, there was blood on the girl's face. "You know very well that I cannot. Not yet."

The girl, Larkin, ignored her gushing nose and the gash on her face. She regarded the mage for some time before asking, "Then why did you steal me? Why bring me here?"

Meraude's back straightened. "You have something that I don't have. Yet."

The girl considered her. "You don't know things." Before the mage could answer, the girl laughed a terrible laugh, something too frightening and awful to be coming from a child. "You'll try to use me to get what you want. I see that."

Meraude regarded the little girl coldly. "What else do you see, Larkin?"

The girl did not answer. Instead, she posed her own question. "Why here, though? I've never seen this place."

They both looked past Aidan to the Seeing Pool, a dip in the middle of the floor cast in silver. He had a bad feeling about what was to become of the girl. He knew her. How did he know her?

"Step over to the Pool."

When the girl did not do Meraude's bidding, the mage grabbed her by the ear and pulled her over to the basin. Aidan stepped out of the way just in time.

"This will amplify your ability."

The girl regarded the Seeing Pool without saying anything, her expression blank. "What am I to do?"

Meraude let out an impatient groan. "You know, fool girl. Look." The girl did not. "Look!"

Shaking, Larkin leaned over the Pool. Her shoulders heaved. "I see nothing."

Curious, Aidan circled around to the other side of the basin so that he might watch the two of them, the mage and the child.

"You're not trying," Meraude accused.

Larkin peered up at the woman. "That's not how it works."

Meraude raised her hand again, but seemed to reconsider her tactics. She lowered the fist and took a step back. "Tell me, how does it work?"

The girl's lip quivered, and she swiped at her eyes with anger. "Why should I tell you? I want my mama."

"Your mama is dead. I think you already knew this, Larkin."

Tears filled the girl's eyes, and Aidan could bring himself to watch no longer. "I wish to wake now," he said, raking a hand through his hair as he stepped back inside the basin. His voice still made not a sound, and he could not feel his own hand in his hair. "What sort of trick is this, Meraude? Why show me this?"

But the mage still seemed unaware that he was even there. Besides, hadn't she informed him that he wouldn't be able to visit her again in his dreams until her servant had reached him? Whoever and whenever that might be.

"*I see....*"

Meraude looked like a cat ready to pounce on its prey.

"*Don't tell her anything,*" *Aidan warned the girl, knowing it was fruitless. He could almost laugh at himself. This clearly was a one-sided vision...if it was, in fact, a vision and not just some common dream.*

"*It's a man.*"

"*Oh, for pity's sake!*" *Aidan turned and tried to mentally rouse himself.*

"*He does not want me to tell you what I see. He looks...confused. Angry. Like he doesn't believe he's here. He – he thinks he's dreaming.*"

Aidan froze. Perhaps this wasn't an ordinary dream, after all.

Meraude pounced. "*How can you be sure? Can you hear his thoughts?*"

"*Of course not,*" *Larkin snapped.* "*People's faces are easy to read. Especially people who have lost so much.*"

"*Larkin?*" *Aidan asked tentatively.*

The girl's eyes rose, and they met his. "*He's talking to me.*"

Aidan swallowed hard. This had to be a dream...and yet, stranger things had happened. "*You can see and hear me?*"

"*Of course I can see and hear you. You're standing right there.*"

Aidan clenched his fists. "*Don't tell Meraude what I'm saying. Make things up. Do not let her know who I am or what I look like.*"

The girl frowned. "*Why?*"

Shaking, he ran a hand over his face and blinked rapidly. "*Maybe this is a hallucination.*"

Meraude was growing impatient. She grabbed Larkin by the shoulder and shook her. "*What is this person saying? Where is he? Why did he appear to you?*"

Aidan shook his head. "*Don't tell her a thing.*"

"*He— He's from years down the way. I think he came here to warn you about something.*"

Aidan sighed in relief. "*That's good. Keep lying.*"

The girl acquiesced. "*He thinks there's a plot to murder you. In your sleep, twenty years from now.*"

A crease formed on Meraude's brow. "*Ask him where he got his information.*"

He shook his head when the girl frowned. "*Don't let her know I can hear or see her. That could ruin the whole game. Ask me what she asked you to."*

"Well, girl, ask him," Meraude said.

Aidan nodded. "Please."

"Meraude wants to know how you got the information."

If he wanted to ask, he had to do so quickly, before the girl gave up the game. "Two and twenty years ago, I made my family vanish."

"What makes you think that?" she asked him.

Meraude cut in. "Think what?"

Larkin held up a hand for the mage to wait. "You can tell me."

"I am Blest. Something to do with the Goblets—"

"The Goblets Immortal, yes. The Summoning one?"

If Meraude had been impatient before, she was livid with unease now. "Is the person who is attempting to murder me in twenty years in possession of a Goblet? How did they come upon it?"

Larkin frowned and sighed. "My mistress wants to know if— Oh, just a moment, milady, he is speaking again." *She nodded at Aidan, who took the chance.*

"Is there any way to bring them back? Can Meraude help me? Will Meraude help me?"

Her frown deepened. "Only the dead can be—" Whatever the dead alone could be, Aidan did not find out. He was roused from his sleep with a jolt.

Opening his eyes, Aidan was disoriented and confused to find himself wrapped around Slaíne, her red hair wound up in his hands. He groaned and untangled himself gently.

Slaíne was still asleep, for once no care written on her face. She stirred as he got to his feet, but he did not remain. He needed to think.

His shoulder throbbed, though it no longer pained him as severely as it had the night before. Truth be told, though, he hadn't slept so well in quite some time. Not that he would tell Slaíne…ever.

Having to make water rather urgently, he left her for a nearby gathering of trees. By the look of where the sun sat in the sky, and by the lack of dew on the ground, they had slept into the late morning. The dream still burned brightly in his mind, and every time he blinked, he swore he could see that pale child staring back at him.

Once he had finished his business, Aidan made himself decent and was going to see if he could rouse Slaíne, but thought better of it. Let her sleep for now. He would think of what was to be done next in solitude.

He felt for Pulls. There were more than he had felt for days, though only one in the near vicinity was human. Slaíne. Aidan shook his head, ignored that Pull in particular, and reached out to feel for other living things around him. Smaller life, like insects and mice, were within a hand's reach underground. But that was not quite what he was feeling for. Just a little larger…. He felt bigger animals, deer and elk, perhaps. Too large. He needed—

"Aha!" He heard them before he felt them: frogs. They would lead him to what they needed desperately right now.

Smiling, he was about to take off in pursuit of them, but remembered Slaíne and ran back for her. When he returned to camp, he hesitated.

The girl was awake, sitting cross-legged, a scowl on her face and the silver blade in her lap. This did not bode well.

Aidan moved in slowly, and for a moment, he wondered what she would do with that sword if she weren't bound to him by the curse. Run him through? The thought sent a shiver down his spine. He hoped he never had to find out. "You're awake," he said, wincing for having stated the obvious. When she didn't respond, he tried again. "About last night— I'm sorry. It was cold and…." *And I enjoyed it a lot more than I ought to have.*

Slaíne's scowl deepened. "Who is Larkin?"

Aidan's brows shot heavenward. "You want to put that sword down and tell me what this is about?"

She looked at the blade as though she'd forgotten she had it. "The only thing they left, it seems. Found it by a tree."

Aidan waited, wondering what had her so perturbed. "Slaíne, I had another dream last night."

Her spine stiffened. "Oh? You think I don't know?" Her grip on the sword's haft tightened, and Aidan quickly Dismissed it before she could cut herself…or him, for that matter. She jumped as the blade disappeared.

It might be wise to head her off with the truth before she could get any jumpier. The girl would get to the truth sooner or later; she seemed to have a knack for that. Aidan knew he would do well to offer at least some of it freely. "It was a little girl with…. What?" Her expression had gone from cross to confused and then smoothed over again.

"Go on."

Aidan shook his head. "I recognized her, but I can't figure out from where. I don't know any children, but...." Why was he rambling? Perhaps Slaíne's mood, or whatever it was, was contagious.

"What was the dream about?" Slaíne asked. "Was *she* in it?"

Aidan sighed. He knew whom she meant. "Yes, Meraude was in the dream. But something was different this time."

Slaíne narrowed her eyes at this news. "What seemed different?"

How to put this without seeming completely out of his right mind? "She seemed, I don't know, younger."

"I thought the Seeing Pool only showed the present and the future. Yer certain you was seeing the past?"

Aidan frowned. "I don't know what I was seeing." The thought that he'd been talking to someone from the past hadn't occurred to him. Could it be?

"And you said she was with a child."

Aidan nodded. "The child – Larkin – said she had been taken from her parents, and.... What now?"

Slaíne had gotten to her feet, agitated all of a sudden. "Sir, what you saw...if you were seeing her with a child...Meraude, she killed the parents, and she killed the children. All of them."

"Whoa, Slaíne, slow down. You're babbling."

She shot him a dark look. "Oh, try and keep up. The Blest. She killed all the Blest. And she hated children. And parents. And everyone. Still does, far as I know."

So, there were other things that Slaíne had neglected to tell him. When would she ever learn to trust him? Probably not until he stopped keeping secrets of his own, he knew. But now was not the time. "Walk with me."

"Where? Why?"

"I'm close to finding water." Aidan turned and took a few steps back to the edge of the clearing, pausing when he sensed she was not following him. "What?"

"How can you think of water at a time like this?"

Aidan stared at her. "Because I'm dying of thirst. Come."

Slaíne hesitated a moment longer, but at last relented and tramped after him. "Where is this supposed water?"

Aidan smiled to himself. "I thought it was scandalous, thinking of water at a time like this."

Slaíne snorted. "I didn't say scandalous. And besides, my throat's as dry as paper."

He motioned for her to be quiet for a moment, so that he might listen to the natural life and concentrate on Pulls. He heard gentle keening directly ahead by several paces. Water had no Pull. Aidan always supposed it was too changing to act as much of an anchor anyway. It had never bothered him before, as he had always been familiar with the areas he traveled. Water had always been plentiful. What he stumbled into now was swamp water. He sighed.

"This ain't drinkable." Slaíne's voice was thick, and if he didn't know her as well as he did, he might think she was on the verge of tears. "Stagnant. We'd get sorely sick if...."

Aidan held up a hand to stay her comments. This would take concentration. "Kneel now."

Slaíne snorted. "Are we going to pray over it?"

"No," Aidan said, fighting a smile, "just do as I say. Cup your hands and...."

Slaíne beat him to the punch, and scooped up a handful of water. "All right. Now what?"

Aidan closed his eyes and concentrated. He felt for Pulls in the water, Pulls so small that he would never notice them unless he was specifically looking for them. And he had to work quickly before it all leaked out of her hands. There! A few dozen potentially harmful things, he was fairly certain. He Dismissed them all, just to be on the safe side. He looked up at Slaine, who was staring at him, a question on her face. "Drink it."

She hesitated. "You just stared at it real hard and now it's safe to drink, is it?"

Now Aidan did laugh, though he was really in no laughing mood. It must seem rather absurd to her. "Just drink it. I got rid of anything that wasn't water."

Slaíne gave him a disbelieving look but didn't need any more prompting. She gulped down what was in her hands and didn't hesitate to scoop up another handful, staring at him expectantly.

Aidan was thirsty himself, but humored her by Dismissing the harmful elements from that handful. He half-expected her to scoop up another palmful of the water, but she instead wiped her mouth clean and got to her feet. So he cleansed the water for himself, not two but five handfuls. That strange drink he'd lifted from the nymphs had left a funny taste in his mouth…going down and coming back up. He grimaced at the memory, and hoped Slaíne did not think of it anymore.

Now that water had been taken care of for the moment, the next concern was finding something to transport it in. He could not simply Dismiss it handfuls at a time; it had no Pull and was tied to whatever vessel it was in. This meant he could Dismiss a wineskin full of liquid, but not the pond itself. Too large. Too unstable a vessel.

"If only I knew where we were."

"Do it matter?" Slaíne asked, and Aidan could tell she was saying it just to irritate him, though he could not imagine why she meant to provoke him.

Aidan ignored the intent behind her words and took them at their literal value. "If we don't want to wander around and die from thirst, yes." He gave her a wry look. "You wouldn't happen to be harboring anything else from me?"

Her eyes narrowed.

"A bucket down your trousers? Or perhaps behind a tree."

"That sword," she said, her color rising, "was just where I said I found it."

Aidan regarded her. "I'm sure it was."

She did not seem to think that he believed her. Her stare was heated, but she veered away from the argument only to start another. "I've not seen no buckets around. No strange *jugs*, neither." Parry, riposte, lunge.

So, she wasn't going to let that one go. He knew full well what she meant, and it was his turn to give her a heated stare. Before he could retort and say something he might regret, Slaíne held up her hands.

"Let's let it be, sir. You've your secrets, I've mine. You have your, er…faults, and I've me own. Fair?" She held out her hand for him to shake.

Aidan regarded her for a moment, a bit of the devil rising up in him. He grasped her hand from where he sat, shook it firmly…then threw her off-balance and into the stagnant water. Laughing from the banks, he expected her to spit and swear at him. What Aidan did not expect was for her to sink below, her arms churning the surface in panic. What had he done? Not bothering to throw off his boots, Aidan leapt into the water, which he found indeed much deeper than he'd suspected.

Something grabbed him from behind, and he almost struck out at it in the dimness, but he knew that Pull. She released him, and they both kicked for the surface.

"What did you do that for?" Aidan shouted at Slaíne, once he'd caught his breath.

She was treading water and laughing at him.

"I thought you were drowning." He splashed her, and she splashed back.

"Should nay have thrown me in," she shot back, her voice rising as well.

She swam out of reach. "Don't ever do that again," he snarled. He splashed at her again for good measure, but she was too far away, so he swam after her.

Screaming, she swam toward the other end of the swampy pond. But she didn't make it before he overtook her.

Aidan grabbed her and dunked her under once, then pulled her back up.

Slaíne struggled against him, thrashing like a prize fish on the line, but Aidan didn't let go. He was behaving absurdly. He knew his behavior was reprehensible. And yet…. It was too tempting. Only this time, there was no strange brew to blame.

"What's the matter?" she said, laughter in her voice.

Aidan answered by touching her face. It was shallower water on this end, and he was able to stand with his head above water. Slaíne was not so able, thus making her vulnerable to his attack. His hands steadied her, held her above the surface and he stared at her, into her.

Her breathing had grown as ragged as his own. Aidan took that as all the permission he needed. For the second time in the span of a day, he leaned in and was prepared to kiss her, but remembered her words from before.

You'll ruin it, she'd said. What had she meant by that? Perhaps he would be wise to find out before he attempted anything again.

Willing his blood to cool, Aidan planted a kiss on her cheek. He met her eyes, and of course could read no betrayal of what she might be feeling. *Typical*, he thought, chiding himself for again overstepping his bounds. "How do we—"

"Transport the water?" Slaíne said.

He released her, and they both swam back to the other side of the pond, Aidan allowing her to reach the bank before he did. When she got out, her clothes clung to her small frame and showed more beneath than was modest. Aidan looked away and gave her privacy.

A thought occurred to Aidan. It was almost too good to hope for, yet the nymphs would have had to dispose of his belongings somewhere. It stood to reason that that somewhere was near at hand. "Slaíne," he said after clearing his throat. He didn't look at her, but took to scanning the woods surrounding. "Where did you find the sword?"

For whatever reason, her tone turned brittle yet again. "I found it by a tree. Why?"

Aidan rolled his eyes but did not pursue the cause of the tone. "Perhaps they hid my belongings nearby."

There was a pause. She sighed, and he felt her moving away from him a ways. When she spoke, her voice was farther away. "It was over here somewhere, though I can nay remember exactly."

He frowned. "The general direction is good enough. I should be able to find anything if I have that."

"You can't feel nothin' now?"

Aidan nodded. "That doesn't mean it's not there. There might be iron involved." He traipsed past Slaíne, ignoring her sharp intake of breath, and stood with his back to her in the gathering of trees. Her Pull, though, was proving as problematic to his concentration as usual. Aidan shook his head. "Slaíne, would you mind moving off a little ways? Your Pull is throwing my perception off."

He felt rather than heard her move back ten paces. Not perfect, but it would have to do. Aidan closed his eyes and concentrated. Again he felt for familiar Pulls but found none. Next, he felt for the absence of Pulls, for a presence that should be there but was not. He stretched himself a little, ignoring everything that was, and— "Yes. There's something here."

His eyes flew open and he followed that repulsion he felt toward that particular metal. It was repelling him as he fought his way toward it, its presence clearer than it would normally have been, since he had been looking for it. The pulsing spot was in the ground, so Aidan looked for disturbed dirt. Sure enough, there was a patch of fresh soil that radiated a 'stay away' feeling. He got on his hands and knees and dug, all the while the force of the repulsion hitting him hard in the stomach.

"You find something?"

Aidan didn't answer at first. He was busy moving mounds of dirt aside, ignoring the small cuts the rocks were scraping into his hands. There! Not two feet below was a chest made of iron, about four by three feet. He hastily cleared away the rest of the dirt, and with a triumphant laugh, he pried the lid off the coffer and found his store of water bladders, his saddlebag and moneys, his knives, some herbs, his fire-making tools, and his cooking patera. He was so happy, he could kiss something.

"Why'd they bury it?" Slaíne asked. She reached around him for one of the bladders, and her arm brushed his, causing his hairs to stand on end.

Aidan ignored his body's reaction and Dismissed all but the bladders. "Perhaps they thought we wouldn't escape if we didn't have our supplies." Who cared as long as they had the much-needed possessions back?

"And you're sure they're dead?" she asked.

"Why wouldn't they be dead? You said it yourself. Their life forces were tied to the light. No light, no nymphs." It sounded stupid coming out of his mouth, but it had to be true. And even if it weren't, it didn't matter now. They were free to be on their way.

Slaíne let out a grunt. "All right. If you say so, sir." Before he could say anything else on the matter, she changed the subject. "Are we still for Wontworth?"

Aidan thought on it for a moment. "Frankly," he said, trying to think of words as not to scare her, "I'm not entirely certain where we should go next."

Of all things, the girl spat into the grass. "Can you, you know, feel for a place near us?"

"I could try. But if no one's near for a few miles, it'll be hard to say."

"Go on, then."

Aidan shook his head but closed his eyes anyway and reached out for Pulls. To his surprise, he found quite a few. The Pulls were weak, but strong enough to tug at him, meaning they were within at least ten miles. Finally, a bit of good news. "There's a village," he said, taking the bladders to the pond, "around seven or eight miles west from here. Its Pull is familiar, and the population is a small size. Might be Wontworth. Might be another town entirely. I'm not putting all my hopes in sheer dumb luck."

★   ★   ★

Slaíne foraged for anything edible whilst Aidan filled the bladders and Dismissed any harmful properties from the water. This took some effort and concentration, and by the time he had cleansed all six, he'd worked up quite the sweat. His clothing had begun to dry, and his head throbbed in time with his heartbeat.

An hour later, Slaíne emerged from the woods with a dead goose hanging from around her neck. She dropped it at his feet, her expression expectant.

Aidan smirked, and Dismissed all the feathers. He Summoned his copper knife and stuck it into the dead bird's flesh. "Don't expect me to gut it."

"Nah," she said. "The innards are the best parts. You mind startin' a fire, though, Ai— Sir?"

His smirk deepened into what might have passed for a smile if he were not so hungry. "You can call me Aidan, you know. That's my name."

Slaíne shook her head. "Nay, sir. Can nay do that."

It occurred to him to ask why, but he had no desire for any more banter, playful or otherwise. So he set about working on a spit to roast the bird on while Slaíne gathered wood for a fire, skirting around each other in silence, the mood in the air uncertain.

He got the fire going and let it die down after an hour, and Slaíne helped him skewer the gutted carcass as to roast it above the small flames. The innards Slaíne insisted on stewing in his patera, something she claimed to never have seen the likes of in her life. The moments dragged. The tension built. Finally, Slaíne broke the silence. "I'll be back," she said, swatting at flies Aidan could not see. "I think I saw some wild onions growing o'er not far from here." She muttered something else, but Aidan could not make out the words.

The bird roasted for an hour, and still Sláine did not return. Had he not been keeping track of her Pull, he might've gone looking for her. He felt her, some yards off in the woods, singing to herself. For whatever reason, it made Aidan uncomfortable, like he was listening in on a private conversation. The words were nonsensical. Gibberish, if he half ignored it. And yet....

> *"Lock and key*
> *The girl in the parlor*
> *Crept on her knees*
> *A'scrubbin' the floors*
> *Woe to she*
> *For listening*
> *At the keyhole*
> *in the door*
> *Oh I murthered a man*
> *Said the smith to the banker*
> *Oh woe to she*
> *The wench at the door*
> *I cheated he*
> *Said the swarthy ol' banker*
> *But who is this*
> *A'listenin' at keyholes*
> *They murthered a wench*
> *A deal was struck*
> *Beware to you eavesdroppers*
> *You'll learn what's more for your luck."*

The tune was all over the place, and her voice was raised and angry in some parts. Honestly, Aidan did not think he wanted to know what or whom she was singing about. It put him in mind to shut out her voice entirely and focus on the pressing matters at hand.

"Find old Cedric's grave," Meraude had said to him. Yet, judging from what everyone had said, and what he himself had witnessed in the dream, the mage was not one to be trusted. But if she had the power to Summon what he could not – *whom* he could not – it might be worth the risk of losing…everything. And that meant finding the

Goblets Immortal. The Goblet buried with Cedric the Elder was the first option, though he had no idea where it might be. The only one who might have known its location was goodness-knows-where, and possibly out to kill all magical beings. Then again, if Meraude had known the grave's location, why hadn't she given the information to him? "She mustn't have any idea," Aidan said to himself.

What was he missing? The mage had mentioned freeing him herself. That did not bode well. He and Slaíne would have to be on the move again, and soon…right after they finished filling their bellies and had hidden any traces of their presence.

And that was another problem: Slaíne. She would resist his plan to find the grave and the Goblets if it meant helping Meraude in any way, shape, or form. Not to mention, it would put her in danger as well. But what could he do? Aidan had no family he could leave her with to watch after her, and even if he had, would the curse take her when he left on his quest?

Staring into the dying embers had a hypnotic effect on Aidan, and he found his eyelids drooping. "No," he said, shaking himself awake. He needed to remain alert. There was too much at stake, too much danger out there for him to take a rest even in broad daylight.

Slaíne began singing again, this time about vilest murder at midnight, and Aidan definitely did not want to hear her thoughts on that matter. Again he tried to shut out her voice, leaning back against a rock.

Maybe Cedric's grave was a trap. Maybe the answer lay with the elves he had tried to cheat. Perhaps he could convince them to give the Warring Goblet back to him, or trick them again somehow.

Aidan closed his eyes, just to rest them. He would remain alert and awake.

The smell of the goose's flesh burning assailed his nostrils and jolted him back to wakefulness. The bird had nearly caught fire, but Slaíne was rushing up just then, her face scratched and dirty.

"You let it burn?"

He opened his mouth to snap a retort, but thought the better of it. He hadn't the energy to argue, and he knew it would get him nowhere anyway. "It's still edible."

She gave him a look but went about saving their dinner. By the time she got to the patera, the organs had grown too tough and dry to eat, so she tossed them into the fire, causing an even greater stink.

★   ★   ★

After waiting for the meat to cool on a stone, they both ripped into the flesh with their hands, stuffing as much of the succulent bird into their mouths as they could. It felt like he hadn't eaten in days, which very well could have been true. It had been hard for Aidan to judge the passing of days and nights with the nymphs keeping the land lit up the whole time.

Slaíne finished first, grease splattered all over her torn and weathered shirt and slacks.

Before thinking it through, Aidan opened his mouth and asked, "Why those clothes?"

The girl looked down at them like she'd never considered her attire before. "Huh," was the first thing she said. "Them's what was given me." Her cheeks grew rosy and she wouldn't make eye contact. "Haven't really thought 'bout it, honest."

Aidan Dismissed the remainder of their meal, along with their still-cooling supplies. "When we reach the town," he said, "we'll find something more suitable for you to wear." For a moment he thought she might take offense at this gesture.

Slaíne did make a face, as if she were not quite certain about the offer or the intentions behind it.

He let the matter drop and got to his feet. "We should probably get moving soon. The day is aging, and we should cover up the remains of camp."

She shrugged and got to her feet as well. They both would not quite look at the other, and Aidan knew she felt as he did: this awkwardness could not be over with quickly enough.

★   ★   ★

It took them half an hour to hide what traces of their presence that they could, neither speaking more than monosyllabic words. After a swig of water each, they followed the human Pulls southwest, stopping twice to rest. The longer they stumbled through the woods, the more convinced Aidan was they were headed for a small town called Abbington, miles away from where he thought Meraude would guess them to be.

Hundreds of years ago, the provincial town had started out as a small collection of buildings that made up a monastery. Shortly after, more of the wood surrounding had been cleared to make room for an abbey. Aidan had traveled once to the resulting strange sprawl of ancient stone giants, patched up after weathering many cold, damp seasons. He'd been a youth at the time. Hopefully now he would be unrecognizable, as he had stirred up quite a scandal when he wouldn't give alms to a nun.

Yes, this must be the way to Abbington. Most woods looked like the other, but this one had a familiar feel to it. They were certain to have a decent place to rest that night.

But something made Aidan uneasy. It went beyond Slaíne, who was quieter than usual as they tramped out of the woods and onto a byway. There was a Pull out there, strong as any regular human's, at a distance behind them. He couldn't be certain, but when they stopped the second time, the Pull stayed where it was as well, as if its owner were trying to be covert. Aidan said nothing to Slaíne; he did not wish to alarm her.

It could be a nomad. It could also be a highway robber or worse. There were strange rumors going around about Abbington, wraiths that came out at night, plaguing the woods beyond with noise and banditry. *Nonsense, probably*, Aidan thought. Still, the sooner they reached the small town, the better.

The person kept their pace, sometimes slipping a ways behind, but always within a mile, now walking parallel with them. If only they would come out onto the open road; then he could put his mind at ease and see who it was and what they wanted. But the fact that they remained hidden made him certain their intent was malevolent.

"What you keep lookin' at?" Slaíne asked.

Aidan started and looked over at the girl. She was keeping pace with him, her jaw tense and her eyes set ahead. "It's nothing," he reassured her.

"Ain't nothin'," she said in a lower voice. "Someone's out there, ain't they?"

So much for not worrying Slaíne. "It's probably just a stray dog or something, thinks we have hand-outs." She didn't buy a word of it, he could tell, but she said nothing on that score.

Though they were both tired and hot and getting somewhat winded, Slaíne picked up her pace by a measure, and Aidan matched it. "Not so quickly," he said below his breath. "The town's just up ahead. Besides, the Pull out in the woods is getting weaker." A lie, but she seemed to latch on to it, as her pace slowed back to a brisk walk and less of the beginnings of a jog.

Ten minutes later, somewhere in the late afternoon, they walked into the bustling village, dodging horse traffic and ignoring the stares that were directed their way. They must look something dreadful after having been in the woods for a day, and during their journeys before that.

Aidan reached into his pocket, where he Summoned a few coins. "Take these and find us a place to stay the night," he said to Slaíne, handing her the money.

"I can nay, sir. The curse—"

Right. That. He needed to be away from her for a while, so he told her to purchase something sweet from the stand out front of the nearest store, close enough to prevent the curse from attacking – her Pull would warn him – and far enough to clear his thoughts.

There was that scandalized look again, like he'd suggested she strip stark naked or hang upside down from a branch. "I ain't a child."

Aidan continued to hold out the money, waiting.

The girl hesitated at first, and then snatched it up as if wanting to have as little physical contact as possible. He did not blame her. He felt the same way.

After enduring one final withering glance, Aidan walked into the first shop he saw: a bakery, where he was greeted with odd stares and some whispers. Aidan tried to ignore the unwanted attention and ordered some pasties from an ample woman with a crooked nose. He couldn't be familiar, surely. It had been going on fifteen years since his last visit. Nonetheless, he remained on the receiving end of some strange looks.

"Are you related to the Wentworths?" the baker asked as she wrapped his wares in grease paper.

"No, ma'am. I am not from these parts." He held out a hand for his change and his purchases. It was a temptation to lower his gaze and hide his face, but he knew that would only make him stick out all the more. Aidan watched as she sorted through her drawer, holding every other coin she handled up to a small gas lamp.

The baker, it would seem, was in no hurry to release him. "Could've sworn you bore a resemblance to their son…what was his name? Jervis?"

"Aye," said a young woman who stood near the counter. She flushed and grinned when she met Aidan's eye. "Jervis, it was."

Aidan shook his head and looked away from the girl. He tried not to show his relief at being mistaken for someone else, but the hints of a smile tugged at his lips. "I am sorry I am not acquainted with the family."

"Mm," said the old wench, handing him the parcel of pasties. "They were a good family. High blood— But all of them was murdered in their beds."

"Aye," said the young woman by the counter. "'Twas quite the scandal, that."

"Sorry to hear it," he said, trying to hide his impatience. He hadn't dealt with many women in the last ten years; he'd forgotten how chatty some of them could be.

"Will there be anything else for you, sir?" The woman bit down on one of the coins he'd handed her minutes before. Once apparently satisfied that they were in fact real, she counted out smaller coins for his change.

"That will be all, thank you."

"Have you any notion how long you'll be in these parts, m'lad?" asked a plump man by the over-iced cakes.

Aidan forced a smile as he accepted his change from the woman behind the counter. "I am just passing through."

The man coughed. "Not one for words, are you?"

"Sir?"

The young woman giggled, her skirt brushing the air next to Aidan as she took her turn at the counter. "Don't mind old Jon. He's into his customs."

Aidan looked at this Jon, feigning curiosity when all he could think about was escape and sleep. "Customs, sir? Have I done something amiss?"

It was the baker behind the counter who spoke. "Didn't give us your name, didn't tell us where you were from, didn't share anything personal about yourself. You see, young sir, we're a nosy folk in this village. We do need our gossip."

Big talk rolled in a wrapper of chit-chat. If only he could simply run out of there and eat a pasty in peace, even if it meant more coldness from

Slaíne. Adult manners, however, dictated that he must stand and take whatever petty nonsense they could throw at him. They were waiting for his answer. "Aidan Powell, at your service."

The fat man's ears perked up. "Powell? Hmm, Powell. Now there's a name worth noting. Any relation to the Powells of Fairbrooke?"

How his mother's obscure name had reached this far south was beyond his comprehension. He hid his unease, despite his rising panic, and replied, "Distant relatives, I believe. I come from farther east than Fairbrooke. Small village, you wouldn't have heard of it."

"Don't bet on it," laughed the woman behind the counter as she finished serving the girl in the overlarge skirts. "Small towns is our business here."

Aidan forced a laugh. *Powers that be, get me out of here without dying of boredom or giving myself away.* "This is a charming town."

"Your first visit here, I take?" said the girl, her skirts again brushing his leg.

Aidan tipped his hole-riddled hat. "Just so. Now, if you'll excuse me, ladies, sir, I'm in search of lodgings for the night."

"The Firestone Inn is run by me father," said the girl with a giggle.

The look shared between the counter wench and the fat old man did not go unnoticed by Aidan. What were they up to? Something underhanded surely was going on.

The girl coughed delicately and moved toward the door. Before Aidan could get ahead and open it for her, the young woman turned to him and blurted out: "Would you mind very much escorting me on some errands, Mr. Powell? I'm afraid there's been some disturbances lately, and it ain't suitable for a lady to be out on her own."

The fat old man hid a chuckle as another cough, and only then did it dawn on Aidan that the girl just might be setting her cap at him. Was there anything in the laws of social etiquette that would allow him to politely decline such a request?

Mercifully, a young man entered the bakery at that moment, pushed past Aidan, nodded to the girl with a smile, and made for the counter. "One of my beaux," she whispered to Aidan, to his relief. "Best not let him see us walking together, Mr. Powell. He's got a jealous streak; don't want him throwing a fit."

Aidan gave her a look that he hoped was good-natured, bid them farewell, and left the shop behind him.

When he emerged, he found Slaíne standing right where he had left her, scowling.

His eyebrows shot heavenward as she thrust the coins back into his hands. "And it's good to see you, too." Aidan sighed and tried giving the money back to her without causing a scene. "I don't take back what I give. These coins are yours."

"I didn't earn those."

Was that all? He laughed and led her away from the sweets salesman, who eyed them both with distaste. "Slaíne, look at me."

She did, her nose wrinkled up. "What?"

"I didn't earn these coins, either. They came from the sale of my family's estate." That didn't seem to change her opinion about taking the money from him. "You should have something to spend. And besides, you *have* earned it."

Her look challenged him. "Have I now?"

They'd come upon a dress shop with ready-made dresses on display in the window. There were pinks and greens and all sorts of frilly, lacy things that women were supposed to love. But Slaíne kept walking even when Aidan stopped, seemingly oblivious. "Here, take these coins and a few notes and buy three dresses."

It was her eyebrows' turn to shoot up to her hairline. "What? Blimey, no."

Knowing it would only irk her and hinder his cause, he suppressed the smile he felt forming on his face. "Here." He reached into his pocket and Summoned several larger notes from Nothingness, which he thrust at her. "Find yourself three or four ready-made dresses. Goodness knows I'm tired of people wondering why you're in slacks."

"If'n it bothers you," she said warily. Without finishing the thought, her hand flashed out and she snatched the money. Only then did Aidan allow the smile to break. "Don't know what the ruddy big deal is."

"Thank you."

"They probably won't let me in, an' you neither. We both smell wretched."

Aidan hadn't thought of that. "At the inn, I'll call for a bath for you— While I wait downstairs, of course."

She snorted. "Don' need no washin'."

"Quit dawdling," he said, beckoning toward the shop. "I'll be just here. Fetch me if you need more money."

With a low growl and a few more muttered words, Slaíne left him and entered the shop.

Aidan waited the better part of half an hour, and still she did not emerge. He resisted the urge to peer through the window, quite aware that the girl was nervous and didn't need him putting his nose in where it was unwanted. So instead, he explored the stands to the side of the building. He was certain not to roam too far. There was still the curse, which latched them together, wanted or not.

"Definitely not wanted," he said, causing the fruit vendor to back away a little. It was just as well; fresh fruit wouldn't last long for his money, anyway, and wouldn't fill a belly like meat. Aidan moved on to the next stall, which sold roasted nuts.

"How much for these?" Aidan asked a bored man in ratty clothes that smelled of burnt wood and silt.

The salesman took his time answering, sucking on his teeth and curling his beard between his fingers. A near two minutes later, it would seem, he at last answered the question. "Which ones might you mean?"

Aidan gestured to the mixed nuts. "These." He felt another human Pull coming his way, and paid it little mind. He was used to Pulls, so it was only natural to ignore it.

"How many for these…plums are they?" asked a woman. Her voice was familiar and almost made him turn to glance, but the nut salesman was speaking and won Aidan's attention back.

"They're not for sale."

Aidan stared at him for a moment, weighing whether or not the man was serious. "Sir?"

"They're not for sale." He removed his cap and wiped the sweat from his brow. "Got anything worth trading, though? Don't take money from strangers. Could be counterfeit."

Aidan nodded. "I see. I have a saddle…." *In Nothingness, you idiot. Are you going to Summon it in front of him?*

The man raised a brow at Aidan and smirked. "No horse?"

"Dead."

He scratched his scruffy beard. "What sorta feller lets his horse die?"

Aidan resisted the urge to argue and stated, "Goblin ambush."

That drew a low whistle from the rough salesman, who replaced his cap and drew a filthy rag from his pocket. "Can I give you some friendly advice, m'lad?" He beckoned for Aidan to lean in before continuing. "Leave this town as soon as possible, a'right? There be wraiths in these parts. Last thing folks here need is for goblins to be brought down on their heads."

What was there to say to that? It had seemed like the goblins had sought him out specifically. Who was to say they wouldn't find him again, this time in a town? "I'll keep that in mind. In the meantime... what would you accept as a fair trade for a pound of pecans?"

The man snorted. "You ain't got the collateral. An' this here fine young lady seems more than likely to give me proper business."

At this Aidan turned, half-expecting to see Sláine, though the Pull was all wrong – too weak and brittle in all the wrong places. Without thinking, he Summoned the silver sword into his hand.

It was the seer he had met at Prewitt Manor.

CHAPTER TEN

The seer was paying with a set of crystal candlesticks, which she drew from a tattered carpet bag. She paid no mind to Aidan, nor did any of the shopkeepers.

Good. No one had seen him Summon the blade; his secret was safe. But he would not be safe long if he did not find Slaíne and flee... if there was anywhere safe left in the world.

"I'll be with you in a moment, *Mr. Powell,*" said the seer without turning. "But yes, why don't you run inside and fetch that young miss? I'll be wanting to talk with her as well."

The salesmen gave strange looks as Aidan hid the sword behind his back – Dismissing it out of sight – and ran around the side of the building. He didn't care. He needed to find that blasted girl. Where had she gone off to?

She was sitting on the shop steps, three paper parcels resting in her lap. Upon seeing him, she picked up the packages by the strings, as if afraid they would bite her. "Mr. Aidan, you look like you've seen a wraith."

"We need to leave, Slaíne. They've found me."

Slaíne's eyes grew wide with fear, before lighting up with a fierce excitement. "Meraude is here, is she? I've been waiting for this moment for a long time. Where is my...." Her voice trailed off as a frown formed on his face. "What? No Meraude?" Her face paled. "Oh goodness, the nymph creatures didn't find us again? I didn't think they was really dead—"

He grabbed her by the elbow and steered her into an ally on the other side of the bakery. "No, Slaíne, Lord Dewhurst is here."

It was her turn to frown. "Lord who?"

Aidan rolled his eyes as she shook off his grip on her arm. "Just the man who says I murdered his family." Only after the words left his mouth did Aidan realize Slaíne would have no idea what he was talking about. He had never filled her in on that particular part of his history.

"Lord Thing says you murdered someone?"

"Lord Dewhurst, and yes. He's here. Or, at least, his servant is. We haven't much time before they find me, and then I'm a dead man."

It seemed to take a moment for her to process the new information, and when she did, she looked angry. "All right. We sneak out an' all, but then you're explainin' what's really going on."

Aidan nodded. "Fair enough. Now hurry." He Dismissed her parcels so they wouldn't hinder her, and they ran for the end of the alley... which ran into a dead end right around the corner where it abutted another building.

"Lord Ingledark," said the seer, who'd crept into the alley behind them, "I come in peace."

He paid the witch's words no mind, but again Summoned Slaíne's silver blade from Nothingness and pushed the girl behind him. "Where's your master?"

The seer's shoulders heaved. She looked much older than when he'd last seen her. Maybe it was a trick of the light, but she seemed to have aged twenty years. "If my so-called master were here, milord, wouldn't you know it?"

She made a fair point. If any Pull was familiar, it would be Lord Dewhurst's; Aidan had been actively avoiding the man for the better part of his life. Still, her word alone wasn't worth going on. He kept the blade raised. "What do you want?"

"Who are you?" Slaíne surprised Aidan by asking the seer. She seemed more curious than afraid, as if Aidan's suggestion of the woman being dangerous wasn't enough for her. Aidan hoped she wouldn't have to find out for herself.

"You mean to run me through, eh, milord?"

"Some sorcerer," Aidan spat. He didn't dare take his eyes off the woman, though he could feel Slaíne moving around him.

The middle-aged woman laughed, of all things. "Sorcerer? You should know better than to believe that for a second, Lord Ingledark."

"Stay back, Slaíne."

The girl did not heed his words, but moved around him before he could grab her with his free hand. "Do I know you?"

The seer frowned. "No. But I know you."

Wherever this was going, Aidan was certain he wasn't going to like it. He moved cautiously as his traveling companion stepped closer to the strange woman. "She's not safe. She's betrayed me once already."

The woman sighed. "Yes, and for that I am sorry. I had not had my bonds broken then."

Aidan groaned as Slaíne moved in far too close to the woman. "I really wouldn't—"

The girl waved him off, all attention on the seer. "What bonds? Like a curse?"

For all the smarts Aidan thought the girl possessed, she was behaving foolishly. Any closer and she'd be within attacking distance from the seer. Slaíne, he knew, had no weapons. The girl was defenseless, so with that thought in mind, Aidan reached into Nothingness and Summoned one of his copper daggers, discreetly so that neither woman would notice. One thought, and he could send the dagger flying at its intended mark…if only he knew that Slaíne would not get in the way.

As if answering his thoughts, the seer said, "You hit the girl in the back with the dagger, milord. Right when you think the shot is clean."

Slaíne turned with a frown for Aidan. "Why do she keep calling you 'milord'? And who did you hit with a dagger?"

Aidan's blood ran cold. "What?"

"Pardon my tenses. You will run the girl through with the dagger if you attempt anything. She'll die in a pool of her own red blood, and you, Lord Ingledark, will have to live with yet another noose around your neck."

Aidan glared. "Did you see it happen?"

The woman said simply, "I am the seer."

What choice did he have? The woman might be telling the truth, and as irritating as the girl was, he did not want to run Slaíne through with a dagger. Without another thought, he Dismissed the smaller weapon, and lowered the sword to his side. "What do you want?"

"What do I want? That is a rather complicated question. I think the real question here is what do *you* want, milord?"

"Excuse me?"

At last Slaíne stepped to the side of the alley, her expression troubled. Now was Aidan's chance. All he had to do was Dismiss the blade, and

Summon it long enough to deal a deathblow to the witch of a woman. But slaying goblins and nymphs was one thing; killing a human, no matter how much he questioned their humanity, was a whole other thing.

"You're a good man." She said it a second before Aidan Dismissed his blade, making Aidan believe that she knew what he'd been planning. "Now, can we please take this somewhere more comfortable and – less confined?" She sniffed and made a face. "And, no offense, but the pair of you stink to high heaven. You'll be wanting to freshen up first, I think." She turned from the pair and led the way into the open market.

Sláine looked back at Aidan, waiting for his lead.

As tempting as it was to take Sláine and flee in the opposite direction of the seer, Aidan decided that he was simply too fatigued to run very far very fast. Besides, he reasoned with himself, it would be good to know what Lord Dewhurst was doing and where he was at the moment. If anyone could answer that, it would be his slave. And a seer. Convenient. He only hoped that he would not be drawn into another trap. "Fool me once," he muttered.

"Sir?"

He shook her question off. "Come on." They followed the woman out into the middle of the square, where she was looking at some frost-bitten rosebuds.

"Ah, what a shame. Some young things aren't meant to last, are they?"

Aidan wondered if she was perhaps using a metaphor. He hated metaphors. They made him think of his uncle.

The woman startled Aidan out of his darker thoughts by gasping. "But look at this. One bud looks like it's going to make it." She prodded the red tissue with her dry fingers. "Yes. Very lovely. This one will bloom into something beautiful." She looked once at Sláine, then threw a wink in Aidan's direction.

The wink, whatever it meant, was missed entirely by the girl, who was frowning at the bush. "Never really liked flowers. They never last. An' they only look pretty. They're feisty buggers, certainly."

"Everyone has their thorns, young miss. Even you, I reckon."

That caused Sláine to look up with a frown. "Who are you? What do you want?"

"Not here, not here. We'll go to that inn that beautiful young woman recommended to *Mr. Powell*. What do you think?"

Aidan was only half-listening; he was busy feeling for Pulls. What if this town was full of iron? Maybe his enemies were in hiding, their Pulls disguised by the repulsive metal.

"Mr. Powell, I said why don't we get indoors? It's not safe being outside at nighttime. We'd be ambushed by robbers, you mark my word."

"Not with you on our side, I am sure," Aidan added dryly.

That made the old woman laugh. "Enough of this gabbing. There is work to be done."

Though he knew he couldn't trust her, Aidan followed, now searching for empty places, the repulsion of iron. Yet as they walked and he felt, he found nothing. Only Pulls. Pulls from buildings, the steady anchors that were not strong enough to hold him in place. Pulls from smaller things, such as supplies and furniture inside the buildings. And there were, of course, Pulls from people, the only real anchors that he would have to let go of if he needed to Dismiss himself.

He walked past all of these, feeling his way without seeing much. Aidan could've closed his eyes if he wished, but it was dangerous relying on the feeling of Pulls; he'd tried it as a younger man, walking with his eyes closed. He had wound up walking straight into a giant puddle that turned out to be quicksand. It was Isaac the beggar – now Isaac the Roma, Aidan recalled – who had helped him out of that mess.

The memory of Isaac made him think of the Goblet that he'd held in his possession for a brief moment. The man had said that he'd liberated the magical vessel from Aidan's uncle. Isaac could not have known what it was; otherwise he wouldn't have parted with it so casually. But why give it to Aidan? It was magical, true, and so was Aidan. He hadn't realized that the thought had been bothering him since their encounter with the elves. He hadn't had time to think. Too much had happened between then and now.

"Is this our stop? Mr. Aidan?" Slaíne was staring at him funny. "Your shoulder hurtin' again?"

"Hmm?" It was then that he realized he'd been rubbing the spot where the nymph's blade had pierced him.

The seer gave him a look that Aidan didn't know what to make of, and ushered them inside the inn he'd been directed to. The woman wasted no time in ordering a private room, a full supper, and a round of something strong to drink – "Not too strong, mind" – and managed the small staff something dreadful.

Slaíne looked at him and smirked. "Must be used to gettin' her own way."

Aidan gave her a wry smile, but did not respond to that. "Don't eat or drink what you've been served until I've had time to inspect it."

She snorted. "For what? Poison?" When he didn't laugh at her joke and his smile vanished, the girl's brow creased. "You think she'd kill us?"

He gave the seer a quick look; she was walking ahead of them, reserving sleeping quarters and irritating the innkeeper. "She betrayed me once. I don't think she'd hesitate to do so again, even with her supposed newfound freedom."

Slaíne's frown deepened into a scowl. "You don't believe her?"

"Two cursed people just chance to meet in a small, obscure village? She's a seer. Of course she knew of your affliction. Why not use it to gain your trust, thus gain mine in return?"

That did not seem to sit well with Slaíne, whose jawline set. "I still say—"

"Well, it's all settled," the strange woman said, returning just in time to keep Slaíne from offering more objections to Aidan's concerns.

The girl wiped her nose on her right sleeve and followed the middle-aged woman into a small yet cozy room in the back of the inn. Once the door had been shut by a servant, Slaíne dropped down in a chair with her back to the door like she had never sat in a chair and relished the idea. As absurd as it seemed to Aidan at first, it might very well be that she'd never actually sat in a chair.

"Now, then, you're going to ask me what Lord Dewhurst is about."

"You read my mind." Aidan's tone was dry, but he kept his face void of emotion. No need to tell this woman any more than she might've guessed. He took a seat only after she sat, and the one he took faced the door. He may have Pulls to warn him, but he would not risk another ambush at her hand. "So, why the change of heart? You seemed rather gleeful to hand me over to my death."

The gap-toothed woman sighed and drew her reed pipe from inside her inner riding jacket. "I was eager, milord, because I was offered freedom in exchange for your life. But you take for granted what I am."

"What are you?" Slaíne asked. Unable to sit still, she got up and started poking at the sad fire in the fireplace.

Aidan sighed. "Slaíne, you're not—"

"Leave her be." The woman lit her pipe, puffed out some blue smoke, and put her muddy boots up on the table in front of her.

Slaíne repeated herself, obviously feigning disinterest as she brought the embers to a healthy blaze with some straw and twigs. "What are you?"

"I heard you the first time, m'dear." The woman grunted, put out her pipe, removed her boots from the table, and looked good and hard at the girl tending the fire. "I saw you for a while now. I'm not sure how this all is going to play out, but you have a part. Yes, I see that very clearly."

The girl turned, her brow now wrinkled and soot-covered. "You see things? Like, things that aren't there?"

She gave Slaíne a gentle smile. "More like things that aren't there *yet*. But not all things. There seems to be no rhyme nor reason to it. But it comes with a price…." She let her words trail off, a thoughtful look on her face. "You see what I'm saying, dear girl?"

"You're a fortune-teller?"

"No, Slaíne. No more than you are a bird."

That caused Slaíne to drop the log she'd been carrying. She opened and closed her mouth a few times, and Aidan wondered what the older woman had said that would have such an effect on the girl. He was about to ask something, but the seer raised her hand to cut his questions off.

"Never mind now, milord. Slaíne, I have something in common with your quest." She was quiet and hesitated before saying more. "You might want to check that Pull at the door, Mr. Powell."

Aidan was on his feet before she spoke. He threw the door open, behind which he felt only one Pull, and found a servant with an ear pressed against the wood.

The strange wire-thin man jumped at the sight of Aidan and straightened up at once. "Ah, er…dinner will be another twenty minutes." He flinched as Aidan gave him a warning glance before slamming the door in his face.

After a moment, when he was certain the way was clear, Aidan sat back down in his chair. "You were saying?"

The woman held up a finger. "Slaíne, you're going to kill that fire with too much compassion. Why don't you sit down as well?"

The girl shrugged and flopped back in her seat. She was fidgety, spooked.

"She's fine," the seer said before Aidan could ask her what the matter was. "So, you're both wanting to know where to find old Cedric's grave."

"Myth," Slaíne said.

The seer shook her head. "History. You'd think people would learn not to argue facts with a seer, of all people. Now, catch me up: How many of the Goblets Immortal have you ever seen?"

"One," Slaíne and Aidan answered together.

"Ah, yes. I wondered if you'd come across one. Those are – harder to see. Iron of the Six. You would've been somewhat repulsed and compelled by it, would you have not, Mr. Aidan?"

Aidan gave a noncommittal shrug. He would tell the seer what he wanted to and no more, and only then when he felt like it.

"Very well. I see you're not going to make this easy for me. There are at least four Goblets, all of their makers slaughtered shortly after their creation, their blood drained dry. As you will of course know, wizard's blood is molten iron…of the most magical sort."

"But don't iron and magic not mix?" Slaíne surprised Aidan by asking.

The seer gave her a knowing look, the meaning of which Aidan still did not comprehend. Again the seer drew out her pipe, filled it with tobacco leaves, and was prepared to light it, before changing her mind. She emptied the leaves back into her tobacco pouch and put away her pipe. "No, I need a clear head for this. Iron and magic, magic and iron. Each repels the other, for magic is pure, and iron is polluted. The two cannot mix for this reason. But wizard's blood – why, it's the purest. Still, 'tis very unruly and unmanageable for even one that is Blest. Unless, he…. Ah, I'm getting ahead of myself." She shuddered and licked her chapped lips before continuing.

"Now, Cedric had the uncanny ability to succeed at anything he set his mind to. That was his Gift, which he imbued the Questing Goblet with. Whoever so drinks of that Goblet takes into himself Cedric's ability…that is, until the affected liquid runs out of their system."

"Which means that people like me should not exist."

The woman shook her head and wagged her finger with a small smile on her face. "You take for granted, Mr. Aidan, your mother."

Aidan's fists clenched in his lap. She had claimed before that she knew how to find his family, wherever they'd disappeared to. That is, she'd mentioned the fact right before betraying him. His tone was clipped when he asked, "What about my mother?"

The seer sighed, exasperated apparently. "She's the reason you can do what you can do. My mother's the reason I can do what I can do. Aidan, your mother was part of the Circle, as was mine."

Aidan held up a hand. He wanted to hear more, but there was yet another Pull at the door, this time with three others behind it.

"It's only the servants," the seer said as Aidan Summoned the silver blade into his hand. "You're going to frighten them to death if you don't put that away."

There was a knock on the door, followed by, "Dinner is served!" Only then did Aidan Dismiss his blade and took his seat once more.

The seer clucked her tongue at him. "So suspicious. No one could buy your trust."

"They could…with my blood. All of it," he said, throwing her previous threat back at her.

That brought some color into the seer's cheeks, but she said nothing.

"Good, I'm half-starved." Whatever Slaíne thought of the conversation, she didn't let on, but hopped to her feet and offended the servants by trying to help.

"We've got it," one of the men said as she tried to take a heavy, hot platter from him.

Aidan rolled his eyes and fought annoyance. "Slaíne, take a rest for once. You've earned it."

The girl gave him a funny look, but then plopped back down in the chair and stared at her fingernails. "They've got it, my hide."

As if to prove her right, one of the servants bumbled and dropped a tureen of peas and butter onto the floor. The young man swore and colored all unpleasant shades of pink and white. "Master's going to see me hanged."

"Leave it," the seer said as the servant got to his hands and knees and started scooping the ruined peas back into their dish.

The man scrambled to his feet and scarpered right out the door, followed by the other three, who took a more leisurely pace. "Call if you need anything more," said the last and snootiest of the four.

The seer made an obscene gesture and muttered a warning at him before the man slammed the door. The words she had spoken before the meal's arrival still hung in the air, but the woman paid them no mind as she grabbed the roast pheasant plate with indecent enthusiasm. "Goodness me, I haven't tasted fresh game since four and twenty fortnights past."

Slaíne regarded the food, then Aidan, as if asking for permission to be hungry. When he didn't respond, the girl plopped three generous dollops of potato hash onto her plate, then half a loaf of bread, before snatching Aidan's clean plate and filling it with food as well. She waited then, looking at him expectantly.

So caught up in the conversation, he'd all but forgotten his warning to Slaíne not to eat 'til he'd explored the food for nefarious Pulls. He took a moment, closed his eyes, and concentrated. There might be some dirt in the potatoes, so he Dismissed that. A bit of something he did not recognize in the pheasant and the carrots, so he Dismissed that element as well. And, just to be certain he hadn't missed anything, Aidan went through the drinks and food stuffs on the table again.

The seer snorted. "What are you expecting to find? I've been here with you the whole time, and one of you's always been watching me."

"Better safe," Aidan said, "than dead."

She gave him a bemused look, and attacked the roast pheasant with her bare hands.

Aidan grimaced. "It's safe."

The woman snorted, spraying the table with partially masticated food. "Of course it's safe."

Slaíne nodded and dug into the food as well.

Aidan wished to join them; he knew he needed the nourishment. But that witch-of-a-woman might as well have dropped a stone into his stomach. What of his mother? What Circle? His shoulder pained him again the more he thought, though he strove to pay the cold twinges no mind.

"Don't mind if I do," the seer said, taking the bowl of potatoes from Slaíne.

How could he trust anything that came out of that woman's mouth? There seemed no point in asking her to explain herself. Yet...what if there were some truth in her words? Aidan could stand it no more. "How did you know my mother?"

Slaíne dropped her fork, and the room was filled with its merry ringing as it hit her tin plate. Aidan didn't need to look at her to know that her eyes were cast down on her lap.

The seer's reaction was to laugh. "Sir, I never knew your mother."

"You just said—"

"I said that our mothers were in the Circle. Had to have been. They're the ones what killed the wizards and kept their Goblets. Really, milord, do keep up with the conversation." She gave him a moment, smiling as if waiting for her words to sink in.

But the words meant nothing to him.

"This 'Circle'," Slaíne said through a full mouth, "was it made of all women?"

The seer shook her head. "Nay, Miss Slaíne, as I think you right well can guess. You do need men for certain things."

Slaíne made a face. "If you say so."

The seer continued. "When a woman who is with child drinks from one of the Goblets, she temporarily takes on its powers. But the miracle growing inside her – why, the Goblet's powers become part of the being's makeup."

Aidan frowned. "All right, if what you are saying is true, what was this Circle of yours? What was its purpose?"

She looked him square in the eyes, searching their depths. "To create a new world order, but of course. Now, before you say another word, let's finish what's in front of us. And despite what you might think, I know precious little of the Circle. It's Meraude what you'll want to ask these questions."

Slaíne snarled at the mention of the mage.

Aidan thought of arguing with the seer, demanding more answers there and then, but his stomach was clenching and practically howling with hunger. So he finally gave in and ate.

$\star$ $\star$ $\star$

Once the ladies had cleared every last crumb and morsel from all of the dishes on the table, and Aidan's stomach could hold no more, the seer insisted that she was quite tired and in need of rest. "I'll still be here when you two awake. Now, my room is across the hall from yours." She passed Aidan one key. "And try not to fight too loudly tonight. The innkeeper's wife is already thinking of turning us out."

One key? "I don't like this." He was not going to leave Sláine with this woman, no matter how much she said she was sorry for the betrayal.

"What don't you like, Mr. Aidan?"

"I don't trust you, with her or myself."

Sláine's gaze flitted back and forth between the two. She worried her lower lip, and seemed uncertain as to what she was to do.

The woman nodded and smiled her gap-toothed smile. "Granted. If ever you were a trusting man, milord, I drove it out of you. But what does Sláine have to do with our supposed feud?"

"Supposed feud? You tried to kill me."

"No, I handed you over to be killed."

"A technicality. I don't want her staying alone with you. In your room or anywhere."

Sláine frowned but said nothing.

The seer threw back her head and laughed, repulsing Aidan with the sight of her blackened teeth and the smell of her fetid breath. "Is that all?"

Aidan folded his arms, quite aware that the girl might make more of his concern than there was.

When Aidan didn't respond, the woman smirked at him. "The girl won't be staying in my room with me." She folded Aidan's hand over the one key. "Good evening. Sláine. Lord Ingledark." And cackling, the seer left them standing together, one apparently confused, the other annoyed.

CHAPTER ELEVEN

"You can have it," Slaíne insisted. The two of them were standing as far from the other as possible, pretending there was nothing to feel awkward about. "I'll sleep on the floor."

Aidan shook his head. "What sort of man would that make me?"

Slaíne laughed, a jarring sound. "Human." She pursed her lips and narrowed her eyes. "You're serious?"

"When am I not?"

"When you're being caustic."

Aidan drew breath to argue, but then released it with a great huff. This situation ought not be. But it was. Every other room in the inn was occupied, and the seer had long since locked herself inside her own accommodations, ignoring Aidan's periodic banging on her door. This shouldn't have been a problem...*wouldn't* have been a problem, if he hadn't been such a thirsty idiot. He could not recall the incident in the nymph's camp without a shudder and prickly stab of shame in his chest. "You are not sleeping on the floor."

"Ne'er slept on no bed anyways."

"All the more reason why you should take it. I will hear nothing more on the matter."

Slaíne scowled at him. "Did it ever occur to you—"

"Hush."

"That I don't want—"

"Not another word."

Slaíne stomped her foot. "This is stupid. I'm allowed to talk."

Aidan gritted his teeth. "I never said you couldn't talk. Talk, talk all ruddy night, if you please."

Her face grew red and her eyes sparkled with rage. "You sayin' I talk too much?"

He groaned. "Women!"

"What about us?"

The tension from the past few weeks caught up with him in that moment, making him fatigued and lightheaded. Her Pull, ever a nuisance and frustration, did not help. The closer Slaíne came, the more he felt like either violently kissing or strangling her.

"What about us?" Slaíne continued to come at him, her face flushed, her eyes full of madness.

Maybe she felt the friction as well. Or maybe she was completely deranged and had no idea how close Aidan was to performing violence.

"Girl," he warned, standing his ground, "I wouldn't push me if I were you."

She threw up her hands and spun around to face the wall. In her haste to turn away from him, her shirt dipped down over her shoulder, the one where she'd been whipped that night by the elves. It had healed over nicely. Her skin was smooth and shiny in that spot.... No, not just that spot. All over, her skin glowed with an impossibly attractive sheen of sweat. She was filthy. He was filthy. And yet....

Aidan shuddered and closed his eyes, willing himself to calm. He needed to cool them both down and fast, before any lines were crossed and he made an even bigger fool of himself. "Slaíne." His voice broke on her name, so he tried again. "I'm going to try the wretched woman again, see if I can't persuade her."

He opened his eyes, and found that the girl had turned around to look at him, her expression curious but still guarded. "I'll just go then." Aidan wasn't moving, but she was. *Turn and leave, you idiot. The door's just there.*

Nearer she came and nearer, her luminous gray eyes searching his own dark ones. Whatever she saw there must have frightened her, because she flinched and looked away. "All right."

With that, Aidan turned and propelled himself out the door, which he shut behind himself with more force than he'd meant to. Instead of knocking on the seer's door, he approached the innkeeper's wife, who was bustling by just then with an armful of towels. "Excuse me, ma'am."

"Eh? Whadduya want?" She smelled of sulfur and looked as though she'd gotten on the wrong side of a pumice stone.

Aidan took a step back from her stench. "I was wondering if a bath could be drawn for my...friend?"

The woman's bushy eyebrows drew together. "Not much hot water to be had here, laddie. Takes me bairns a right good hour's worth to heat enough water for two tubs."

"Just one tub will be required."

Her eyebrows shot heavenward. "You and your friend be sharing, then? That's not hygienal." She stopped to hock up a lungful of phlegm into one of the clean guest towels, which she straightened and moved to the bottom of her pile.

"Right. Still, I would pay—"

"Of course you would pay. Blimey, I ain't running no blasted charity here. For the love of Petere!" Again she hacked and spat. "All right, a silver piece will cover the bath."

"A silver for one bath? You've got to be joking."

The lady shrugged her broad shoulders. "Take it or leave it, that's what water's worth in these parts. Bathing is a luxury." She sniffed and made a face. "I'd assume you of all guests would realize this."

Aidan resisted the urge to barter and haggle. "Fine, one silver for one bath."

The innkeeper's wife nodded, her nose still thrust high in the air. "Very good, sir. I'll throw in a cake of soap for two pence."

"Done, madam."

★　　★　　★

While he waited for the water to be heated and the copper tub to be filled, Aidan did not reenter the room nor did he bother the seer again. The hall was narrow, but at the end of it there was a chair and a side table covered with a small assortment of books, so that was where he made himself comfortable. Unfortunately, he realized as he settled in, most of the books were poetry. The rest that weren't, the books with crisper pages and stiffer spines, had only to do with one topic: botany. *What sort of inn keeps study books?* But reading materials were far and few between in Aidan's line of work – wandering – so he opened one and tried to absorb himself in it.

While he sat and tried to read, he kept himself open to the feel of Pulls. There was nothing particularly strong within his reach... well, beside one, but that he ignored as much as he was able. But the reading material was dull, and he was tired. So, despite the boisterous nature of the folk down the stairs, Aidan found himself nodding.

Coldness crept from his shoulder and down his limb, but he did not wake.

Instead, Aidan found himself standing where the barn on his estate had once been. Hunger tore at his stomach, his weakened limbs shook with effort as he carried a stack of wood indoors. Somewhere, deep inside, Aidan knew he was asleep, that this half-starved body he walked in was but a shadow of the past. But soon he lost himself in his memory self, and they became one, trudging to do the work of a servant.

The night air was crisp, yet thirteen-year-old Aidan was covered in sweat from the evening's work. Uncle had been in a mood again. He must suspect, he must know that something was not quite right with his nephew. But Aidan had not lost control for at least a year, and even then it had never been in front of the dour man, who surely would see Aidan burned at the stake if he found him out. It was a dangerous waltz that he danced.

"Aidan! Say, Aidan, I brought you something."

Aidan dropped his load in relief and stumbled to the iron fence. It never felt right, meeting near the metal, but at least it didn't nag him like every other blasted object and person did. "Tristram, you shouldn't have come."

"Fine way to greet your only friend. Here, Mum will horsewhip me if she finds out, but I stole two hand pies that were cooling in the kitchen."

Aidan smiled a wry smile as his corn-haired friend shoved the pies through the slats. "You mean she'll whip you if she knows you dared set foot in the kitchen."

Young Tristram shrugged. "What are you waiting for? Mr. Powell will swipe them from your hands, soon as look at them. Eat."

Despite being destitute for three years, Aidan still had a streak of pride in him. Taking things, even gifts from friends, didn't come easy. "I thank you, friend. You really shouldn't have risked it."

Tristram laughed, causing Aidan's lips to twitch before he tore into the cold pies. "So, the lord of the manor. I hear he's ill." He eyed Aidan with interest. "Doctor York's been out to see him on several occasions."

"'Tis news to me. I am usually kept out of the way when anyone calls."

"The old man's a coward."

Aidan lifted one shoulder half-heartedly. "I suppose."

"It's a ruddy disgrace, him using and abusing you as he does."

"I'm cheap labor."

Tristram surprised him by spitting like a commoner. "It isn't right. The estate and the title are yours."

"Not 'til I'm of age."

"But you'll die before then. You should just kill him. Put something in his drink. No one will be the wiser, and if they knew your plight...well, they wouldn't blame you."

The pastry turned hard in Aidan's mouth, and that which he'd already devoured sat like a millstone in his stomach. "I have enough blood on my hands, thanks."

With an exasperated sigh, Tristram put his hands on the bars of the fence and leaned forward. "You don't even know if it was you. I mean, you didn't actually see—"

"What I saw," Aidan cut in, "was a burning barn explode. I sent them somewhere, Tris. I just – I just don't know where." He tucked the remainder of the pastries in his torn pockets. "Thank you for thinking of me. I really must return to my work."

"He beat you?"

Aidan flinched at the mention, but laughed. "When he can find me, which isn't often." He still hadn't told his friend about his trick. It was difficult, and perhaps dangerous, but every time his uncle went into a drunken rage, Aidan would use his ability to make himself disappear. It was uncomfortable, but it had saved him several beatings.

Tristram did not share Aidan's smile. "I worry about you."

"You worry about everything."

Tristram wouldn't back down. "That's not true. You do all the worrying, save when it comes to yourself."

"You need to forget—"

"Boy, where have you gotten to? The fire's dying in here." The old man's voice carried all the way down to the road. Uncle sounded drunk. And he hadn't had his supper yet. He'd be meaner than a wet cornered rat.

"I really must go."

"Think about what I said."

With a smirk, Aidan turned back. "Which bit?"

Tristram looked at him meaningfully and started walking backward. "You know." He mimed putting a glass to his lips, then grabbed his throat and writhed.

Aidan gave him a stern look. "When I wish to be hanged, I'll think on it."

"Boy!"

"Coming, Uncle." Aidan returned to his dropped firewood, recovered it, and trudged up the hill back toward the house. Four stories tall, the gray stone mansion had fallen into disrepair over the last three years. For all his talk of investing and making himself properly rich again, Aidan's uncle had failed miserably. He lost twice as much as what he invested, and the staff was reduced to four people: a serving wench, a butler, a farmer, and Aidan.

"What took you so blasted long? Did you have to grow the trees?" The old man let out a bark-like laugh and rapped his walking stick in time to his merriment on the floor. He frowned as he looked up at his nephew. "You look too much like your father, the scoundrel. Dark hair. What Powell would wish to have such dark hair? As black as sin, your unruly mane. Chop it off. All of it."

Aidan ignored the man's ramblings as he set about building up the fire again. He jumped when he felt the stick strike his back.

"Impertinent fellow, turning his back to me, ignoring my words as if he were my equal. What do you think, boy? You think you're something special, do you?"

"No, sir." Aidan ignored the throbbing pain where he'd been struck, and repaired the blaze. "Shall I see to your supper, sir?"

"'Shall I see to your supper,' he says. What, you haven't begun it already? Should have been done hours ago."

Aidan wished to argue that he only had one set of arms and one set of legs, but he was not a fool. In truth, the maid had told him she would see to the dinner preparations. He ought to have known better than to trust her.

Hurrying out of the room before he could suffer another whack with the stick, Aidan did not watch where he was going and walked right into a late courier who was sniffing about the entry hall. When the funny-looking man spied Aidan, he straightened up at once and put on an air of self-importance. "Where is the lord of the manor?"

"You make it your business, sir, breaking into this house and demanding to see the master of the manor?"

The man frowned and looked down his nose at Aidan. "Is the master in or is he not?" He waved around the piece of correspondence, lily-white parchment with a black wax seal closing it at the fold. "Mr. Dewhurst requires an immediate answer."

"What does that old fool want?"

That earned him a clap on the ear. "You scamp! Such cheek. Such nerve. I ought to—"

"I shall bring the lord of the manor the letter, unless you wish to be met by a drunken Mr. Powell in all his wrath."

The man peered around Aidan, who stood his ground. Eyes narrowed, the self-important delivery boy bent down to Aidan's level. "You speak so of your master?"

Aidan laughed without humor. "Master? In faith, I hope not. Shall I have the letter, or shall I not? I've a many good things to do, and—"

"Mr. Dewhurst expects a reply."

"Does he, now?"

"Your master owes my master quite the sum. S'put my master in a terrible mood."

That made no sense. Mr. Dewhurst loved it when people owed him money, especially Aidan's uncle. Before he could snatch the letter from the man's hand, a loud, drunken grunt sounded behind him.

"What's takin' the fool boy so long? Got lost on his way to the kitchen."

Aidan tensed. He should have been paying better attention to the man's location. In truth, the messenger had thrown off his sense of where things – and people – were in the house. "Uncle, I—"

"Who's this? Collectors? I haven't any money, take the boy, if you must, but I haven't a penny to my name."

Aidan had the pleasure of watching his uncle turn ashen gray, spittle spraying from his jowly cheeks as he prepared to plead his debt away.

"I've, er, a message for you, milord. From Mr. Dewhurst."

That caused the man's spine to straighten considerably. "Dewhurst? What does that old sot want?" The old man sneezed.

The messenger, who had already been baptized with a wave of spit, took a quick step back. "My master said you owed him."

"Owe Dewhurst? I've paid him back in full." The drunken man laughed heartily, and staggered into Aidan. "Tell that old wart that he's remembering wrong."

Now the messenger fidgeted and went rather pale. "Sir? My master said that on pain of unemployment I should deliver this message to you and not leave until I had a reply." The letter passed by Aidan, so close he could have snatched it, but of course he didn't. His uncle received the missive instead, snapped open *the seal and read. And as he read, his expression went from merry to somber, to contemplative.* "Boy, fetch me my writing kit."

Aidan turned to go, but was caught mid-stride. "Sir?"

"No, no. Just go to Dewhurst yourself."

That made no sense. "And what should I tell him?"

"Tell him," *said Powell, tearing the letter into pieces,* "that I send my regards and my nephew, and if he's too stupid to figure out the answer for himself, then he deserves everything that's coming to him."

Aidan's sense of dread increased, and he found himself arguing for reasons to remain on the estate that night. "You haven't had your supper."

"Cook can deal with it."

"We had to let Cook go last week."

"Then Thomas will deal with it."

"Thomas doesn't know how to cook."

That drew the ire out in the old man. Swinging his cane, he drove both Aidan and the courier out the front door, swearing and spitting until, at last, he shut and bolted the door behind the pair of them.

If Aidan didn't know any better, he would say that his uncle had taken to singing sea shanties behind the closed door. "Well, that was not in character." *He made for the front gate, where he expected to see a saddled horse waiting. When he found none, he turned to the messenger.* "You came on foot?"

The man laughed. "'Course I came on foot. A servant's not worth wasting a steed on."

"Right." *Aidan was liking this less and less by the moment. But Dewhurst's manor was not far. Aidan would reach the place within the half hour, provided he was not waylaid by highwaymen.*

"Mr. Aidan? You awake?"

Aidan opened his mouth to respond that, yes, he was awake. But instead he turned to the messenger and said the words he knew would seal his destiny: "I'll take the back road, then. No need to show me the way."

"All right. I've got some business to attend to at the local pub. Just be sure to see yourself in the back door. It's the staff's night out, so no one will be there but my master and his missus."

"Mr. Aidan, you're dreamin'." Someone shook his shoulder.

His shoulder had grown cold again, so cold that it prickled and burned. All was dark, and he opened his eyes to find himself full-grown, sitting in a strange inn at the end of a hall, with Slaíne staring down at him.

"Where am I?"

"You was sleepin', sir. Ought I not have wakened you?"

He blinked the sleep from his eyes, the memory of the dream clinging to the backs of his eyelids. It had seemed so real! Well, it was real; it had, in fact, happened, nigh nineteen years past. He closed his eyes again and pressed his palms against his closed lids. "No, you're fine. I just – I just was dreaming strange things. Perhaps it is good that you woke…me." His eyes had popped open and he was staring at someone who was Slaíne and yet was not Slaíne.

Where there had been dirt and muck, there was clean skin the color of milk, never mind a few smatterings of orange freckles that made her look like she was flushed. Her hair, once tangled and matted, was wavier than he had first thought it, and not as auburn. And though she was back in the filthy clothing of a boy, somehow she did not look so masculine.

Idiot, stop staring. Before he could make a total fool of himself, Aidan got to his feet and pretended to see something over her shoulder.

Slaíne's gaze followed his, curious. A maid wandered past at that moment, giving Aidan the excuse to pay attention to something else. "Excuse me? Miss? What might the hour be?"

The maid gave him a look of utmost contempt. "I reckon it's about dusk, sir." She shrugged. "Might be earlier. Might be later." And with that, she hoisted her broom over her shoulder, turned, and headed down the remainder of the hall.

"Somethin' wrong, sir?" Slaíne asked.

Yes, something was very wrong. Next time he saw that wretch of a seer, he'd give her a good verbal thrashing, putting Slaíne and him in this situation. What would people think, now that she was so obviously not a boy? Not that she had ever looked like a boy, not really. This could ruin more reputations than one.

"There's more water, if'n you need," she offered, her brow crinkled with worry. "Don't think the water's all that filthy."

Aidan nodded. "Right. Well, I just— Oh, for the sake of all, I almost forgot." With a quick look around, he concentrated for a moment, then Summoned the parcels he had asked her to purchase earlier. If he was to ruin them, he might as well do the job thoroughly.

Slaíne's eyes popped. "Er, that's all right."

"If you don't want them, perhaps our all-knowing friend might be interested...." The words were scarce out of his mouth before Slaíne snatched the dressmaker's boxes from him.

She smirked and flushed. "Don't think these are quite her color."

Aidan nodded solemnly, his lips twitching in spite of himself. "Of course."

Slaíne laughed, a forced sound, before turning on her heel and returning to the rented room. The door slammed shut behind her, and Aidan swore he heard the bolt being thrown not long after.

While waiting, he did not sit down this time. He did not wish to return to that strange memory or dream, or whatever it had been. It was at least the third occurrence since the nymph queen stabbed him in the shoulder with that ice-cold blade. The thought of the weapon alone made Aidan shiver and rub the invisible wound.

The creature had inflicted it moments before her death. Were they that spiteful, those creatures of light? She could have struck him to kill, right through the heart, he had been vulnerable to her attack. But it seemed almost as though she had chosen to merely wound him...for what reason, though? The more he thought on it, the less spite seemed likely. She had known what her weapon would do to him, dredging up vivid images of the past; that much was obvious. Was it a warning? Maybe it was a gift, though Aidan could see no merit to it, other than tormenting him further.

He had thus far not dreamt of the biggest trauma of his life, merely skirting around the corners of the memory. He hoped he never would re-encounter the shock that had jolted him. "Jolted," Aidan murmured. The word dredged up yet another memory. Where had he heard that word recently?

The answer came to him easily enough: someone had said it in his first vision from the past. But who and why? The more he tried to home in on those details, the farther they seemed to flit away from his reach, and the more his mind wandered in opposite directions. He thought of the first vision – or had it been the second? – where the little girl had seen him through the Seeing Pool. Had that been a trick of Meraude? He thought not. It must have to do with the icy wound.

And thinking of the little girl was when he realized that he knew who that little girl was. In fact, he knew not only who she was, he knew exactly *where* she was.

Aidan shot forward, cursing, and began pounding on the seer's door. "Seer!"

"Go away, milord. It's time for the bats to be about."

"I know who you are."

A pause. "Well, good for you."

Aidan stopped pounding for a moment, then resumed when he felt her Pull moving back toward the bed. "Open this door or...."

"Or you'll what?" she said. "Make a bigger scene than what you've already made? Go to bed, sir. We'll discuss your impeccable memory in the morning."

Heads popped out from different rooms, and shouts and jeers were thrown at him, along with bits of trash. "Pardon," he offered a half-dressed man who was giving him the eye of death. Once he was certain the inn guests had returned to their activities, Aidan leaned into the door. "Why didn't you tell me we'd seen each other before?"

Footsteps hesitated on the floorboards, and the Pull came nearer. "What are you on about?"

Aidan pressed the words delicately through the door. "If you knew it was I you'd seen in the Seeing Pool as a child, why didn't you say?"

There was a long sigh, and the door opened a fraction. "Would it have made any difference? More likely it would have muddied the future. Besides, life has a way of unfolding. Best let it, milord. Best let things that are meant to be, be."

"You tried to kill me, after knowing I was...." He was what? He could not even finish the thought. She had helped him once, her as a child in the past, him as an adult in the present.

"As much ill as you think of me, I did not relish the thought of another one of the Blest being murdered. Too few of us left."

Aidan let out a low breath. "Us? So you were one of the children? You are one of the Bl—"

The crack widened, but not by much. "What of it?" She seemed even older now, more tired.

"When you said you are no fortune-teller...."

"And one I am not. Seer's a fun title, but it does not make up for what the Circle has done – and Meraude, in her turn. Now, before you go telling all of the world our secrets, be mindful. It is no coincidence that the goblins found you and then the nymphs. You've got a mark on you, one that won't wash off. Don't go attracting any more attention. We're easy enough to find as it is."

Aidan opened his mouth to say something, though he could not think what, so he closed it at once.

The woman, Larkin, gave him a knowing smile. "That's better. We'll discuss our next course of action in the morning. Until then, I suggest you stay in your room, the both of you."

Aidan nodded. He did not know what to make of this woman. He needed time to think, to clear his head. What he really needed was a walk out in the wild, with no Pulls but nature's to contend with.

She shook her head. "You know as well as anyone what would happen to her if you up and left in the night."

"I wasn't going to—" Oh, what was the use? She'd seen what she had seen; perhaps there was a version of him in the near future that abandoned them both, the girl and the seer. He wasn't sure how Larkin's ability worked.

The woman nodded. "Good. I haven't seen much, but you need to keep your door bolted. No matter what you hear in the square. Tonight, your focus needs to remain on the Goblets." She nodded and muttered to herself and, hands shaking, she slammed the door in his face and took her own advice by bolting it. There was a terrible wail on the other side of the door, and the floorboards crunched as the strange woman's Pull moved away.

He raised his fist one more time to knock and ask if she was all right, but he thought better of it and turned back to his own quarters. The door was still shut, and he dared not try the handle. Distraught and confused, Aidan turned and moved back toward the chair. That is when Slaíne's Pull slackened and the bolt was thrown open. No one emerged. The Pull retreated, back toward the solid mass whose Pull must be the bed.

Frowning, Aidan approached the door with a soft tread and rapped gently on the doorframe. "Slaíne? Mightn't I—"

"Door's unlocked, sir."

He pushed the door open. It groaned on its hinges, and Aidan heard a few muttered complaints from their neighbors. He shut and bolted the door. When he turned around, Slaíne was in the small bed, her back to him.

Upon quick examination, Aidan found that there was a blanket and a pillow sitting on the chair near the fireplace, which was now crackling merrily. He looked over at the tub of water, which was murky and tepid to the touch. It would be easy enough to Dismiss the dirt and oils from it. Perhaps he would…in the morning, and without the girl there, of course. Now all he wanted was to lie down and sleep

With a soft grunt, he placed the pillow down on the floor and settled down on the small area rug before the blaze. He covered himself with the blanket, noticing she had left him the thicker one. The gesture wormed its way into his heart, and he tried very hard to think of something other than the warmth spreading through his chest.

As he settled, sleep crept up on him, drawing him into a dreamless rest. And resting on the edge of unconsciousness, he heard a soft voice singing.

> *"A gent had me soft heart in his pocket*
> *Tiddily do tra la day*
> *A gent had me poor heart in his pocket*
> *O it bled, and he did not do nothin'*
> *Woe, woe, tiddle do tra la day*
>
> *O me heart, he reft it in three small parts*
> *Tiddily do tra la lee*
> *O me heart, left berefted and wasted*
> *Bled dry as paper, no love left for me*
> *Tiddily do tra la la lee."*

★   ★   ★

Aidan woke from his sleep feeling rested and untroubled. But the world, he observed upon rising to his feet, was still dark. With no frame of reference other than the sky, Aidan moved to the window, saw the waning moon on its decline, and guessed it to be two in the morning.

A glance at Slaíne, and he was reassured that he had not been too noisy in his movements. She must have grown overheated during the night, for her coverlets were thrown over, revealing the greenish yellow of her long-sleeved day dress.

He squinted in the darkness, looking around for the boxes. They were piled on the floor next to the dresser. Curiosity got the better of him, and he approached them as he would a sleeping beast. With one look over his shoulder, he was at ease that Slaíne was good and truly asleep, and he pulled back the brown wrappings of the dressmaker's boxes.

One dress was blue, the other a deep green. *What am I doing?* he wondered to himself. He'd given her the money, asked her to buy herself dresses; did he think she would cheat him? What had he been expecting to find? Frivolities? He knew little of the girl, and yet…and yet he knew without a doubt that she would never swindle him. Desiring to no longer explore his intentions or feelings brought on by his sneaking, Aidan moved back to the window.

When he looked out, he noted there was more activity in the square than had been there before. The dresses forgotten, he watched as people took to running. Some poured out of the inn. Their footfalls and grumblings echoed below. Aidan felt the men's Pulls. Yes, they were all men; he could just make out their attire in the lamplight. But why the mob? He closed his eyes and felt for others. It was in that moment, when he realized each man was carrying something, that the shouting began.

Instinct took over as he Dismissed his belongings and hastily tugged on his boots. He tucked his one bronze dagger in its sheath before Summoning his copper dagger and sidling up to the door. He listened.

Slaíne stirred and mumbled something unintelligible before sitting bolt upright in bed. "What's that noise?"

Aidan held up a finger for her to be quiet.

Men were still shouting, hasty footsteps were falling, and the sounds of chaos filled the night. Aidan moved to the window again. The mob had scattered, and men clothed in black filled the square. "Bandits," he said, watching as the pillaging began.

"Bandits?" Slaíne didn't sound afraid as he might have expected; rather, she sounded annoyed.

There was a firm rapping on his door. "Arm yourself! The wraiths are here."

Aidan sheathed the dagger and Summoned the sword. Wraiths? Were there such things? If so, there was no fighting them. Feeling as though he was forgetting something crucial, he unbolted the door.

"Sir, don't," the girl said. "You can nay go out there."

He smirked over his shoulder at her. "Nothing's going to happen to me."

Her frown deepened. "Aye, there will. If there ain't no one to watch out for you." She stumbled out of bed and rubbed her eyes. "Right. Where's my sword?"

Aidan shook his head. "No, you are to stay here."

"But the curse—"

"I won't go that far."

Slaíne raised her eyebrows. "Sir, what if you don't have no choice?"

That was complicating things. He was wasting precious time where he could be helping. Even now the harbinger was running down the hall, banging on doors for a second time. It was all Aidan could do to remain there, calmly discussing how to go about this. "What is to be done?"

"Bring me or don't go. Not that hard, actually."

Aidan groaned. "If I don't go down there, men might die. I have—"

"Abilities, yes. Ones you don't want to go flaunting."

Aidan bristled. "I never flaunt them."

Slaíne gave him a hard stare. "Never said that. We're wasting time." She made a move toward him, the dress slipping and pooling around her legs in the moonlight. There she stood in her underthings, scowling. "Curses."

It took a moment for Aidan to regain his wits and look away. "See? You are in no position to fight."

"I'll just wear my old clothes."

This was going badly. Shouts had been taken up in the distance, and the town's warning bell tolled. Every second he wasted here might cost someone their life. But taking her with him was out of the question. "No, you are staying here."

"But—"

"That is an order, Slaíne."

She recoiled from the words as though they had bitten her. "So, it's still this?"

"Slaíne…." Whatever he was going to say, he knew it would not be enough. She'd never been his to order about; he'd never seen her that way. And yet, here he was, abusing her to save her. He shut the door and threw the bolt. With men yelling for aid, he ignored them. He was a fool. A blasted fool. "What would happen if I went out of bounds?" Aidan wanted to make sure. He needed to know, if he were to have an easy conscience.

The girl scowled and would not look him in the eye. "Don't know what you mean."

Aidan took a deep breath and tried again. "If you'd run off any farther that day or if I had left you lying there, what would have happened?"

The bell tolled again, footsteps thundered down the halls. And yet he stayed, waiting for her answer. When she did not offer one, he approached.

"I want to do the right thing." When he reached out his hands to take her by the shoulders, Slaíne stumbled away from him. He froze.

"What do it matter?"

"Don't be petulant."

Her gaze met his, but there was no spirit in her eyes. When she spoke, it was in monotone, as if she had recited it time and time again before. "The terms of the curse would have been broken beyond mendin'."

"And the consequences?"

She looked away and shrugged. "No more pain, at least."

He stiffened. So, it was as he had expected. If he, in his haste, had left her alone and strayed outside the bounds of the curse's limits, Slaíne would have died. How close he had come to possibly killing her!

For an eternity they stood there, the first sounds of battle clashing outside their window. The seer had been right; Aidan should never have even undone the bolt. With a sigh, he ran a hand through his hair and turned back to the fire. "You'd best find a way to, er, fasten that – your, gown. It needs doing up in the back, I assume." And hating himself most fiercely, ignoring the Pulls without and the guilt within, Aidan Dismissed the sword, settled back down by the fire and prepared himself for a dreadful daybreak.

Her Pull moved closer then stopped. How did she tread so noiselessly? "That's it, then?"

"Please, go back to sleep…I mean, if you wish to."

Slaíne moved back toward the window, and when she spoke, her voice was tighter than a fiddle string. "We're not going to help them?"

"I'm going to wait this out and see what comes tomorrow."

She murmured something and clambered back to the fire. For a moment there was a respite from all the shouting and clashing weapons; perhaps the town folk had managed to drive these wraiths, or whatever they might be, away.

She spoke. "I want my sword."

Aidan Summoned it again and set it on the floor next to him. "There. If that makes you feel safer."

Slaíne snorted. "I want to help."

"I know."

"*You* want to help."

He was silent. "I've changed my mind."

"Changed my mind, he says. Liar."

Aidan rolled over into a ray of moonlight. She hadn't taken the weapon. "Slaíne, this is not our fight." He hated himself for saying it, but she'd made him realize how hasty he'd been to act.

"You don't believe that."

He looked up at her. Slaíne had pulled her dress back up and was holding it closed with one hand behind her back. "Slaíne, you have said it yourself. What if we became separated?"

"Don't—"

"Please, let me finish. If we became separated, the curse would strike you down. I will not live with that. I'm not stopping you from going down there and fighting."

"Aye, but you are. Not goin' is as good as sayin' I mustn't."

Aidan groaned and rolled over again. The world outside had grown eerily quiet. He could no longer feel all the Pulls he had sensed earlier. Perhaps the villagers really had rallied and managed to drive the nuisances away. "Can we not have this conversation? Please?"

"I won't let them people die, just 'cause of some stupid curse. If'n we don't help, it's on me. My fault."

That brought Aidan to his feet. In a flash he was in front of her, in her space. "Don't. Ever. Say that." He was angry. Nay, furious. But not at her; it would never be her fault...never if they lived for another ninety years would it be on her.

She mistook his anger and quick movements and threw up her hands to shield herself. But, as a credit to her bravery, she stood there, ready to take whatever she thought he was about to deal on her.

Realizing his mistake, Aidan put gentle hands on her wrists and pulled her arms away from her face. He attempted a weak smile when she would look at him, and placed a chaste kiss on her brow. "Please, let me worry about blame. Try to rest." When she didn't move, he put a finger beneath her chin and tilted her face up to look at him. "They'll be all right. I can already feel the enemy Pulls retreating."

Slaíne seemed to drink in his words like a dying plant, her eyes glassy as one mesmerized. Outside, the returning shouts of victory broke the spell, and her gaze moved away again.

Aidan released her and took a few steps back. "Good night, Slaíne."

She turned her back to him and returned to bed. "'Night, sir."

CHAPTER TWELVE

The next morning, Aidan awoke feeling as though he had sleepwalked a thousand miles. His sleep had been undisturbed by any dream, for which he was very grateful, but he was weary to the bone. For a moment, he thought of lying back down, but he heard Sláine moving about, and he knew she would desire to have the room to herself for a while.

After freshening up – as best he could, all things considered – Aidan went downstairs, took care of some personal business, and went to see about ordering his company's breakfast. Glares met his quick gaze, and the innkeeper's wife was even less friendly than the previous night. He knew the cause. No surprise, really, he thought. There was whispering, and a few marked-up faces turned away at the sight of him.

Ignoring all this, Aidan returned to his room, and heard two voices within.

"Hold still," said the seer.

"Let go," Sláine snarled.

Aidan was seized with fear and tried the door handle, but the door was bolted. "What's going on in there?"

"Not now, milord. There's a wild beast to be tamed."

Aidan frowned before clarity dawned on him. "Tell the beast that breakfast should be ready within the half-hour."

"Won't take nearly that long – if she would only quit squirming. It's gotta be tighter, girl. Quit your fidgeting."

A grunt. "Nay. Not that tight," Sláine said with a startled gasp. "You *are* a witch! You got me hair in the laces."

Suppressing laughter, Aidan left the two shouting at each other and went to the chair at the end of the hall. As Larkin had said, it only took another ten minutes to do what she could with Sláine's dress. Soon the seer stormed out of the room, wringing her hands. "So many tangles! She never brushes that crazy mane of hers."

Aidan mashed his lips together before he could smile or chuckle at the agitated seer. The seer was a seer, though, and she gave him a shrewd look.

"And don't look at me like that, milord. Hair is a very serious business." She shuddered. "Well, at least, to most decent people."

"Heard that," Sláine shouted through the keyhole.

Aidan leaned against the door frame and regarded the older woman. "You look tired."

She scowled. "Never, Mr. *Powell*, comment on a lady's appearance other than to praise it to the heavens." The woman straightened out her skirt and glared at a large stain. But she did look tired. Exhausted, even.

Aidan sought to seek the reason whilst smoothing things over. He began with caution. "Forgive me, madam. I was out of place. I merely meant that last night was difficult for all of us. I assumed you had as much trouble sleeping as I did." There. If that would not do, nothing he could say would.

Larkin narrowed her eyes at him. "Stayed in your room last night, did you?"

He winced. "Mostly."

She scoffed. "'Mostly', he says. One does not mostly do much of any single thing. I mostly died. I mostly cut off my hand."

Aidan raised his eyebrows. "One could mostly cut off their hand...."

"Oh, you rascal. I saw—" Her eyes grew distant and she clamped her mouth shut.

"Did you see the row I had?" Aidan asked.

"See? No. Heard? Yes."

Aidan groaned. "I didn't know I was being that loud. Forgive me."

"Nay, not I to forgive. Ask her. She's the one that you wronged."

That did not sit well. The words chaffed at Aidan, and he shook his head. "I did nothing other than what I thought to be right."

The seer regarded him again with one of her cold, piercing looks. "Trust her." Before Aidan could answer that he did – mostly – Larkin cut him off. "Tonight, when the wraiths return, take her with you."

Aidan shook his head. "No."

"You might be surprised."

"Absolutely not."

The woman's shoulders heaved and she smiled. "She does have the sword."

"Yes, but a sword does not a swordsman make."

Larkin laughed. "She might be better than you at it. Do not judge before you've seen."

"If something happened to her—"

"Pssh! It would no more be your fault than if I crossed the road and was run over by a stray apple wagon. You can't save us all, milord."

Aidan clenched and unclenched his jaw. This was not the conversation he wanted to be having this early in the morning, if ever. "You changed the subject on me. What happened last night when I left you? I heard—"

"No decent man would listen at keyholes and then repeat what he heard."

The door behind Aidan creaked open. "Heard what?"

Aidan moved out of the way, and Slaíne brushed past him. She still wore the yellow dress, though the light gave her face a better color. It was more flattering than he had realized in the dimness of the night previous. He cleared his throat as if to speak, then thought better of it.

The seer raised her brows at him, though Slaíne was mercifully unaware. "Are we on the road today? I 'spect we'd be wanting to find the grave."

Larkin shushed her. "No, today is not the day to try for it. We need a strategy, in case we encounter any foe. Not to mention that none of us has a clue as to the location. We'll need a map. We'll need a certain Lord Dewhurst for that. He has a map, though I doubt he understands how to read it. We'll take that somehow."

"Good luck with that," Aidan muttered. The women looked at him, and he raised his hands. "Your old master has a map. Perhaps others have a copy as well."

The seer was already shaking her head and finger at him. "Let us speak of it here no longer. We'll talk over matters at the appointed hour. But for now, milor— All right, *Mr. Powell*, you could do with, er, some—"

Slaíne sniffed. "Yes, he does kind of stink, don't he?"

Aidan laughed. "Is that all?"

"Men," Larkin said, taking Slaíne by the arm and leading her down the remainder of the hall. "Don't take too long, breakfast is in twenty."

"I know," said Aidan, amused. "'Twas I that told you."

But they were already gone.

Aidan cursed and returned to the room and bolted the door behind him. The water, as he expected, was freezing, but he thought it unreasonable to ask the servants to empty the bath and heat more water for him. So he Dismissed the filth from the tub, stripped down, and took a quick, brisk bath.

Once he'd finished, he had nothing to dry off with, and was forced to return to his own filthy clothing. But, after a little concentration, he was able to Dismiss the worst of the grime and dried sweat away, making the clothing more presentable and less offensive to the ladies' sense of smell.

After he'd done that, to his surprise and relief, he found a shaving kit lying on the dressing table. He hadn't had a good shave in – well, since visiting his hometown and Tristram.

As he lathered up, Aidan thought of his old friend. He'd been putting off thoughts of the traitor for a while now, but the scraping of the blade against his skin brought the memory of pooling blood in an inkwell.

How stupid he had been to put his friend in the position to do something like that. And how stupid was he now, letting the seer into his circle. Aidan did not wish a circle. He did not need a circle, and yet here he was.

"I need to get rid of her," he muttered to himself. He knew that the seer could not be trusted. She had proven that during their first meeting. "She hasn't tried anything yet," he told his reflection. The blade was dull, and the shave was not as close as he would have liked. Aidan grumbled and went over his face a second time.

It was true: Larkin had not tried anything yet. But just because she'd been acting under a master's orders before, it didn't make her any more reliable. And that was another matter: *Had* she been acting under orders to distract Aidan so Dewhurst could capture him? And if so, what was to stop her from lying about being under those same orders still? He did not think she would try anything at the moment; for whatever reason, she wanted help reaching old Cedric's grave. She would not be the first person to ask for Aidan's help in that matter.

"Meraude," he muttered, splashing his face with cold water. If either Lord Dewhurst or that witch wished for the Goblet, it was best to make certain that neither got hold of it. He could refuse Meraude, since she had no idea of his current location and had no longer contacted him by way of the Seeing Pool. But the seer. She could see things before they happened. But how much? Would she know he planned on leading her in circles away from where he suspected the Goblet to be? Even now, she could be sitting down there, watching the future shaping before her very eyes…if that was how it worked. Somehow, Aidan doubted it.

Well, there was nothing to be done about it at the moment. He dried his face, threw on his vest, and went down for breakfast. For a moment, he panicked, feeling so many Pulls, and none of their owners looking any friendlier at him than they had earlier. Some of the men outright pointed and snarled their disdain at him.

"Coward," one muttered.

Aidan let no emotion show on his face and made for the private room where they'd dined the night previous. The seer was sitting at the table, smoking a pipe and prattling on about some nonsense. She seemed rather pleased about something, but stopped talking when she noticed that Aidan was standing there in the doorway.

Slaíne, on the hand, was worrying her lip and wouldn't look Aidan in the eye. This did not bode well. The last thing he needed was a mischief-maker on his hands, and he suspected the seer was just that.

"What's this?" Aidan said, trying to keep his voice even.

Larkin laughed like a drowning bird through a mouthful of smoke. He thought she rather looked like a dragon in that moment, and suddenly wished for the silver sword. But the fancy passed without either seer or Slaíne noticing anything awry.

"What's so amusing?"

"Nothing's amusing, sir. We're – that is, I am worried." She shot a look at the seer, who shrugged.

Aidan crossed his arms over his chest. "I can see that you are worried. What has you so?"

"Them out there, they're saying right horrible things about you."

It felt as though a millstone had been lifted from around his neck. He actually chuckled. "Is that all?"

Slaíne's brow puckered. "But they called you a – well, a…." She shied away from the word. He would not.

"Coward," Aidan finished for her.

It was the seer's turn again to laugh. "See, miss? Our man doesn't care what others say or think of him. The only opinion of himself that he cares about is his own."

Aidan rubbed his shoulder, which prickled with painful coldness. "When I sort out whether that was meant as a compliment or an insult, I'll respond appropriately. Where is breakfast? I ordered it to be here nigh thirty minutes ago."

The girl managed to meet his eye that time. "Madam had to re-order it."

That rose Aidan's brows. "Whatever for?"

"The innkeeper's wife, she doesn't like you much." The seer winked at him. "I told you not to get on her bad side."

Aidan swore before remembering he was in the company of women. "Forgive me."

"Oh, don't worry; I say a lot worse than that." And with that, Slaíne turned back to the fire and fiddled with the poker.

He chose to ignore that comment. Instead of responding, he sat down and poured himself a cup of cider, felt for any strange Pulls, found none, and drank deeply.

"Your own fault, milord, for not fighting last night. All of the able-bodied men, stranger and local alike, took arms against the sea of wraiths and drove them bravely away into the night." She smirked. "Or, so they tell it. More likely the wraiths realized they were outnumbered and went to gather stronger numbers. Give me some of that. Yes." She, too, poured herself a glass of cider and drank deeply. "Will you fight tonight?"

"Firstly, you told me to stay indoors last night. Secondly, who says they'll return?"

"The woman who knows, that's who."

That did not sit well with Aidan. He did not wish to remain here another night. The sooner he could get rid of the seer, the better. "What was your vision about last night?"

The woman coughed on her own smoke. She sat there wheezing and thumping a fist to her chest before she was able to quit, and then stared up at Aidan with watery eyes. "What makes you say I had one?"

Aidan gave her a wry smile. "Because you said your visions came with a cost, and I assume, judging from the wretched pain you sounded to be in, that the cost was paid last night for another one."

Larkin did not regard him with a friendly eye as she took a calming sip of cider and put her pipe out. She tucked the instrument back in her pouch. Grimacing, she shook her head. "It was all nonsense, really. And don't feel smart for figuring out my curse that easily. Each of us that's Blest has got some price to pay for it, Lord Ingledark. You know as well as any."

There was a loud crash, which caused Aidan to jump and turn to Sláine. The seer, not surprisingly, had not moved an inch but took to picking at her nails.

"What's wrong?"

"Nothin'," Sláine said, though her brow was creased. "Just knocked over my chair. Clumsy today, I am." She righted the furniture and sat down on it.

Aidan decided to not look at her a moment longer than was necessary, and took a seat of his own. "Right, so. You say Lord Dewhurst has a map."

The seer favored him with a curt nod. "The one which you believe is impossible to get. You who can Summon and Dismiss at will."

Aidan shook his head. "You do not know how my particular brand of magic works."

"Then enlighten us."

He gave Sláine a sideways glance, and was surprised to find her still pensive. But he ignored her discomfiture and began an explanation of his own abilities. "In order to get rid of something, I have to Recognize it." He paused. "Say I wanted to Dismiss a chair in the next room here in this inn. I could concentrate, find a Pull, but if I didn't have a line of sight and have never explored that chair's Pull before, I might Dismiss only part of it, or something else entirely."

Through this explanation, the seer nodded and continued picking at her nails. When he paused, she looked up. "Go on."

"Well, say you could get me within half a mile of the map, I wouldn't be able to Call or Dismiss and then Summon it to myself. I don't know its Pull, follow?"

"It's not familiar," Sláine chimed in.

Aidan afforded her a small nod, but his gaze returned at once to Larkin, who was smirking. "What? You have some solution to this problem?"

"No, I just like the thought of you getting your revenge."

That caught him off guard. "What do I need revenge for?"

"For what Lord Dewhurst did to you and your reputation, that's what." She turned to Slaíne. "Didn't he tell you why he's a wanted man?"

Aidan raked a hand back through his hair and drained his cup. This woman. The nerve, suggesting that he need to avenge himself against the dandy. Yes, the idea was tempting. But that he would actually take the law into his own hands? The thought was ridiculous. He said as much, and the woman laughed in his face.

"Get the map, Lord Ingledark. Do to that fiend what he would have done to you, had you not run fast enough. Take back what is rightfully yours."

"What's she sayin', Mr. Aidan?"

"It doesn't matter, Slaíne. Seer, I have no taste for vengeance. If you, on the other hand, have need of it, I won't stand in your way." They were silent then, the three of them, for Aidan motioned for them to be so; there were several Pulls at the door, familiar Pulls from yesterday. "Just the servants bringing breakfast." They all let out a collective breath of relief and went back to their previous occupations.

After the servants had laid down their wares – plates full of potato hash, ham, wheat cakes, and honey – they left, and Aidan could feel that they were out of eavesdropping range. The three continued their conversation.

It was Larkin who first spoke again. "Fine. The girl will cause a distraction, you will get into the house and retrieve the map, and I will deal with his so-called lordship. Sound like a good plan to you?"

Aidan had no intention of following her plan, but he did not offer his dissent. Instead, he scratched at his chin and looked thoughtful before answering with, "Let me think on it. I am not entirely certain that is the best course of action at the moment."

The seer eyed him curiously, but let the matter slip. "Right. Now, why are we letting this fantastic feast grow cold before our very ravenous eyes? Let's tuck in."

★　　★　　★

Later that day, while the seer took a rest after complaining of a headache, Aidan Dismissed all of their belongings and took Slaíne out into the town square. They passed hagglers who called out to them, pushing their wares, some getting in Slaíne's face and demanding she try on such and such a necklace or brooch.

Aidan smirked. Slaíne pushed on, ignoring the hawkers. "Rude," she said, far from sounding or looking flattered.

They walked in silence until they neared the edge of town. That was when Aidan turned to Slaíne and said, "Let's walk a little farther, shall we?"

She raised her eyebrows at the words, frowned, but followed him down a small lane. "What's the matter?" They came to a standstill next to a small garden, whose keeper watched them with consternation. That would not do.

Aidan gave the man a rueful smile and led Slaíne further still, behind houses, through hanging laundry, until they emerged on a side road. "Forgive me, I wanted to make certain we weren't being followed."

"Who'd want to follow us?"

He gave her a pointed look.

"You mean you didn't want the seer to see where we was going?" She worried her lip for a moment. "Won't she, you know, know anyway? She's got that talent, after all."

He shrugged. "I wanted this at least said without her within hearing distance." Aidan looked around again before getting to the meat of the matter. "She probably already knows that I do not trust her."

Slaíne snorted and stopped when he gave her a funny look. "'S obvious."

"Right. Anyway, I fear she means to lead me into another trap."

That startled her. "She ain't said anything that made me worry about that. But you're the one what's got history with her."

"I am not willing to place my life in the hands of someone who has already betrayed me. That is why I propose we form our own plans."

She looked at him, amazed for a while.

He wondered what he'd said to shock her so.

"You want my opinion?" she asked.

He nodded. "Of course."

Slaíne went quiet for a moment, her brow wrinkling. "No one's asked my opinion before."

Aidan waited patiently for as long he dared allow, feeling all the while for Pulls, and keeping a sense out for Larkin's Pull in particular. Her Pull, mercifully, was nowhere to be found in the near vicinity. If he concentrated hard enough, Aidan was certain he'd be able to find it back at the inn.

"How can one make plans without a seer knowing?"

"I don't think her foreknowledge works how you believe. If she is one of the Blest, like me, then maybe her ability has its limitations. I can only Summon and Call what I can recognize or what feels familiar. Perhaps she can only see what concerns her directly."

"Then why find us? She must've used her abilities to cross our paths, and we nay concern her direct-like."

"But we do concern her directly. Because she *chose* to see us. If my theory is a correct one, she was sent to find us. But if we were to bring in a third party, one that we would make certain had no direct contact with her...."

Slaíne's brow furrowed further. "I don't know, sir. It would be a risk."

"Agreed."

"What would this third party of yours do?"

"They would be waiting to rescue us, should anything ill befall you or me. There is no way to know for certain. The risk would be finding a person we could trust, and also trust that our all-knowing friend is not all-knowing." He sighed and felt the weight of their situation rest on his shoulders. Perhaps it had been a fool's errand, walking out here, hoping to share some of the burden. Slaíne seemed to still be in the master-slave mindset, and he felt true pity for her. "Anyway, I just wanted you to be aware, should I need to contact anyone or do anything tricky, that I'll need you to be my eyes and ears with Larkin."

The girl nodded, but she did not seem pleased. "All right."

It did not seem possible that Slaíne would betray him, given the nature of her curse, but he decided to make future plans on his own and to only bring her in on them when necessary. "I know she seems...all right, but I don't trust her."

"Then I don't trust her."

Aidan smirked. "Glad to know we're agreed on the matter."

"Always."

He ignored that last remark in favor of feeling for any unwanted

Pulls in the near vicinity. He recognized the seer's right away. She was on the move. "Come," he said, leading Slaíne into the open street. At once they were accosted by more salespeople, the majority of them latching on to Slaíne, whose temper seemed on the rise. Before she could slap a particularly forward apothecary, Aidan stared the man down, using his full height to his advantage. That got the man to back away.

The seer's Pull was leading him away from the main ways. He wondered if she could see him and if that would put him and Slaíne in danger. Just to be certain, he Summoned his dagger when he was certain no one could see him, and tucked it into its sheath on his belt.

He could feel Pulls near the woman, but none of them were familiar. It would be prudent, he decided, to wait for her on the outside of the alley, pretending to look over fruits with Slaíne, who he planned to keep oblivious to his plan. "Fancy a look at peaches?"

"They ain't in season," Slaíne reminded him.

"Right. Strawberries?"

She nodded and they approached the man selling them from the back of a cart. He sold them by four-quart baskets. It would seem, no matter how Slaíne haggled for only three handfuls, then six, then nine, that the salesman would not budge.

Aidan kept the girl and the man talking, pretending to eye some overripe fruit, all the while keeping a sense of where the seer was. She was moving out from the alley, and she carried a lesser Pull with her. So, his ruse had been for naught; the lady merely had acquired some purchases.

When he felt her emerge from the alley fully, Aidan interrupted the haggling.

"We'll take two baskets."

Slaíne looked at him, surprised. She seemed ready to argue, to cite the fact that it would be imprudent to buy so much fruit when it was only the both of them. But she held her tongue.

Even the salesman seemed surprised that an out-of-towner would purchase that much, but he didn't say anything either. Money exchanged hands. Aidan lifted the baskets from the wagon, examined them, put one back for finding a moldy berry toward the bottom, then picked out a more suitable one, and they were on their way.

Aidan smiled sideways at Sláine, knowing she was curious as to what he could mean by this.

"Are you gonna.... You know, tuck them in that place where things go when you...you know?"

Aidan laughed. "Nothingness? No, these berries aren't for us. They're a peace offering."

"Oh." She said nothing more, but Aidan knew she had not been the least enlightened. It was at this moment, when he heard his first name being called, that he allowed himself to turn and acknowledge the seer. She'd been following several paces behind. Her hands, to his surprise, were empty. But there was a weight there, a minute difference from the weight on her person before: an unfamiliar Pull. The woman was concealing something similar to what she'd had on her person before. But what?

"We are returning to the inn for the time being, Larkin. I am glad to see you are on your feet again."

"'Twas the strangest thing," the woman said, joining them. "I had this rather sudden headache, and then it was gone."

Aidan knew that she knew he was skeptical of her. Better to show some of it than to make her think that he suddenly trusted her, which would raise her own suspicions. *Difficult game, this*, he thought. He allowed himself to frown. "A headache?"

"Milord, you would do well to trust someone in this world." Good. She had perhaps taken some of the bait.

"Trust," he replied, "is not something to be doled out like a common good."

Larkin snorted. "True. But if you keep it all to yourself whilst you live, why, that isn't living so much as existing."

That chaffed at Aidan, and he opened his mouth to form a sharp retort. Sláine, however, seemed to scent trouble in the wind, and cut him off.

"You want help carrying them strawberries, sir?"

He hid a smirk to the side. "No, but I thank you, Sláine, for the offer. I would be no gentleman if I allowed you to carry them."

"I ain't no lady, so there's no worryin' there." She laughed, but he would not.

The seer cleared her throat. "You think too meanly of yourself, miss. You fail to take in account your family tree. I wonder...."

That dampened the mood. Aidan could feel spirits sink almost as surely as he could feel Slaíne's Pull tug at him as he got a little too far ahead. Uncomfortable, he stopped and waited for her to catch up.

"What you know of my family? They're dead."

They were in sight of the inn now, and a few men shot Aidan dark looks before slithering away to drink in alleys, or worse. He paid them little mind, leading the ladies, to their obvious surprise, to the servants' entrance at the back of the establishment. They were greeted there by a merry woman with a great ruddy complexion.

"Are you the fine cook whose wares I've had the honor of enjoying?" Aidan asked, setting the baskets at his feet.

The woman batted her lashes. "Oh, stop it. You're makin' me blush, good sir."

Aidan grinned. "I hope this is not too forward, but I saw these delicious strawberries and thought you might have use for them."

The blush deepened. "For the inn? What are you chargin'?"

His smile deepened, and he ignored the incredulous stares the women behind him were surely directing at him. "It's a gift. One for you, one for your good lady. A Mrs. Bostworth, I believe?"

Cook let out a hearty laugh. "You know the way straight to a fat woman's heart: food. Mrs. Bostworth will be right pleased to see these." She leaned in, her flesh stinking of onions and spice. "Don't tell her me said so, but she'd be eyeing the lot of berries since they was wheeled into town."

"I give you my pledge that I shall say not a word of it. Shall I just carry these in for you?" He hoisted the baskets and was prepared to be led into the kitchen, but the cook stopped him in his tracks.

"Nay, Mr. Powell. Ain't proper and you know it." She laughed and took the baskets from him. "I'll send your compliments to the missus."

"Very good of you, ma'am." The deed done, he bowed, Slaíne and the cook curtsied, and they went on their way.

"What was that about?" Slaíne asked, her expression significantly smoothed over since the distressing words from the seer.

"Genius or stupidity," Larkin said with a laugh.

"Sir, you coulda kept them berries in – well, in that place." She'd lowered her voice and gestured around vaguely.

He raised his eyebrows. "Sometimes, Slaíne, allies are more valuable than produce."

They walked on together in silence, re-entering the inn and inquiring after second breakfast, as the seer had a hankering for something more. The kitchen was busy preparing the evening meal and tea, and didn't serve anything hot for the noontide meal, but they were more than welcome to cuts of cold pork and cheese and some fruit. The three agreed to this easily and retired again to the back drawing room, which turned out to be occupied by five men playing whist.

Upon seeing Aidan, two of them looked away, but one outright called Aidan a coward. Aidan shrugged, letting the words roll off him. And he would have been more than happy to ask for the food to be taken to their rooms, as his shoulder had begun prickling again, but Slaíne made a move for the offending man.

"Take that back, you tub o' lard."

"Oi, whatchoo callin' me that for, you vampire?" His companions nickered with laughter at this.

"Slaíne," Aidan warned, taking the girl by the arm. To his surprise, she shrugged him off. "This isn't worth it."

"Yes, Slawn, it ain't worth it," said the "tub o' lard."

"Look 'ere, you toothless ear snout, you bludgeting, blue-faced nit."

The man rose and got back in Slaíne's face, his own growing redder than a plum. "You control your missus, man. Worthless slut."

Before Aidan knew what he was doing, he'd released Slaíne and had taken a fistful of the man's shirt front. "Would you like to say that again?"

The seer tutted. "Men and their quarrels. Worse than old women. Makes one think they've nothing better to do."

"Tell your mother to be quiet," said the dealer in the game. None of the men had risen in defense of their friend, but continued to play their game.

The man Aidan had by the collar was squirming like a worm on a hook. "Gerroff! Gerroff. I meant no harm."

Aidan felt a hand on his arm, and he knew from its Pull that it belonged to Slaíne. Without hesitation, he released the man, who crumpled to the floor, wheezing. "Go back to your game, which I see that you are losing quite successfully at." What was wrong with him? How quickly he had been provoked, and at such a small word. Yet as he thought of what they'd called Sláine, his blood rose to a boil again, and he was forced to brush past the women, ignoring their comments on the ordeal as he thundered up the stairs.

It had been foolish of him to engage in any type of violence. The last thing he needed was the law's attention, especially considering he was wanted in these parts as much as in Breckstone. He'd best steer clear of trouble from here on out. He breathed deeply. Somewhat calmed by his quick jog up the stairs, he pulled out his key and entered his room. He was surprised to find the maid in there. "Miss?" he asked as Sláine and Larkin came up behind him.

"Wha's she doin' in here?" Sláine wondered, none too quietly.

"Cleaning, ma'am," the starch-stiff woman said. Her back was ramrod straight, but her expression had gone from bewildered to belligerent. "'Tis my rightful duty, 'tis."

Aidan felt a headache coming on. "Yes, of course."

"You sure travel light."

Aidan raised his eyebrows. "Miss?"

"There ain't nothing in 'ere." Her tone implied that she did not trust people who carried little with them.

Sláine stepped around Aidan. "A fire burned our house to the ground. What we wear is all we have left."

Larkin sighed. "Does it really matter? It isn't no job of a serving girl to be asking such pointed questions. Now, off with you. Shoo!"

Aidan and Sláine stepped to opposite sides, and the maid hurried out of the room with a great huff.

"Nosy beast." The seer shook her head.

"You didn't know she was in there?"

Larkin scowled at him. "I can't foresee everything. You didn't sense her in there?"

Aidan folded his arms. "Her Pull wasn't particularly strong, so no." He wasn't about to say that he couldn't feel it because Sláine's was tugging at him so hard, he half wondered if she had some control over it and was annoying him on purpose.

The woman stepped inside and looked around the room. "Nothing seems to be missing."

"'Course something's missing. Maids are like that."

That amused Aidan. "You ever steal anything, Sláine?"

She glared at him. "Never was a servant, sir. Just a slave."

"Are we going to discuss what happened downstairs, or are we going to gloss over the fact that His Lordship nearly took down a man a head shorter than he?"

"Oh, enough," Sláine said.

The seer tutted and perched on the window seat as Sláine took the chair near the door. "Milord, we can't have you going after every man who questions the girl's honor."

Aidan rolled his eyes. "Noted. Now, can we discuss what actually matters?" The woman stared at him blankly. Sláine did not look at him at all, but picked at her sleeve. "Tomorrow I have decided that we are to leave this town. I never like to stay in a place for too long."

"The law might find you."

He nodded once. "Or worse. Now, you say that Dewhurst keeps the map in his mansion?"

The seer regarded him for a moment before speaking. "Yes. The old lard tub keeps it in a locked drawer in his study. Should be easy enough to get to…once we've managed to house-break, that is."

Sláine groaned. "They'll hang us for that."

"Not if we don't get caught."

"And you have a way of ensuring that?" Aidan looked the woman squarely in the eye, as if he might be able to draw the truth from their depths, or at least discern it.

Larkin stared right back at him. "After tonight, I will tell you the plan."

Aidan forgot himself and swore.

"Now, milord, you take certain things for granted, such as the fact that I don't quite trust you. What's to stop you from taking my plan and fleeing tonight under cover of darkness?"

He looked heavenward. "And tomorrow you'll share this plan of yours?"

"I will tell you then, and not a moment sooner."

He did not desire her plan, inasmuch as he desired to test the mettle of her words. For all he knew, she would lead him straight into another trap, and he hoped to be the one to turn the tables on her once he'd figured out how she meant to do it.

Shortly after, a different maid brought up a sampling of meats and cheeses for their requested midday meal. She set it on the side table, gave Aidan a funny look, and left as quickly as she had come.

Though far from hungry, Aidan figured he would need his strength, should he find himself forced to fight wraiths. Not that he planned on facing them. He had enough on his mind, and fighting spirits was the last thing he wished to do.

Slaíne was the first to reach for the food on the tray. "Right. So, what if the wraiths return tonight?"

"We'll do as we did the night previous," Aidan said, trying to keep his voice even. When Slaíne began to protest, he held up a hand and interrupted her. "We can't join every adventure that comes our way. We've more important things to think about and prepare for than some local conflict."

With a disgusted grunt, Larkin joined Slaíne and scooped up a handful of dates. Aidan knew full well what she thought of the idea, but he would not yield. Unless forced, he could not afford to. Fortunately, the seer did not voice her thoughts, and they were able to enjoy their meal in peace.

★   ★   ★

Later, when he was assured that Larkin and Slaíne were occupied in the seer's room, Aidan sat down and composed a short letter. It was a risk that it should even find the right party, but he addressed the brief and cryptic missive, sealed it, and handed it over to a maid to be posted.

The serving girl eyed him askance but did as he asked, a ten-pound note tucked in her fist. "Anything else, sir?"

Aidan produced an even larger note and passed it to her. When the recipient's eyebrows shot heavenward, he gave her a serious look and said, "For your secrecy."

★   ★   ★

That evening, Aidan shut and bolted his door and prepared to settle down by the fire. He had just thrown the blanket over his legs, when he heard the eerie shrieks in the distance.

"It's starting," Slaíne said from her position at the window.

Aidan didn't respond, determined not to engage. But he could feel her gaze burning into the back of his head. With a shiver, he pulled the blanket farther up his neck.

"Sir, please. I know you're not afraid...." She stomped across the creaking floorboards as calls were taken up and down the hall outside. "What makes you stay inside?"

Aidan glowered at the small blaze before him. "What makes you say that I'm not afraid?"

"Because you're not a coward," she said simply.

That made Aidan laugh. He rolled over and looked at her waifish figure standing over him, hands on her bony hips. "Being afraid has nothing to do with cowardice, and sometimes it is our inaction that shows just how brave we are."

"Nonsense. You heard what everyone's calling you."

Aidan gave her a stern look. "Put no credence in others' words." He sat up a little and propped his head up with his hand. "Besides, what does it matter to you if I am a coward?" Aidan had meant the words playfully, but they were not taken that way.

There was a glint in Slaíne's eyes, and if he didn't know any better, he'd say she was on the verge of tears. When she spoke, however, the girl's voice was steady, if not pleased. "I know you think the Goblets are more important."

"I do. We'd be wasting ourselves on a cause that has nothing to do with us." Before she could interrupt, he continued in a rush. "Think about it, Slaíne. If any of the Goblets fall into Lord Dewhurst's hands, or any wrong hands, for that matter, so much harm could be done. I, at least, don't even know the full extent of what could happen."

Slaíne was silent for a moment, the look on her face pensive. But soon she shook her head and replied, "Let's stop pretending this is about the Goblets, eh?"

Aidan shifted his position, sitting up entirely. "If that's not it, then what is it?"

"It's you and your conscience."

That brought Aidan up short. "What do you mean?" he said with an impatient sigh.

Footsteps thundered down the hall. Several someones banged on their door as they passed, and the wraiths continued to shriek in the near distance.

Slaíne did not speak at first. It was as if she were weighing her words with some care before committing them to the charged air. When she answered him, she spoke forcefully. "You blame yourself for everything. Maybe you's not afraid of conflict, but you's afraid of failing us." Her face colored crimson up to her fiery hairline, but she jutted her jaw out at him, as if daring him to say she was wrong.

She was not. At least, not entirely wrong with her bold presumptions.

Aidan sighed heavily. "Slaíne, what would you have me say to that, hmm?"

The girl shrugged and seemed to deflate. Perhaps she wouldn't pursue this any further than it should go. She opened her mouth and dispelled him of that hope. "What happened to your family?"

Aidan stiffened. "Don't."

Drawing her arms around herself, Slaíne continued. "You keep mutterin' in your sleep. Something 'bout your fault…and Sam."

"You really don't want to go there."

She laughed without humor. "I'm already there. Larkin says you think you killed 'em." Her eyes were large and her voice was unsteady. "Let it go, sir. You can nay change the past."

He made a movement toward her, uncertain what he really wished to do. This was neither the time nor the place. They had many things to think about, and his family – well, they were taboo, not to be talked of by someone, *anyone* in such a callous way.

"Move away from the window," Aidan snapped.

The maddening girl, she threw the windows open and perched one foot on the window seat. The cries were no longer distant. It would be wise of them to blow out the light and pretend the room was vacant, lest they be bothered. The girl gave him a knowing look, but didn't move.

"Away from there! They'll see you!" Aidan grimaced as he threw the curtains closed. "This isn't a game. You could die."

Of all things, Slaíne laughed, and not for the first time was Aidan dubious of her sanity. "Pleasure knowin' you, then." And with that said, she leapt from the window and into the dark night.

"Slaine!" Aidan shouted. He could not hear her body hit the ground over the din of shouts and metal on metal, nor could he see her, not in the dimness. For a terrifying second, he thought of jumping out after her, but what good would it do for both of them to have shattered bones...or worse? With a shudder, Aidan tore from the room. He thundered down the stairs, all the while entertaining dark thoughts. Her Pull remained strong; was it that she lived, or would her corpse prove just as compelling?

Moments raced past like horses, and after battling through a barricade consisting entirely of apple crates, Aidan found himself crouching on the front stoop. He stilled his breathing for a moment, closed his eyes and felt for Pulls. The important, most pressing one was mere feet away. As he began to follow it, he realized that the Pull was slackening at an alarming rate.

The night was pitched into shrieks and black cries, and for all the good his eyes did him, he felt her seconds before she bowled him over.

"Oomph."

"Shh!" she hissed, crawling off his prone form.

Aidan righted himself into a more dignified crouch, squinting in the night so that he might better observe her state. "How did you— Are you hurt?"

She repeated her previous request for silence, but broke it herself. "I don't see nothing."

The night flared into a bowl of crimson glow, a wreath of smoke kicking up in the breeze as the scent of burning wood assailed Aidan's nostrils.

"At least we can see now."

"They're torching the town, Slaíne."

Slaíne nodded but with a shrug said, "Well, gotta take our blessings where we canst get 'em." They were both on their feet, racing toward the flames.

Aidan did not think it would affect him so, the sight of a building being reduced to ash. But his shoulder prickled as badly as his conscience, and he was irresistibly drawn into a half-vision, one that overlaid what he saw before him. A barn, burning.

Ten-year-old Aidan ran for the doors, thrust them open, only to be slammed with a fist of smoke. Coughing and wheezing, he managed to call out, "Mother? Father? Sam?"

No response.

Mind spinning, Aidan ran back down to the creek.

"Sir?" said Slaine, her figure blurring before his eyes.

Aidan shook his head. Where was he? Oh, yes. The wraiths. Putting out a fire. He needed water.

A rock leapt from the creek, striking him in the shoulder. His own voice was shrill as the spot throbbed painfully.

"Sir, stop. You're gonna hurt yourself."

He shook his head to clear the cobwebs from his mind. "Memories. They're just memories."

Slaíne gripped him as he started to sway on the spot. The screams were piercing, and they were close. So many voices crying out for blood.

"Sir, now you're hurtin' me."

Fighting a rising panic and nausea, Aidan blinked his eyes several times in quick succession, hoping to see straight. His vision cleared somewhat. He found himself Calling Slaíne. They stood now, hip to hip, elbow to elbow, as two welded together. At once he Released her, and they both stumbled, regained their footing, and followed the screams and the heat.

Up to this point, they hadn't met any hostile forces. Now, rounding the dressmaker's shop, Aidan sensed and saw at least a dozen Pulls. They were cloaked in dark brown, the fabric hanging loosely on their apparently lanky frames.

Aidan stopped Slaíne before she could run into them. Perhaps her eyes were not as good as his, or perhaps he sensed more than he saw.

The creatures saw them now. Some held torches, others brandished swords. Aidan felt for the Pull of their weapons. No iron. Copper, tin. Children's toys. No, they were not to be worried about. The fire, on the other hand, was a problem.

Aidan Dismissed six swords within the span of three seconds, then went for the torches. One, two, three, four. He Dismissed them all, and now all the light came from the burning building.

The wraiths were surprised, shrieking as their hands suddenly fell empty. Soon, however, they recovered their wits, but Aidan was already upon them. With some difficulty concentrating, Aidan Summoned Slaíne's silver sword. He dispatched two of the wraiths with four mighty strokes. Slaíne, he could sense, was moving toward the burning building.

Faced with the challenge of an armed man whilst possessing no arms themselves, the wraiths screamed and fled, tripping over the hems on their long robes as they went.

Aidan looked for a moment down at the two he had slain. He flicked back the first one's hood with the tip of his sword and found an ordinary man, his face a mask of death. Aidan swore. "Slaíne. Get away from there. You're going to burn yourself."

But Slaíne wasn't listening. Her attention was focused on the third story of the building, whence came the shrill cries of a woman. The building was burning and collapsing around her as she moved onto the window's ledge. She held a small child in her arms.

Aidan's chest tightened. They were far too high for him to climb to them in time, even if he possessed a ladder. And the wraiths were returning in numbers. Cursing, he positioned himself beneath the woman in hopes of catching the child.

Slaíne was already on the move. She stepped back several paces and then charged at the building. Instead of running into the brick siding, the girl soared high into the air, scarcely touching the wall in her ascent. In seconds it was over. Slaíne secured the babe and shot back down to earth, slowing a split second before she would have hit the ground.

There was no time to take this miracle in before the mother in the window made her own desperate escape. Aidan followed her Pull as it came crashing to earth, and adjusted his position accordingly. The woman fell with a scream. Aidan's knees buckled as her weight hit his arms, and his muscles burned and strained at the contact. Both Aidan and she collapsed onto the ground in a heap as the wraiths began to ring them in.

"My baby," the woman gasped, snatching the infant and pushing her way through the wraiths, who didn't seem interested in her.

"How did you do that?" Aidan shouted as he felt her back press against his. He Dismissed the weapons of more wraiths, but this time, only one or two fled. "Slaíne?"

"Can we first focus on not dying, sir?"

He shook himself out of a momentary stupor. "Can you get us out of this circle?"

"Nay, sir. I ain't strong enough to carry us both."

Aidan cursed. He felt for the wraiths' Pulls as he slashed out at them. All of them had normal human Pulls; he could not get rid of them as easily as he could the goblins. There was a shriek and a grunt behind his back, and he could tell from the girl's Pull that she had soared upward again.

"Too many of 'em," she shouted.

Aidan grunted his agreement. Slaíne continued to drift out of the wraiths' reach, while he lashed out at them. Meanwhile, the building continued to burn. He could Dismiss himself, but that would only buy him an hour. And there was Slaíne to think about. He did not know how her ability worked, so if he left her for Nothingness, there was no telling what sort of trouble he'd put her in.

The moments crawled by like years, but the cloaked men were pushed farther back as he fought. And as the moonlight hit their eyes, he knew once and for all what they were really dealing with. "Bandits."

"What?" There was another grunt behind him, and it was then that Aidan realized why no one had managed to grab him from behind: Slaíne, however she was doing what she was doing, was dropping as a deadweight onto their attackers, only to soar straight up again before they could touch her.

It was a good tactic, but she sounded tired. He was tired too. Sword or not, these mere mortals would soon deal a death blow. And it was a wonder: Why had all of them been drawn to Aidan and Slaíne? Aidan felt few Pulls beyond the vast circle enclosing them. And where was the rest of the town, the ones who had called him a coward when he had not fought alongside them the previous night?

He dispatched his twenty-first man and that is when he realized that he wasn't only fighting bandits: they were fighting the town as well. "Slaíne," he called over the screams. But why? "I'm going to clear a path for myself. Follow overhead."

"How are you gonna do that, sir?" Another grunt followed by a curse and the tearing of cloth.

She had a fair question, to which he didn't yet have the answer. He was, however, a gentleman – as much as he could be called one – and did not want to frighten or distract her. "Just trust me."

"Blimey," said the girl. "These aren't no wraiths. These be town folk. For shame." There was a sickening crunch as Aidan assumed her boot connected with someone's nose. Before he could come up with a plan, shouts took up in the distance, breaking up the riot around him.

"The inn's a-fire! The inn's a-fire!" cried several women, their words being taken up by the town folk, who made up the vast majority of the mob. The wraiths had begun to flee, and the villagers left them for the inn with apparent reluctance. He Dismissed the sword and shouted at Slaíne, "To the woods!"

Slaíne didn't need telling twice. She hit the ground running, and Aidan sprinted beside her. They ran into the night, Aidan feeling for Pulls that might lie ahead or behind. All was still; no one followed nor laid traps before them.

They ran 'til she could no more, and they took to walking, saving their breath until they were a good two miles away from the town. Then, Slaíne ventured to speak first. "High as I were, the inn were nay on fire." Her voice was thin and breathless, and Aidan did not answer at first. He was more concerned as to why the villagers had turned on him, the only obvious answer being that they were afraid of Slaíne and himself. "Think it were the inn-keeper's way of thankin' ye?"

Aidan nodded, though he knew she could not make out the movement in the moonlight. He was more out of breath than Slaíne, and a cramp had formed in his side. He grabbed her arm to halt her, and leaned against a tree.

With a sigh, Slaíne collapsed to the wood's floor.

Aidan Summoned a water skin for them both to partake of. Though his throat was raw and his mouth parched, Aidan passed the vessel to her first, and she drank deeply before passing it back to him with a muttered thanks.

After he'd gorged himself on water, emptying the skin, he took a moment to again catch his breath. "You noticed the town has turned against us."

Slaíne sniffed. "Folks're always skeered of what they don't understand."

Aidan could only nod and sigh. "Word of this will reach Dewhurst. We need to be clear of here before daybreak." He flopped onto his back and felt for approaching Pulls. A handful had come nearer their current location, but no one had ventured within a mile. It was a good thing; Aidan was less than certain if he could fight another man, let alone run to the next town. And that was another thing: now that he was infamous, his description – and probably Slaíne's – would be circulated far and

wide; there would be no more staying in towns. As usual, Aidan would
be skirting civilization…and perhaps reduced to poaching and worse.

"Blast. What if our friend did nay make it out of there all righ'?"

Aidan groaned. "Let her fend for herself."

Slaíne tsked, and tapped his forearm with her boot. "She knows
where we're goin'. Could be tortured an'—"

"I know," he said without heat. "We'll have to plan our next moves
carefully, though we move forward blindly." He Dismissed the spent
bladder and sat upright. "But we'll discuss strategy when we're safely
away from here – and rested." Two Pulls had crossed nearer, and Aidan
rose. "We should leave now."

"All right." Slaíne accepted his hand, and he pulled her to her feet.

She was heavier than he had remembered, and it made Aidan wonder
if she'd been using her strange ability to aid her before. He released her
hand, more as an afterthought than anything. The pace he kept was slow
yet steady, and Slaíne matched his steps evenly.

The wind hissed through the trees. Unseen beasts scurried in the treetops,
making nary a sound, though Aidan was well aware of their presence. The
Pulls behind them had paused, and Aidan took that as a signal that he and
his companion should pick up their pace by a good measure. If anyone were
examining the area where they had lain but twenty minutes before, the
pursuers would make out their trail and be on them shortly.

Worry and a fast pace led to nothing. They stopped twice, once to
drink more water, the second time to eat a handful of day-old bread
each. It stuck to his throat and scraped on the way down, but Aidan
only allowed himself and the girl one mouthful of the second bladder
each. It wouldn't do to run out of water at night. Not here. Not with
danger so near.

Aidan laughed, a strange sound as Slaíne plopped down beneath a
tree. "Glad I thought to Dismiss our things before things got crazy."

"Our things?" she parroted. "I don't nay have no things." It wasn't
said with sarcasm or heat. She sounded confused. "Never did have no
things." Silence. "Ah, but I did have a dog once," Slaíne said after a
moment. Aidan looked at her, but was scarce able to make out her
silhouette in the dark. "Well, it weren't really my dog, but he liked me
much better than the Four." She let out a heavy breath. Her fingers
snaked through the grass, back and forth, back and forth with a slight

whisper, as if she were still petting the creature's back. "Woke up from a real deep sleep one night. There were smoke and screams and curses. And all I could think about, where's the dog?" She went silent here, and Aidan wondered if he should ask her what happened. As it turned out, there was no need. The girl offered the remainder of the story up herself. "Found him the next morning, burned to a crisp. Were a silly thing, but that's what, you know, Jolted me." By the light of a star, he caught the glint of the whites of her eyes, wide and glassy.

That caused Aidan to shiver. "Jolted you?" he repeated, by and by.

Sláine didn't reply. She didn't need to.

Aidan drew his arms about himself, the spring breeze raking against his sweat-drenched clothing. "I take it that you have a history with the Goblets Immortal as well." Releasing himself from his own embrace, he lowered himself to the ground and lay with his hands flat at his sides. "How—"

"Me mother drank from the Drifting Goblet. Must have. Or her mother before her did. It's the same sad tale." Another heavy sigh and she moved nearer. "Girl finds herself kidnapped by strange cult. 'Drink of this' says such and such a so-called friend. The girl, soon realizes she is with child. They knew before she, and it don't matter how much she might object to a strange child, the Goblet she drinks from." She paused in her narrative, and Aidan thought it appropriate to ask,

"And Meraude was one of the children from the Circle, too?"

Sláine moved closer still and froze. "That is the queer thing of it. Nobody rightly knows, or won't tell me. Could be either. There aren't many of us left that she hasn't slaughtered."

"And yet here we are."

"Here we are."

Aidan wrinkled his brow in thought, and soon turned to Sláine, reaching in the dark that he might touch her and find relief from her nagging Pull. He gave up after a sore moment, and continued. "Why is it, do you think, that we have crossed each other's paths? If there are so few of us, then what are the odds of our having met so?"

"Not good," Sláine admitted. They were silent after that, each lost in their own thoughts. And slowly, ever so slowly, Aidan found himself relaxing into sleep's embrace, though the night was cold. It was irresistible. It was inevitable, as inevitable as breathing.

CHAPTER THIRTEEN

In this vision or whatever it might be — Aidan couldn't decide what to call these mind-wanderings into the past — there was a woman. She was at once familiar and unfamiliar. The stranger paused before saying with a smile, "Well, Aidan. Are you not happy to see your auntie?"

Aidan rejoined that he did not recall being in possession of any such creature.

The woman, birdlike in visage and in dress — and giving off the air of one who would take flight at the slightest provocation — smiled her raptorial smile and said, "Why, nephew, you do not recall your father's sister?" She tsked and fussed and, spreading her great arms out like bright plumage, demanded that he come forth and embrace his long-lost relative.

Aidan was not deceived; this woman was not a memory. He had never seen the likes of her in his life. Nor was this a dream, as his prickling shoulder warned him. "What are you?" he said coolly. "And don't lie to me."

The wing-like arms dropped, and with it the pretense. "Aidan, of course you would not know me. And you are right on one score — this is not a dream nor a memory. On another score, however, you find yourself quite incorrect. I am your aunt...."

Aidan's mouth worked a few times before closing again. He shook his head. His father did not have a sister. He would have mentioned — should have mentioned.

The woman, as if reading his thoughts — perhaps reading his thoughts, indeed — twinkled her eyes at him and said, "Ask me no questions, I'll tell you no lies."

If he weren't suddenly so afraid, he would have scoffed and demanded that she leave him and his head to himself right there and then. However, a creeping dread crawled up his spine, and he resolved hat, whoever she might be, he would not trust her.

She tsked again. "Really, nephew. Don't be so taciturn." She sniffed delicately. The room in which she sat and he stood at a respectful distance was his childhood bedroom. There was the four-poster bed, the nightstand, the stone fireplace and the iron poker. It felt so real, he could feel repulsion to the metal,

*and the metal to him. The woman laughed in the white velvet loveseat upon
which she sat.*

*As Aidan watched, the scene shifted. They were downstairs in the library.
Now they were in the kitchen, where Molly, his nurse, was stealing scraps from
the table. She looked at him once, then went back to her rummaging. Lastly, they
stood outside a burning barn behind a young boy with dark locks, screaming for
his parents as the very earth trembled.*

*Aidan turned in this vision and asked the woman, now standing, "What
are you?"*

*Smiling, she tapped her nose. "I am shadow. I am shade. You are the door.
Open, my son. Open your eyes."*

He awoke and nearly jumped out of his skin. It took him a disoriented
moment to figure out what he was seeing and feeling.

Slaíne, normally the cynic and door-watcher, lay against him in the
grass, shivering in her sleep as she hugged herself. The early morning
air bit at him as well, but neither that nor the strange vision were what
held his attention. Had the previous night's revelations ripped down
some barrier between them...at least, in her mind? Aidan did not know
how that made him feel. But those thoughts were meant to be saved for
a later date, for the girl tossed in her sleep, lashing out with her arms
violently and nearly clapping him with her elbow.

But a moment passed, and Slaíne sat upright with a jolt, her eyes
opening wide in alarm. She gasped, and her breath clouded the frigid
air. She looked over at Aidan, frowning, then scooted away, her face
wrinkled up in obvious distaste.

Aidan sighed. Well, it would seem nothing had changed materially as
he had first thought. No need to fret, then. "Good morning."

Muttering, the girl stumbled to her feet and into a nearby cluster of
bushes. Aidan knew better than to follow her.

After taking care of some necessary business, he summoned one of the
precious water skins from Nothingness. He took a small gulp and waited
for Slaíne to return, which she did presently, a frown upon her face.

She gave him an odd look, and then shook her head. "Right. What
are we to do now?"

Aidan's chest heaved. It would be dangerous, returning to Breckstone,
never mind breaking and entering Lord Dewhurst's property. The last
time he'd been there.... Aidan shuddered at the thought. All these

thoughts took but a split second to pass through his mind, before he spoke. "Slaíne."

"Sir," she threw back.

He arched a brow, but said nothing of her tone. "I cannot ask you to put yourself in peril."

Slaíne groaned.

Aidan held up a hand to waylay her protestations. "However, our – er, connection and circumstances being unique, I fear that cannot be avoided."

She looked at him with her piercing gray eyes, and Aidan nearly lost his resolve. What right had he to ask her? Yet, though little did he know of her, he knew well enough not to tread lightly and dance around the issue. He latched his courage on her strong will and continued.

"Dewhurst lives about four miles from where I grew up. If we are to travel there...."

"Aye?"

"We will need to be discreet and swift. I traveled to Breckstone recently to sell my estate to a friend."

"Could he help us?"

Aidan laughed. "That friend has, shall we say, other interests now."

It was Slaíne's turn to raise her brows, but she said nothing, though curiosity burned in her eyes.

"No, you and I are the only ones we can trust now. I am not well known there anymore, though there may be circulations of my image. I am not known, however, for having a traveling companion." Here he looked at her pointedly. "If I were to travel as your servant—"

Slaíne laughed at this without humor. "That's likely."

Aidan gave her a dark look and continued. "Think of it. No one looks to or at the servant, but to the master or mistress. It would, of course, be somewhat inappropriate, a lady traveling alone with no other female company...."

Her eyebrows rose higher still.

"But we shall raise questions no matter how we go about this, and less so if you and I switched roles, so to speak. Besides, your dress is fine enough, and my clothing's worn enough, that this might just work."

Slaíne puffed out her cheeks and released a gush of breath. Her frown deepened. "What of...ye know?" She pointed to her mouth, and Aidan understood at once.

"Your dialect isn't common around here."

"It's low-class, that's what it be."

Aidan shook his head. "In these parts, no one but a traveler would have come across it. What are its origins?"

Her face darkened, and her lips formed mutterings as to discourage Aidan from asking further.

"Slaíne, this is important. If we are to decide upon a cover story, I am going to need all the information you can give me."

The look on the girl's face lightened a little, but she said nothing and reached for the bladder, which he provided. After taking a silent swig, she said, "Well, me mam and fadder were high, I s'pose. But I don' much recollect them. The elves...." Slaíne paused to growl through her teeth. "They had their own language when speakin', and I can nay rightly say I caught onto any of it. What I did understand was as you heard when you was 'round them." She sighed. "Other than that, we talked to folk in many a different town, me mostly doin' the talkin'."

Aidan nodded. "You've had a Roma's life."

Slaíne made a face. "Don' reckon I ever met the kind, sir."

While she was talking, Aidan felt for Pulls, still found no human ones near enough to raise alarm, and Summoned some rations he'd stored: an apple and a slice of cheese each, which he'd wrapped up at the inn and Dismissed when no one had been watching. He offered Slaíne her half of the meager meal, and she treated it like a feast. "Let's walk," he said through a mouthful of apple.

The girl only nodded, licking her fingers as they took off.

Yester-year's leaves crackled and crunched lustily beneath his boots, and branches reached out to snag his traveling cloak. Annoyed and hindered, Aidan Dismissed the garment from his body.

In contrast, Slaíne made nary a sound as they traveled, and the brush seemed to treat her more kindly than it did him. She swore through a mouthful of ancient apple, her face enraptured. "Almost good as new."

Aidan nodded. "Hunger will do that to your taste buds. Nothing tastes so good after burning off a whole two days' nourishment in the course of two hours."

She swore again, and Aidan bit down on the corners of his mouth.

"You'll introduce yourself as an islander."

"Which island?"

Aidan shrugged. "I don't think it really matters. The coast is far from here, and few will have ventured hence." He finished his apple and Dismissed the core, wishing to leave no evidence behind of their passing through. "You were traveling with a larger company, but were waylaid by bandits. You, myself, and a few others escaped."

Slaíne spat out a seed and chucked the apple's core deep into the underbrush. "Where are the others, then?"

"I doubt anyone will inquire this deeply into your affairs, but for caution's sake, tell people they are on the road south."

She nodded. "The vaguer the better?"

"The less said the better. If you get caught in a lie, don't lie further to cover it. Stick to the truth as much as you are able. Such as your name."

She raised an eyebrow at him. "Right, keep my name. And what about you, sir?"

Aidan grinned. "Refer to me as little as possible." He waylaid her misgivings with a wave of the hand and a quick reassurance that people were not so nosy in larger towns, which is where they were headed.

The girl frowned. "All right. So I pretend I'm a lady, keep me name, you's my servant, and then what? How do I get the map from Lord Thing?" Now her feet were crunching, and she was minding the way more than she had previously. Her shoulders hunched forward, and her face creased against the slight breeze that reached down among the low-hanging boughs. Her hair became ensnared by one of those woody hands, and Aidan was forced to stop and help her untangle herself.

After some time, having freed her, Aidan spoke again. "I need to know where the map is in the house. If I can find its Pull, Dismissing it will be nothing. But since it's unfamiliar to me...."

"That's where I come in."

"This is going to be dangerous, Slaíne. Are you sure you're equal to—"

"'Course I'm equal," she snapped. "What else?"

Aidan let loose a laugh and finished the crumb of cheese he'd allotted himself.

At this point in their travels, the area became marshy, and Aidan refilled his water bladders, Dismissing any harmful elements. His spirits were hopeful. The weather was fine enough for traveling: not too cold as to numb, but neither too warm as to cause him to work up much of a sweat when moving. The flies, however, were intense in this area. They were of the biting variety, and Slaíne cursed like a sailor as they swarmed her.

"Can you nay do nothing about these blighters?"

Aidan shook his head and stoppered the last bladder. "No. For whatever reason, I cannot Dismiss any living creature…save for myself." The moment the words were out of his mouth, he was surprised that he did not wish them back. It had been his secret, his safe-hold. Secrets had always been his escape route, and to throw important ones such as that around – and to a strange girl above that – was most likely the worst thing he had done since selling his estate to Tristram. And yet, regret did not follow.

★　★　★

It was nearing dusk when they reached the main road, which Aidan had been hoping to avoid. His travels rarely took him this far south, and the way was unfamiliar to him. For a moment he stood on the precipice. The wind shifted, and he regained his bearings. "Tanderine blossom."

"What?"

Aidan looked around and, sure enough, spied the yellow blossoms pushing up through the thick underbrush. He smiled a real smile for the first time that day. "Tanderine blossoms grow thickly in a small area outside of town. I haven't traveled there much since my twenty-fourth year, but I am quite certain we have just stumbled upon it."

Slaíne wrinkled up her nose. "Smells pretty, I suppose. Why have I never seen 'em before?"

"Because they're specific to this part of the world. They've been cross-bred again and again, to get that sweet a smell."

"They're sort of ugly…like shriveled up-old hags with a skin fungus."

Aidan chuckled. "Appearances are deceiving. There's great healing in their nectar." After a beat, he reached down and plucked one of the blossoms from the earth and studied it. Then, reflecting further on their goodness, he picked with fervor, stuffing the flowers in his hat. If he'd had these when he'd run into the Romas…. Upon further reflection, that was what the antidote was most likely made of.

He didn't have to look to know that Slaíne was following his example.

The glowworms had already made their appearance, and Aidan knew there would be no more traveling that day. They would eat their supper – a heartier slice of cheese and two more apples apiece – after building some structure against the night, which looked to be a cold and wet one. This close to town, he did not wish to light a fire, and with the dampness, it would smoke something terrible.

"Care to help me?" he asked, setting the overflowing hat on the ground.

Slaíne added her handfuls to the heap and waited for him to Dismiss the whole lot, which he did without show this time. "Right. What're we doin'?"

He pointed to a cluster of trees and asked her to gather brush and any large sticks she could find. Aidan went about, trying to find branches on the ground, and he thought Slaíne would follow suit. But soon he felt a strange fluctuation in the tension between their two Pulls, and turned around to find her scurrying up the side of a tree… without actually touching the trunk. Amused, he stopped his work and bit his lip so that he would not laugh.

Slaíne had found a thick branch and was standing astride it. She looked down at him, and though he could not be certain, she might very well be smirking at him. "Watch out below."

"Be careful. Perhaps you ought to find another— That branch looks too thick to be of use."

She appeared not to be listening as she floated up another two feet, then four, aligning her feet with that branch below.

Time to put a stop to this. "Slaíne, you cannot possibly break that branch. Come down before you—"

Too late. She shot down at the branch at breakneck speed, and the branch creaked ominously. Again she floated higher, and again she shot downward.

"Slaíne," he warned. "You're going to break something."

"Yep!" she shouted, then, "Timber!"

Aidan ran back a few paces as the branch crashed to the forest floor, scattering leaves and scaring birds in its massive wake.

A moment later, Slaíne floated down, panting yet grinning. Her smile, however, melted, as she looked at the waist-thick branch with her tongue stuck out from between her teeth. Slaíne sighed and shrugged. "Too big and heavy to move, ain't it? Guess we'll have plenty o' firewood."

At that, Aidan burst out laughing, and she had to smile again.

Aidan hated to discourage her, but the noise was sure to have drawn unwanted attention. Anyone living on the outskirts of town would be drawn in their direction to investigate the noise, and attention was the last thing they needed. With a sigh, he shook his head. "I fear this won't do."

Slaíne's brow creased. "What, sir?"

"We should move on perhaps a little further tonight." As he said the words, the sky began to spit down on them…not a heavy rain, but a thin mist. He caught a shiver and smiled at her ruefully.

She nodded and followed him away from the fallen branch.

Before crossing the main road, Aidan felt for Pulls, satisfied himself that there were no travelers within their immediate reach, and they both crossed the way, trembling against the cold and damp and trying to leave as few tracks as possible. By the time he thought it a safe distance to stop, there was but a bit of daylight left. They ate their supper, such as it was. Slaíne shook so hard that Aidan feared she might miss the apple entirely and bite her lower lip instead. It was not a satisfying meal. Aidan didn't know when they'd be able to restock their food supplies, seeing as he was a wanted man in Breckstone; they had to be thrifty.

Once they'd finished eating, Aidan found a giant evergreen, beneath which they would sleep. He crawled under after Slaíne, who swore as the needles prickled her.

"Can you nay get rid of 'em?" The second he collapsed next to her, she surprised him by grabbing and clinging to him, her breaths coming in clouds that hung in the air above them. "Well?"

Her hands were cold against his chest, and her thighs against his waist were…. Lucidity left him for a moment, and he forgot what she had asked him.

"Ouch!"

Aidan jolted back to reality. "Try not to move about so much."

She swore at him through chattering teeth. "These blasted needles will be the death of me."

With a sigh, he felt for their thin, fragile Pulls and Dismissed as many as he could sense. It didn't take long, and as soon as he finished, he tried extricating himself from her tight grasp, which was rather strong for someone so slight. But she appeared to have fallen asleep, so he gave up trying.

The hours trickled by like sand down the throat of an hourglass. Aidan watched through the branches as the sun finished its descent, and the moon climbed to its highest point, and all the stars lit up a cloudless sky. The night dug its nails into him, leeching the warmth from his body. At once he was thankful for Slaíne's warmth and strove to think nothing more of the situation.

Dew fell. The night-dwelling creatures pitched their songs into a cacophony of sound, until, the moon sinking, the creatures grew still and left Aidan to believe the sun's dawning was near.

The night through he tried running the plan through his mind. It was a feeble one at best, downright deadly at its worst. But they needed that blasted map...if Larkin hadn't been lying about it in the first place.

Perhaps, Aidan mused, *I should simply Dismiss all the paper and parchment from the house.* It was an idea, a somewhat workable one. Yet there was a problem: What if the paper was concealed by iron? Or what if the map was not made of paper at all, but painted on oilskin? There would be no knowing. He could try Dismissing all the paper and oilskin he could sense, and sort through it at a distance, seeing if he had discovered the document. But how much paper might Dewhurst's manor contain, and what then if the map was not among that which he had Dismissed and Summoned? It would look suspicious to Dewhurst if all the paper goods had gone missing from his home, and the issue of theft would be raised. Naturally, all the vagrants, Romas, and foreigners would be rounded up and questioned, drawing so much attention to Aidan and Slaíne as to prevent their attempting the theft a second time. No, they would get one chance at this, and they had better get it right. No map meant no Goblet. No Goblet meant an angry Meraude, no answers, and another bounty on Aidan's head.

These thoughts worried him until first light, keeping him from any semblance of sleep or rest. He meant to stir early, hoping to pace about and get rid of some of his nervous energy. It was not meant to be, it would seem. Slaíne, as usual, slept as one dead; freeing himself from her would mean waking her, and he didn't relish the idea.

At last, when the sun had cleared the trees, the girl stirred, rolled over, and sat up with a start. For a moment, she looked about as though uncertain of where she was or who Aidan was, her eyes wide and wild. After that moment had passed, she came to her senses and stopped shaking and casting him odd glances. "Well, that was strange." She did not expound.

He wasn't going to ask, but as they scarfed down their sad excuse for a breakfast – one shriveled and drying pear each – Slaíne still didn't seem quite herself. He sighed as they crawled out from beneath the pine. Exhaustion would be his constant companion, it would seem, until this whole sordid affair was behind them. That is, he reflected, if Slaíne was still up for participating in the theft and deception.

Her words accosted him out of nowhere. "You've strange dreams, no?"

Aidan eyed her as she brushed the pine needles he'd missed from her dress front. "Yes, I have." He paused, waiting for her to go on. When she didn't, curiosity got the better of him, and he resigned himself to inquiry. "Why? Did you have some strange night vision?" He meant it playfully, but she frowned up at him.

"Aye, strange indeed. But it weren't no vision – I don' know what's to come. Ain't no ruddy seer."

Perhaps teasing hadn't been the best approach. She seemed to clam up now, her jaw set taut and her posture rigid. Ah, well. If she wasn't going to offer any more, he wasn't going to ask anything more, but he couldn't shake a dark feeling that came over him all at once. Aidan put out a hand to stop Slaíne, drawing a curse from her. "Slaíne, did you dream of Meraude?"

She let out a groan. "Not that old hag again. You dream of her?"

"Not last night."

Slaíne narrowed her eyes at him. "Did you sleep at all last night?"

What did it matter to her? Aidan shrugged. "No, I did not. What has this got to do with anything?" She didn't answer. "Answer me straight. Did you dream of Meraude?"

She bristled. "'Course I did nay dream of that wretch. I dreamt about the woods." She shot him an accusing look, and took off toward the road, seemingly forgetting her curse as Aidan ran to catch up with her.

"Easy."

Slaíne growled at him. "I'm not a horse."

Aidan rolled his eyes. Why did she always want to start fights? "No," he said after a measure, and that is when he noticed the great rip in her dress. "You are not. Forgive me." He waited a moment longer before changing the subject. "I think you should change."

She stopped mid-stride and looked over her shoulder at him. "Change what?"

Aidan put up his hands. "Please, hear me out. We've been in the woods for a while now, and, I – I don't know how to say this but...." Why was he starting to laugh now? There was nothing funny about the tear in and of itself, but she was already in such a foul mood, apparently, that one more thing going wrong was ridiculously horrible. It was so awful, it was funny.

It was Slaíne's turn to roll her eyes. "I've got a tear in me dress, haven't I?"

Aidan turned away as she started cursing, shaking with laughter. What was the matter with him? He attempted to calm himself, turned and was surprised to see her staring at him expectantly. His eyebrows shot heavenward. "What?"

"Sir, you gotta help me."

He still wasn't understanding. They'd come close enough to town that Aidan could feel more individual Pulls milling about not more than a mile away. They had better start moving. "What is it?" he pressed.

Of all things, Slaíne stomped her foot and threw her hands up in the air. "You, sir, are going to have to help me get dressed."

★   ★   ★

Half an hour later, after much awkwardness and snarled instructions, Aidan finished lacing up the back of Slaíne's blue dress, and they both stood away from each other, fuming. Now was not the time to be divided by something so silly. Still, Aidan could scarce look at her without laughing or scowling, and she would not even favor him with a glare. So into town she walked as instructed, Aidan following as close behind her as he dared, keeping his head down.

He'd given her some instruction as to what to say and do if stopped or confronted, though he doubted the latter. If anything, the men would tip their hats, and the women would nod or turn to gossip about this unknown woman in their midst.

They passed through the town's iron gates, which always remained open on this end, as they were too heavy and cumbersome to close every night and open every morning. The cobbles were well worn from much foot, horse, and carriage traffic. At this early hour, with the sun still on its ascent, there were not too many people about. A few of the tall buildings boasted ten windows apiece, and some of the upper ones had been opened so that maids could empty chamber pots or shake out rugs.

Aidan hadn't been through this part of town for years upon years. He hoped that no one would remember him. He would have to rely on Slaíne's acting skills – which he wasn't sure existed – to get them through if anyone suspected him.

The town had changed quite a lot since he'd last passed through. New buildings had sprung up, giving the outer ring of the city a claustrophobic feel, too many sights and too many Pulls surrounding them. There were some familiar sites, like the carved stone fountain in the middle of the square that depicted two lovers kissing, something Aidan had always rolled his eyes at.

"Sir?" Slaíne murmured.

"Aidan," he replied. "Better yet, call me something different altogether."

There was a brief moment where she paused mid-step and turned around to look at him, perplexed. "Sir— Rutherford, I mean."

Aidan grimaced as her shoulders began to shake with laughter. "Yes, milady?" He'd affected a lower-class accent, obviously startling his traveling companion, who paused again and looked over her shoulder at him. "Milady?"

Slaíne shook herself and stepped out of the way for an open carriage and horse rolling and trotting through the middle of the square. The driver raised his hat to Slaíne as he rattled and jingled past, and in response, Slaíne all but ignored him. Perhaps she would do all right after all.

"Rutherford, what if our friend is following us?" Her voice was so low, he had trouble at first deciphering what she was saying. When

Aidan did not respond at once, she rephrased the question. "You know, our know-it-all friend?"

"Yes, I know what and who you mean, but keep your eyes ahead." They both side-stepped horse droppings and a group of gossiping stable hands, who also raised their hats to Slaíne, who in turn ignored them as someone in her station of life would.

"Love of all, but I feel foolish, lookin' like I'm talkin' to meself." Her shoulders heaved. "What of Larkin? Think she'll show up and betray you?"

Aidan clenched his hands into fists. "Very likely."

Another thoughtful pause. "Then why are we doing this?"

"Because this will be our only chance...if she is, in fact, not on our side." He had to be quiet now, as there were more people about in this area and it would not look proper for him to be talking to his mistress without apparently having been spoken to.

The cobbles here were more worn, and a few of the stones had come loose or gone missing entirely, making the way treacherous for someone not in good walking shoes, like most women. Aidan recalled Slaíne's shoes, which were more practical than what he'd seen the fashionable Ton wear. Should they need to run, their escape should not be hindered in that way.

Aidan stiffened when he felt a familiar Pull. It was coming from one of the shops, if he was not mistaken. Ah, yes, the blacksmith's. He squinted in concentration, exploring the Pull. He remembered to keep his gaze lowered as they moved on, leaving the familiar behind. He did not know anyone who lived in this part of town. At least, not that he remembered.

Before he could determine the Pull's source, it disappeared. Were they hiding? Aidan's blood seemed to freeze in his veins, and it took every modicum of self-control that he possessed not to Summon the silver sword and run for the hills. Instead, he settled for matching his stride with Slaíne's and telling her to quicken her pace, which she did with nary a backward glance.

The pathways through town now multiplied, the street widened and then gave way to clusters of buildings in the center of it. Aidan was now on hyper-alert, feeling not just for Pulls but the absence of Pulls, certain there must be iron concealing unwanted persons. Yet as they hastened to the right fork in the road teeming with servants and a carriage or three, Aidan could feel no repulsion and saw nor felt anything amiss. He tried to relax. He tried telling himself that this would work out, but when he felt Slaíne's Pull getting too far ahead, he did the last thing he knew he should do: he pushed against the small crowd and caught up with the girl, grabbing her by the hand.

Slaíne frowned, looked down at their entwined fingers, but did not question it nor pull away. She said something he could not make out over the din. When he did not respond, she tugged him over to the side of the road, and they stood facing each other next to a water pump and trough. "How much farther?"

Aidan shook his head, which he tried to remember to keep down. "I cannot say, ma'am," he said, remaining in character. If anyone were to eavesdrop and discern that they were headed for Lord Dewhurst's estate, they could very well be followed and lose whatever element of surprise they still might hold.

Slaíne nodded. "Ah, right." She began to wipe her nose on her sleeve, a nervous habit of hers, but caught herself, seemed to think the better of it, and shot Aidan a guilty look. "You feel any – thing?"

Again Aidan shook his head. "No, ma'am."

"And we keep on in this direction?" She worried her lip for a moment, her wild hair catching in a breeze made by passersby. Where had this surge of people come from? Wasn't it a trifle early to be out running errands? Aidan couldn't be sure; he'd been away from this sort of civilization for quite some time now. "We'd best keep on the move. And try to walk less as one with such urgent purpose."

"Do I walk with purpose, now?" she scoffed. "Sorry my acting skills are nay to yer likin', s— Rutherford. Shall we?"

They walked for some time, Aidan receiving no more than a handful of initial curious glances from the women-folk. Men tended to keep their minds on task; the women would be the first to sound the alarm, if something were amiss. Aidan donned the role he played best: brow-beaten, worn-down, life-weary man. This kept him hidden. Slaíne, Aidan realized too late, would draw more attention the narrower the town became. Not many in these parts were red-haired and pale of complexion.

Sure enough, as the number of Pulls decreased, the covert stares and the occasional pointing increased. "Who's that, you think?" a wee child asked its mother, tugging on her grimy apron. The woman at the cobbler's shop, whom the babe was addressing, took one look at Slaíne and pulled her young indoors. "Vampire," Aidan heard her spit before slamming the door behind her child.

Whether or not Slaíne heard the word, Aidan was uncertain. If she did, he wondered if it bothered her. If so, she did not let on.

Past the cobbler's, down a narrow back street, Aidan noted that the houses truly were growing few and far between. "There will be a bit of the wood coming up ahead," he said, catching up with Slaíne.

She bobbed her head in acknowledgment. "What then?"

Aidan glanced over his shoulder, though he knew from the Pulls surrounding them that no one had been following their progress. "Our passing through town will – *should* go unnoticed. But once we've reached that particular patch of wood, there will be sentries." He gave Slaíne a meaningful look to make certain she followed.

The girl frowned. "They belong to Dew—"

Aidan hushed her. "Yes, that man. If I still know him, he still likes to make a show of his power. You might be questioned, asked to state your business and the like." He grimaced, failing to mention that he himself would probably be searched. No need to plant even more worries in her head.

"And I'm to tell these sentries that we was waylaid by Romas, an'— Ah, bugger." She chewed on her lower lip again as she thought. "I can nay sound proper. We'll be ratted."

"Not if you keep talking. Act confident. Take no lip. Attitude will get you everywhere with these thugs."

Slaíne shot him a meaningful look. "And they nay will look on ya?"

He let the comment roll with a laugh. "We'll be fine." They slowed their pace. Aidan's thirst was growing under the heat of the rising sun, but he would not risk Summoning a water skin and possibly give himself away. Again he checked for Pulls. None familiar, save for Dewhurst's, who must be on his estate, such was the distance. He felt for Larkin's Pull; nothing. Good…unless she was hidden by the presence of iron. And there was no return of the Pull he'd experienced back in town. But still he did not drop his guard, releasing her hand.

"Where did you live?"

Aidan cringed. "On the other side of town."

Slaíne nodded, her brow creasing. "An' you were lord of this all?"

This was the last topic he wished to discuss with Slaíne or anyone, for that matter, now or at any time. So instead of elaborating, he gave her a non-committal shrug.

Slaíne took the hint and pressed him no further.

The busyness of the town fell away, along with several hundred human Pulls, leaving them in the thick of a small wood. Aidan sensed four new Pulls hidden in the trees near them, and the artificial call of a bird seemed to cause Slaíne some confusion. She started to look among the leaves, but Aidan coughed a warning, and she returned her eyes to their path.

Several human Pulls ahead at the manor were drawing together at a point high above the trees. *Archers*, he thought ruefully. What could have possibly set them on their guard...unless Larkin really had set a trap and didn't need to be present for it to be sprung. Aidan ground his teeth. He was about to take Slaíne by the arm and steer her back whence they came, but a Pull was quickly making its way toward them, and one was moving in from behind. They were good and surrounded now.

To Aidan's surprise, Slaíne came to a halt and put up a hand for him to stop. Then, entertaining the air of someone both spoiled and bored, she opened her mouth and said snappishly, "If you would be so good as to show yourself, sir or sirs, I would be most obliged." Silence. She let out a heavy sigh. "How's a lady to feel, being followed around in the shadows like she's some sitting duck? Out wi' you, I say." There was another silence, and Aidan feared Slaíne had erred in her presumptions. Twigs snapped as two Pulls from the side and one from ahead rushed toward them. Hands sweating and itching for Slaíne's silver sword, Aidan bowed his head and tried to look the part of the foolish servant.

The two men, both guards from either side of the wood, made it to them first. They wore the regal red cape and the golden-brown tunic and slacks of Dewhurst's guard and had the swords to go with them. The weapons, however, were not drawn, though one of the men rested his hand on the pommel. "What have we here?" he asked, amused.

"A vamp and her pet?"

The two laughed for a moment until Slaíne joined in, a note of menace in her lilting voice. The men's laughter became more uncertain and soon cut off altogether. One coughed. The other grimaced.

At last, Slaíne's laughter died and she placed her hands upon her hips. "If we're quite done wi' this merriment, I would like to know if I mayn't pass in peace."

They were bulky men, overfed and underworked. Both wore chainmail over their dirty tunics. That had to make them sweltering hot beneath and perhaps a good deal cross. As it was, both faces were blotchy red and beads of sweat had formed on their exposed skin, sure signs that they were no match for Aidan if there was to be a fair fight. And there wouldn't be.

"Rattish, Lefere, enough of your posturing."

Aidan started and looked up at the sound of the new voice before lowering his head again and staring at his muddy boots. It had been a woman's voice speaking to the men, something Aidan had not anticipated. This voice held authority, and that could only mean one of two things: either Lord Dewhurst kept a woman as head of the guard, or…. He shuddered at the thought.

The hem of a white gown came into view, and Aidan chose to stare at it. No, definitely not head of the guard. Dewhurst had remarried. The rake. The devil!

He stopped his mad stream of thoughts. There was a conversation going on, and he must attend.

The woman was saying, "I hope my guards have not been giving you too much trouble."

Slaíne let out a chirp of a laugh. "It isn't anything I ain't heard before."

"I hope you don't mind my saying, but you don't sound like you're from around these parts."

"Oh, I'm originally from Ilitris."

"I have not heard of that place. Where is it?"

Aidan grimaced internally. Slaíne needed to speak with more authority.

"Ilitris is a small mountain town. Not many've heard of it." She must have sensed some of Aidan's frustration, for she interrupted the woman's next question. "I'm sorry to cut in, like. But I's beset by highwaymen not five days prior. I'm to meet up with the rest of my convoy 'fore the week is out, and we'll like as not replace what was taken."

"You poor dear. Have you reported the robbery to the proper authorities?"

Aidan tried not to tense. If she lied and said yes, that could be easily checked into, especially by someone of this lady's status. If Slaíne told the truth....

Slaíne spoke. "Nay, ma'am." Here she leaned in and said in a conspiratorial voice, "It's been my experience that foreigners ain't treated none so well in these parts." She pulled back. "Besides, I did not know who I should report the robbery to."

The two guards, who had been standing at full attention when their superior arrived, now were fully at ease, shifting their weight from side to side and throwing muttered insults at each other. Their mistress ignored them.

The woman's age was impossible to gauge from her face, though the slight strain in her voice put her, in Aidan's estimate, in her forties. From what he made out in his short glimpse of her, the woman seemed in decent physical shape and could easily pose a threat if Slaíne were to engage her, which he prayed she would not. A moment of awkward silence passed, and Aidan knew Slaíne should be the one introducing herself. This could be going much better than it was. "Pray, forgive me. I have not yet introduced myself. I am Lady Dewhurst."

"Milady." Slaíne made a half curtsy, but did not introduce herself.

"And your name might be...?"

"Slaíne Cuthbert, milady."

There was a small pause. "Welcome to the heart of Breckstone, Miss Cuthbert. Are you in possession of anything I should know about?"

"Milady?"

"Are you carrying arms? You know, swords, daggers, and the like."

Slaíne gave out a short laugh. "If I did, we would nay have run afoul of those highwaymen, I dare say. And I would think me clothes would be baggier."

Lady Dewhurst returned the laugh, though it was twice as short and more than affected. With care, Aidan monitored the lady's Pull and the Pull of her clothes and the possessions she carried on her. Lady Dewhurst, it would seem, carried nothing openly. But with a little probing, Aidan felt the repulsion he was expecting but dreading: iron. From the size, he would hazard to guess it was a small dirk in its sheath, and it was strapped to her ankle. He should be in little danger from her. Well, unless she bent down on whatever pretense she might assemble.

"Very well. I assume I won't have to search you. Only your man."

Aidan willed Slaíne not to react.

"Rutherford has nothing to hide." Even as she said it, the two guardsmen of the Dewhurst estate stepped forward, kicking up dust as they came.

Aidan remained calm and still, trying to affect a resigned, servile manner. These thugs had several weapons apiece, as he had observed, and, unlike earlier, the swords and daggers could not be dealt with by Dismissal…not in front of the wife of the man who was after his blood.

The one on the left slammed into Aidan, causing him to lose his balance and his footing and topple to the ground. He shielded his face as they jumped him.

All the while as they searched him with unnecessary roughness, Slaíne remained silent, just as he would have wished her to. Putting up a fuss over a mere servant would not serve them well in the long run.

It was when they'd searched him once through and through and they started the search all over again, that Slaíne did speak up.

"Are we quite finished here?" Her words were laced with disdain with an undercurrent of boredom. "Really, you'd a'think they's afraid of one scrawny, unarmed manservant."

To Aidan's surprise, the men got to their feet, giving Aidan a light kick apiece before returning to their mistress's side. "He's clear, milady."

Aidan knew he was going to feel the effects of their near-brutal search later, but he feigned indifference as he scrambled to his feet, still keeping his gaze downcast.

"Well," said Lady Dewhurst. "I apologize for any misconduct on my men's part. They are, after all, just men and can't always control themselves."

"Quite." The tone was polite enough, though Aidan could tell that she was fuming inwardly.

"My husband and I were just sitting down for our mid-morning tea, Miss Cumber."

"Cuthbert," Slaíne put in.

"Rather. If you would like to go around back to the kitchen, Cook should have something to refresh you."

This was it. This was their chance. Aidan tried not to get overly excited or anxious; any reaction on his part could send things spiraling out of control quickly. Instead, he contented himself with staring at Slaíne's boots.

"That would be lovely. Thank ye for yer kindness, Mrs. Dewhurst."

Aidan winced. It was an obvious slight Slaíne had just made, addressing the woman by a lower rank. Lady Dewhurst, however, seemed to be ignoring it.

"Have you no horses?"

"Goblins ate him."

"Oh, how vulgar." A pause. "Him? You only had one horse?"

The ladies' Pulls moved out of the woodsy area, and the two guards stalked off into the bracken. Aidan followed after Slaíne, keeping a respectable distance.

"No, the horse what was eaten were mine. The others could nay be spared."

Slaíne was better at lying than he at first thought she would be. That put him in mind: Had she been lying about anything to him, and if so, would he be able to discern it? But he was getting distracted. Shutting out Slaíne's Pull, Aidan reached out and explored the manor, which he had not set foot in for around two decades.

There were many human Pulls concealed within and scattered without. He felt Dewhurst's moving to and fro in one long line. That concerned Aidan for a moment, for a pacing man was an indecisive man, and an indecisive man was a worried man. Did he suspect Aidan's presence? No, he was getting ahead of himself. He'd better attend to the bigger threat he was sensing: repulsions. Beneath his boots, concealed deep within the earth, he at once felt as though he were not fighting gravity so hard, that he was being pushed away from the earth. To his wonder, Slaíne did not seem all too steady on her feet either, which distracted him yet again. Did iron affect her abilities as well?

He had just wondered this when the ladies came to a halt.

"The kitchen is around back. Welcome to Dewhurst Manor."

"I'm much obliged, I'm sure," said Slaíne in the same forcedly civilized tongue as their host.

Aidan rolled his eyes at the ground as Lady Dewhurst's Pull retired inside the house and Slaíne's moved forward and to the right.

"Stuck-up," Slaíne said a little too loudly.

Aidan resisted the urge to hush her. He followed her to the back of the house, all the while feeling the repulsion of the metal beneath. Dewhurst must be expecting him someday, why else would he outfit everything with iron? It occurred to him, though, that if the metal affected both him and Slaíne, two so-called 'Blest', why wouldn't it affect the seer, Larkin? She had, after all, been in servitude to Dewhurst for goodness knows how long. Aidan was missing a piece, a vital piece, but he could not wrap his head around the situation. Slaíne's Pull and the iron's repulsion proved too much of a distraction, and he could scarce think.

Servants scurried here and there, paying the two strangers little to no mind. Some carried laundry baskets, the contents of which they hung on a line, while others carried dead chickens by the feet, and others still buckets of water and armfuls of wood.

Slaíne led the way to the kitchen with little difficulty. She gave Aidan a look over her shoulder that said, "How do you want to do this?" But he shook his head; he was still making a plan, having not expected to be received at all into Dewhurst Manor, least of all through the kitchen. An idea struck him, however, when one of the maids dropped her share of firewood.

"Oh, blast," she swore, swiping at her sooty brow.

Aidan took a chance. "Mightn't I help you with that?" he said, tweaking his dialect yet again to match hers.

The woman, apparently exhausted, nodded. "Just put it by the stove, and make sure to stack it neatly. Cook'll have yourn hide if'n you don't."

Aidan bobbed his head and retrieved the scattered logs from the ground, and the kitchen maid scuttled off on her harried way. Arms full, he nodded at Slaíne, who followed him into the busy kitchen. The cook, or one of the cook's helpers, was laboring over an enormous iron pot and was too busy to notice two strangers slip into her domain. And to make things even better, the din was extraordinary. Banging pots and pans, sizzling skillets, crackling fires, clacking knives, and the chatter caused quite the racket and masked Aidan's words to Slaíne. "Stay in the kitchen. If anything goes wrong on my end, I'll give you a Tug. If anything goes wrong here—"

"I'll move for the door, and you'll feel the change in my Pull."

Aidan nodded.

"What're you dawdling for? Put the logs where they belong," barked a matronly woman with a tray of burnt vittles, which she thrust at Slaíne. "I s'pose you're the wandering woman who expects tea, even though it might be putting us out of 'ouse and 'ome."

Aidan gave Slaíne a look that he hoped conveyed the message, 'Behave yourself,' stacked the wood, and found the servants' staircase, which he assumed would lead him into a network of other staircases, one of which would hopefully lead him to Dewhurst's study – wherever that might be.

He met no one on the first stair, which led him to a landing. The landing was occupied by two women who were puffing pipe smoke like dragons and tearing the master of the house to shreds with their tongues. They were dressed well enough for servants, both in black dresses with white aprons. Aidan assumed they would ask him where he was going, they being in a more authoritative position than the woman whose wood he'd carried. If they did stop him, he had an answer ready.

But it turned out that he needed no excuse. The two women spared him but a moment's glance before going back to their gossip.

Mindful that Slaíne's Pull remained stationed about where he had left her, Aidan mounted the next staircase, which was to the left and behind him. The stairs were worn from much use, and here he ran into more servants, swearing at him for getting in their way. Still no one stopped him.

He was still on the back side of the house, the servants' network of stairs and passageways. Dewhurst's study might be this high up, if Dewhurst were a traditional man and liked to do things fashionably. If not…well, Aidan would check the floors below and the one above as well.

This landing was deserted. He could feel the Pulls and repulsions below, distant tugs at his person, besides Sláine's tug at his core, but hers he was growing accustomed to. Aidan reached out and felt for human Pulls on this level of the house. There were none. Then he concentrated and discerned bits of iron repelling him from here and there, nothing larger than a penknife. But he did not allow himself to breathe easy.

Through warped glass windows, he heard busy chattering in the yard. He spared one look through the pane, satisfied himself that no alarm was being sounded, and moved with purpose through a dark, narrow doorway, which led him into the living part of the manor.

The place was resplendent, full of rich and beautiful tapestries, a glass chandelier that extended from the ceiling and down the length of a grand, weaving staircase not five yards ahead. Again he paused, felt for human Pulls and found none but two solitary ones on the floor below him. He'd best tread with a lighter foot than he had done so far.

Aidan ignored the human Pulls for a moment, then reached out and felt for paper, oilskin, and even leather Pulls. The room heaviest with paper Pulls came from the far end of the hall. He would check there first, work his way back as quietly as he was able, checking each room through the keyhole. Opening many doors would increase the risk of making too much noise and getting caught.

He took a steadying breath and began. The room at the end of the hall, the twelfth door on this level, was full of papers, stacked from floor to ceiling. He would never sort through all of this without getting caught, so despite what he'd planned earlier, he found every paper and oilskin Pull in the room and Dismissed them all. Hopefully, by the time someone discovered them missing, Aidan and Sláine would be long gone. Just to be certain, he felt for iron repulsions that might be concealing something. He felt none and moved on.

The next room was a guest bedroom. He doubted Dewhurst would store anything of importance in there, but just to be certain, he checked for Pulls and repulsions. There was some paper, which he Dismissed, but no repulsions.

Aidan went on like this for every room. He'd been so preoccupied with his task that he'd forgotten to pay attention to the two human Pulls on the floor below him. Alarmed, he reached out, and felt that they had retreated down to ground level.

Aidan checked on Slaíne's Pull. A second, unfamiliar Pull was sitting or standing stationary next to hers. This would be normal, he reassured himself, seeing as the kitchen had been in a frenzied state of preparation. Besides, Slaíne seemed to have the wits to handle herself. Aidan moved on.

With care, he crept back down the servants' staircase and made his way to the next floor. Again he met no human Pulls.

Encouraged by this, he began the process all over again, starting at the far end of the hall and working his way back. Most of the rooms were bedrooms that held little to no paper, but consistently more iron. It was the last door, the door next to the servants' entrance that he knew to be Dewhurst's study via a look through the keyhole.

He tried the door. It was locked. Aidan felt for iron in the lock's innermost parts. There was none. He was about to Dismiss parts of the lock, but hesitated. If he Dismissed the parts of the lock into Nothingness, he could Summon them back, but there would be no replacing them within the mechanism. In short, Dewhurst would know that his lock had been tampered with by supernatural means. He would know an enemy was near.

Again he felt for Pulls, sensed just one below him on the next floor, but now there were three on the floor above him, the one he had quit ten minutes before. He'd better move more quickly.

Aidan closed his eyes and felt for something in Nothingness that might serve to pick the lock. Nothing. If only he had thought to purchase and Dismiss a few women's hairpins into his cache. *No time for regrets now.*

Opening his eyes, Aidan felt first for iron repulsions. There was a large one, right in the middle of the room, low, perhaps below the floorboards. *A safe?* Aidan wondered. He wouldn't doubt it. This had to be where the map was hidden. Aidan needed to get into that room.

Aidan went ahead and Dismissed the inside of the lock, turned the knob, and stepped inside Dewhurst's office. It was a cluttered room, something that surprised Aidan. Papers stacked high up to the ceiling, boxes of what felt like different metals in various shapes and volumes, and a neat shelf of books, all covered in dust. "Hmm." Aidan focused on those immediately. Dewhurst, as far as Aidan knew, was not a learned man. It was no wonder the volumes were dusty. And yet…something was off about them.

He knew he might as well do the job thoroughly, so he Dismissed all the papers in the room, excluding the pages of the books. In the back of his mind he noted that there were fewer Pulls in the kitchen downstairs. Slaíne's Pull and the stranger's Pull remained in the same spot.

Concentrating was taking an effort, as the powers he'd used thus far had muddied his thinking. Paper was, as objects went, not too substantial and should not cause so much mental exhaustion…when Dismissed, Summoned, or Called in small batches. He'd probably taken care of at least thirty dictionaries' worth of paper into Nothingness. The mere suggestion of the thought put a heavy weight on Aidan's mind, and it was with difficulty that he returned to task.

Those books were off. The first shelf, the topmost one, was covered in dust, and there were no strange Pulls coming from their pages. The second shelf was the same. But the third shelf looked cleaner than the others. Aidan glanced at the titles of the books: they were old with worn binding, their gilt letters fading into oblivion. He picked one up and turned the page. *Durgo the Cunning's Rise and Subsequent Downfall: A Historical Account.* Unknowledgeable as to whom this Durgo the Cunning might be, Aidan replaced the book and again reached out with power and felt a small iron repulsion. Blinking, he ran his hand along the books until he found the source: a small iron key, which had been tucked inside the spine binding of the second-to-last book on the right.

Wasting no time, Aidan seized the key and Dismissed the rug covering the metal repulsion in the floor. He paused a moment, listening and reaching out for human Pulls. There was no one on the floor below him anymore, so he Dismissed the floorboards and found the source of the repulsions. It was a small iron safe box, about the size of Aidan's torso. He got onto his hands and knees and tried the key, which clicked the lock open. Something in Aidan's mind screamed, *Too easy!* but he ignored the warning bells and removed the oilskins inside. Several maps with the vaguest of hints scrawled in the legends. "This must be it," he muttered, Dismissing the lot of them.

He'd taken enough time. Slaíne would be getting worried. Aidan did not bother Summoning the floorboards or the rug; he might drop them by accident, thus making enough noise to draw unwanted attention. So he crept out of the room, shut the door, mindful of human Pulls, and returned to the servants' side of the upstairs. They might have to run fast and hard, but somehow Aidan thought not. Everything was going well.

He was on the second stairway leading down when he felt human Pulls fast approaching. He could retreat back up the stairs and hide behind a curtain, but if he were caught hiding, that would for certain raise the alarm. If only he could think straight! He could not Dismiss himself, lest he risk the wrath of the curse that bound Slaíne to himself, could not Summon the silver sword lest.... It was too late. The two women were upon him. They were the servants he had seen gossiping earlier, and this time they regarded him with a wary eye.

"Whatchoo doin' up this 'igh?"

"I got lost," Aidan said, remembering on the second word to keep up the lower class accent.

The two women looked at each other. "Well," said the second, smaller woman, "don't let mistress know you was lost. She'll think you was stealing stuff."

Aidan shook his head. "Thank you much." And with that reprimanding, he trotted down the remainder of the staircase, wound round the corner, and took the one returning to the kitchen. Too late did he notice the iron repelling him, marring and twisting Slaíne's Pull. He looked up with a start.

"Oh, I'm sorry, sir," she sobbed before Lady Dewhurst could stop her, the dagger pressing against Slaíne's throat.

CHAPTER FOURTEEN

For one calculating moment, Aidan stood there, keenly aware that he needed to do something and fast. But his thoughts were so muddied, his mind was so tired, that the only thing he could think to do was Dismiss more. Nothing he could Dismiss, however, would do them one lick of good. Lady Dewhurst could not be Dismissed, neither could Slaíne nor the iron blade digging into her porcelain throat. He could Dismiss the chair Slaíne sat in, giving her captor a surprise that might work in his favor…if not for the blasted blade! Any surprise movement could cause the instrument to dig deeper into her flesh, causing damage that Aidan did not want to think about.

"Think carefully, Mr. Ingledark. This blade is sharp, and her skin is only so thick just there."

He glared at the odious woman. And it occurred to him, a cruel, ugly thought: he could dash out of there right that moment, leaving Slaíne to her fate. Did he really owe her anything? Yet as soon as the idea formed in his mind, it died and vanished. He could not leave her. As an alarm was taken up by Lady Dewhurst and he remained where he stood, unflinching and unmoving, he flattered himself that it was Slaíne's stupid Pull that rooted him to the spot. He could not be honest with himself; he would not.

As the house was surrounded with human Pulls armed with iron, and shouts were taken up, and the pig on the spit was allowed to burn and perfume the air with its acridity, something that had been wriggling loose inside Aidan gave way entirely. Whatever control he possessed over his ability was gone. Blood pounding in his head, Aidan Dismissed. Aidan Dismissed the table at which Slaíne sat, her face a blur from behind the film over his glazed eyes. The pig vanished, then rematerialized on the counter, splattering boiling hot juices and fat onto those standing too close. A scream, feral, primal filled the room. Every last piece of non-iron cutlery vanished. A dozen kitchen knives were Called, soared across the room inches from Aidan's breast before shooting out from him and planting themselves in several different human Pulls that he could find. The scream became a roar of rage, as the Pulls lessened in vitality. Someone was openly weeping, and clarity returned at last to Aidan. The screaming ceased.

The film cleared from his eyes. Slaíne was the one crying, her eyes full of remorse and…. Goodness, she was terrified of him. And that was the last impression he had before something repulsive and hard hit him over the head. The rest was stars and darkness.

★   ★   ★

"This ain't goin' so well," said a familiar voice. Aidan knew he was in the dream world because he found himself back on his former estate and the barn was whole and not an ash heap. He blinked his mind's eye and beheld four stooped forms covered in rags. Aidan groaned.

"Not you four."

"Least he hasn't lost the whole of his mind."

"Quiet, Reek," said the elf who called herself Treevain.

"What are you doing in my head?" Aidan demanded. "How did you get here?"

The four exchanged crafty looks before the fattest one said, "We're dead, that's why we're here. What is you doin' here?"

"That question was of a rhetorical nature," said the tall one helpfully.

Aidan sighed. "It's my head."

The four elves' heads bobbed as if he were very smart and wise to have realized this obvious fact.

Shoulder prickling and cold, Aidan shook himself. He needed to wake up; something told him that he was in dire straits in the conscious realm.

Reek seemed to realize he was trying to rouse himself, because she shook her head and put her hands on his arms to keep him from jerking around. "Wait. Wait! We've been trying to reach yous."

"You've got what is ourn!"

"Aye," shouted two of the four.

Treevain told them to do something rather rude, and they quieted. "Do not give Meraude the Goblets, Aidan Ingledark. She's got the Warring Goblet now and will soon try to possess more. Give her nothing she requires."

Aidan sighed. *"Why should I listen to anything you four say? You tried to kill me, for the love of all that is—"*

"All's fair when you take someffink that ain't yourn." The hideous creature sniffed. *"Tea ain't the same wiffout Slaíne."*

"Oh, aye," said the fat one mournfully. *"But there would be no enjoying tea in this realm, no how."*

"Being dead does have an effect on the tasting and the eating and the drinking," offered the shortest.

"The point is, Lord Ingledark, you owes us four favors. And you'll repay that debt by finding the Tower and entering the Seeing Pool."

"The Seeing Pool?" Aidan repeated.

"Yes, we reckon you know where that is."

"That is where Meraude is," Aidan pointed out.

The four nodded. *"Oh, we know. So don't bring no Goblets there."*

"She'll kill me if I arrive without any Goblets." For whatever reason, his vision began to grow fuzzy. The four elves blurred, and their anxious voices grew concerned.

"Blasted iron."

"Ruins all good Scrying missions."

"Oh aye."

The pulse in Aidan's head thrummed a painful tattoo and the world began to fade to black again. He became acutely aware that he was moving toward iron, perhaps an entire room of it, not of his own accord. Yet in this state of limbo, he could still make out the elves' warnings not to trust Meraude, not to give her the Goblets Immortal, and so forth and so on.

The four said they were dead. That raised many questions, none of which Aidan could form into words coherent enough for the creatures to hear and comprehend. At the same time, wherever his conscious self was being moved, he was no more able to prevent it, such was the state of things. He felt the temperature shift from warm and stuffy to cold and damp. The colder it grew, the harder it was for him to hear the elves' pleas, and the more Pulls and repulsions he felt.

Aidan attempted to move his fingers, but had no control over any part of himself. Slaíne's Pull was not too far away, but he could not hear her, just the muffled voices of determined men. He smelled the dampness, and it clung to his skin.

"Is he still breathing?" asked a stout, cheerful voice. Dewhurst.

"Yes, milord."

"Set him down there, and we'll see if we can rouse him. You've secured the girl upstairs?"

"With difficulty," said a thin, nasal voice that Aidan did not recognize. *The elves' faces surged into view and Treevain shouted the last words he would hear before waking: "I held on to the maps. Lot of good they'll do ya now...."* And with that, the pain became at once more than a dull, distant throb; it bloomed into an earth-splitting headache.

"He lives," said a snake-like voice.

Aidan felt cold iron pressing against his back, repulsing and yet restraining him. Furious, he realized he was manacled to and with the metal. Before opening his eyes and revealing that he was in fact awake, he felt the Pulls around him. There were four of them, including Dewhurst. Sláine's Pull, he realized, was farther away than he would have liked, yet it felt as strong as ever.

"Rouse him. I want to make sure there's no permanent damage." It was Dewhurst who spoke as iron exchanged hands.

A great shudder rippled through Aidan's body. He'd never felt so many repulsions in his life. It left him feeling as though he was being pushed upward with many icy hands whilst at the same time being pulled down by them.

A wave of water hit him in the face. Sputtering and choking, he gasped for air. The room was as he had imagined it: iron walls, iron floor, but mercifully there was no iron ceiling, which would have made Aidan feel like he was being crushed more so than he already did.

"Dry him off. I don't want him catching his death."

Aidan resisted straining against his bonds as a foreign human Pull approached and threw a cloth over his head. For one wild moment, he believed the man meant to suffocate him, and he was prepared to Dismiss the fabric, but there was no need. The man finished absorbing the water and quickly moved away from Aidan.

The thought that he might Dismiss himself into Nothingness was cut short by Dewhurst, who must have guessed what he was planning. The stout man stepped forward – Aidan could feel his Pull, if not see him from his prone position. "I wouldn't try anything...tricky, Ingledark. We've got your traveling companion trussed up nice and tight, as you

must be able to tell with that remarkable extra sense of yours."
Dewhurst loomed over him, a smug look of satisfaction painting his
features. He had grown old since last Aidan had taken a good look
at him. The lord of the land's brown hair had faded to a dull gray
and was thinning in places, and his Pull wasn't as substantial as it had
once been, despite the added bulk of weight. Heavy bags sat under
his watery blue eyes, and lines ran from his eyes to his brows and
along the edges of his mouth.

"What do you want, Dewhurst?" Aidan said, keeping the venom
out of his voice, for he knew it would get him nowhere. His head
continued to pound as the lord spoke, his voice of such a timbre and
volume it made Aidan's pain increase doubly.

"Not yet, Ingledark. We'll get to that soon enough." He paused
here and ran a hand down the collar of his fine linen robe. The man
always had been immaculately dressed, and there were few things
Aidan disrespected more than a dandy. He drew Aidan's attention
to point above him on the ceiling. "See a door, my lad? Means of
escape? Comfort? No, I didn't think so. Those aren't the real things
that you want, are they? I wonder...."

Aidan rolled his eyes. "Quit with the theatrics, old man. I fear the
boards you tread will not hold your girth."

Of all things, the man laughed an amused laugh. He leaned
over Aidan, much to the captive's discomfiture, his eyes raking in
goodness knows what details. "You don't seem to have aged much.
What are you? Twenty-something?"

He looked over at his men, one of whom quickly piped up
with,"Three and thirty, milord. If Prewitt is to be believed."

Dewhurst nodded. "Yes, time has been kind to you. I, on the
other hand...." There was another staccato burst of laughter that
sounded only half-sincere, and it faded out as the man frowned.
"Tell me, Ingledark, what do you want?"

Aidan would not play this game. He felt the Pulls around the
room and above the room. Slaíne's was stationary and it at once
felt like it was in the room with him yet separate somehow. He did
not know what to make of that, so he moved on to the men. He
could Dismiss their clothes, humiliate them, focus hard on their hair
and leave only tufts behind. But those pranks would only mentally

exhaust him and haze his thinking, and Aidan needed every ounce of mental strength he could muster.

"Don't look so worried, Ingledark. I'm not planning on killing you."

"Change of heart?" Aidan snapped.

The man shook his head with a rueful smile that Aidan knew better than to trust. "An increase of knowledge. But you have not answered my question, though I believe I am already in possession of the answer."

This was going to grow tedious rather quickly. Aidan hated cat and mouse games, treading lightly on words that could be his saving grace or his undoing. He winced involuntarily as a new pain shot up his skull.

Dewhurst let out a sigh. "I see I shall have to put forth your answers for you."

"Be my guest," Aidan muttered.

The lord snapped his fingers, and one of his men approached with a goblet made of iron. Aidan's expression must have betrayed his reaction to Dewhurst, who snorted with derision. "Do not worry, my lad. It is not one of the Immortals. It's an ordinary iron goblet containing something to relax you…and perhaps your tongue."

Aidan's head was lifted, and the goblet was placed to his lips, which he mashed together. He knew what was coming next, though it did not stop him from gasping.

Dewhurst had his nose pinched, and after a minute of holding his breath, Aidan was forced to open his mouth, and the alcohol, ran down his throat before he could Dismiss it.

He was able to cough and spit some of it out, but another chalice was lifted to his lips, and another torrent of tepid liquor slipped down his throat, and then another. Before long, his thoughts were jumbled. Dewhurst's face swam before his eyes.

"I'll tell you what you want, Ingledark. You want control. Of your life, of yourself, of your…heart." His ensuing chuckle was a dark one. "I hold all three in my hands." He flexed his fingers inches from Aidan's face, then tightened them into a fist. "Now, I will tell you what *I* want." Again Dewhurst snapped his fingers, and more iron was brought forward.

To Aidan's revulsion, Dewhurst now held an iron dagger the size of his hand, and he was cleaning it off with a rag and more medicinal-smelling alcohol. If the man wasn't going to kill Aidan, what was left?

Was he to be tortured for information that he did not possess? He tried to scheme quickly, to come up with some means of escape, but his thoughts would not clear, and his pulse thrummed in his ears as the dagger was held up to a candle.

"Essence of cloves," Dewhurst said to the man behind him. They were taking no chances; everything that they did not wear was iron.

Essence of cloves was poured on the uppermost part of Aidan's forearm, almost to the joint. Now Aidan did start to struggle. He strained against his bonds as if he might break them, but he knew it was in vain.

Dewhurst lowered the blade. "Someone hold the boy still. I don't want to kill him by accident. You, you just there, you've the goblet still? Good. Good."

Realizing what Dewhurst meant to do, Aidan tried Dismissing anything that had a Pull, but he was too sluggish. The blade pierced his arm, drawing a gasp from his lips. He could scarce feel the liquid running from his veins as the men held him down. He felt giddy and lightheaded.

"Yes, very nice." Dewhurst's voice was pleased and deadly to Aidan's ears.

Aidan thought he would go mad as the intermittent *ploink, ploink, ploink* of his blood dripping into the goblet filled the silence. His vision started to fuzz over, and he gave an involuntary shudder that even the brutes holding him down could scarce withstand.

After an eternity, the bleeding ceased, and he was bandaged up by the lackeys and covered with a scratchy blanket that smelled of earth and rot. Something firm was propped up under his head, and he could see Dewhurst studying the crimson in the cup.

He noticed Aidan staring at him and dipped the glass in a salute. "To your health." And he drank.

Aidan watched Dewhurst drain the cup without flinching, and thought he might lose consciousness again or the meager contents of his stomach at the very least. But Aidan did not faint. He needed to see if it worked.

Dewhurst dropped the cup as one burned and, hands shaking, he held them up to a light on the wall. "Interesting." He turned an eye to Aidan and, with a look of utmost concentration on his face, Dewhurst reached out as if he could grasp the air.

Aidan felt a weak Tug at his collar, but he stilled it with a Tug of his own.

Dewhurst frowned and focused on something else. With a cry of delight from Dewhurst and his men, a candlestick on the wall's ledge fell over and sizzled out. He looked at Aidan knowingly for a moment, as if he'd just been dealt into a secret that had eluded him for years.

Aidan's headache worsened tenfold, and his eyes would not quite focus. He kept the expression on his face neutral, but Dewhurst must've known what horrors were playing out in Aidan's mind.

As a boy, Aidan had stumbled upon his abilities by accident. He did not recall the sense of glee that Dewhurst was most obviously experiencing. All he remembered was terror and pain, as he could not prevent objects from flying at him.

The men with Dewhurst applauded their master, who managed to make one of their capes fly out behind them. This feat must seem amazing to them, but it did not seem to impress Dewhurst. His face darkened and he cut off his men's applause. "Upstairs, all of you."

The three guards thundered up a staircase that Aidan could not see but could sense. "What do you think of that, m'lad?" When Aidan did not answer, Dewhurst came at him, brandishing another knife. "Well?"

"You're disgusting and pathetic, but it wasn't anything I didn't know already." The words had no feeling in them; Aidan was exhausted and wished unconsciousness would overtake him then and there. It did not.

With a laugh, Dewhurst brought the blade to rest against Aidan's jugular. It was cold and repulsive, and Aidan wanted to wrench away, but he knew better. "Tell me your secrets."

"What secrets?" Aidan asked.

"Don't play the fool, Aidan Ingledark. Tell me, how do you make things disappear and reappear? Shouldn't I be able to do that now?" He looked thoughtful for a moment and then increased pressure on the blade. "Do I need more blood?"

Aidan rolled his eyes. "How would I know? I've never feasted on another's lifeblood before like a ruddy vampire."

That earned him a smart slap upside the head.

Aidan grunted. He'd bitten his tongue by accident.

Dewhurst continued talking as if Aidan had not insulted him. "You drank of one of the Goblets Immortal, then." It was not a question. So, he did *not* know as much about Aidan as the seer did. That made Aidan wince; he hadn't trusted that woman a jot, and yet she hadn't shared the most important details about his and her abilities to this man. Dewhurst must really be Larkin's enemy. And if Larkin had been on his side and not Dewhurst's, perhaps she could have helped them after all.

Aidan was struck again. Stars swam before his eyes, and he let out a small involuntary groan.

"Tell me why I don't have your abilities." Dewhurst's agitation was showing, a weakness that Aidan could exploit if only he could think through the pain and the alcohol.

When his vision cleared, Aidan was silent, trying to gain whatever control he could over the situation. But when Dewhurst flew at him a third time, he blurted out in frustration, "How on earth am I supposed to know?"

Dewhurst lowered his hand and studied Aidan. When he spoke, his voice was distant, as if he were thinking out loud and not actually speaking to his prisoner. "I was certain it had to be in your blood, and it is…just not as potent. You drank from a Goblet Immortal, the magic flows through your veins. What was she not telling me?"

She? Could the madman mean Larkin? Aidan thought it was likely, but if so, perhaps the seer had been *forced* to tell. He shuddered. What of her own abilities? Did Dewhurst not know what Larkin was?

"Perhaps I just need more practice," Dewhurst was saying. With that, he reached out his hand again and Pulled Aidan's cravat, which gave a weak tug and then lay still. With a gasp for breath, Dewhurst set his jaw and gave it another go. This time, the cravat obeyed Dewhurst to a greater degree, though it was not what the lord must have wanted. He gave out another great gasp for air and reached out until he grew red in the face. This time, the cravat listened to the enemy's Calling, and choked Aidan until he could not draw breath.

Gray and black spots hazed Aidan's vision until, with much huffing and puffing, Dewhurst Released the fabric. "Well."

Aidan coughed and gagged. It felt like an invisible hand remained at his throat, a phantom presence that reminded Aidan that Dewhurst could and probably would do it again. He braced himself, ready to hold his breath in case he needed to pass out.

However, Dewhurst didn't seem to be recovering from his gasping and panting. "That was impossible," he sputtered. "Is it like that every time?"

Aidan did not know what he meant. Pulling, Pushing, Calling, Dismissing, Summoning, Releasing…it had no physical repercussions for Aidan. *Perhaps each of the Blest has a different price to pay for their abilities.* Yet as Dewhurst recovered, and Aidan thought on the matter more, the more it seemed that it might just be Dewhurst over-thinking things and putting too much physical strength into his process. Never in a million years of torture would Aidan ever advise the brute on this, lest he become more powerful. A shudder rippled through Aidan's body, and he coughed several dry coughs.

Red in the face and trembling, Dewhurst approached Aidan again. He looked years older than he had moments before, sweat dribbling down his brow and cheeks. The man reeked of perspiration.

Aidan knew he was missing something vital, something that had to do with his blood. While Dewhurst had been choking him, Aidan hadn't thought of fighting back. Why was that? He could have easily Dismissed the cravat and stopped the man. But a part of him had been focusing on what he imagined Dewhurst was thinking.

"You will tell me more later." And with that, the man's Pull retreated up the stairs.

Aidan closed his eyes and let himself drowse as the alcohol and fatigue at last won out.

CHAPTER FIFTEEN

As always, he'd gone fishing by the creek without permission. That is what happened in past reality and in his recurring dreams; and like in both reality and his dreams, Aidan made his way home after the screams had been taken up and gone at once silent. This is where the dream split off from reality. Instead of returning to find the barn ablaze and his uncle staring at it with a lost look, the old man was now smiling a sad yet sympathetic smile. He looked right through Aidan, to his very soul. "They're dead, Aidan." It wasn't his uncle's voice that spoke, though.

The voice was all at once familiar and alien. It sounded like...almost like his own. But the dream moved on and was again like the usual one he experienced. He ran into the barn, which should have collapsed on his head, but instead burst upward and outward as he experienced the Jolt. He could not control his powers for the first week he had them, and had slept in the woods for fear of discovery. As it was, his uncle had thought the barn's explosion had been due to the fertilizer the family always kept stored in mounds. Aidan had run out of there before he could find out the truth that he, Aidan, was a freak and possibly a murderer.

His dream feet carried him down to the creek, where rocks pelted his arms and legs. He could not control their Pulls, and soon collapsed, sobbing for his mother, whom he believed he had blown up in the barn explosion. Everything tugged him in distinctly different directions. There were Pulls from humans, which only took him half a day to figure out, and there were Pulls from nature and animals. The inanimate Pulls, he realized on the second day of hiding, were the weakest, and without meaning to, he ended up Dismissing half of the rocks on the mucky banks.

When he did return home, he was bruised and filthy, and his uncle had already established himself as head of the household. Dewhurst had been appointed lord of the land, and Aidan was nothing to anyone. He didn't speak for weeks at a time, and eventually he realized his uncle's true colors.

In the dream, his uncle looked down at Aidan, who swept the floors, his arms bone-tired from the day's labor. Again the voice that was not his uncle's spoke through the man's body: "Let them go, Aidan. They're dead."

Aidan awoke from the dream. He was alone, sore, and hungover, but he was no longer chained to the iron slab. Now he lay on a makeshift mattress on the floor, his ankles in irons, but his hands were free. "Odd," he muttered, then leaned over and threw up all over the floor. Again and again he retched until there was nothing left in his stomach, so he gagged for a solid five minutes.

Closing his eyes, Aidan lay back down on the mat. His head throbbed and he felt as though someone were clutching him by the throat; other than that, he seemed to be in all right shape...until he felt the throbbing in his right arm. Dewhurst had bled Aidan from his left arm, but now the right one was bandaged as well. *I must have been out harder and longer than I first thought.*

Sláine's Pull gave him a small jerk. It was on the move, and it was farther away than he knew it should be. The curse would surely take her. With a weak cry of panic, Aidan stumbled to his feet. It did no good. Before he could open his mouth to shout her name, he attempted to Call her. It worked for a moment. He felt her skid closer to where he was kept prisoner, but the iron was interfering, and he realized he might have given away a secret: that he could Call another living being. No doubt Dewhurst would be interested in learning how to do this. Aidan had no idea how he'd done it. Before Sláine, he'd never managed to Call another living soul.

He was about to shout for her again, but it occurred to him that perhaps the curse had transferred ownership to Dewhurst. If that were the case, it created a whole array of new problems.

The Pull moved away, and the iron all but entirely muted her presence from his awareness. Bereft, Aidan let out a strangled gasp. He was alone. He'd never been so empty and alone in his life. There were human Pulls moving about overhead, but they were insubstantial, featherweights in comparison. Aidan was gutted. Unbidden tears formed in his eyes, and he fought them in vain for a brief moment before letting them spill.

While he cried, he thought about his next move, his dream from earlier forgotten for the time being. How was he to get out of this mess? "Not through weeping like a child," he muttered as he rubbed the tears away with the backs of his hands. Once more he sniffed, and then he concentrated on Pulls.

The Pulls around him were nothing: the blankets, the straw, the pillow, a candle, and much to Aidan's surprise, a plate of food and a chalice full of water. He cringed at the sight of the crust of bread and thigh of chicken. His stomach lurched, and he was afraid he would begin vomiting all over again. Aidan closed his eyes, and his nausea evaporated.

Yes, the Pulls were nothing he could do anything with. He reached beyond the repulsions from the iron, but there was nothing that could aid him, not above or below, and not in the inner workings of his bonds. Perhaps he could find something to pick the lock with, though he doubted it. Dewhurst was stupid, but his advisors were not. They would have interrogated Tristram for every detail he knew. Aidan snarled at the thought of his former friend. Tristram, the one person who knew the contents of his bag of tricks, the one who had betrayed him. The heat was not in Aidan's anger, though, and soon he'd calmed enough to think clearly again.

Slaíne would be used as leverage, but to what extent, Aidan wasn't sure. Dewhurst couldn't know much of the girl's curse, unless the girl herself had been forced to share that information. With the curse's possible and probable transfer, she would be all right. However, if Dewhurst had an inkling of what power Slaíne's Pull had over Aidan, it would be used. She would be killed…. No, worse things would be done, and Aidan knew that he would give in and that it didn't have everything to do with her Pull. There was something else, something that Aidan did not wish to explore.

He would keep Slaíne out of his questions, out of his mind, and maybe there would be no need for him to give in to Dewhurst's demands. As he thought of Dewhurst, footsteps thundered overhead, and half a dozen human Pulls approached, all bearing iron. On instinct, Aidan drew back against the wall, then forced himself to lie back down and feign unconsciousness. Perhaps he could observe Dewhurst and his men before they roused him, and thus gain some advantage.

A heavy door creaked on its hinges, and iron-tipped boots thundered down into the iron dungeon. Aidan kept his eyes lightly closed and his breathing slow and even. Yes, there were six human Pulls, one of them Dewhurst's, which had changed since he had last sensed it. *He's frustrated, but he's going to act triumphant.* Aidan didn't know how he knew, but he was certain that Dewhurst was going to try to trick him into believing he'd made progress with his stolen blood and the abilities they afforded him. It was all Aidan could do not to gag at the thought of his blood being drained for this wretch.

Soft words were spoken between Dewhurst and one of his men, whose clothing's Pulls felt more expensive than a servant's, and Dewhurst's peculiar Pull approached him. Another moment of silence passed, and an iron boot tip tapped into his thigh.

Aidan jerked awake and glared up at Dewhurst, something he knew that the man expected of him. As predicted, Dewhurst wore a smug smile and showed no signs of discouragement. Perhaps he had made progress, and Aidan had been wishful in his thinking.

"You've slept long enough." Dewhurst turned his back to Aidan and took a few steps toward the stairs. He turned again, and opened his mouth to say something haughty, when a scream was taken up overhead. Whatever Dewhurst's plans had been, he looked rather put out. "What is this ruckus? Guard."

One of his men stepped forward. "Yes, milord?"

"Go and see what that was about."

The man saluted and then ran upstairs as more voices were raised in the distance.

Dewhurst turned his attention back to Aidan. "I trust that you rested well? No? Well." He chuckled. "You're probably wondering how long you've been out."

Aidan was only half-listening. With a jerk he realized that Sláine's Pull had returned, and he could tell at once that something was wrong. The Pull was as strong and distracting as ever, but something was different. Confused voices shouted over each other as Dewhurst attempted to drone on. Something hit the floor above them with a sickening thud. Someone swore and called for a doctor.

At last Dewhurst gave up all pretenses and called to one of his advisors, "Find out what the devil is going on and report back."

The man nodded and ran up the stairs himself.

Aidan could no longer contain himself. He had to know, precautions be hanged. "You do realize," he began, his tone frosty, "that my traveling companion is cursed."

Dewhurst's eyebrows shot heavenward for a moment, but he quickly reassembled them to carry an air of indifference. "Is that so?"

Aidan was prepared to say more, but decided against it. Why had Slaíne failed to mention this fact to Dewhurst? Was she trying to get herself killed? He no doubt had sent her on some errand about the household, far from this iron cage where they both now waited, and the curse had been called into effect. Had Slaíne even tried resisting orders? If not, why not?

Fortunately for Aidan, Dewhurst was distracted by two sets of footsteps thundering back down the stairs. "What is going on?" Dewhurst demanded.

The guard spoke before the adviser could. "That girl, she escaped her bonds and—"

"What? How? You were supposed to be escorting her to—" Dewhurst cut himself off and gave Aidan an appraising look.

The guard shifted his weight from foot to foot, before his master turned back and struck him across the face, as if he had been present for the escape attempt. Blood poured from the man's open mouth, and he stumbled backward a step before righting himself. No one came to his aid.

"Speak up, man."

"She tried returning inside, milord."

Dewhurst let out a small laugh before turning back to Aidan. "Why would she do that? You mentioned a curse."

Aidan just shrugged. He had said too much, and now it would be used against him. Why was he so stupid? He'd like to blame it on the lingering hangover and mental exhaustion from yesterday, but he would not be generous with himself. Instead, he kept his face clear of all tells and emotion and waited to see what Dewhurst would do or say next.

"Never mind, Ingledark. I shall get to the bottom of this mystery myself."

"If you please, milord...." said the adviser.

Dewhurst looked distracted. "What? Yes, go on."

"Captain caught her again, but before they could make much progress, she fell over and started convulsing."

Why hadn't Slaíne warned them? Dewhurst was her master now; he'd need to know this sort of thing in order to avoid hurting her by accident. On the other hand, if he found out, she would be used as leverage somehow. There was no winning this. He must speak. "Her curse is bound to me."

The men stopped talking and looked over at Aidan. Dewhurst turned last, his face wrinkled with confusion and distaste. "Oh? Interesting. Did you curse her yourself?"

Aidan translated it as: "Will I be able to as well, now that I'm drinking your blood?" Aidan decided he'd better not give that impression.

"No, it was not me, it was someone else. The curse transfers from master to master." He hated himself, but it needed to be said. He wondered what Slaíne would have wanted him to say on the matter.

Dewhurst seemed finished with those sorts of questions, but his advisers weren't. One of them, a tall man nearest the steps, spoke up. "If she belongs to Lord Dewhurst now—" He gave an acknowledging bow to his master. "what are the terms of the curse?"

For a moment, Aidan hesitated before speaking. "I don't know that she's Dewhurst's. I am almost as in the dark about the terms as you are."

"Enough," Dewhurst cried, breaking from his smug façade. "I need to know more about the Blest. How does this all work?"

"Milord," said two of the advisers, their tones warning him to be careful.

Lord Dewhurst waved their concerns aside. "Why should we be talking about curses when time is pressing? I need answers, and I need them now." He stamped his foot, making Aidan think of a petulant child.

"Milord," said the tall adviser again, "might I have a word?"

Rage flickered across Dewhurst's reddened face, but he consented to be led aside and talked to.

The three advisers spoke to him in low, urgent tones, but Aidan could not make out more than a word here and there.

Dewhurst was impatient, but why? The more Aidan strained to hear, the more he got the feeling that Dewhurst was terrified yet full of power-lust.

It would seem that the advisers were done talking to their master, who seemed unable to remain still for long. The four of them turned back to Aidan.

"Bring the girl down here," Dewhurst barked at one of the guards. He took to pacing as his orders were carried out.

Aidan tried to keep his expression blank. He wasn't stupid; he knew what they were going to do, and it would be all his fault. *My fault.* The mantra repeated itself in his mind. Hadn't he already done enough damage? Slaíne, just collateral damage. Aidan felt sick, but he didn't know what else he could have done.

He observed Slaíne's Pull as someone carried her down the stairs. There was no decrease in the Pull's strength, though it had definitely gained a different quality. It took him a moment, but soon he picked up on what had changed: the curse's ownership had transferred to Dewhurst. Aidan was no longer in control.

Slaíne was as limp as a ragdoll, though the occasional tremor would cause the man carrying her to nearly lose his grip and drop her. The guard lowered her to the ground at Dewhurst's feet, and the seizures stopped, but her eyes did not open and her breathing didn't slow.

Dewhurst observed her with disdain. "So, you're cursed, eh?" he said to her. "Well? Speak."

"I don't think she can hear you," Aidan cut in before he could strike her.

"I didn't ask you." Dewhurst turned and spoke in low tones to who Aidan decided must be his head adviser.

The man tugged at his salt-and-pepper beard and nodded as Dewhurst spoke. "That very well could be, milord. Excellent deduction."

This wouldn't do. Aidan needed to hear what they were saying and what they intended to do. Still keeping his eyes off Slaíne – he knew that one look at her could ruin his focus – Aidan tried inching closer to where the men were talking.

The adviser said something about 'maps' and 'interrogate'. Dewhurst cleared his throat and countered with something that sounded like, "She can't know," and shuddered.

Aidan moved closer still, mindful of Pulls and appearances. No one was paying him much mind, which was a relief and at the same time suspicious; perhaps they did not view him as a threat.

As if in response to Aidan's unspoken thoughts, Dewhurst looked right at him and smirked. His advisers left the room with a look at their master, and Aidan was left alone with Dewhurst and two of the guards.

"Let's not play these games, Ingledark." He snapped his fingers, and one of his guards brought over a stool, which he flopped down on with an ominous groan. "You took something of mine which is valuable beyond measure, and I would like it back. If you don't give it back, well, there's no saying what I will do to your traveling companion." He laughed at the last two words, as if to imply there was something more to her than that.

Aidan affected a bored expression. "Not one for originality, as always."

Dewhurst snorted. "We checked your person, and you're obviously not carrying the household's treasury of papers and oilskins. You sent them away. Bring them back. Now." Dewhurst drew an iron dagger from the sheath at his ankle and handed it to one of the guards.

The guard gave his master a confused look for a moment, but realization dawned on him as Dewhurst gestured to Slaíne's prone form. She looked so helpless and pale lying there. They could do anything to her, and he would be powerless to stop them...unless he played his cards very carefully.

"Enough with the dramatics, Dewhurst. Here are your papers. Now, be a good tyrant and tell your man to stand down." With a blink, Aidan released all the papers and oilskins that he'd been keeping in Nothingness, being careful not to Summon anything else. He felt the silver sword's comforting presence in his stores, and it gave him some reassurance that they were not entirely at this man's mercy.

Apparently Dewhurst had thought Aidan would need more persuasion than that, as he blinked with surprise and let out a low, "Oh."

The man with the iron dagger awaited Dewhurst's directions, the blade raised.

Dewhurst snapped his fingers twice, and the man stood down, lowering the weapon. "Well, we'll see if everything is in order. You, Philip, or whatever it is your mother calls you."

"Milord?"

"Take these papers upstairs and have Rumpolt and Stearns sort through them. Tell them to pay particular attention to the oilskins, and I don't want to see any forgeries. Everything will need to be checked for accuracy."

"Yes, milord." And with that, the guard began scooping up mounds of paper and dividing them into piles he could carry.

Dewhurst paid the guard no mind, his attention still on Aidan. Despite having all of his dratted papers back, the man did not seem in the least bit pleased. He glowered at Aidan, and when he spoke, his voice was low and full of venom. "What can you tell me of the Goblets Immortal?"

Aidan sighed. "I know even less than you, I am certain."

Dewhurst thrust up a finger to waylay his excuses. "Nonetheless, Aidan Ingledark, I know your family was part of the Circle. You must be in possession of some knowledge, even if you are unaware of its importance. Think, man. Think!"

"All I know is third- and fourth-hand information. I was young when my parents died." He gave Dewhurst a pointed look. "And before their death, I displayed none of my abilities." Was that saying too much? Perhaps it was, but Dewhurst did not seem to catch that Aidan had to be Jolted. Maybe that's what needed to happen to anyone who sought to wield a Goblet's powers. He would use that information for leverage… later. Right now he needed to find a way to get himself out of this mess. The problem was, no immediate ideas were coming to him.

Dewhurst regarded him with a thoughtful expression, though the frustration was still there, just held back. Sure enough, when he spoke his tone was even. "All right. I'll let you know what I know, and then you can fill in with whatever I missed."

Despite himself, Aidan perked up at this. Perhaps Dewhurst knew more than Aidan did. Perhaps it would be Aidan who learned something to his advantage. Dewhurst did, after all, know about the Circle, and Aidan had only heard that cult mentioned recently.

"There are six Goblets, each with different powers." He began ticking them off on his fingers. "Warring, Summoning, Drifting, Seeing, Questing, and Enduring. Each Goblet bestows its powers upon he who drinks from it. Am I right so far?"

Aidan nodded, though it was a lie. He had drunk from the Warring Goblet, and he certainly did not possess any new abilities. Slaíne had told him that the Goblet's powers only lasted until the drinker's body expelled whatever it had imbibed from the vessel. The only lasting way to have powers, it would seem, was to have absorbed a Goblet's contents when forming in the womb. Aidan stopped Dewhurst to ask a question of his own. "What was the Circle's purpose?" Though he was fairly certain, from his vision and from what Larkin had said, that he knew.

Dewhurst frowned at being interrupted, but he answered anyway.

"Well, we can be civil, now can't we?" He paused, as if hesitant to give Aidan anything he wanted. At length he spoke again. "To find the Goblets and unite them…or, so my source tells me."

Aidan guessed but did not voice that Larkin had been the so-called source.

"There were mostly women in the Circle. Goodness knows why."

That made Aidan's stomach churn. So, he was right. The Circle had been a mere cult to breed Blest children. Aidan remembered what his mother had said in one of his visions, for now he was certain it had been of her: Lady Ingledark had spoken to her brother, Aidan's uncle, of escaping. That answered the question of whether or not she was a willing participant. What of Aidan's father, then? They'd been married and happy when Aidan was a boy. Had they escaped the Circle together? "What happened to the Circle?" Aidan asked.

When Dewhurst spoke, he growled. "What does it matter? It's done with. Now, it's your turn to answer my questions. Enough of your cheek."

Slaíne still lay motionless on the floor, but her breathing at last began to slow. She let out a tiny moan.

Dewhurst ignored her. "Six Goblets, united called the Immortal. That can only mean one thing – drink from all six, and you'll have eternal life." He gave Aidan a thoughtful look before continuing. "But why don't the powers stick? I drank your blood and I possessed powers for approximately three hours. There must be something I'm missing." They sat in silence for a moment, Dewhurst staring into nowhere while Aidan looked for his chance to strike.

Would it be possible to kill Dewhurst here and now? The guards didn't seem alert, and Dewhurst himself was leaning forward, right within strangling distance. The thought made Aidan break out in a cold sweat. He'd taken lives before in self-defense, watched the light leave a person's eyes and felt their Pull slacken and fade to the point where they no longer anchored him. He was almost certain he could Dismiss a corpse. It wouldn't do to have witnesses. If the guards left, Aidan could strangle the man, Dismiss his body – evidence that could get him hanged – and hope that Dewhurst had the keys to Aidan's shackles on his belt. There was a definite repulsion around the man's midsection. Perhaps that is where the keys sat.

A shudder rippled through Aidan's body. He had no love for Dewhurst, but the thought of killing a man who hadn't a fighting chance left Aidan feeling hollow for having considered it. It wasn't mercy or pity, he reasoned with himself as the silence wore on. It wasn't sporting.

The thought and the moment passed. Aidan caught Slaíne blinking, her eyes distant and unfocused before closing again. No, it would not do to make an escape now, not until he was certain that Slaíne was in any shape to run and that her curse would rebind itself to him.

"I'll be frank with you, young man." Dewhurst's words startled Aidan and he nearly leaped to his feet. Dewhurst smirked. "My powers are only a shadow of what I've observed in you. I need the Summoning Goblet, the sooner the better." He rose to his feet and took to pacing, treading in Aidan's pool of sick without realizing it. "Until then, your blood will have to do."

Aidan told Dewhurst where he could go, earning a whack to his already sore head.

"You will teach me how to...." Dewhurst paused, waving his hand around as if he would be able to physically grasp the words he was looking for. "You know, what you do when you make things disappear and reappear."

Aidan shrugged. He was not going to help the man out with his vocabulary, even if there was no choice but to help him with the task.

"Whatever you call it." Dewhurst's eyes flashed, and a cruel smile spread across his face, exposing small teeth. "You are not stupid, no matter how much I wish to believe it. You know exactly what will happen if you do not give me your full cooperation."

Aidan pushed his luck. "Why do you need the Summoning Goblet?"

"Hmm? What's that?"

"I said why did you single out the Summoning Goblet? You said you wanted all six." That earned Aidan a kick in the shin.

"I do not see how that is any of your concern."

There was worry there. Something had Dewhurst scared, something that possession of the Summoning Goblet could assuage. But what?

Aidan resisted the urge to rub the spot where Dewhurst had kicked him, though it smarted something terrible. Instead, he studied the man's face. Dewhurst did not look worried. His expression and his posture did nothing to betray anxiety. What had Aidan so convinced that this man was in all actuality terrified?

"My staff will bring down some breakfast shortly," Dewhurst surprised him by saying. He read the expression on Aidan's face correctly. "Must keep up your strength. But if you refuse nourishment, well...." He looked sideways at Slaíne. "If you refuse, she doesn't eat either." He let out a booming laugh, as if this whole ordeal were quite amusing to him. He snapped his fingers, and his two guards were at his side.

"Milord?" they chorused.

He held up a finger, indicating they should wait for his words. He addressed Aidan. "How far?"

Aidan frowned, wondering what he could mean. Then he realized that Dewhurst was referring to the boundaries of the curse, how far he, Dewhurst, could be from Slaíne before it took hold. So, he wasn't as stupid as he looked. "No more than ten yards," Aidan replied, though he believed the distance to be longer.

Dewhurst considered him for a moment, nodded, then turned to his men. "Carry the girl upstairs after me. Then send Cook to me. I have special instructions." Without another word to Aidan or anyone, the lord of the manor turned on his heel and sauntered across the dungeon floor and up the wooden stairs, his one guard carrying Slaíne after him.

The other guard remained for a moment, regarding Aidan with interest. He waited until the footsteps on the stairs had retreated, then reached inside his vest.

Aidan watched him warily.

Without a word, the guard handed a small iron box to Aidan, who accepted it with some reluctance. "Open it," the man mouthed, his expression earnest.

Aidan did so, and was surprised to see a slip of paper. He looked up at the guard, his mouth starting to form a question, but the man snatched the iron box out of his hands, tucked it back into his pocket, turned heel and left.

At once Aidan opened the slip of paper and read, "Stay put. Don't resist."

He groaned and crumpled up the paper in his fist. For a brief second, he'd thought he might have an unexpected ally in the manor. Was this another one of Dewhurst's tricks? Perhaps he had been trying to give

Aidan false hope. Just to be on the safe side, Aidan tore up the note and hid the pieces in what appeared to be an ancient chamber pot.

An hour later, a grumpy woman in a filthy apron carried a tray containing a plate and cup, but no cutlery. She slammed the tray down in front of Aidan and backed away. "You're lucky you're gettin' anything," she barked.

Aidan raised his eyebrows at her but said nothing.

"Don't you look at me like that. Well, go on. Eat."

Aidan did not move.

With an exasperated sigh, the woman pulled a horsewhip out of her back pocket and came at Aidan. "I'm not ter leave until you've et every last crumb."

Aidan looked at the plate. There were two pieces of burnt toast, a slab of fatty bacon, and two fried tomatoes. He did not wish to admit it to himself, but food sounded wonderful just now. If he had been unconscious for as long as he thought, then he hadn't had a substantial meal in over three days.

Slowly and deliberately, Aidan nibbled away at the toast, all the while watching the cook to see how fast he could get a rise out of her. Perhaps it was not the smartest thing to do.

The woman, built more like a burly man than anything, brandished the whip more than once, her lips pursed. "Master said you stole important papers."

Aidan looked her up and down, then gave the woman a non-committal shrug.

Her expression soured even more. "Eat faster. Like I haven't got better things ter be doing than watching thee pick at yourn food."

Aidan washed down the rest of the toast with a swig of water, which he first studied for strange Pulls. This sent the woman over the edge. She raised her whip to strike, but Aidan Dismissed it before it could come within in an inch of his face.

"Thanks for that."

Eyes wide and body trembling, the cook all but tripped over herself to get away. "Devil's work! What are you?"

Again Aidan shrugged. He finished the rest of the meal, no longer able to hide his hunger, and the woman watched him, her eyes filled with horror.

The second he drained the remainder of water from the cup, and there was not a speck of food left on the plate, the cook snatched up the tray and fled up the stairs, faster than he'd thought her girth would allow.

So, not all of the staff knew what Dewhurst was up to. As Aidan searched for something to pick the manacle's lock with, he wondered if he could use that information to get a few of them on his side.

*   *   *

The next day ran on much like the previous one: long and tedious. Only this time he saw neither Dewhurst nor Slaíne, and the cook was replaced with a confused-looking scullery maid who barely regarded Aidan. Aidan ate burnt toast and a cold sausage, explored Pulls, searched his stash in Nothingness for something that might aid him, and came up with schemes that he immediately gave up because he knew they were futile. If only he could think straight. He'd never felt so powerless and so foggy-headed, and he knew why: iron.

On the fifth morning of his captivity, Aidan woke up to five men standing over him, the repulsion of iron in their grasps. One man sat on his chest, one sat down on his legs, and the other two bled him. Aidan did not resist as they had apparently feared he would. He couldn't escape or think clearly enough to Dismiss the blood, so what was the point of fighting them? Once they'd gotten what they wanted, the men cleaned up his arm, bandaged the spot, and left with the iron chalice of crimson.

Dizzy and lightheaded, Aidan lay there, willing himself not to throw up his breakfast. Two hours later, the scullery maid from the previous day came down with a tray of food: cold cornmeal mush, a fatty hunk of braised beef, and two small carrots. While Aidan ate, he attempted to make casual conversation with the girl, though she seemed more interested in watching the ceiling than answering his roundabout questions. After he'd finished the food, and drained the cup of water, she took the tray and its contents and made her way up the stairs.

When she had left, a maid came down and emptied the chamber pot, much to Aidan's relief; it had been full and sitting there for two days now. She did not even give Aidan a glance, but finished her task as quickly as she could manage. When she returned half an hour later with the pot empty and scrubbed out, Aidan tried a different tack than he had with the scullery maid. "Thank you," he murmured, but she ignored him still.

The remainder of the week wore on like this. Every other day, Aidan was bled. Every morning and afternoon and evening, meals were brought and cleared, and he was cleaned up after. It was like being a guest in a very perverted inn, one that charged in pints of blood.

It was on the morning of the eleventh day that Aidan felt Dewhurst's Pull overhead. Aidan was still lightheaded from being bled, and was recovering on the stinking mass of blankets. Flies buzzed around his prone, unwashed form, but he did not bat them away. He was growing weaker. Every day he felt it. Not only was he losing blood, he was losing muscle. He was not being fed enough to maintain what body fat and muscle he had, and the iron was certainly not helping. In short, Aidan knew himself to be on a slow, exhausting path to being bled to death. But Dewhurst's Pull meant something was happening. Maybe he would come down into the dungeon, and that would give Aidan a chance to try one of his most desperate ploys on the man: tell him everything and hope he'd be set free. Even as he considered it, Aidan knew it to be futile.

As he lay his head back down, shouts were taken up overhead. Slaíne's Pull returned, and jerked him to an upright sitting position. Dewhurst was livid about something, and Slaíne was shouting something back. There were scuffling sounds overhead, and it sounded like someone had hit the floor with a thud. "Slaíne," Aidan groaned, shaking his head.

There were more shouts, and Dewhurst's Pull headed for the set of stairs leading down into the dungeon, Slaíne's Pull quick on his heels, flanked by two guards. "He'd just better ruddy well tell me," Dewhurst was bellowing as he thundered down the stairs.

"He don't have it, or else he'd a'given it to you," Slaíne spat.

"Don't mouth off at me, fool girl." As Dewhurst entered with a lit candle in one hand and a handkerchief in the other, he looked at Aidan, who thought the man's head might explode, it was so red. "Where are the blasted maps?"

Aidan blinked. "The Goblet maps? I gave them to you."

"You gave me back all of my papers, but the two maps in my possession you have withheld. Where are they?"

Perplexed, Aidan closed his eyes and felt in Nothingness for paper and oilskin. There was nothing made of those materials in his cache, so he opened his eyes and shook his head. "There's nothing there."

Dewhurst swore and stalked closer to where Aidan was sitting. "Those are my maps. I need those maps. You will give them to me at once."

Despite himself, Aidan's voice rose as well. "I told you I gave you everything back. I don't have your blasted maps."

"Liar." Without warning, Dewhurst turned to Slaíne and backhanded her.

"Leave her out of this," Aidan warned.

She tumbled to the floor, and only then did she look at Aidan. Both of Slaíne's eyes were black, and her lip had been split open.

"Are you all right?"

Slaíne nodded once and looked away, as if ashamed. She didn't flinch as Dewhurst kicked her in the ribs.

"Don't. Touch. Her." Now Aidan was on his feet, preparing to Summon the silver sword and have done with this once and for all, consequences be hanged.

The two guards reached for their own iron weapons.

"It ain't worth it, sir," Slaíne said.

"Silence, both of you. I need to think." Dewhurst had taken a few steps back from Aidan, whom he seemed to regret visiting. He paced back and forth, the color that had filled his face draining. "I need those maps. They're – they're mine. I need them."

He's lying. Yes, Aidan was certain of it. "Who are you holding the maps for?" Aidan asked after weighing those words carefully.

Dewhurst stopped pacing and looked at Aidan as if he were mad. "I'm not holding them for anyone, boy. Now, you obviously are lying to me about not having them. Bring them back at once, or I'll—"

Aidan held his hands up. "Calm down, old man. I told you I don't have the maps. I didn't have enough time to look at all the papers and oilskins I took."

"Bah. Nonsense."

"Why would I lie when you're holding so much over my head?"

That made Dewhurst pause and consider his words. He did not want to believe Aidan, Aidan knew innately. Dewhurst wanted to hate the orphan boy he had tricked into handing over his title, the boy he'd framed for murder. He hated him and his noble blood. If Dewhurst had a sword, he'd run Aidan through right now, blood and Meraude's demands be hanged.

Aidan shook himself out of the small trance he'd just entered and looked at Dewhurst, amazed. "You're working for Meraude."

Only upon hearing her name did Dewhurst betray any fear in his features. Yet after a moment, he smoothed the worries out of his face and shook his head. "You are a misguided child." *How does that Ingledark brat known about Meraude? I haven't mentioned her, nor the fact that I was supposed to aid this boy or stay out of his way.*

Aidan blinked himself back into the moment, having fallen again into a trance. He opened his mouth to accuse Dewhurst, but then it occurred to him: if he could somehow get a read on Dewhurst's thoughts and feelings, it would be best to keep the man in the dark about that fact. Aidan shut his mouth and shook the cobwebs from his brain. How could he be sure of this new ability? Where had it come from?

Dewhurst interrupted his thoughts. "Those maps are crucial to your survival – to *her* survival." He gestured toward Slaíne, who now stood outside of striking distance. "I suggest you check your cache again."

Sweat formed on Aidan's brow, though the air down there was cool bordering on cold. What could he do to convince the man of the truth? "I don't have the maps," he repeated, desperation leaking into his voice.

The look Dewhurst gave him was incredulous. "Do you think me stupid? Those maps did not sprout legs and walk out. Someone took them. Who else has been in my study?"

"Maybe a servant—"

Dewhurst waved the suggestion away. "My servants are loyal to a fault. I will give you three days, Ingledark. Three days to consider all the horrible things I could do to the both of you to get the maps back. And don't think for a second that I would hesitate to follow through." Dewhurst and Aidan stood there for a moment, sizing each other up, before the lord turned on his heel and stormed toward the stairs.

Slaíne gave Aidan one last pitiful look before trotting off after her new master. The guards didn't even look at him before turning and filing out after their employer.

Aidan waited until their Pulls had all but disappeared before swearing. Three days? He'd searched his cache in Nothingness thoroughly. There was nothing even remotely map-like stored there.

Something else nagged at Aidan as he lowered himself to the floor. Who *did* have the maps? Had Larkin stolen them before leaving Dewhurst's estate? If so, then she had truly set Aidan up to fail and be caught, and his hopes of trusting her now were dashed entirely. He thought back to his interactions with her. On one of the last days he'd seen her, she'd found him and Slaíne in the market place in Abbington, a new Pull on her person. It had felt like paper. Perhaps....

No, Larkin wouldn't have been so stupid as to carry the maps on her person. Besides, she would've had to have them sent to her in Abbington, because she most certainly didn't have them when Aidan first ran into her there. Unless she had them hidden somewhere.... No, someone else had taken the maps.

What did I get out of the vault? Aidan mused. It had looked like a map. But it couldn't have been, if Dewhurst was honest and hadn't recovered the map from the papers Aidan had stolen. Maybe Aidan's stash in Nothingness was compromised somehow. "Nothingness." Aidan sat upright as an ancient, gnarled voice came to mind. *"I held on to the maps. Lot of good they'll do ya now...."*

He'd thought that Treevain's voice in his head had been a hallucination brought on by stress, and the same with the woman who had claimed to be his aunt. Perhaps they'd been real. Aidan rested his head in his hands, racking his brain for other indications that this might be true.

The images and visions had been silent since he'd been imprisoned the previous week. They had changed in quality and quantity since the nymph had stabbed him in the shoulder with the ice blade. As he thought of the wound, Aidan rubbed it absently, though it did nothing more than give a tiny throb. "That must be it. They have to be connected. All of it."

He thought some more. *The elves said they were dead. Maybe they are. Maybe I can talk with the dead because of the blade wound.* Aidan shook his head. If that were true, why would he have just seen those hideous creatures instead of someone that had meant something to him? *Maybe not any sort of dead person,* he mused, thinking more clearly than he had in weeks, despite the iron. *But what sort? They must all have a common denominator.* Aidan felt he had most, if not all of the pieces to this puzzle, but they were all gray sky with no breaks in the pattern.

Fatigue overcame him, but still he sat and tried to puzzle out his muddled thoughts.

Soon after, the scullery maid brought down Aidan's afternoon meal – a cold potato and a dried-out slab of salmon, and a gulp of vinegar wine in a dented tin cup. She stood watching him as she always did, making certain he didn't squirrel away any scraps of food anywhere. When he finished, she took the tray, and he thanked her as was his habit.

The maid paused on her way back to the steps, and for the first time, he heard her speak. "You know," she said, "you're the only one in this household that thanks me for anything. Why?"

Aidan didn't answer, but shrugged.

She laughed but grew silent and thoughtful a moment before speaking again. "I could get whipped for this, but I have a feeling you won't tell."

Aidan tried not to look too eager, but nodded all the same.

With a sigh, the maid crept back over and said in a lowered voice, "Not everyone here likes his lordship. You might find some allies in the village." She made a face as she said this, probably realizing that he had no way of getting in touch with anyone outside of that room. Or perhaps she'd caught a whiff of his stink, as he'd been down there long enough without a bath to be offensive.

"Thank you," he said again, drawing a smile from the maid.

She seemed torn for a moment, obviously weighing her words before committing them to the air. "If there's anything I can do, let me know – and don't you thank me again just now." They shared a laugh, though Aidan's was more relieved than amused. Manners had never come easy to him.

Aidan felt a human Pull pause overhead and he pointed at the ceiling and mouthed, "Listening."

She nodded and shouted for the listener's benefit, "And there's more where that came from," perhaps a bit too dramatically, before winking and then fake-storming up the stairs.

When she left, Aidan sat back, his thoughts more scattered than before.

CHAPTER SIXTEEN

Aidan was asleep when they came for him that evening. He hadn't meant to doze off, but it wasn't a surprise, considering all his body was putting up with. The men wore masks, and the atmosphere around them was charged and excited as the first fist connected with his jaw.

Aidan rubbed where the knuckles had struck, knowing it had been a practice tap, to see how he would react. "What do you want?" he asked, rising to a sitting position as the figures retreated a few steps.

No one responded at first, but brown and blue eyes stared at him from beneath the masks, four sets, all jittery and drunk on some emotion.

"Is there a leader among you?" Aidan studied their appearances as well as their Pulls. Three Pulls belonged to Dewhurst's soldiers, and one was a servant's. He stared straight into those eyes and saw no wavering and no pity there. "If you're going to beat me senseless, I'd at least like to know there's some order behind it."

"Y-you dare speak to us, you fey scum," the servant, the tallest among them, demanded.

Aidan laughed without mirth. "So, that's what Dewhurst is telling you I am?"

"Don't contradict your master," the same man spat.

"Are we going to do this or not?" whined one of the guards, coming at Aidan. He made to kick him, but Aidan grabbed his leg and twisted it, causing the man to fall to the ground. The first thing he had learned from his uncle: never underestimate someone who looks feeble and beaten. But he knew they would not make that mistake again.

Aidan hadn't a moment's respite before the others sprang at him. He was strong, but did not possess the strength of four men even when he wasn't half-starved and bled, so they managed to pin him down.

"Oh, this is fair," Aidan snapped. "Four against one? Cowards."

That earned him a real punch to the eye this time. The man on his chest raised his fist again, his eyes gleaming with a fanatical light. "Let go, J—" The servant stopped himself from finishing the name.

Aidan grunted. "You're not here on Dewhurst's orders?" His eye throbbed painfully and was already starting to swell shut.

"You breathe a word of this to anyone, and we'll kill your sweetheart." The servant and the younger guard laughed, before the other two hissed at them to shut up. "All right, all right," said the servant, lowering his voice as the young guard snickered. "You tell anyone, fey, or make a sound as we proceed, and your redheaded witch'll find herself hanging."

Before Aidan could reason with them, they started in. They beat him with fists, making sure to keep his face untouched besides the lone bruised eye, evidence of their handiwork. Aidan struggled against them in vain. But they were not long into the beating when Aidan felt a tug in his gut that had little to do with the wind being knocked out of him. *Sláine.* He groaned silently. *Stay with your new master.* What was she thinking, risking the curse's wrath?

His shoulder burned with icy pain before Sláine even made it to the first step. With strength that could not be his own, he threw the four men from his prone form, and they lay scattered and bewildered. Just as quickly as the burst of power had come over him, it left.

Sláine hadn't paused in her approach, a frying pan brandished high. The sight would have made Aidan laugh, had she not brought it down with force on one of the men's shoulders. There was a resounding crack, and Aidan knew she had shattered the man's bones. "Out," she barked over the injured man's cries.

One stood up to her, reaching for a dirk, but his comrade put a hand on his arm and spoke to him in a low voice as another guard came to the injured servant's aid. Without another word, the four fled up the stairs, not bothering to muffle their footsteps.

Sláine's wild eyes took in Aidan, and she dropped the pan but did not move, as if frightened of him. When she spoke, her voice was hoarse. "I'm sorry I could nay get here sooner."

"How did you know anything about this?" Aidan managed to grind out. His voice seemed to snap her out of whatever apprehension she might be feeling, and she approached.

"One of those guards warned me. I read his note too late, I see."

Now Aidan did chuckle, only to stop at once and wince. "Not too late. I'm not yet dead, as you can see."

His attempt at humor fell flat with her, and she scowled. "Lot o' good I been to you." She sniffed, and leaned over him. Her eyes took in his face and she nodded. "Right." And without explanation of what she was up to, the strange girl pulled a paring knife out of her bodice and ripped the remainder of his shirt away.

"What are you...." He grew silent as her fingers whispered across his bare flesh, tracing purple bruises that had already blossomed on his chest, before probing for broken bones. It would have been more painful, had her Pull not been so comforting and familiar...and had her touch not felt so inviting. He focused on that as she traced lower and lower, and then back up again. His breathing grew ragged, and as hers did not, he guessed she thought the groan he let out was born of pain.

"Nothing's broken," she said after a moment. She eyed him askance but did not question why he was looking at her like he knew he was looking at her.

"How did you manage getting down here?" he asked, willing his blood to cool. This was no time to be thinking amorous thoughts that scared even him.

Slaíne looked at him like he had suffered a concussion and even put a hand on his brow. "I took the stairs."

Again Aidan laughed, and again he groaned. "I meant the curse. Did you break the curse? Is that how you were able to leave Dewhurst and come down...here? What?" She was blushing and looked sadder than he had ever seen her.

"It's attached back on you."

Aidan blinked. "What? How?"

"Never mind that. I need to plot, and you need to rest." She took the hole-riddled blanket at his feet and covered him up.

"I've slept enough."

She let loose a dark chuckle and shook her head. "I doubt that, somehow."

Despite her command to lie back down, Aidan eased himself to a sitting position, though his body protested. He had not been in the presence of anyone whom he knew he could trust for too long to sleep through it. "Are you all right?" His muscles screamed at him as he reached out and touched her face, the bruises that had yellowed. To his surprise, she did not pull away but watched him.

"Gets beaten and asks if I'm all right." Her voice was thick as he leaned in.

He licked his lips. "They hardly touched me." Sense and pretenses be hanged. He'd wanted her from the moment he'd been gripped by her Pull, and perhaps it was fear of what was to come that made him desperate for her, but he didn't care. Aidan tilted her head to the side and pressed his lips to her throat.

Slaíne shuddered, but didn't object as he kissed his way up to her mouth, then pressed his tongue against the line of her lips. Her lips parted and the breath rushed out of her as he kissed her like this was the last time he'd ever see her. All of his pain disappeared as he poured all of his passion, fear, and hope into that tiny mouth. His hands were rough with Slaíne as they seized her waist and drew her closer, her Pull maddeningly strong. She was all but in his lap, and blood thundered in his ears as her hands pressed against his chest.

With a gasp she pulled out of the kiss and watched him, wide-eyed. He did not release her waist, and she did not try to pull away, to his relief. "Sir...." Whatever she was going to say, it seemed she lost the courage to say it. She changed the subject. "Why haven't you used the sword yet?" she whispered. "You could have been free days ago."

Aidan shook his head, ignoring the flash of pain that rippled down his neck. "And leave you here?"

She squirmed. Her voice was barely audible as she said, "Then it's my fault."

"Slaíne, even if I could have managed to get my hands on the key to my bonds, I would have numerous guards to contend with. And say I got past them. I am too weak right now to run far and maintain the speed needed. You are not to be blamed."

Slaíne worried her lower lip and wouldn't meet his gaze now. Her hands slipped down into her lap. "So it's hopeless?"

Aidan shook his head but cringed, a moment that did not go unnoticed by Slaíne.

"They beat ya harder than you're tellin'."

"I don't feel any pain." It was true. The only thing that hurt was his head, and that was the only part of him that wasn't so close to Slaíne.

Maybe her powers came with some healing ability that she had failed to mention to him.

She quirked an eyebrow. "Aye, but ya will." The voice of experience.

Aidan shuddered again. "How do I—"

"Not now, sir. You need to rest." She started to pull away, and he reluctantly released her, only to be overcome with a wave of pain and nausea that threw him onto his back when she was no longer touching him.

He groaned and grabbed her hand to stay her. "Don't go." The full weight of what had just happened crashed down on Aidan's shoulders. Had she not shown up, would the guards have bothered to stop? He would have failed them, his family, Slaíne. All of them. As he closed his eyes, the girl lay down next to him and pressed his shaking hand against her heart.

"I ain't going anywhere, sir."

★   ★   ★

When he awoke the next morning, Aidan found he was nearly crushing Slaíne against him, his body curled around her. He moaned and unwittingly lost grip of everything he held in Nothingness.

Slaíne jumped as the sword clanged on the ground next to her. "Sir," she hissed, reaching for it. "You need to send it back or use it."

Aidan had grabbed her hands and was holding them pressed against her. He was trying to send the sword back along with everything else piled up in the room, but it was proving difficult. He hadn't realized that the toll on his mind had been as taxing as on his body.

Footsteps and shouts sounded up above, and human Pulls drew near as Aidan Dismissed the sword, the saddlebags, the saddle, and that was as far as he could get before the guards came rushing in, followed by Dewhurst.

"What was all that...." The lord stopped short at the sight of the patera, wood, and odd belongings strewn across the floor. He swore. "Where did you get all this?" It was then that he noticed Slaíne, who was still trapped in Aidan's arms. "What the devil? How did she get down here?" Dewhurst struck the nearest guard across the face with the man's own dirk. "Search through this – this filth and see if the maps are there."

Aidan had a strange impression of Dewhurst. He looked furious, his face red and his nostrils flared, but there was a hollowness in his chest, an ache as he stared at Aidan and Slaíne, the latter of whom had gone rigid. Aidan didn't know what to make of it, until the man's feeling disappeared completely and was replaced with icy terror, though his expression remained livid.

"Who turned on me? Who dared touch my prisoner without my consent?" So, he'd spied the bruises. He shook from head to boot. "She's going to kill me."

The guards were on their hands and knees searching through everything Aidan had accidentally Summoned. They said nothing, not even as their one bleeding comrade got down on his knees as well, dripping blood everywhere as he searched.

Blood. It occurred to Aidan then why he was able to guess what Dewhurst was feeling and thinking so easily: his blood was in Dewhurst's system. What other advantage might this give Aidan? He did not know, but for now he settled for latching onto Dewhurst's thoughts in what he hoped was a subtle enough way as not to draw attention.

Get the maps, the impression of Dewhurst's thoughts pressed into his mind. *Get the maps, and it won't matter if we slaughter Ingledark here and now. I will be her equal, at least.* Absently, Dewhurst patted at his pockets. There was a presence in there, a mix of iron and another metal. Difficult, that.

Aidan could try to Call what he guessed to be the key, Summon the sword, and run the man through while Slaíne unlocked his shackles. He explored the key's Pull and repulsion as Dewhurst continued to pace. No good. The metals were too closely bound. If he gave it a Tug, the non-iron part might respond, but the iron part would stay in Dewhurst's pocket, and Dewhurst would know what Aidan was attempting. If only he could fool Dewhurst into handing the key over....

As if in response to Aidan's silent wish, Dewhurst removed the alloyed key from his pocket and held it out. He stared at it for a moment, his face void of expression. With a blink, it was back in his pocket. Dewhurst looked befuddled for a moment before shaking his head and turning back to his guards and swearing. "What's taking you so long? Have you found it?"

The bleeding guard stood whilst applying pressure to the wound on his face. "There's nothing, sir. Well, not nothing."

"Well, what is there, then?"

The other men stood, too, their faces red from exertion. "Well," said one, "there's lots of hay. Which means he has a horse."

Dewhurst's face turned as red as raw meat. "What the devil sort of good is that going to do me?"

The man quailed and took several steps backward. "If he's got one, why did he not ride in on it?" The question was raised on the end of the sentence, the man obviously stressed and tense.

"Who the ruddy well cares? I'm looking for paper, not horses."

Aidan released Slaíne, after whispering in her ear, "This is our chance. Wait for my signal then approach Dewhurst."

She gave him a confused look but nodded.

Aidan closed his eyes and homed in on Dewhurst's thoughts. They weren't as clear as they had been moments earlier, but Aidan latched on to them anyway and tried directing his own wants and ideas toward the man's mind. He'd never controlled a human being before, but he had controlled objects, and he used the same intuitions and principles. Hearing Dewhurst complain of a stomachache in his mind, Aidan gave his thoughts a Push as he would Push a piece of paper, lightly and delicately.

Dewhurst's hands went to his middle as he towered over his guards and continued barking at them.

Aidan held on to Dewhurst's thought and pretended as though he could see it. *Put your hands lower, in your pocket again.*

Dewhurst obliged.

Sweat formed on Aidan's brow, and his head was beginning to ache. *Now, slip out the key and hold it out behind your back.* His head screamed at him to stop, but he knew he might never get a chance like this again. With all of his mental might, he Pushed the thought at Dewhurst until, at last, the man slipped a hand into his pocket and again produced the key. *Behind your back. Put the key behind your back.*

Again Dewhurst unwittingly obliged.

Aidan nudged Slaíne, who rose to her feet and sneaked up behind Dewhurst.

Still holding Dewhurst's mind in his hands, Aidan used the last of his strength to will Dewhurst to release the key and then forget about having done so.

Fortunately, Slaíne guessed what Aidan was up to and managed to catch the key before it could fall, and returned to Aidan before one of the guards noticed her. She was back beside him in a blink. "Now what?" she asked.

But Aidan couldn't answer. All strength had left him, and he began to cough. *I hope Slaíne's hidden the key away.*

Gone were Aidan's impressions of Dewhurst's thoughts and whims. They were replaced by a dull ringing in Aidan's ears as the nausea subsided. He gagged twice and then was still.

Dewhurst swore. "Someone, clean this mess up." With that said, his Pull retreated as he ran to and up the staircase.

Despite the command, the guards didn't remain behind; Aidan felt all of their Pulls retreat, and heard their feet scrabbling up the stairs not seconds after Dewhurst had used them. It was now only Slaíne and him.

"What did you do?" Slaíne whispered, her voice awed. "Ne'er seen nothing quite like that."

Aidan attempted a chuckle, but it came out as a grunt. He blinked several times to clear his vision, but everything looked filmy and distorted. "Are they gone?"

"Yeah. Guess they can nay stand the smell down here no longer." She then called them something rather colorful, and this time Aidan did manage to laugh.

"Do you have it?" he murmured.

"The key? Yeah. Should I use it?"

Aidan hesitated as she placed a cool hand on his throbbing forehead. "It might be best to wait until I've regained some strength. What are you going to do, carry me out of here?"

Slaíne was silent. "He said three days he'd give you before…well, you know."

"Yes, well—"

"Oh, for the love of mercy, what are you afeared of?"

Aidan groaned, and Slaíne pulled away her hand. "I'm in no mood to argue, so—"

"Never mind all that." With that said, she took the key, went to his feet, and undid the shackles binding him. "There. Now, would you mind bringing that sword out, or do I gotta do everything myself?"

She stared at him expectantly, until with a roll of his eyes, Aidan Summoned the sword.

Slaíne picked up the blade after it had clattered to the ground. "Right. They will have heard that, no? Get up."

Indeed, there were more shouts overhead, and several Pulls returned to the mouth of the cell. "C'mon," she insisted.

Trembling, Aidan raised himself to a sitting position. From there, he got to his knees, his muscles protesting. But soon he was able, with Slaíne's help, to rise to his feet. Just in time, too.

Though the guards who had retreated were slow in their return, Aidan had just managed to ready himself as the first one came into view. "What's all this?" the one in front asked.

Mercifully, Slaíne had thought to hide the blade behind her back. Even so, the men were eyeing her warily. "What? You afeared of me?" she said.

One laughed. The other one looked taken aback at her cheek.

Aidan knew what she was going to do before she moved, and he was helpless to protest or stop her. So as she ran the first man through with her silver blade, Aidan Dismissed the belt holding up the other man's trousers.

The first one collapsed with a gasp, red blooming from his stomach as he toppled forward onto the floor. The second one stumbled out of his drawers and moved to pick up his blade, which had clattered to the ground, but Slaíne was already upon him, slicing him across the throat.

The guard's hands went up to his neck as he sputtered blood, and she pushed the blade clean through his throat until it emerged on the other side. Dying, the man collapsed.

Aidan latched on to the deceased's Pull, Dismissed it, and watched as the light left the second man's eyes, Slaíne hastening his end like a dread angel of mercy. Once that man had passed, Aidan latched on to that Pull and Dismissed the second body. His head spun and his muscles spasmed beneath his own weight, but they'd only spent two minutes of precious time. "I don't know if this is a good idea...."

But Slaíne would hear no complaints. She pocketed the key and came to where Aidan stood swaying slightly. Mercifully, his vision had cleared, and he could feel some of his strength returning, though not what had been lost in the weeks of being under-fed, bled, and remaining inactive. Putting one arm around his waist whilst holding the sword in the other, she helped him hobble toward the prison door, which remained ajar. No calls of alarm had been taken up, so they made their way up the stairs.

With each awkward step he took upward and away from the iron, the more like himself Aidan began to feel. But it wasn't enough. He was getting lightheaded, and his knees began to buckle.

Slaíne swore below her breath and nearly lost hold of him. "Sir, you gotta keep goin'."

But he sank onto the step he was on and clutched his head. His ears rang, and a vision overtook him. It was of a man, perhaps in his twenties, standing on Aidan's family estate.

"Need some help?" the man asked sotto voce.

Aidan could feel himself being shaken, knew that Slaíne was there somewhere, tugging on him and urging him forward. Weary beyond belief, Aidan could do nothing but nod.

The familiar stranger gave Aidan a piteous smile before saying, "This is going to feel peculiar." And with that, Aidan returned to the moment, Slaíne standing over him instead of the stranger.

"Blimey," she murmured, her face red with exertion. "Can you walk?"

Aidan opened his mouth to answer, and that is when he first felt it, the sensation of becoming too large for his own skin. He had experienced something similar the night previous when the guards had come in to beat him, but that had only lasted a moment. A great swelling of strength and energy took over him, clumsily controlling his movements. Soon he was upright, walking with Slaíne as though his body were making its own decisions.

Slaíne gave him a confused look, but moved ahead of Aidan, sword raised as they crept around a corner. "Can you feel any Pulls, sir?"

Aidan closed his eyes and concentrated, but whatever or whoever was controlling his body was interfering with his ability to feel any Pulls...or have control over them. "I don't think I have my abilities right now."

"What? How's that even—"

"Later. Can you get us out of here?"

The house was full of various noises: maids, perhaps, running around overhead; cooks and kitchen wenches chattering over the clatter and clank of earthenware and metal pots; and there were male voices, right around the corner. Aidan frowned, having no sense whatsoever where anything or anyone was. "This is disorienting."

Slaíne hushed him and stepped forward to peek around the corner, and swore beneath her breath. "This way," she mouthed.

Aidan followed her, or rather, whoever possessed control over him did, and they made their way toward where Aidan thought the kitchen might lie. They had no sooner neared the savory aromas of roasted meat and potatoes, than a voice rumbled from behind them.

"How in the blazes...?" It was Dewhurst, and his expression of surprise turned to one of indignation and rage.

Slaíne grabbed Aidan's arm with her free hand. "Run!"

He didn't need telling twice. Aidan ran after Slaíne, overtaking her at twice his normal pace. "Slow down," he had to tell the stranger controlling his movements.

"Are you sure?" the man's voice echoed in his head.

"I'm not leaving her in my wake. Slow down," he said, knowing Slaíne must think him mad. He shrugged against his own volition.

"Fine. You might want to pick that girl up...if you don't want to get caught, that is."

"I'm not strong enough right now, I—"

"No, you're not, but I am."

Dewhurst was screaming for guards, his footsteps falling fast behind them. Any moment now, he would emerge from behind them, grab Slaíne – or worse – and they would be done for.

"You're being dramatic, Aidan." And with that, he halted against his will, turned, and picked up Slaíne as if she weighed nothing more than a sack of feathers. With barely a moment's pause, he was back to running toward the kitchen.

Slaíne was shouting turns at him, and he was taking them. Servants scurried out of their way, and those that weren't quick enough Aidan bowled over with inhuman strength. They had made it out the kitchen door, finding the kitchen empty, when they were met with a surprise on the back lawn.

Darkness had begun to fall, and surrounding the estate were men armed with bows and flaming arrows. At the sight of Aidan, they let out a cry.

"*Sorry, mate. This is where I leave you,*" said Aidan's possessor, and the extra strength leaked out of him like new wine from an old wineskin. He collapsed beneath Slaíne's weight, and that is when the fiery arrows began to rain.

CHAPTER SEVENTEEN

To Aidan's amazed eyes, the missiles bounced off the roofing, skittering and rolling as they made contact with the thin metal plating. But some of the arrows were true and found weaknesses, barren spots in the house's armor.

When the men surrounding them took their aim again, they aimed for the top levels of the house, which soon caught ablaze. Screaming servants streamed out of the smoking manor. The guards weren't far behind.

If they didn't want to get pierced by the arrows meant for their enemy, Aidan knew he needed to move. But it would seem that Slaíne was rooted to the spot. "Slaíne, we need to move."

"They're burning it down with people inside," she said so softly, Aidan could hardly make out what she had said. She turned to leave his side, and Aidan knew what she meant to do.

Aidan latched on to her Pull and Tugged it hard, sending her flying back toward where he was struggling to his feet. "Slaíne!" he bellowed.

"Lemme loose." She thrashed against his invisible hold on her like a fiend, but he continued to reel her toward safety, for they were nearly trampled as people poured out of the flames. "They'll burn them alive. Let go."

"Think, woman. Think! We need to get out of here or—"

"I am thinking," she snapped, pushing off him. After giving the burning manor one last piteous look, she turned, put her arm around Aidan, and helped him limp out of harm's way.

No one was trying to extinguish the blaze. No one was fighting the men who had surrounded them and shot the arrows. It was as though some spell had fallen on all of them...or as if one had been lifted. Dazed, they wandered away from the heat of the fire and then stood, eyes transfixed on the catastrophe.

From the front of the manor there came a great cry, and soon Aidan felt Dewhurst's Pull joining the company in the back yard. "Thieves, fire, foes! What are you standing around for, you stupid lumps on a log?" The man swore. "Put the fire out!"

No one did anything.

Slaíne collapsed, the sword still clutched in her hands. Beside her, Aidan felt a sudden surge of energy that had nothing to do with whatever force had possessed him before and everything to do with the fact that he could end this. That energy propelled him toward Dewhurst.

Some of the guards hissed at Aidan and spat, even. But none tried to stop him. Aidan did not hesitate, for he knew Dewhurst's men were not loyal, and though they hated Aidan and his 'magic', they were surrounded by their enemy. And judging from the familiarity of at least a dozen of the Pulls, Aidan knew who that enemy was and that his secret missive had been received.

"It's over, Dewhurst," Aidan shouted over the roar of the blaze. "You and your men need to put down your iron if you care to see another day."

A murmur went up among Dewhurst's men, and Aidan knew that his allies were drawing back their bows. He reached out and felt for the hated man's Pull, and found that he was cowering perilously close to the blaze.

Though weakening, Aidan sensed the remnants of his own blood still in the other man's system and gave it a good tug. With a cry, Dewhurst shot through the brush and bracken, barreling over three of his men.

Aidan hobbled over to where Dewhurst lay, now by himself, as his men had distanced themselves. "Start talking."

"Don't kill me," he blubbered. "I wasn't working for myself. I—"

"Oh, quiet. We both know that's not true."

Dewhurst whimpered, and Aidan knew it was a ruse. He felt the repulsion of iron in the man's grip, and knew Dewhurst was waiting for the right moment to strike. By now, the heat from the house fire had grown unbearable; they would have to move on shortly. "D-don't you see?" Dewhurst said. "She's going to kill you. Maybe – maybe if we fight together…." Now the disgraced lord did quail beneath Aidan's glare. "Don't you see it? You have to trust me."

"Trust you? This is – unbelievable." Aidan took a step back and held up his hand to block out the heat.

Slaíne tugged at his shirt. "Sir, either we're helpin' or we need to go." Her Pull retreated several steps back, and he was inclined to follow, leaving Dewhurst to the Romas who still surrounded them. But something stopped him. The repulsion of the iron that Dewhurst was hiding was all wrong, that much was becoming evident by the beatings of his heart. This was more than just a repulsion he was feeling. The mystery object also possessed a Pull.

Dewhurst was still cowering, his face red and blistering in the heat. He didn't touch it or look at it, but the man had a rather large lump in his jacket, whence came the repulsion joined with a Pull. What was he hiding?

"Sir," Slaíne pleaded.

Curiosity gnawed at him, but Aidan knew he needed to get away from the heat. He nodded and turned away. "Very well."

"Please, don't leave me to these – savages." Dewhurst motioned around at the Romas, who had drawn back a few paces but remained with their bows drawn, perhaps waiting for a clear shot. "You're a better man than that, Ingledark."

Aidan had turned but now resumed walking.

"Don't turn your back on me, lad. She's going to kill you. All of you. I've got what you need to stop her. You need me, for pity's sake. Take me to my horse in the stables. I've more information I can give you there."

Aidan sensed a repulsion before it could hit him between the shoulder blades. He ducked, dragging Slaíne down with him. That was when the Bartlett Band of Romas let their next volley of arrows fly.

Shrill cries filled the air as all of Dewhurst's men – the ones that had survived the first attack – fled. At once the amount of anchoring Pulls dropped down by thirteen, all presumably belonging to now-deceased men. Aidan looked back at the carnage and saw that Dewhurst had been struck in the shoulder, his wound weeping copious amounts of blood. His eyes, now glazed with pain, swept past Aidan and he let out an incoherent plea.

Aidan spat in his direction and looked away.

Slaíne helped him to his feet as the Bartlett Band of Romas retreated. Isaac Pensworth nodded at him, placing two fingers to his temple in salute. It said it all: "My wrongs have been righted."

Aidan nodded his agreement, and watched Isaac follow after his ragtag band into the wood. He would have to catch up to them and thank the man personally for coming to his rescue, late though it was. Now that the score was even, Aidan could not help but wonder where they would stand: friend, foe, or something else entirely.

The sky was darkening with the threat of rain as the last Roma disappeared from sight. A wind swooped down upon them, and the flames danced like sprites in a frenzy. Only they and the servants remained, and never before had Aidan seen such a lost-looking flock. The past be hanged, but he could not help them. *My fault.*

They would not look at him, but moved farther from the blaze. Perhaps they would find work in town, live with relatives, start anew. That sounded appealing to Aidan, being given a fresh start. In a way, perhaps he had been. He was, however, still a wanted man. That warrant would darken his name 'til the end of his days, striking Breckstone off the list of potential places to live. A nomad's life would continue to be his until he got his family back. Then perhaps he could settle down in his mother's home village where he was yet unknown and unnamed.

"Sir?" the girl asked him. "Sir, what're we to do?"

Aidan's shoulders heaved. "We find the Goblets Immortal. But first we find a horse."

It took him five minutes of hobbling before they reached the stables. The ostlers had abandoned their charges, which snorted and hoofed at the ground in distress, a few rearing up at the sight of strangers. "Shh," Aidan soothed, though the beasts were beyond comforting. Perhaps they smelled smoke from the house.

"What has them so?" Slaíne wondered, leaving Aidan to stand on his own. "They're right frothin' at the mouths, they are."

Aidan sniffed the air. The smoke hadn't reached here yet. Something else was bothering the horses...something that smelled like the beginnings of decay. Aidan looked around for the source of the noxious odor and caught a glimpse of a great mound of hay. The hay was obviously hiding something, as bits of linen and leather poked out here and there. Upon closer inspection, Aidan's stomach churned. "Bodies."

Slaíne came up next to him. "More dead bodies?"

"So it would seem." But the sun was setting. There was not enough light to make out the features of these unfortunates. Aidan searched the Pulls and was startled. "I know these people."

"You recognize their Pulls?"

Aidan nodded mutely, though he knew she would not be able to pick up the movement in the waning light. He swayed on the spot and thought he was going to faint. "They feel like...." He patted his own chest, ran a hand over his heart to make certain it was in fact still beating. "These Pulls are familial."

"Come again?"

He turned to Sláine, a scream building in his throat. "Sláine. These Pulls feel like...me."

Her eyes grew wide, and that is when the light in the sky ran out. "They can't be you, sir. You're here. You're not dead."

Aidan was only half-listening. "They're both me. But they're not me." He shook his head, and then it dawned on him, and he sank to the ground in despair. "I think I've found my parents."

There was no explaining it, no accounting for how it could be so. Yet the fact remained: he knew those Pulls and they were his parents'. But how?

The horses continued their frantic hoofing and snorting. The air grew cold. Aidan's arms were all gooseflesh, and he could not stop shaking as tears of rage clouded his vision. "Dewhurst. Dewhurst killed my family."

Sláine, who had been silent for a moment, spoke the question he couldn't find his voice for. "Are ya certain? I thought you said they disappeared when you was but a boy."

"Their bodies are here," Aidan snapped. "What more proof do I need?"

"I'm not sayin' it weren't Dewhurst," she countered, her tone soothing. "But, if'n you don't mind me saying, these bodies are newly dead from the looks of things." She approached Aidan and stooped down next to him on the ground.

Blinking away the tears, Aidan let out a long sigh. "Maybe they've been alive all this time and he just now killed them?" Even to his own ears the words didn't sound right. It was an enigma that he would perhaps never solve. Why had Dewhurst done this? The thought of Dewhurst nauseated him. Bile rose in his throat.

Slaíne rubbed his back in soothing circles, and he did not stop her. It didn't matter now what he did or didn't feel. Meraude had lied. There was nothing left for him. The Goblets Immortal held no answers about bringing his family back, and there was no point in tracking the magical vessels down.

"This isn't over," Aidan said after a moment, perhaps startling Slaíne, who let out a soft gasp. Wiping his mouth, he stumbled to his feet and stared into the darkness where his parents lay. They could not tarry here much longer. The fire brigade would have been called by now, and the yard would soon be packed with volunteers fighting the blaze. The rain had ceased falling, and a nasty wind had blown in from the north.

With a choked sob, Aidan latched on to the bodies' Pulls and carefully Dismissed them into Nothingness. He could bury them later.

"What are you going to do now?" she asked him.

He did not respond, but Summoned the silver sword.

"Aidan, what are you doing?"

Jaw clenched, Aidan staggered out of the stables, paying no mind to whether Slaíne was following him or not. When he returned to the manor house, the yard was empty but for the dead bodies…and Dewhurst.

The hated man was crawling on all fours, making his way toward a puddle of water, perhaps to calm the heat blisters swelling on his face. He didn't deserve the relief.

Traces of Aidan's blood still remained in Dewhurst's system. Aidan latched on to the familiar Pull and gave the man a good tug in two different directions.

Dewhurst screamed as his breastbone cracked, the sickening sound only just audible over the roar of the blazing house. Aidan was not through with him.

He could find no words for Dewhurst, and physically exhausted as he was, he had no energy to spare for the man's much-deserved demise. He made Dewhurst aware of his intent through their peculiar mental connection a moment before forcing Dewhurst to raise his hand and Summon the silver sword from Aidan's hand into his own chest.

Gurgling crimson, Lord Dewhurst toppled over onto his side, shuddered once, and breathed his last.

Exhaustion overwhelmed Aidan, and he heard a ringing in his ears. If not for Slaíne's Pull, right at his elbow, he might have passed out.

"Sir," she said, her voice watery and blurred. She then said something he couldn't catch and handed him something cold and repulsive and yet Compelling: a Goblet, he realized. "Sir."

Aidan shook his head like a dog getting rid of fleas.

"Didn't deserve the mercy. But...blimey, what are we going to do now?"

Aidan did not answer for a moment, his thoughts in turmoil. His path was more muddled than before, and his mind could scarce form a coherent sentence. But there was one thing he would hold on to. Only one thing mattered now. "Sam isn't with my parents' remains. I think Meraude might have him." *Lies.* He knew it. Slaíne knew it. But finally they were on the same page about things. Aidan cast a sideways glance at her, a slow, deadly smile stealing over his features. "Let's kill the mage."

ACKNOWLEDGMENTS

Julene Louis – your sage advice and insights made this book stronger.

Victoria Vogel – your steadfast belief in my abilities has made me a more confident writer.

Ruth Johnson – your faithful encouragement has kept me from throwing in the towel more often than you will ever know.